Dusk

The Hollow Trilogy: Book One

Brent Kruscke

The Hollow Trilogy: Dusk

ISBN: 978-0-692-36022-4

This is a work of fiction. Names, characters, places and
incidents are the product of the author's imagination or
are used fictitiously. Any resemblance to any person
living or dead is purely coincidental.

Printed in the United States of America
2nd printing May 2015

Special Thanks

Michelle Rutkowski and Lynn DeGrande,
for your words of wisdom

Christopher Wright,
for your guiding hand

And Kara Swain,
for your unwavering love and support

For mom and dad,
For everything you've done for my dreams,
and always being my loudest cheering section.

Thank you.

DusK

Prologue

Upon a hill, overlooking the small town of Pointe's Hollow, sat a house of indiscriminate misfortune. The house had been forgotten by its neighboring town. It sat on the shore of Lake Michigan, quiet and desolate, watching over everything below.

The great house had but one tenant. He was who watched over the town. He stood between it and the horrors most believed did not exist. Shadows that paraded about in the light with the rest of the world, unseen.

Cool moonlight spilled into a dark and mostly empty room. It held a couch, a coffee table, a few odd pieces, and a blank spot high on a wall above a fireplace. One of the pieces was a small end table positioned in front of a window. On this table sat a telephone.

This phone, although important, was a standard model. It was simply a slate black, rotary phone, the kind found in houses on Main Street America circa 1976.

In retrospect to its ordinary look and feel, the phone was Pointe's Hollow's lifeline. It connected the town's guardian angel with the town's strong arm. It didn't ring often, but when it did, it never led to good things. It was the calm before a storm, and, of course, on a fateful night in late November, thunder rumbled.

The phone rang.

The sound of the bell mixed with the plastic handset rattling in the cradle created a symphony of chaotic yet brilliant noise. The music of the ring bounced about the empty house, falling on the man's uncaring ears. Ears that didn't want to hear the phone.

The phone rang again.

This time the ears had a harder time ignoring the ring. They heard, and they tried desperately to ignore.

The phone rang a third time.

The ears could no longer ignore it. It could be only one thing: bad news. That made the man hesitant, but he knew it would only be worse if he didn't answer it. The man the ears belonged to shuffled through the halls and entered the room. He was a large man, but in presence only, not in stature. His body was slim with haunting features. He carried a half empty bottle, not the first of the night, in his left hand.

On the fourth ring, Pointe's Hollow's strong arm picked the handset off the cradle, canceling the noise. It faded to nothing, and the house sat quietly.

Sighing, while rubbing his forehead with the hand holding the beer, he spoke into the phone, "Yeah?"

"It's me," the guardian angel said.

The strong arm took a long drag on his bottle. Once he was done, he said, "I don't know what you think of my social life, but I don't get many callers."

The caller's response was a mottled apology mixed with spiritual words of encouragement. There wasn't time for this, and there definitely wasn't time for God. Not in the man's house. God left this house a long time ago.

"What do you want? I'm a very busy man."

The strong arm looked at the bottle and took a swig of alcohol. The caller could hear the liquid sloshing back and forth as the man raised and lowered the bottle.

"The answers you seek, my son, cannot be found at the bottom of a bottle."

"You won't blame me for not taking your word, Father." The last word came out as a slight hiss. "I feel like my questions are ones with answers one must discover for oneself."

The man was not being overly rude to the caller on the phone. It was just the nature of their relationship, their normal to and fro.

He took another drink from the bottle, emptying it. The empty bottle clunked on the small end table as the man set it down. The brown bottle looked strange in the blue moonlight.

A low sigh was audible on the other end of the phone. "Something has happened."

He had known it was going to be bad news. It always was. He was not a man you called with good news. His number was not one you dialed when you were announcing the birth of a child or a job promotion. This was by design. He was meant to be invisible. Dealing only with the scum between the toes of his town.

"You don't say," the man finally said. He was making light of the situation, which was most definitely a life or death situation, but he didn't care.

The caller told him what had happened. It was bad news. Very, very bad news. The man's hand instinctively went to his hip. It was there, just as it always was, but it felt so good to make sure.

"Did you hear me?" the caller said, concern in his voice. Most would be frightened, but not him. He had been associated with these dealings for far too long to be frightened by this. But he was the king of concern.

"Yeah, yeah. I heard ya."

"Do you know what this means?"

"Yes," the man said, growing somber. "I know."

They said their good-byes; then, each hung up their respective phones.

The man stood by the table for a moment, not sure what to do next. He reached down and pulled out a revolver from a holster on his right hip. It was large, made of harsh steel and a sandalwood grip. He had other weapons, including his creative and cunning mind, but this was his favorite.

With the ease of practice, he popped open the gun's chambers and spilt the contents into his palm. Six shells fell and rattled against each other in his hand.

After a moment of consideration, he deposited the shells into the inside pocket of his jacket. From another pocket, he pulled out a handful of new objects. He slid five into their respective chambers and then held the last one out for inspection.

I know all too well what this means, the man thought.

Through the window, he could see the large, full moon perched in the night sky. The man's focus switched from the moon to the bullet in his hand. It had a brass casing like all the others, but what made this bullet special was the slug. The crowning slug that hung out of the casing was an object designed for one purpose and one purpose only. To kill.

But what truly set this slug apart was that this particular slug, along with its brothers and sisters sitting cozily in the revolver, was made out of pure silver.

Chapter 1

Mrs. Denver, a stout, plump woman, waddled across the front of a small classroom. Her frame resembled the oddly proportioned frame of a pear, with a round, robust bottom half that sloped up to a smaller top that exploded into a brown nest of a hairstyle. For a woman who looked like she would feel more comfortable on a couch with a TV guide in her hand, she really loved to walk the span of the room's blackboard. Back and forth she would walk. From one end to the other.

The entire board was covered with the shavings of the diminished stub of chalk she held in her right hand. These shavings formed countless mathematical symbols and numbers. She started with a seemingly simple equation at the top left of the board. Then, growing in expansion and difficulty, she bounced from end to end scribbling examples for the students.

The students in the rest of the room followed along diligently, some a little more diligently than others. Sarah Cohen, the guaranteed valedictorian of the Class of 1978, followed Mrs. Denver as if she was a preacher reciting the holy prayer from the good book.

Then, there was Jerry Collins. A local, pot smoking child of the revolution. Jerry was trying to understand what Mrs. Denver was saying. He had repeated this class twice, and he'd be damned if he was going to sit through it a fourth time. Even though he really wanted to get it, the numbers and symbols looked like hieroglyphics in the Great Pyramids of Giza. He tried to find the definition behind 'cos' and 'sin,' but all he could really think about was getting out of here to have a smoke.

The other students varied between the two of them, except for one. Nicholas Wake. He sat in the back of the class, in the chair closest to the door, one leg stretched out from under his desk as if he was ready to bolt for freedom as soon as the old, silver bell sang its tune.

His head was down, and his shoulders were hunched. He was deeply involved with something. It just happened to be something different from Mrs. Denver's lecture. It wasn't because he didn't understand the work; in fact, he probably could have taught the class himself. He understood the subject; he just didn't care for it. English and history were what he enjoyed.

What had his attention so fully was a sketch he had been working on all hour. It was a stunning penciled likeness of Mrs. Denver. Pear shaped body in all its obtuse glory. She had one hand raised addressing the class. That hand, wielding chalk, bounced around on the paper with the help of small, motion-curved lines like a comic book character.

Behind the disfigured teacher, the blackboard's color was sucked into a central point as if being sipped through a straw. The black of the board squeezed tight and then detached from the wall, forming a fiendish creature. Arms spread wide, each ending in frightening claws. The creature hung above Mrs. Denver, white eyes made of chalk bent into a scowl above a mouth that hung open, drooling. All of the features were made up from the symbols that painted the board.

He often drew pictures in class. Art had been a talent of his from early childhood. He never had any intention of using this gift for a career later; it was just a hobby that had entertained him in times of boredom. Like now. The drawings weren't always ones of such evil circumstances like Mrs. Denver about to be devoured. Sometimes, he drew landscapes. Fictional places mostly. Fake worlds spanning wild hills and filled with fantasies. He thought he'd enjoy drawing real places, but having lived in Pointe's Hollow his whole life, there wasn't much from which to draw. Truth was, he'd always rather be somewhere else, and he was mostly. At least, in his mind.

However, when he actually sat down to think about it, most of his drawings of people were in monstrous situations. He chalked this up to his selection in stories. A lot of his time had been spent with his nose in books from the local library or with eyes glued to a television set watching *Darkness Falls*. Many kids his age had switched over to the bandwagon of the science fiction movies. *Star Trek* was a popular show among kids, and other movies like *Planet of the Apes* caught kids' attention. Strange, faraway worlds with unique story lines and characters encapsulated the deprived youth.

Nicholas had seen *Star Trek* and enjoyed it, but the black and white monster movies that Graveyard Jerry announced during his late night sessions were what he really loved. Ghouls, ghosts, monsters, demons, vampires, werewolves, banshees, and all other general hauntings made his skin crawl and his adrenaline pump.

So, it was no wonder his sketches became slightly morbid in the daytime when his nighttime was filled with such monster movies as *Blood from the Mummy's Tomb*,

Afraid of the Night, and *The Werewolf in Washington*. He had just watched one the night before. At the moment, the title escaped him, but he did remember blood dripping from the walls and....

"Nicholas!" Mrs. Denver's shrill voice cut the air like claws.

Nicholas looked up from his drawing, resetting his large, black glasses from their downward slide on his nose.

Luckily, Mrs. Denver was still at the front of the class and not over his shoulder looking down at his art. Her hands were on her hips, and most of the other students had turned to look at him. Nicholas felt himself shrink back in his chair as if his body believed it could disappear.

"Welcome back to fifth period algebra, Mr. Wake. Normally, I would gain great pleasure in strolling back, plucking what has grasped your attention so thoroughly today, and promptly escorting it to the nearest wastebasket."

Mrs. Denver's proper speech almost made getting a verbal beating from her even worse. Her ability to make you feel obscenely stupid while she chastised you made her the worst teacher to get on the wrong side of.

"Quite lucky for you, however, you have caught me on a generous day," she continued, folding her hands in front of her. "If you can solve the equation on the board, then I'll let you keep whatever filth you have on your desk. How's that sound, hmmm?"

Would sound a lot better coming from somebody else, Nicholas thought. But he also thought, given the circumstances, he should count his blessings.

"That sounds fair to me, Mrs. Denver." His voice quivered a little in the beginning, and he felt foolish.

Mrs. Denver smiled a smile of arrogance, as if she had caught him in a trap. Nicholas was worried she had.

"Well, then," Mrs. Denver stepped aside to reveal the equation, "fire away, Mr. Wake. Factor the expression."

Nicholas scanned the board. In the shaken script of Mrs. Denver, he read

$$6x^2 - 13x + 5$$

He halfheartedly read the equation twice and then a third time. Without a glance down or a scribble of outside work, Nicholas said, "Three X minus five and two X minus 1."

The smile on Mrs. Denver's face slid off like a melting chunk from an iceberg plunging into the ocean.

"That is correct," Mrs. Denver said, agony filling the emptiness she emphasized between words. She hesitated for another moment, staring at Nicholas, and then she turned back to the board, continuing her lecture.

Even after coming out on top with Mrs. Denver, Nicholas still shrunk back a little. Yes, he had shown Mrs. Denver she wasn't the only one in the room who could factor equations, but in that same instance, he showed the rest of the class how smart he was. Nicholas never thought himself a genius, but he always did seem to know the answers.

Other kids didn't like when someone knew all the answers. For some reason, people feared intelligence. At sixteen, Nicholas didn't understand this fear, but with the look of, 'You better watch yourself,' Nicholas got from Danny "Pointe's Hollow's High School Quarterback" Finch, he had no question of its existence.

The only one who didn't fear his intelligence was Emily Gordon. A beautiful girl, with fair, red hair and green eyes, Emily was the exception to almost every rule in the book. Every time Nicholas was called upon to give an answer, her look toward him would always shine among the rest. She would turn, flick her hair in the lovely way girls do, smile, and turn back. A diamond in the rough was Emily. The classic story of beauty and the geek.

After a few more minutes of grueling lecture from shrilling Mrs. Denver, the bell rang, and Nicholas was out the door before the rest of the class had turned around. He made it to his locker, grabbed his school bag, and headed out the front doors.

Even though he didn't have a car, Nicholas headed toward the parking lot. He never resented that he didn't have a car. He knew it was far too much money for his aunt, and he had no job. Besides, everything in Pointe's Hollow worth getting to was easily reachable by bike. Once he got to the lot, he let out a long breath.

Freedom, he thought.

He unlocked his large bike chain with a small key from his ring. After wrapping the chain around the frame and reattaching the lock, he mounted and pedaled off.

The bike, a worn, red monstrosity, took off smoothly as it always did. The bike had problems only when real speed was gained on large downhills, and then it was a slight wobble in the front tire. Nicholas was sure he could fix it if he took a moment and looked it over, but once he got home, it always seemed to slip his mind. With a shift of his weight, he turned left, heading for downtown.

Downtown was actually a small collection of buildings lining the sides of Harbor Street. The buildings were the bare necessities of a small, rural town. There were two apparel shops, where most of the townspeople purchased their clothes. Further down, a barber shop sat on one side of the street, and directly across from that was a salon. Two favorite food joints and a bar were the sources of food and camaraderie for the locals. A general store and a hardware store rounded out the street, separated from the rest by a vacant lot.

The vacant lot had always been there and probably always would. Its ownership had been haggled over and argued about for years. No one really knew who owned it or what could be done with it. So there it sat, empty and useless.

A chain link fence stood on the back side. It hung loose and rusted, teetering on the edge of falling down. In the front, there was a short, wood-planked fence that looked almost as old as its companion on the back side. Things had been tossed between these guards for years. Bottles; newspapers; empty food containers from Shores, the local burger joint; and even an old, sunbaked washing machine sat in the barren wasteland between Berk's Bakery and the Pointe's Hollow General Store where you could buy a toothbrush and motor oil just an aisle apart. As a kid, Nicholas thought it held some magical powers like all the world's troubles were put there to be made right. Now, he saw it for what it was: a conveniently placed dump.

There were more stores along the shore by the docks. Little things that were used more during the tourist season, if you could even use 'tourist season' to describe what Pointe's Hollow had between the months of May and September.

Pointe's Hollow, or The Hollow as the locals referred to it, was a tiny speck on the map off the side of the highway, on the northern left side of the state. The main street, Harbor Street, ran from the highway, flanked by fast food restaurants, motels, and gas stations, to the blessed shore of Lake Michigan. Many visitors stopped off the highway to get gas or fatty foods on their way to Mackinac Island or the Upper Peninsula for their real vacation spots. The few who did vacation in The Hollow quickly realized there was nothing to see and left for greener pastures further north.

Even the shoreline was not the sand-filled fantasy of most coastal mental images. The northern side of the docks was sand, but it intermingled with weeds and other vegetation. You could walk barefoot through this section, but it was hard to escape without being pricked by plants or rocks.

Dusk

The town was hard to find. Not only because of its diminutive size, but because of its surroundings. A dense forest surrounded the town on three sides, while the fourth looked out onto the cool water of Lake Michigan.

Four roads led into The Hollow. Most who did find themselves on one of those barren ways wouldn't make it all the way to town, fearing the possibility of breaking down in the middle of nowhere. Menacing trees hung over the road as if part of a snare, ready to snatch an unsuspecting driver right off the road.

On that fourth side, where the land broke off to the cool water of Lake Michigan, was the Pointe's Hollow wharf. The wharf was split into two sections. The larger held docks and warehouses for ships fishing along the coast. During the good seasons, many fishermen could be found filling up the stools in Richie's Bar. But they'd be here for only a day or two and then be gone.

The smaller section of the wharf, which sat north of the larger, held the residential boats. It sat mostly vacant. Boats were a luxury, and luxuries were not something townsfolk could afford. Some fished for a living, but they kept their vessels in the larger section with the seasonal ships.

Yes, sir, Pointe's Hollow was a little piece of something, but heaven was not the place that came to mind.

Nicholas's bike tires bounced and thudded over the cracks in the sidewalk. He passed through the town: Richie's, the aroma of beer and pool chalk wafting out the open windows; Croft's Clothing and Apparel; the rolling red and white sign in front of Snippers; and, finally, 27th Lumber and Hardware. His side of the road turned into housing and across the road, the vacant lot stood, haunting.

He glanced behind him, checking for cars, and then crossed the street. People padded the sidewalk more thickly on this side, so Nicholas stayed on the street, grazing by the sides of the cars parked along the curb. He reached Claire

Street and turned right, heading for his aunt's house. In minutes, he was out of 'downtown' and that was it for the Pointe's Hollow tour.

His aunt's house was in a small subdivision on the northeast corner of town. A small collection of buildings with crossing, grid-patterned streets, the neighborhood was named Woodlawn Grove. Quite accurately named, for all the streets were named after common trees. Oak, Willow, Birch. The list went on.

Nicholas's aunt's house sat in the back on the corner of Elm and Willow. It was quaint, stylish, and everything his aunt ever wanted.

She always said, "I'm close enough to the water to feel the breeze on my face, but not so close that I have to worry about seagulls using my yard as their own personal crap zone."

When Nicholas was younger, he'd always smile at this. Now, he'd just shake his head and think, *That's Aunt Sherri. Crazy, but oh so lovable.*

His aunt had taken him in after his parents had died in a car accident. A drunk driver slipped to sleep at the wheel and struck his parents' car head on. Both of them died instantly; the drunk driver walked away battered and broken, but alive. He was sure the situation was not his aunt's happiest time. She had lost her sister and now had to raise her nephew, giving up her late twenties bachelorette lifestyle. But if she resented Nicholas for that, he never saw it. In the beginning, she even tried to be more maternal than she needed to be, but it became clear quickly that, even at his young age, Nicholas could mostly take care of himself.

After storing his bike in the one-car garage to the right of the house, he went inside via the side door, coming in on the kitchen. He was greeted by the smiling face of his aunt. She stood in the middle of a messy kitchen in a flour-coated apron and a messy bun with music blaring.

13

"Hey, Nicholas," she said with a wave, "I'm making cookies. You wanna help?"

Nicholas smiled, "No thanks, Aunt Sherri. Let me know when you get around to tasting." He carefully sidestepped her and the mess surrounding her, making his way to the living room.

"Will do. How was school?"

Nicholas shrugged. This was his usual response to her questions about school or his day-to-day happenings.

She responded with, "Well, there's always tomorrow."

She stretched, turned up the music, and went back to baking with a revived swing in her hips.

Nicholas went through the living room, passing a couch, a television, and a collection of family pictures. He gave his frozen-framed parents a passing glance as he always did and then continued upstairs. It was always hard to look at them for too long. He wouldn't admit it to himself, but it was even too hard to think of them for too long, so he tried not to.

The bathroom went by on the left, followed by a hall closet on the right. The end of the hall forked into two rooms. His aunt's room was to the left, and her craft room was to the right. The craft room had begun as his room until he had discovered the drop ladder attic door. When he first saw it, he imagined great wonders awaiting above it. In actuality, it held only a few boxes of clothes and dust.

For his thirteenth birthday, he had convinced his aunt to clean the attic and turn it into a bedroom. She was excited to have a free room for her crafts, which had taken over the dining room table since he had moved in, but she was not excited to go up there. She had never enjoyed attics and had no idea why Nicholas would want to live in one, but in the end, she had agreed.

Nicholas reached up and grabbed the small chain dangling from the door in the ceiling. The door swung down with a collapsed ladder on top of it. He unfolded the ladder, placing the end on the carpeted floor of the hall. Softly pressing his weight on the bottom step, the ladder clicked into final position, and he quickly climbed to the top.

The ceiling of the attic slanted at extreme angles to a point that mirrored the roof on the outside. The walls were just tall enough that, even with the extreme slant of the ceiling, Nicholas was able to stand at any point in the entire room. He had to bend his neck only slightly right next to the walls.

Posters hung tacked to the walls and ceiling in an organized pattern. *Dawn of the Dead, Dracula, Creature from the Black Lagoon,* and *The Blob* were just a few of the titles displayed about. His bed was pushed up against the back wall with a dresser extending from the foot of the frame. Atop the dresser sat a television. The wall to the right of the bed was covered with book cases, stuffed with books and models. Across from that, against the opposite wall, was a desk.

After refolding the ladder, he threw his bag on his bed and went to the desk. He sat, looking over the mess of pages and pencils scattered about.

On the back, left corner of his desk sat a typewriter. It had been his father's. Nicholas's aunt had brought it to him a few years ago, and Nicholas had put it in that exact spot. He had never touched it after that. It was too eerie. He was not able to say what made it eerie, but he knew it was. So he let it sit.

Lifting his glasses, he used his thumb and forefinger to rub his eyes. He felt drained. His hand fell away, and his glasses dropped back into place. He got up from the chair, leaving his desk and the typewriter behind him. Without knowing he was going to, he went to the circle window in the west-bearing wall of the room.

The window looked out on the lake. Luckily, the ground slanted enough so Nicholas could clearly see the harbor. Ships both of commercial and residential were navigating the shallow waters of the docks. The sun was dropping in the sky, and it gave the entire scene a warm light.

Out in the middle of the bay stood a small island. On the island stood an erect tower of massive size. The lighthouse was probably the oldest part of Pointe's Hollow. He had gone to the island on a school field trip in his younger years. The old bricks of the tower and the adjoining building looked as if they came from a time unknown to man. They stood slanted, cracked, and hollow. It was an unsettling place. The orbiting light of the lighthouse's lamp twirled about, alighting the cliff edge to the north of the lake.

Overlooking the wharf, atop the rocky cliff, stood an old house. It was one of legend around Pointe's Hollow. It had been there for years. People would speak of the place as if it was haunted. Not even the bravest would go up to that house. Looking at it now, Nicholas felt a cold shiver run down his spine. He looked down to the lighthouse again.

As Nicholas was looking out at the lighthouse, a large fishing boat was pulling into the commercial dock section. He smiled, thinking that tomorrow there would be some new faces around town, and he was not surprised to be excited by this. In a small town, new faces were an enjoyable reprieve from the mundane.

He left the window, en route to see if *Darkness Falls* was on as he waited for his aunt to call about cookies. The old TV he had inherited took a moment to light up, but when it did, Graveyard Jerry was in mid monologue introducing the next film in his selection.

"And, yes, I know what you're thinking. Quite a grave situation old Dale found himself in in the end of that one." Graveyard Jerry drew out the word 'grave' into a vibrato. He smirked, "Hopefully, our hero will have more luck in our next film, *Full Moon Massacre*."

Graveyard Jerry's voice graveled along and broke only

for him to let out a bloodcurdling howl. That being followed by his trademark cackle made Nicholas smile as he maneuvered deeper into the bed.

"What do you think?" He waited as if the viewers would respond. "You wanna know what I think? I think," Jerry paused for over-dramatic tension, "you're gonna have to watch to find out!" He cackled again.

The movie started with resounding music from a small label production company, followed quickly by a bone chilling note over the title card. After a few minutes, Nicholas had completely forgotten about the large ship docking. There was no way he could know what that ship had in store for his town and for him.

Chapter 2

THUD!

Nicholas jumped in surprise, almost falling out of his chair. The book slipped from his fingers. Pages fluttered about, causing Nicholas to lose his current spot.

"Oh, I'm sorry, lad. I didn't mean to scare ya," Mr. Lloyd, the librarian, said. The large stack of books he had been carrying now stood askew on the table. "Guess I'll never get use to being quiet at this time of night." He was a wiry framed, elderly man, with a long nose, spiraling white hair, and thin-framed glasses.

It was Friday, and the school day had dragged on relentlessly. Nicholas had decided he was going to spend the after school hours at the library. This was not unusual for him. Now, it was after closing, and he was still here, his nose firmly planted within the pages of a novel.

If he was not at school or home, most likely he was here at the library. For such a small town, Pointe's Hollow had a large library. A two-story, old brick building designed with classic architecture held enormous bookshelves stocked with thousands of books. The only breaks in the shelves were three sets of large, rustic oak tables set with lamps and a small, colorful, carpeted area for children.

Most nights, the library closed at eight o'clock sharp, but Mr. Lloyd was always here later taking care of different odd jobs. After a few times of Mr. Lloyd asking Nicholas to leave once the Roman numeral clock above the check-out counter hit eight, he had asked if he would like to stay late and continue reading. Nicholas had accepted the offer and taken full advantage on numerous occasions, sometimes even helping Mr. Lloyd with jobs around the library.

On this night, he had thoroughly lost himself in the bindings of Mary Shelley's *Frankenstein*. Not his first time through the classic, but it seemed every time he read it, he got something new out of it. The story was simply fantastic, and the themes of loneliness and death were riddled with great moments.

"That's alright, Mr. Lloyd. I should have finished up a while ago anyway. I'm sure my aunt will begin to worry soon."

"I see you're reading *Frankenstein* again," Mr. Lloyd prodded. In addition to allowing Nicholas to stay late in the library, Mr. Lloyd had always taken great interest in Nicholas's life. He always asked about his readings, his home life, how school was going, and what he planned to do after senior year. In honesty, Nicholas didn't know what he planned to do, and he told this to Mr. Lloyd time and time again.

Nicholas liked Mr. Lloyd. Out of everyone in Pointe's Hollow, Nicholas seemed to trust Mr. Lloyd the most, aside from his aunt, of course.

"Yup, still finding things I missed last time."

"I believe there are certain books where you always will, my boy, and that one may be one of 'em."

There was a slight twinkle in his eye, as if Mr. Lloyd knew more than he was letting on. "Some stories speak louder to certain people. I believe this one has spoken to you," he paused and seemed to consider what he said. "Come to think of it, I'm sure that's not the only one you've flipped through on multiple occasions."

Mr. Lloyd was being coy. He knew very well Nicholas had been through pretty much every monster book in the library on more than one occasion.

"I guess you just have a way with books," Mr. Lloyd smiled, causing his face to crinkle.

"Maybe," was all Nicholas could think to say. He looked at the stack Mr. Lloyd had placed on the table.

"You need help with those?" Nicholas offered.

Mr. Lloyd looked down at the books. "No, no. I'll be quite alright. You just be along now. I don't want your aunt coming after me 'cause you lost track of time. Just the one tonight then?"

Nicholas reclaimed *Frankenstein* from the table, "Yeah, just the one."

"Uh-huh." Mr. Lloyd lowered his head, so he could look over his glasses, "I guess I best be taking those back to their spots then, hm?"

Nicholas turned and felt a warm wave come over his face. There was a pile of books beside him on the table. Eight large volumes he had taken off the shelves with every intention of reading them, but had forgotten once he had *Frankenstein* in his hands.

"Yeah," Nicholas began, "I forgot about those ones. I'm sorry, Mr. Lloyd, I shouldn't have grabbed so many."

"Not at all, Nicholas, not at all. I've always admired a strong appetite for reading." The sly smile of his crept across his face again. "Now begone with ya."

Nicholas left the table, grabbing the book and his bag as he did. As he made his way to the front door, Mr. Lloyd called after him.

"Of course, you realize," Mr. Lloyd yelled after him, "I

await the day I'll be putting a book away with your name on the spine."

"See ya, Mr. Lloyd. Thanks again for everything," Nicholas said, not acknowledging the last thing Mr. Lloyd had said. It wasn't the first time the librarian had mentioned something about Nicholas writing, and Nicholas assumed it wouldn't be the last.

The old man began to collect Nicholas's forgotten books, shaking his head, thinking of what a good kid that boy was.

Nicholas suddenly felt the blast of cool air from the lake as he exited the library. He finished zipping his bag, with *Frankenstein* freshly tucked within the other contents, and then swung the shoulder straps into place. He zipped his jacket up a little higher to help save his neck from the cold. It was mid-November, and the small town was ready for a frigid winter.

After taking a seat aboard his bike, he debated which route to take home. The roads or the woods. He could follow the roads all the way home. It would be a smooth ride, but it would take a while. The woods would be rougher, but quicker.

He checked his watch, 10:36.

He had decided. The woods it was.

Nicholas kicked his pedals in reverse, caught a revolving pedal with his foot, and pressed it until it caught. He let his other foot leave the ground and began pedaling toward the path through the woods.

Nicholas had taken this shortcut many times and with the moonlight to help, he easily found the entrance. When he did find it, the hole seemed smaller and almost foreboding. It was as if the woods themselves didn't want him to pass through. After a moment's hesitation, he turned into the hole, and it appeared to widen to its original size, allowing Nicholas to ride smoothly into the woods.

Dusk

The dirt, mixed with leaves and twigs, crunched under Nicholas's tires. The tires seemed to slip out from under him with every bounce, but with the awkward nimbleness only a teenager is capable of, he plowed through the trail. The woods were quiet, which he thought was rather strange, but he hardly paid it any mind, thinking of his aunt and his warm bed.

A cool breeze slithered through the branches of the surrounding trees. A gust wormed and wiggled and then smacked Nicholas in the face. His eyes squinted against the blow.

Suddenly, something caught his attention from the corner of his eye. Nicholas turned, whipping his head to his right.

Nothing.

But he had seen something, hadn't he? Movement. It was movement between the trees. It had been fast, but it was sizable movement.

Sizable? Nicholas thought to himself. *It had been huge. Gia....*

He was unable to finish the thought; he had taken his eyes off the road for too long. His front tire struck a large root protruding from the ground. The bike bucked and threw Nicholas forward as if he was an offering.

"Take the boy," the bike seemed to say, "it's not me you want; it's the boy."

Nicholas had only a second to smile at this before impact shook his bones. He bounced off the dirt like a ball and flew even further. His glasses jumped off his face, abandoning the sinking S.S. Nicholas before his final plunge. He took two more bounces, one on his shoulder and another on his hip, before he came to a stop on his back.

"Damn it," Nicholas whispered.

It barely came out. The wind had been knocked from him, and he could hardly breathe. After a moment, he was able to open his eyes. The moon glared down from above him. The face of its cratered surface seemed to mock his plight, as if it was its root-disguised foot that had tripped him.

Nicholas slowly got up on his elbows. Everything hurt. He shot one more look up at the grinning moon, giving it a 'What are you looking at?' smirk, and then looked away. He'd be gone quickly if he began fighting with things as imposing as the moon.

Nicholas made it to his feet and cautiously stretched his back. The pain was enormous, and just as he thought he couldn't take it anymore, there was a slight pop and his muscles began to loosen. He thanked his lucky stars he was still young enough to take a fall like that and walk away mostly unharmed.

When he finally turned around, he saw his bike had done an exact copy of his roll. It laid only about two feet from where Nicholas had laid just a few seconds before. Seeing the bike there, Nicholas could see that he was in a sort of clearing. It was nothing spectacular. Probably only six or seven yards across and ten yards long, but in the thickness of Pointe's Hollow woods, that was a clearing.

Nicholas hunkered down low to the ground. He was nearsighted without his glasses, and he needed to get as close to the ground as he could if he was going to find them. He easily found them. Finding one's glasses seemed to be a talent all glasses-wearing people developed over time. Once he had them in hand, he quickly wiped of the lenses with his shirt and replaced them on his nose.

Nicholas looked around and saw nothing out of the ordinary within the trees or in the mangled maze of the branches. He looked back at the bike. He sighed, "What am I going to do with you?"

He tossed up his hands in frustration and then let them fall to his side, smacking his thighs. Truth be told, this wasn't the first spill he had had on this bike, and it would not be his last. He took another moment with his hands poised on his hips, shaking his head at the bike on the ground.

The bike looked so apologetic laying there that Nicholas had to forgive it. Dropping his hands from his hips, he went to retrieve it.

A cool shiver ran up Nicholas's back and licked his ear. It stopped him dead. Had he heard what he thought he had heard? No, that wasn't possible. But, yet, Nicholas knew what he had heard. It happened again.

"Nicholas," the wind whispered.

Nicholas whipped around; the path was clear. Gooseflesh ran up his arms with an intense ripple. He could feel himself want to shake.

It's just the wind, Nicholas, he thought. *Just the wind and an overactive imagination.*

The air was now silent. Nicholas let out a breath. When it stayed quiet, he turned back toward his bike. No sooner had Nicholas dismissed what he had heard when it came again, louder.

"Nicholas."

Nicholas turned. "Hello?" he said, voice trembling. He thought about bringing his hands up to defend himself, but couldn't move his arms.

The voice began to mock him and others popped up.

"Hello?" one mimicked.

"Nicholas," another called.

"Nicholas!" a third barked.

They seemed to come from all around him. He was turning on his heels. He went left, and then a voice would come from his right. When he turned right, the voice would be on his left.

"Nicholas."

"Hello?"

"Nicholas."

The voices began to speed up and grow louder and louder. It became so overpowering that Nicholas couldn't stand it any more. He could feel his eyes begin to burn with tears. Terrified, angry, and alone, Nicholas wanted nothing more than to stop the voices.

"Nicholas," the voices continued. They seemed to beckon him, but to or from where Nicholas couldn't tell.

Nicholas's hand went to the sides of his head. His eyes squeezed shut. This couldn't be happening. Nicholas was rational. Although he watched scary movies, he didn't believe in this, did he? Twenty minutes ago in the library with a book in hand, he didn't. Now, in the woods, with those damn voices - "Nicholas," "Hello" - he believed.

Just as he thought he was going mad, the voices stopped. They hissed out of existence on a smooth gust of wind. Nicholas cautiously opened his eyes.

Nothing was there. Just his bike sprawled out in its spot in the clearing. He dropped his hands from his ears. The night was eerily quiet now.

Thinking it over, thinking he was safe, Nicholas let out his held breath. That's when a low, guttural growl came from behind him. The tiny hairs on Nicholas's arms and neck pricked to attention. He slowly turned like a character from a horror movie. What he saw was exactly that, a horror movie.

Back in the shadows of the forest, two gleaming, yellow eyes glowed from the ebony abyss. Nicholas's shoulders followed his neck around, followed by his hips, until he was facing the eyes. They were large and menacing. They were relatively low to the ground. Whatever it was, it seemed too small to be a person.

Run! Nicholas screamed at himself. *Run, for heaven's sake. Run!*

But Nicholas couldn't take a single step, let alone run. He was petrified like an old piece of wood. All he could do was stare into the fiendish eyes. They blinked back in response to Nicholas's stares. A flash of black gave Nicholas great hope that he had imagined the eyes.

Slowly, another growl quivered into resonance as the eyes moved forward. Claws (or were they hands?) came into the clearing illuminated by the moonlight. They were grey and hairy and wielded long, black nails.

From the hands, arms protruded; from arms, shoulders; and from shoulders, a torso. The rest of the body followed, but Nicholas didn't see it because his focus was captured by the thing's face. Its face was an elongated muzzle.

It was a wolf. No, it was a giant wolf. No, even that wasn't right.

The posture was wrong for a wolf. The back was hunched as if the being was not meant to be on four appendages. To solidify this fact, the beast in front of him pushed off the ground with its forelegs and stood on its hindquarters.

It was a thing of fiction, imaginary, not real. Nicholas didn't believe it, wouldn't believe it. The beast's growl grew into a wild howl of ferocity. As the sound reverberated through Nicholas, he realized that sometimes fiction was reality and sometimes reality was fiction. Nicholas accepted this as he stood mere yards away from a seven-foot tall werewolf.

The werewolf was tall and thin, nothing like Lon Chaney in *The Wolf Man*. Covered in hair, with bent legs and muscular arms, the beast stood poised, ready to attack.

Nicholas wanted to run, but knew, on four legs or two, the beast would run him down without breaking a sweat. Nicholas could only stand there. Stand there and hope, hope for a miracle.

The beast, however, had other plans. It stepped back with one foot and then leaned forward, bellowing a roar of distaste. Nicholas's hair flew back in the blast of foul air. It was hot and smelt of meat. The roar was still continuing when the beast took off toward Nicholas. It bounded forward heedlessly, head down and arms outstretched.

When the beast was only a few steps away, it dived toward Nicholas, flying through the air. Nicholas could see the gleam in its yellow eyes.

Nicholas wanted to run, but knew he couldn't. He wished he could at least close his eyes, but he stood still, transfixed by the impossibility of the situation.

Hopefully, it would all be over quickly.

BANG!

The sound was an earthquake shaking Nicholas's entire world. A burst of blood and flesh ripped from the monster's body, flying out wildly. The weight of the hit caused the wolf's flight to stray off course, and Nicholas felt the air ripple past him as the beast missed.

It hit the ground beside him and slid, digging up a small section of earth. Sounds of whimpering and anger protruded from the wounded animal.

BANG!

BANG!

Two more beats of the resounding noise rang out in the small clearing. One sent up a flash of dust from the earth and another struck home in the pelt of the beast. It responded with a roar of protest and pain. The werewolf's legs scratched at the ground as it tried to gain its footing. It prevailed in its struggle and rushed off into the woods on all fours.

As Nicholas watched it go, there was a rustle behind him, and for a moment, he feared another beast was coming for him. He turned and saw not a wolf, but a man. The man was garbed in a long, dark coat. He stood in the clearing, hair shaggy, face unshaven, and eyes mad with glee. A large revolver sat perched in the man's outstretched arm, vomiting smoke.

"Get down," the man said in a gruff voice. Nicholas

heard him and wanted to comply, but he was too stunned to move.

The man closed the gap between them and put his hand on Nicholas's shoulder.

"I said," the man pressed on Nicholas's shoulder, "get down!" Nicholas was shoved to his knees.

The beast turned his trajectory from straight into the woods to circling the clearing.

BANG!

The gun in the man's hand went off. The bullet popped splinters from a tree between the man and the beast.

BANG!

The fifth bullet whistled through the air, over the back of the beast. The bullet caught a branch, and it exploded into oblivion.

BANG!

The final shot bounced off the bark of a tree and clipped the monster in the hindquarters. It roared in pain.

The man lowered the smoking pistol and snapped open the chamber. Brass casings spilled out in a shining sprinkle. The pieces clinked and clattered as they fell.

The beast's ears perked at the sound. It stopped its mad dash, skidding in the underbrush. Glaring at them, its top lip curled up into a snarl. Nicholas could see this from his crouched position. He began to rise now. The mysterious gunman was between him and the beast; he was no longer in the way. The man was scrounging in his pockets.

The monster began combing the ground with its front paw, in preparation of assault. Nicholas saw this and saw the man still trying to find his first bullet.

"Is it...." Nicholas began quietly. The man didn't respond. He found his first bullet and slid it into the chamber. That was answer enough for Nicholas.

The werewolf reared back and began another onslaught. Nicholas tapped the man's shoulder now and pointed out, "It's coming back."

The gunman found his second bullet and loaded it next to the first. He said, "I know," seemingly unconcerned.

The monster rumbled forward, pounding heavily against the ground. In quick succession, the man found the third and fourth rounds. Nicholas could feel the ground shaking below his feet with every bound of the beast.

"Hurry," Nicholas said.

The man found his fifth bullet, but had difficulty getting it into the chamber. The wolf was almost on them. In a few moments, they would be a rabid werewolf's road kill. Nicholas began to bounce on his heels.

"Hurry, man. Hurry!"

"I am trying," the man said, slightly annoyed, but light, as if this was normal for him. Vibrations shook Nicholas's calves. The man's fingers dug in the seemingly endless pouch of his pocket.

The final bullet was pulled from his coat's recesses. The man looked it over, "Hello, beautiful."

Despite Nicholas's terror, the man took another moment to kiss the bullet. In front of them, the wolf prepared to pounce over the final distance.

With a slight click, the sixth bullet fell into place. The wolf released the tension in its hind legs and flew at them. Nicholas had a moment of deja vu as he saw its mouth open again.

Faster than Nicholas could see, the man closed the chambers, raised the revolver, and fired.

BANG!

The shot rang out, seeming louder than any of the others. The slug flew forth, blowing out the back of the monster's skull. The force of the blast forced the monster back on its original path, head back, body rolling. The body fell on the ground with a soft plop. It gave a final, involuntary twitch and then went limp.

Dusk

Nicholas stood breathless, unsure if what he had just experienced was real. His savior stood, gun pointing straight up, smoke billowing out of the barrel. He looked majestic in the moonlight. Nicholas wanted to reach out and touch him, half expecting him to disappear.

The man dropped the gun, twirling it effortlessly on his finger. It slipped home in the holster hanging low on the man's hip. After another pause, he turned to Nicholas.

Nicholas looked the man over. He was tall, but he was quite slim underneath his coat. His clothes were wrinkled and unkempt. His face had a gleam of youth, but the lines carved into it were filled with the hollowness of many years. He was a man of legend and folklore. A cross between John Wayne and Sherlock Holmes, Nicholas decided. Dangerous and brilliant. A catastrophic combination.

"Are you okay?" the rough voice of the gunman asked. Nicholas heard him, but didn't answer.

"Wha…." was all Nicholas could manage. He was in a daze.

"You okay?" he asked again. "You're not gonna hurl, are you?"

Nicholas could only look at him, confused.

Hurl? Why would I hurl?

Nicholas's eyes wandered around the stranger to see what he hadn't wanted Nicholas to see.

Behind the stranger, the body of the beast had changed. Instead of the large, hairy body that had laid there just a moment before, there was a naked man. His body was pale and completely nude from head to toe. The back of the head was encompassed by a dark hole, surrounded by strands of wet gore.

The blood rushed out of Nicholas's face just as it was pooling out of the dead man's head. The ground below Nicholas's feet began to shift, tilting one way, then another. His head felt three times its normal size. He wanted to talk, but his tongue was thick, his mouth dry. Little black dots popped up into his vision. Everything began to spin.

Nicholas had just enough consciousness to hear the man say something that sounded like 'shift,' and then his face met the ground and everything went black.

The feeble screen door smacked the frame with a hard rap as Earl Hutchins left Richie's, out the back door. He stutter-stepped down the old wood steps, and once he felt dirt below his feet, he almost fell forward. The only thing that held him up was years of adapted skills at walking inebriated.

The neck of a bottle was pinched loosely between his two stubby fingers. Earl raised the bottle, bent his back, and drained the final droplets. He puckered and licked his lips as he lowered the bottle.

Without a cautionary glance, Earl tossed the now empty bottle over his shoulder. His aim was usually good, but this time he missed the large green dumpster pressed up to the back of the bar. Brown glass shrapnel exploded into a hazard all over the ground.

With his drink finished and discarded, he stretched, belched, and stumbled off. He had an aching pain in his bladder. He needed to take a piss, needed to bad. Richie's bar was obviously stocked with a good size bathroom with three different porcelain drains Earl could have graced with his urine, but that wasn't Earl. Earl was what he liked to call a rougher. At the ripe age of fifty-six, he had spent most of his life outside.

His father put it best when he used to say, "There ain't nothin' better than taking a piss with a cool breeze on your pecker. Well, maybe a good lookin' woman, but that's all I say."

Earl chuckled heartily at the memory and almost knocked himself over from the force. He regained his footing and continued toward his destination. He crossed the back lot of Richie's and then crossed Coral Street into the forest. A lot of people in The Hollow were leery of the woods.

Bunch of worry wart sissies, Earl thought as he drunkenly fought through the brush.

After the first layer of plant life, the area between the trees opened up, and he was able to walk more freely. The rough terrain of the forest floor was a little harder to traverse. A couple of times, Earl had to catch himself on a tree to save himself from going all the way to the ground.

On the third time, he caught himself with a strong hand on a large lump in the trunk of a tree. Earl looked at the tree and chuckled.

"I'm sorry, madam," he began, words slurring slightly, "I didn't see you standing there."

He patted the tree's trunk with a thick hand. His muscular arms vibrated with the hits. Earl had been a sailor once upon a time. Years of rigging sails and hauling fishing nets had turned his arms into small trees themselves, his muscles lining his arms like the grains of the bark on the trees.

A burp came up from his gut, and he stifled it with one of his thick-fingered fists. His other hand arose in an apologetic gesture.

"Excuse me if you will, miss. Must have found myself at the bottom of a few too many," he said, laughing. "Hey, you wouldn't happen to know where the little boys' room is around here, do ya?"

The tree obviously gave no response. There wasn't even a breeze, so the wiry branches stood eerily still.

"You do?" Earl said, excitement growing. He turned, "Right over there, you say? Second tree on the left? Is that so?"

Earl put his hands on his hips as if he was contemplating this. After a moment, he nodded, agreeing with the tree's answer.

"Well, thank you loads." Earl turned to go mark the second tree on the left. He suddenly turned back. "Now, don't you go anywhere," he said, pointing at the tree, "I'll be back to talk with you after I take care of some business. I wouldn't want you to leaf while I'm gone."

Earl bellowed out a laugh that shook his sizable gut in heaves.

"Get it?" he asked. The tree stared back at him, almost with a look of derision. Earl waved the tree away and found himself at his make-shift urinal. He unzipped his pants and began his business.

The forest was silent, except for the sound of running urine on bark. Earl didn't notice the silence; he was too focused on his business.

"Earl," no louder than a whisper, came on the wind.

Earl heard it, but paid it no mind.

"Earl." More lyrical this time, it beckoned him. Earl looked back at his former companion. The tree just sat there as before. Shrugging, Earl finished his leak, gave it a good shake, and zipped up his pants.

"Earl," the voice said again, louder.

Earl whipped around, swaying on his heels. He was looking at the tree again.

"You say something, darling?" His drunken state quickly began to wash away as fear sunk in. He took a step toward the tree, still swaying, but less now.

The tree looked the same as it had before, or did it? There was something different about it. The tree couldn't have moved, but it seemed to have shifted. That was crazy. Of course, talking with a tree is also crazy, but Earl didn't think of this.

Dusk

The shadows, Earl thought, and he was right. The difference on the tree was the shadows. Earl looked up, right into the face of a full moon. Before, the moon had illuminated the tree quite fully with little disturbance between them. Now, the tree was covered in mostly shadow.

"What in Sam hell," Earl said aloud to himself. He walked over to the tree, with a few stumbling steps. When he reached it, he saw his own shadow grow tall on the trunk.

His hand raised to touch the tree. He had a quick moment to think that this might be a bad idea, and then his fingers were on the bark.

As soon as he made contact with it, something happened. The shadows on the tree rushed away. They seemed to be pulled from the front of the tree to the dark side, disappearing. Earl's eyes widened.

How many drinks had he had? He couldn't remember. He quickly vowed that if he got out of this, he would never drink again. An empty promise, both he and God knew that. Earl had often made this promise and always found himself back on a stool at Richie's with a drink in his hand.

While Earl was vowing something he would never do, he became aware of his own shadow. But it couldn't be his shadow, for it was no longer mimicking him. Earl raised his hand in an experiment. The shadow's arm didn't move. Earl began to wave his hand. Again, the shadow did not move.

Earl dropped his hand. His mouth felt dry. He wanted a drink. Suddenly, as Earl stood there, his shadow raised its hand of its own accord. Earl could only stare, still as stone, as the rogue shadow closed its hand into a fist. The first finger on the shadow's hand shot out, making Earl flinch. The shadow began to wag its finger and shake its head side to side as if to say, "Tsk tsk, Earl. Tsk tsk."

Earl blinked, hoping the hallucination or mirage or whatever it was would be gone. But no matter how many times his eyes closed, when he opened them again, the shadow was there. Still shaking its head. Still wagging the derisive finger.

SNAP!

The sound made Earl jump. It came from behind him. Earl, being a rougher, knew what the sound was as soon as he heard it. It was the snap of a twig. The only problem was that twigs did not snap on their own. Earl could feel the powerful presence of the other now.

The shadow stopped its wagging finger to point behind Earl. Earl felt the sweat drip down his face, roll around his eye, over his cheek, and drop from his jaw line. A lump formed in Earl's throat, and he forced it down.

God, I'm sorry for bothering you, but I think I'm gonna need some help, Earl thought pleadingly as he began sprinting wildly through the trees. His arms and legs were still rubbery from the alcohol in his system, but that didn't stop him from running.

He cursed himself for having the third, fourth, and fifth drinks. His feet bent and his ankles rolled over the forest floor. By sheer willpower, he stayed up. His hands touched and pushed off from trees in an attempt to make himself go even faster.

Behind him, he heard twigs cracking, heard leaves rustling and could feel the thing getting closer and closer. He didn't dare look back, though. He didn't need to. He knew the thing was there.

To his left, he saw the small light above the back door of Richie's bar. He still had a lot of woods, a street, and the back lot to traverse, but Earl believed if he got to Richie's, he'd be safe. He pushed himself even faster.

The thing was right on his heels. He could hear it. But he could see the small hallway leading to the back door out of Richie's. He could see his stool, butt print slowly fading, but still there. And he could see the tall, frothing glass he was going to order as soon as he sat down.

Dusk

Now, if you don't believe God is a grudge-holding deity, Earl would have done everything he could to convince you otherwise. For no sooner had he envisioned the drink he vowed to never have again than he lost his footing and fell, sprawling to the ground.

As he fell, Earl thought of another of his father's sayings. This one just as simple and true to this day as it was the day his old man had said it. "Life's a bitch."

Earl fell flat on his chest and then rolled in the underbrush. Once Earl came to a stop, all he could do was turn and face his attacker. But when he turned, nothing was there. Earl could see the path he had taken through the woods. Saw disturbed leaves, broken branches, but nothing was chasing him.

Earl breathed heavily. A smile cracked across his face.

Just the alcohol, Earl old buddy, he thought.

The relief was overwhelming. Earl looked down at the ground, attempting to catch his breath. When he looked back up at the woods, he still saw nothing. His smile grew.

He looked to the right, nothing. He looked to the left, nothing. Earl chuckled slightly. As he looked back center, something caught his eye. The color drained from his face, and his smile disappeared.

It was his shadow, black and disconnected. It stood staining a tree disconnected from Earl as he sat on the ground. But that wasn't the worse of it. The shadow was pointing again. Pointing behind Earl. Earl didn't even turn. He felt warm, wet breath cake the back of his neck. There was a sharp pain and then only blackness.

Chapter 3

Nicholas woke up in a flash. His hand went to his head where a pounding was deep within. He sat up in bed, swinging his feet over the side.

"Jinkies!"

Nicholas looked up from the floor to his television. Images swam before him, murky and deformed. He reached out for his glasses, grabbed them off his bedside table, and placed them on his face. *Scooby-Doo, Where Are You!* was on. It was Nicholas's ritual to watch *Scooby-Doo* every Saturday morning. The characters were groovy, and the monster-themed mysteries were something that fell right into Nicholas's wheel house. The only downside of the show: the monsters always ended up being guys in a mask at the end. But it was something Nicholas could look past.

Did I leave the TV on? Nicholas thought, but he couldn't remember. He actually couldn't remember even coming home last night. What was the last thing he did remember? He remembered going to the library and talking with Mr. Lloyd. He got on his bike and then....

Eyes, claws, bullets, and a head covered in gore flashed across his mind. The power of the memory threatened to knock him out.

"Zoinks!" Shaggy, a character from the show, said from the television.

Zoinks is right, Nicholas thought.

Nicholas got up from his bed and clicked off the television. He wasn't in the mood for Scooby and the gang. Now that he was standing, he realized he was still fully clothed, jacket and shoes included.

How did I get back?

Nicholas then realized the last thing he remembered was passing out in the middle of the woods. Nicholas thought harder and remembered the gunslinger who had saved him. Had he been the one who brought Nicholas back home?

How did he know where I lived?

All of a sudden, Nicholas's savior had become very frightening. His knowledge of Nicholas's home and the deadly skills that Nicholas had seen the night before were a scary combination. Nicholas thought about the man being in his house, in his room. It was a terrible feeling of invasion. He felt like he needed a shower. He wondered if his aunt would be....

Aunt Sherri. The thought was so obvious and violent that he almost fell back from the brutality of it.

Without another thought, Nicholas darted for the hall. He quickly unfolded and descended the ladder and headed to his Aunt Sherri's room. It was empty. The bed was made and nothing seemed disturbed, but it wasn't enough to ease his worry.

Nicholas slapped the door frame and rushed down the hall. He descended the second set of stairs and made it to ground level. Whipping through the living room, he stopped in the doorway of the kitchen and saw his aunt standing by the stove, cooking, unharmed, and her hair done up.

He let out a thick breath of worry. He suddenly realized he was out of breath, and he leaned against the wall, inhaling deeply. Sherri turned around to look at Nicholas, her face slowly changing from cheery to worry.

"Nicholas, are you okay?" she said.

Nicholas smiled and waved his hand at her, "Yeah, I'm...." He had to take in another breath. "I'm... fine. Just... tripped... tripped on the...." His hand was waving and pointing at the staircase.

"Uh, huh," his aunt said, looking the boy up and down. "You think you might want to get changed? I know you got in late, but that is no excuse to be a mess."

She pointed at Nicholas with a spatula.

Nicholas looked down at himself. He was already aware he was in dirty clothes, but he hadn't realized until this moment he was also caked in dirt and grass stains.

"Well, you know," Nicholas began, "boys will be boys." He smiled.

"Preaching to the choir, Nicky," Sherri said.

"I'm sorry about being out so late," Nicholas said, fishing for more information.

"No worries. I was a teenager once, too, you know. Of course, I never stayed late at a library. A drive-in maybe, possibly a random basement, but never a library."

The library?

His desire for answers only made him more confused. So, he continued, "Yeah, well you know me and my books."

"Yes, I do. I'm just glad we have a place for you to go. Especially with Mr. Lloyd being over there all the time. A good guy, Mr. Lloyd. He's quite fond of you, you know?"

"Mr. Lloyd?" Nicholas asked before he could stop himself.

"Yeah, Mr. Lloyd." Sherri turned around and looked at him with a strange glance, "He likes you. I thought that'd be more than obvious after last night."

Dusk

Yes, of course. Nicholas thought. *Now if only I could remember last night.*

"Yeah, he's great." A bad recovery, but the only thing Nicholas could think to say. Luckily, his aunt took the bait without question. His aunt was one of those people who, if you let them say a few words, would preach for hours.

"Yup, I caught him outside by that old beater truck of his after you had already gone up to your room, without saying good night by the way, don't think I missed that, Mister." She pointed her spatula at him again, this time in an accusatory manner.

"Sorry," Nicholas said, with a slight smile.

"Ah, well, it's in the past. Just don't let it happen again, hear me?"

"I hear ya," Nicholas answered.

"Uh, huh." Turning back to her breakfast frying in the pan, she said, "Anyway, I caught up with Mr. Lloyd outside, and he explained you helped him out with some inventory. I swear I worried about times like this when I started looking after you, but if I knew then that the worst thing you'd get into was working at a library, I'd have laughed myself to death."

Nicholas was nodding, but he didn't understand a word of it. He had been at the library last night. He had gotten a book and had talked with Mr. Lloyd a bit before he left, but Mr. Lloyd refused his help. Then, Nicholas happened upon the mess in the woods. Although he hadn't gotten a really good look at the man, Nicholas was sure that Mr. Lloyd was not his savior.

The only explanation was that Mr. Lloyd knew who the gunman was or at least had some idea of what had happened last night. He would have to go talk with Mr. Lloyd as soon as possible if he was going to get any real answers.

"Nicholas?" his aunt had continued. He looked back up to her now. "Don't you think?"

Nicholas was a good liar, but he wasn't that good, "Think about what?"

"Mr. Lloyd, strange. Nice, don't get me wrong. A saint to take you under his wing like he has, but always seems to be hiding something."

Nicholas was still only half listening, but he could at least answer now. "Yeah."

"Look at me gossiping like a school girl. Mr. Lloyd is privileged to his secrets just like the rest of us, and I'll just have to live with that."

"Yeah," Nicholas said again.

After a shower and a change of clothes, Nicholas pedaled away from his house toward the library and Mr. Lloyd, hoping to get some answers.

As Nicholas approached the library, he eyed the forest off to the northwest. The trees were a large, formidable force. The outer limits being the front lines, standing strong and tall. The canopy of the trees shrouded the inner woods in darkness, and they seemed to beg for someone to enter them. For someone to enter and be caught.

Trapped.

To the right of the front door, Nicholas locked up his bike at the rack and entered. He peered about the place trying to find Mr. Lloyd. Behind the desk, Linda, Mr. Lloyd's assistant, sat penning something in tiny scribbles, but Mr. Lloyd was nowhere in sight.

Mr. Lloyd's absence from the library was a rarity. There used to be a rumor in the high school that Mr. Lloyd actually lived in the library. Of course, Nicholas knew this was complete garbage considering he himself had spent many nights here in the library and seen Mr. Lloyd leave for home with his own eyes. This, however, didn't discredit the fact that the library without Mr. Lloyd was strange. He had to be around here somewhere.

Or maybe he's sick. Nicholas thought this could be a

possibility. *Or he's de....* Nicholas didn't allow himself to finish that thought. He would have discarded it entirely except for the itching feeling that if anything he remembered from last night was actually true, Mr. Lloyd's death was not out of the realm of possibility.

Nicholas began searching the library trying to escape his sneaking suspicions. He searched the entire first floor with no success. He even waited outside the public restroom to see if Mr. Lloyd had been in there when he entered the library. Again, no success. He finally decided to look on the second floor.

The second floor, always so silent, made Nicholas's hair stand on end. He perused the large shelves of books, looking up and down the rows for any sign of the librarian. As hope was fading, Nicholas saw a pile of books at the end of one of the rows. He went to the next row over, which incidentally enough was the last row, and found Mr. Lloyd shelving books back into place.

Seeing Mr. Lloyd there, taking part in his day-to-day routine, suddenly made Nicholas angry. Here was Mr. Lloyd acting like yesterday was just another day. Acting like Nicholas didn't almost die yesterday. Acting like everything was just fine.

Although Nicholas was angry, he restrained himself from yelling out as he approached the librarian. Nicholas made it all the way to a few feet behind Mr. Lloyd, who didn't even glance up. Nicholas stopped and opened his mouth to say something, but nothing came out. His mouth closed, opened, and closed again without saying anything.

"I'm guessing you came here for some answers," Mr. Lloyd said, without turning around.

He had a large novel in his hand and was inspecting its binding. If Nicholas hadn't already been speechless, he certainly was now. Mr. Lloyd's tone was solid, but apologetic. This made Nicholas ashamed of his earlier anger.

He realized this wasn't just another day for Mr. Lloyd, either.

Now, up close, Nicholas could see the faint, dark circles under Mr. Lloyd's eyes, and his chin had a very fine layer of stubble. Even though it seemed Mr. Lloyd was offering what Nicholas had come for, he was unable to ask for it.

Mr. Lloyd turned from the book in his hands, looking over his thin-framed glasses at Nicholas. Nicholas didn't shy away from his look, but he did shrink a little adjusting his own glasses. His fury from before was all but gone. Although Nicholas hadn't said anything, Mr. Lloyd gave a slight nod of understanding.

"I was afraid of something like this," he said, turning back and placing the book in his hands on the shelf. "I knew if I stayed here, sooner or later something like this would happen again."

The book was placed safely between the other volumes on the shelf, but his hand still rested upon it, as if the book was precious to him. The word "again" rang through the quiet room.

Mr. Lloyd turned back to Nicholas, "I always knew it would be you. I wish it wasn't. I wish this hadn't happened to you, but I think, in a way, it was always meant to."

Nicholas couldn't be silent any longer.

"What would be me? I don't even know what happened last night. You're not making any sense."

Mr. Lloyd sighed, his years weighing in his eyes. "Come, we shouldn't speak of it here. We'll talk in my office."

He turned away, leaving the piles of books, and motioned Nicholas to follow with a wave of his hand. After a moment of hesitation, Nicholas did.

Mr. Lloyd's office had the feel of being lived in. Unlike most offices, it felt like this was where Mr. Lloyd spent most of his time. Nicholas supposed he did. It sat near the front door on the first floor, right behind the front desk.

Two walls were covered with ceiling high bookshelves. The third, opposite from the door, had a large window spanning its length. Below the window stood another bookshelf. Nicholas thought it strange for a man who worked in a library to surround himself with even more books in his office. But on further inspection, Nicholas could see that although there were many books on the shelves, there was a lot of empty space and knickknacks spaced about.

In front of the back wall sat a desk, impish in comparison to the large bookshelves surrounding it, but Nicholas supposed it was all the space Mr. Lloyd needed.

There was room for papers, a cup of pens and pencils, files stacked three high, and a clear area for current projects. At the very edge, a small triangle name plate stood with the name 'Melville Lloyd' engraved above 'Head Librarian.' Nicholas had never known Mr. Lloyd's first name. Everyone referred to Mr. Lloyd by his title and last name. He guessed with a name like Melville, Nicholas would go by 'Mr. Lloyd' as well.

Mr. Lloyd sat in the large desk chair behind the desk and motioned Nicholas to drag an antique armchair from the corner. Nicholas did, placing the chair directly in front of the desk, so he and Mr. Lloyd were straight on. A conversation of the magnitude they were about to have called for nothing less.

For a moment, neither spoke. Nicholas stared at Mr. Lloyd as Mr. Lloyd scanned the shelves on the left side of the room. Nicholas was about to say something, something he did not want to say, when Mr. Lloyd spoke up.

"I first came to Pointe's Hollow in 1946." His voice didn't waver, but there was a sense of sadness in his words. "Thirty years ago that was. My God, how time flies looking back." A sad smile cracked his face.

"People always talk about if they could go back and do

things differently, they would. They have a mental list of all the times they'd like to change. Now, I haven't lived a perfect life, nowhere near." His smile faded. "But there is only one thing I would change if I could."

Mr. Lloyd finally turned away from his books and met Nicholas's eyes. "If I could, I'd go back and never stop in this godforsaken town. I would leave Pointe's Hollow in my rearview mirror and never think of it again."

Nicholas could see the seriousness in Mr. Lloyd's eyes. He could also see the fear. It made Nicholas afraid. He wished he could forget it all and walk away right now, but he stayed, needing to know more.

"In my first year of living here, my wife had gotten pregnant and nine months later, we were blessed with Jacob, my son." As Mr. Lloyd continued his story, he turned back to his books. "We thought this was a good omen. Thought it was a sign that this was where we should be. My wife was always one for the signs. Believed that if she was supposed to do something, God would send her a sign."

Another smile came, this one tender, but it was just as short-lived as the first one.

"I was working on the docks at night, along with working for the school's library. The baby had been a little more expensive than originally anticipated. They always are, so I was trying to get some extra money."

He sighed, looking down at his fingers. His fingers on his right hand were picking at something on his left.

"I was coming off my shift, almost home, when I heard the scream." Mr. Lloyd's eyes glazed over as he went back to that night. "The front door was ajar, hanging by a single hinge. I pushed through, ignoring the gashes in the wood. I went straight to Jacob's room. I saw bits and pieces all over. The crib was smashed, and there was a wet shine to the splinters." Mr. Lloyd's voice wavered, but he continued.

"That's when I saw it. At first, I couldn't comprehend

what it was."

Nicholas shifted in his chair, remembering that he had felt the same way just the night before.

Mr. Lloyd talked, long breaks between his words. "Its skin was covered in scales. Its hands, giant claws. Fingers and toes webbed. And eyes, black as coal. I wanted to run as soon as I saw it. It turned and looked at me."

Mr. Lloyd paused in his telling. He seemed to be struggling with something. His hand came up and wiped over his mouth. Nicholas thought he saw a slight shake, but he couldn't be sure.

"My wife, Laura," he paused as the name came from his lips, "Laura was laying limp in the thing's arms. Its mouth was parted with teeth, like daggers, shining, stained red."

Mr. Lloyd couldn't hold it anymore, and a tear spilled from one of his eyes.

"At the time, the worst thing I could think was it had bit her. The bastard bit her." The quiver in his voice was clearly audible now. "But then, then I remembered the crib and how it shined when I first entered the room."

Nicholas heard what Mr. Lloyd was saying, but it took a moment for him to understand; then, he knew. The beast had eaten Mr. Lloyd's son. Nicholas's stomach flipped, and he felt like vomiting.

With a sense of urgency, Mr. Lloyd continued, "After that, I went into a blind rage. I took my knife from my belt; I had it on me for gutting fish at the docks." Mr. Lloyd's hand raised in a wielding fist. "I charged and tackled the monster. In the mess that followed, I was able to bury the knife into the thing." His fist came down on his other hand. "It threw me off and rushed away. I chased it all the way to the lake until it disappeared into the water."

With the worst part of his story over, he was able to calm a bit. Nicholas was glad; he hated seeing Mr. Lloyd like this.

"When I returned home, I found my son gone, my wife dead, and my life as I knew it over."

Mr. Lloyd looked down now, finishing his story. Nicholas looked down, too. Nicholas's fists were clenched. He released his fingers, revealing red palms. After a moment, he looked up. Mr. Lloyd was already looking at him.

"I tell you this so you understand," Mr. Lloyd said.

Nicholas finally found his voice, "Understand what?"

"That there is something very wrong in Pointe's Hollow."

"What do you mean?"

Mr. Lloyd fell back in his chair. His story and the events of the previous night were taking their toll. "I don't know, not exactly. I only know that it's true."

Nicholas was irritated by Mr. Lloyd's coy words, "How can you know? I mean what you're saying, about your...." But no matter how annoyed he was, Nicholas didn't want to hurt Mr. Lloyd by bringing up his family again. "It can't be true. Monsters aren't real. They're the things of movies, of books." Nicholas threw up his arms to emphasize his point, pointing out the books all around. "They're fiction. Imaginary."

Mr. Lloyd looked at Nicholas. "Yes, they are," he said finally, taking Nicholas off guard.

"Yes, in most circumstances, they are," Mr. Lloyd continued. "In most places, they are just as you say, fiction. Imaginary. But not here, not in Pointe's Hollow."

Nicholas looked at Mr. Lloyd, confused. Mr Lloyd continued to elaborate. "Like I said, I don't know everything. I'm not saying I do. I don't even know if I'm one-hundred percent right. But this is what I have been able to find out." Mr. Lloyd shifted himself in his chair and continued.

"There are certain places where the lines between fiction and reality blur. I don't know what causes it. I'm not even sure what the blur fully entails. But what I do know, and what you know, is reality is just a frame of mind."

Nicholas stared at Mr. Lloyd for a while. What he knew was that what Mr. Lloyd was saying was crazy, some delusion of a wronged widower spoiled by time and age. That had to be it. But what Nicholas also knew was there was no better explanation for what had happened last night.

"Who is he?" Nicholas said before he knew what he was saying.

"Him? Well, to be honest, I don't rightly know. Before last night, I had only seen him once before, about three years ago. He came to the library, real late one night. He slipped through the front door as the last person left. When I saw him come in, I was instantly cautious. He was," he paused, hand waving, trying to think of the word, "haunting. Had there been any money in the library, I would have thought he was there to rob me. But there was none."

Mr. Lloyd got up from his chair. He walked over to the bookshelf on his right and picked up something from it. He walked around the desk and handed it to Nicholas.

It was a knife. Nicholas spun it around in his hands. The handle had little splotches of coral on it, and the blade had become rusty. It had the look of spending too much time under water.

"That was the knife I put into the back of the beast that killed my wife and son," Mr. Lloyd said. "When that, that thing disappeared into the lake, it took that knife with it. I got it back thirty-seven years later, when that man came into the library."

Nicholas looked at him, stunned. Mr. Lloyd smirked.

"Because of that day, and after last night, I'm pretty sure he's on our side."

Nicholas looked at the knife again. His thoughts drifted back to the previous night. He raised it, handing it back to Mr. Lloyd. "Good thing for us."

Mr. Lloyd took the knife and placed it back on the stand on the shelf. He walked around the desk and took his seat again. Nicholas could see that Mr. Lloyd wanted to end the conversation, but Nicholas had more questions.

"So, where can I find him?" The question had come out more intensely than Nicholas intended. Mr. Lloyd noticed the intensity, but didn't comment.

"You can't, or at least I don't know how. So far, it's been he finds you, not the other way around."

Nicholas was upset by this fact. Again, Mr. Lloyd noticed, and this time, he did comment.

"Why do you want to find him?"

"I'd just like to thank him, I guess." Nicholas said quickly. He knew he had spiked Mr. Lloyd's interest, and he didn't want to allude to his real intentions.

"You guess?" Mr. Lloyd said, and with that, Nicholas knew he had been caught. Nicholas sighed and looked at his feet.

"That's what I thought," Mr. Lloyd continued. "Now, Nicholas, listen to me very carefully." Mr. Lloyd leaned over his desk and waited for Nicholas to look up from his feet. "Do not go looking for trouble. You knock on the devil's door, he will answer. Do not tempt him."

Nicholas looked at him.

"Promise me, Nicholas."

Nicholas knew it was wrong to lie, especially to a friend, and he did regard Mr. Lloyd as a friend. It felt very wrong when he said, "I promise."

"Good," Mr. Lloyd relented, but with a hint of sadness.

All of a sudden, Nicholas wanted the conversation to end. He stood, thanked Mr. Lloyd for his time, and said he must be going. Mr. Lloyd smiled and said it was no problem.

Nicholas was almost to the door when he stopped and turned back toward Mr. Lloyd. Mr. Lloyd had moved to some matters on his desk and didn't look up until Nicholas spoke.

"Mr. Lloyd?" Nicholas began. Mr. Lloyd looked up at him, eyebrows raised. "Why didn't you leave?" He took a moment and then decided to clarify. "I mean, after your family was.... Why didn't you leave? Why did you stay?"

Mr. Lloyd looked at Nicholas for a long moment, so long that Nicholas was afraid he had offended him. He was about to take the question back when Mr. Lloyd smiled. The first real, honest smile since their conversation had begun.

"I'm not sure, but if I'd had to guess, I'd have to say it's the same reason you are going to go looking for trouble tonight."

Nicholas was nervous all of a sudden. He wished he had just skipped this last question. "I wasn't going...."

Mr. Lloyd stopped him with an upraised hand and a shake of the head. "Honestly, I expected nothing less." Mr. Lloyd smiled, an old, weathered smile, and turned back to work.

Nicholas released a breath and smiled himself. He raised a hand, gave a little salute to Mr. Lloyd, and then left the office without a look back.

From his office window, Mr. Lloyd watched Nicholas get on his bike and ride away. He would have given anything to save the boy from the world he was about to walk into. Unfortunately, he didn't have that option.

The boy's question had been one he had asked himself many times. Why hadn't he left? There had been nothing holding him here after his family's death.

Mr. Lloyd sighed, rubbing his temples with his thumb and finger. In the months after his family's untimely death, he went through a rough time. Anyone would, he supposed, but he had been really low.

He hadn't told anyone about the thing he had encountered. On top of everything, Mr. Lloyd had not wanted a trip to the loony bin. The idea of anyone taking him seriously was absolutely absurd. No one would believe him. He wasn't even sure he believed himself. When the police had asked him what had happened, he fabricated a story of seeing a man rush from his house as he returned home. The police believed him, following through with the case, but, obviously, in the end, coming up with nothing.

Even on days cops came to his house with good news, news of leads on the case, he had been somber. Because the leads, no matter how solid, would lead nowhere, and he knew this. For all the answers he needed had sunk to the bottom of the lake. There were times on the worst of days when he had gone out into the water in drunk tantrums and tempted the beast to come for him as well.

Nothing ever came.

Mr. Lloyd dropped into his chair. Belief in what he saw only came now because of the man who brought his knife back from the depths. He looked over to the shelf where the knife now sat. Its old and dull blade stared back with a heavily-weighted glare. The knife had been a symbol for many things. First, Mr. Lloyd's sanity. Second, the beast's death and the triumph of justice. But finally, it was a reminder of what he had lost.

He wished he could throw it away. He wished he could leave The Hollow. He would never have remarried; that was without a doubt. Laura was always the only woman for him. But he could have had a chance at some sort of happiness. Most of the time, he enjoyed doing what he was doing, but there was always a looming darkness as long as those woods surrounded him.

Just like he told the boy, there was no way to prove or

to be sure, but he knew something was wrong with Pointe's Hollow. It all spawned from those hallowed woods. Mr. Lloyd looked away from the knife and turned to gaze out the window again. At the far edge of the far field, he could see the tree line.

The reason Mr. Lloyd hadn't left was nothing sentimental or psychological; it was because of those woods. Although Mr. Lloyd had never admitted it, not even to himself, he knew those woods were at fault for his continued existence in The Hollow.

His eyes scanned the tree line from right to left, then left to right. As he scanned, he never had the feeling he was looking at the same section of trees. Even when he looked at one section moments before, those trees looked different the next moment, as if something had changed. The feeling was unsettling, but what was even more unsettling was the feeling of something looking back.

Mr. Lloyd had never tried to leave, but deep down, he knew if he had, those trees wouldn't have let him. They wouldn't let anybody leave if they didn't want you to leave.

Chapter 4

As Nicholas rode away from the library, his mind felt like mush. So many things had changed so suddenly that he was unsure how to feel about all of it. Mr. Lloyd was a sound man, respected by everyone in town. If he believed the town was evil, then it most likely was.

But that only raised more questions than it answered. How was a town evil? People could be evil, sure. History was full of evil people. But a town? A place? No, it wasn't possible.

Neither are werewolves, Nicholas thought, *and neither are sea creatures or monsters or whatever it was that Mr. Lloyd had seen so many years ago.*

It seemed that the ideas of reality and fiction were being crossed in Pointe's Hollow and, like it or not, Nicholas found himself in the middle of it all.

Nicholas turned onto Harbor Street. It was more densely populated than his first pass through. The Clark brothers, Willy and Howard, two elderly chaps who loved to fight with each other almost as much as they loved each other, were in a heated checker match outside the barber shop. Nicholas could hear their voices from the other end of the street, but could pick out only a few words.

As the brothers fought, people meandered about on the sidewalk, and shops were abuzz with the life of a small town on a late Saturday morning.

Nicholas needed something to calm his nerves and take his mind off the events of the night before. He skidded to a halt in front of Shores. An ice cold Coca-Cola would be the perfect thing for a troubled teenager dealing with the shock of finding out the things that go bump in the night are real.

After locking up his bike on a light post in front of the diner, he pushed through the glass doors and was bombarded by the rattling chatter inside the diner. It was about eleven thirty, so the lunch crowd was in full force. All but one of the tables were full, and only a few stools sat vacant.

Nicholas took a seat, and after a moment, Mike, the diner owner, came over to take his order.

"What'll it be, Bud?" He put both hands on the bar and leaned forward, taking full notice of Nicholas. Even after years of owning, running, and cooking for a small town diner, Mike was still able to have the demeanor of completely enjoying his job. Yup, Mike was one of the few people who was doing something he truly enjoyed. Nicholas admired that.

"Just a Coke, Mike."

"Coming right up." With that, Mike was gone.

Nicholas grabbed a napkin off the bar and retrieved a pen from his jacket pocket. He began to scribble on the napkin while waiting for his Coke. Before long and without realizing what he was doing, a moon behind strips of clouds in a starless sky and a shadowy figure below manifested itself onto the napkin. The figure was strangely wolfish, but wasn't exactly what Nicholas had come in hoping to forget.

"That's really cool."

Nicholas looked up from his napkin expecting to see Mike back with his Coke, but instead was surprised to see Emily Gordon perched on the stool next to him. So many times Nicholas had seen her face. Picked it out from the rest of his class, but not once had he been this close to her.

"Your picture," she said, pointing to the napkin in front of Nicholas. He realized he had been staring at her without saying anything.

"Yeah?" he was finally able to muster. He looked from her back at the drawing and then back up to her. "It's okay, isn't it?"

"Okay? It's awesome." She was smiling now, completely engrossed in the picture.

"You think?" It wasn't the best thing he could have said, but it was the only thing he could think of.

She looked at him like he was being intentionally coy, "Yes, I do." Again, she smiled.

Nicholas smiled now, too. He couldn't believe she was sitting there right now, talking with him. Oddly enough, out of everything that had happened in the past twenty-four hours, this was the hardest thing he had to digest.

"Yeah, it's a little bleak, though," Nicholas stated, trying to amend for the dark nature of the drawing.

"Yeah, it is," she said.

Nicholas quickly jumped on the band wagon, "Definitely. A bit morbid even."

He spoke as if the mood of the picture put him off. He didn't want Emily thinking he was a freak like the rest of the kids at school thought.

"I like it," Emily said. "I love all that horror movie stuff. Dark nights, monsters looming, and all that. Absolutely love it."

Nicholas began to backtrack on his approach, "Yeah, me too."

Emily raised an eyebrow as if Nicholas was toying with

her. This wasn't going well. Luckily, Mike returned with his Coke.

"Sorry it took so long; a bit backed up today."

"No problem, Mike," Nicholas said.

"And for you, Miss?" Mike said, always the attentive server.

Emily answered him by saying, "I'll have what he's having."

Mike nodded and walked away. Nicholas watched him go and then turned back to his Coke. Emily on the other hand, never took her eyes off Nicholas. Nicholas didn't notice her looking, and even if he did, he wouldn't know how enthralled with him she was.

"Kind of funny," Emily began. Nicholas looked at her. "Such a small town, in the same school for years, and I don't think we've ever talked before."

The comment caught Nicholas off guard. He wasn't exactly sure what to say, so he just stared at her. She smiled and looked away, hair falling about her face the way only a blossoming teenager's can. Nicholas was intoxicated with her.

"So, you think they're real?" Emily said, tossing her hair back over her shoulder.

"What?" Nicholas saw Emily was looking back at his drawing. An icy cold ran over him. A flash from the night before flew by, and he felt the blood rush from his face.

"No," Nicholas choked out. He looked up at Emily and saw she was looking at him quizzically. He smiled, "Of course not."

Emily's smiled began to fade as if this answer upset her. Then, something came to mind, "However, we can never really be sure what lingers in dark corners and what calls nightmares home."

There was a pause, and then Emily smiled, and Nicholas did the same. They both laughed.

"That's good; very poetic, Nicholas." She looked away from him and back to his drawing, then back up to him with a new smile.

"You ever wonder about the house, the one up on the ridge?" The specification was unnecessary. Nicholas would have known which house she was speaking of without another word. Every kid had wondered about that house. Charlie Landon, a kid who had moved away from The Hollow around four years ago, said he saw a light on in a window as if there was a lone tenant up there, wallowing the nights away.

The epiphany hit Nicholas like a weight. He had been wondering what his next step would be in this adventure he found himself in. Of course, the logical step was to find this mysterious gunman, but Nicholas hadn't the slightest idea where to look. Now, he knew exactly where to start.

Nicholas was going to answer Emily, but Mike returned with Emily's drink.

"Here you are, Miss Gordon. Looks like your father's right outside waitin' for ya."

Emily turned, and Nicholas also looked outside. On the other side of the large glass window of the diner sat a police cruiser. Leaning on the side of the car, large brimmed hat pulled down to his sunglasses, stood the sheriff. Never had there been a more imposing man. His stature was large, and his face was stone. Along with his hat and glasses, he sported a full, stout mustache. He raised his right hand, motioning Emily to come out.

Emily turned back, rolling her eyes. She grabbed her Coke, muttered a thanks to Mike, and hopped off her stool. She took two steps, stopped, turned back, and came right up next to Nicholas.

"Could I keep that?" Emily pointed at the napkin.

"Ah, sure," Nicholas said. She snatched up the napkin in a flash.

"Thanks," she said, through a smile, and was out the door in a few strides. She walked up to the sheriff. He took off his glasses and greeted Emily.

After Emily got into the car, the sheriff looked back into the diner at Nicholas, replaced his glasses, circled his car, and drove away. Nicholas let out a held breath.

Mike let out a thick, hearty laugh. "Oh, Sonny, you're playing with fire with that one." His laughter grew even louder as he walked away shaking his head. Nicholas looked back from Mike to the window, where the sheriff had just been. He couldn't see the house up on the cliff; he wasn't even facing the bay, but he knew it was out there. Waiting.

"Yeah," Nicholas began. "You don't know the half of it, Mike."

Emily's thoughts were back with the boy at the diner. So, when her father called her name, she was startled to realize he had done so three times.

"Huh?" she mumbled, coming out of her trance.

Her father looked over at her through his large sunglasses. It was a look that would have intimidated almost anyone in town. Emily was the exception to the rule, however. She looked back, smiling sweetly.

Sheriff Gordon sighed, knowing he wasn't winning. "I asked who that was back at the diner."

Emily looked away, knowing where this conversation was going. "Just a boy from class."

"Uh, huh." Sheriff Gordon scratched his chin with a thick hand. Emily could tell he wasn't going to let it drop.

Emily decided it would be best in the long run to give up. Besides, it wouldn't be long before 'The Lone Sheriff of

Pointe's Hollow' would know everything he wanted and needed to know about Nicholas. Secrets didn't last long in a small town and even less when your father was the sheriff.

"His name is Nicholas," she finally said and took a sip from her Coke.

"Ah, the Wake boy," Sheriff Gordon said. There was something in his tone that led Emily to believe he knew who it was even before he asked. He said nothing else. Not because he had nothing else to say, but because he knew it drove Emily crazy.

"He's nice," she offered, watching her fingers peel the label from her bottle, as if it was nothing more than a casual comment.

Sheriff Gordon nodded, pleasantly content with the way the conversation was going. Emily hated that she was losing. She always lost, but she fought all the same.

"Really smart, too," she continued.

"Smart, you say?" He was mocking her now.

"I do say," she shot back, followed by a honed glare.

Again, he turned and looked at her over his sunglasses. They both stared down one another until Emily cracked and began to smile. Her father took only another second and followed suit. Emily broke eye contact and looked back out the window.

Her father wanted to say more. She could sense it.

She had admired Nicholas Wake from afar for quite a while now. She was never afraid to talk with him; she just never knew how she would approach him. She got lucky today in the diner. He looked so rooted in his work, she had almost decided against saying anything to him. Then, the picture had caught her eye.

It was horrifyingly beautiful. For that one moment, her admiration for his art outweighed her uncertainty about her approach. Without realizing it, she had sat down and started talking.

Dusk

Her thoughts circled around every word they had exchanged. The entire encounter happened over and over again in her mind, like an old record that stayed in the player for days. Her hand reflexively came up to her chin and she leaned, her elbow placed on the window. The look in her eyes dripped from glancing to dreaming.

They rode the rest of the way home in silence, both lost in their own thoughts about a boy who had just finished a well-deserved Coca-Cola.

After undoing his chain, Nicholas mounted his bike and looked westward toward the coast. Far off he could see the peaks of the old house on the cliff. A large shiver ran down his spine, but he shook it off.

Scanning the cliff, he tried to pick out the path to the house. The thick foliage of the surrounding woodland made it nearly impossible. He sighed, swallowed his fear, and set off.

A few moments later, he was out of town. He passed houses and the docks, and, finally, the street was shrouded by trees on either side. They flew by at differing speeds depending on whether he was going uphill or down.

In accordance with the middle of nowhere atmosphere, he also passed three dead opossums, a couple of squirrels, and even a half decomposed deer. His only break in his ride from the constant passing trees was a small section of shrubs that seemed to have overtaken about an eight foot section of woods.

About an hour and a half later, Nicholas stopped to catch his breath. He paused after a large trek up an incline. During his break, he turned back and looked over his shoulder. He could see most of the town from here and even some of the bay.

Something was off. After all his time riding, he had not seen a single cross street or even a turn off from the road. It was strange, because Nicholas knew if the house had an entrance, it had to be on this road. The house did exist, so it only made sense for it to have an entrance. Even if the road was dirt, it wouldn't be so grown over that it was unrecognizable, would it?

Nicholas was becoming discouraged. He didn't want to have to find this place; it was out of his control. Why would the world make this even more difficult than it already was?

While he stood perplexed by the current situation, he also found himself at a crossroad of the mind. He had the choice to continue forward, further away from the safety of his home or to turn back and pray he had missed something. Nicholas looked down the road ahead of him to see if he could pick out a cross street. There was nothing.

His stomach rumbled, making his decision for him. He turned his bike around and travelled back the way he had come, head hung low, defeated.

As he pedaled back, he again passed the decomposed deer and some of the other critters. He was coming up on the small patch of shrubbery when something caught his eye.

Within the shrubbery, there was an unnatural vertical line of wood. Usually, this would be chalked up to a tree or a branch in disarray, but this was too perfect. Nicholas slowed his pedaling while he further investigated the shrubs. Within moments, he could see the entire structure was fake.

He skidded to a stop and closed the gap between himself and the fake shrub. He walked his bike the rest of the way. The closer he got, the more obvious the falsehood became.

The vertical line within the shrubs that had caught his initial attention was actually one of a pair. They were the inner sections of a fence made of old wood and covered in vines from top to bottom. The odd placement of the fence was outdone only by the further oddity of its camouflage.

Once he fully inspected the fence, he glanced on the other side, finding a thin layer of branches covering the stone drive hidden within the trees. If he had been driving, which most did at high speeds, he wouldn't suspect a thing. But here, up close, on foot, there was no mistaking a cover up.

Unfortunately, the discovery had not made Nicholas excited or even happy; it only made him more concerned about his adventure. If the path to the house was hidden, somebody had to be behind it. Someone who had something to hide.

There was a moment when Nicholas almost put the whole thing behind him, turned around, and went home. But as all moments do, this one passed. He continued forward, first rounding the fence, not wanting to touch or disturb it, and then rode up the gravel drive.

Stones sputtered and spit from his back wheel as he pedaled along. After ten minutes, he could see the end of the drive. The gravel rounded in front of a black, wrought iron gate, eight feet tall and rusted with age. Long poles extended tall and crowned in a dented arch. On either side of the gate ran an equally tall brick wall.

Nicholas took a moment to hide his bike in a small brush pile to the side of the drive. After his bike was secure, he returned to the gate and thought about his next move. It wouldn't be an easy one. The gate was not only old and rusted, so it might not move at all any more, but even if it would move, it was locked with a chain. Not just a chain, but links of metal that were so large that they looked like they would be more fitting attached to the anchor on the Titanic, rather than on this gate.

Hesitantly, Nicholas approached the gate. He grasped it with both hands and gave it a little shake. There was no give, not an inch. Again, he shook the gate, harder, but with the same result.

He stepped back with his hands on his hips. In frustration, he lashed out and kicked the fence. Gazing up the height of the fence, Nicholas debated about climbing it. It was possible, but it would be difficult. There were no horizontal bars, only vertical ones, so he would need an enormous amount of upper body strength to make the climb. That strength he did not have.

Frustrated, but not willing to give up easily, he began to walk back and forth in front of the fence trying to devise another plan. After a few passes, Nicholas noticed some bricks placed unevenly within the wall to the left of the fence. They looked rough, as if they had been beaten. A small bit of rubble lay in front of that part of the wall. Within the debris, he saw stones with letters carved in them.

He left that side of the fence and went to the other. He saw that this wall was still solid. The stone was full and written upon it was:

WINTER'S HALL
EST. 1899

He mouthed the words and ran his fingers across the etching. After a moment, he returned to the less fortunate wall. The rubble's features looked much easier to climb than the surface of the full wall.

Without a second thought, he mounted the first few stones and began to ascend. He was surprised how easy it was for him to climb the wall. As he reached for the top, the stone below his right foot shifted, and he almost fell, but was able to stay up by a finger's breadth.

His feet softly plopped on the other side of the wall into a pile of dead leaves. It was only now, on the other side of the wall and in the yard of the towering mansion, that he thought about how much trouble he could be walking into. Nicholas swallowed hard. After a moment, he moved toward the house.

The house looked even larger up close. Three stories tall with countless windows and a yellowing color. The entire house looked alive. It was from a different time altogether.

A different world, Nicholas thought.

The main structure of the house, or Winter's Hall as the sign proclaimed, rose to a single peak. A rounded porch cover ejected from the front. Large cylinder towers rose up to a tremendous height. There was a taller part to the right of the main section where a sizable window sat. Its shape was that of a German expressionist film, pointed top with a flat base. It wasn't a mansion as much as it was a castle.

He had no idea how long he stood there. He was right in front of the house of so many childhood stories. Looking up, he took in the entire place, inch by inch.

If he hadn't been looking at that particular side of the house, he would have missed it - movement around the right side of the house. It wasn't a shape per se, more a wisp of mist.

"Hello?" Nicholas called after the movement.

No answer.

I came this far, better go all the way.

With one more passing glance at the house, he took off running toward the corner.

As Nicholas rounded the corner, he got another glimpse of the mist, but this time he saw what he thought was a leg. Suddenly, Nicholas had the feeling he was chasing someone around the house.

Not someone, he thought. *Something.*

The thought scared him, but didn't stop him. He took off again, and this time when he rounded the corner, the mist was nowhere in sight. Catching his breath, Nicholas scanned every inch of the backyard. Nothing.

He evaluated the backyard. A small, cobblestone path wound through the grass like a snake. The grass was long, but still tame. The garden patches speckled throughout were a different story. They had gone wild, overgrowing their small sections because of neglect. Nicholas looked around as he walked along the path.

That was when he heard a scuffle behind him. Nicholas froze. A cold sweat broke out along his brow. Everything became very quiet in the yard. Nicholas couldn't hear the wind anymore, nor could he hear the birds in the woods. All he could hear was his quickening heart beat and then the click of a gun hammer being pulled back.

Chapter 5

"Turn around, slowly," a voice rang out, making Nicholas jump.

It took all his strength to spin around. The mysterious gunman from the night before stood about ten paces away in front of an open back door, wielding an armed pistol of deadly proportions. An undeniable urge to crumple onto the ground came over Nicholas. But his body stiffened as hard as stone.

"You have five seconds to give me a reason not to sprinkle you across my lawn," the gunman continued.

Nicholas had to speak. He knew if he didn't, he would be dead. Suddenly, he was angry that he came all the way up here. How could he be so stupid? He shouldn't have come up here, alone, with no one back home knowing where he was. Mr. Lloyd might have an idea, but he couldn't do anything to save Nicholas, anymore than Nicholas could save himself.

The man raised the gun, motioning to Nicholas.

"Don't shoot, don't...." Nicholas stammered. One of the man's eyebrows raised.

"What are you doing here?" the man said.

Nicholas relaxed, but it was still hard for him to get his words out. "I just, I just wanted," Nicholas started, but stopped. What did he want? Answers? To thank him? Nicholas wasn't really sure.

The man looked Nicholas over. It was invasive. Nicholas felt the man's blue eyes crawling over him, weighing the danger of the teenager in front of him. Slowly, the man's hand fell to his side, and he shifted his weight to one foot.

"Come on in," the man said, much to Nicholas's surprise "If you aim to ask your questions, it'd be better to do so somewhere I can put my feet up and enjoy a drink."

With a flick of a turn, the man disappeared into the house, leaving the door open. Nicholas stood there, internally debating about running back to town and the safety of his bed. Then, his overactive imagination kicked in and the image of the snarling wolf tearing apart his bedroom window and ripping through his life made him think otherwise. With a quick intake of breath, he walked into the house, closing the door behind him.

The interior of the house was as haunting as its exterior. Underneath a layer of age, the old house was clinging to its former beauty. Its efforts, however slight, were in vain, for the age and unkempt nature of the place were evident everywhere. Cobwebs linked piles of dust that canvassed the sparse furnishings sprinkled about the house.

Nicholas stepped through the dank house and immediately thought back to all the monster movies of which he was such a fan. His entire being was telling him to turn back, to run, to escape. But he pushed forward anyway. Maneuvering through a few hallways, he emerged into a great entrance hall. It held a single staircase curving around to the second floor along the right wall. Small windows spaced evenly about the case cascaded the room in silver light.

Dusk

Looking around, Nicholas saw many doorways. One door stood slightly open, while the rest sat closed and desolate. Nicholas took a final moment to look behind him and wonder if he was getting in too deep. In the end, Nicholas assumed that he was indeed getting in too deep, but that was just fine with him. He went to the door, leaving behind the life he knew for one he didn't.

Nicholas pushed the door as he peeked in. The slight hiss of a bottle opening echoed through the room. Nicholas watched as the man plopped down on a rustic, red couch. The cap from the bottle clattered across the small coffee table. As he tossed the cap aside, he kicked his feet up. They landed on the table, causing the cap to rattle.

The rest of the room was mostly empty. Nicholas assumed the doorway in the back led to the kitchen, which explained where the man had gotten the beer. The couch and coffee table combination across from a single armchair, a small table in the corner with a phone on it, and an empty fireplace were the only things occupying the room. The sense of emptiness was heavy in the room. Its dimensions were far too large to be filled with only the few objects.

Nicholas did notice some oddities. A square vacancy above the fireplace was discolored from the rest of the room, the accusatory fingerprint of a missing picture frame. His eyes must have lingered on the spot too long, for the man on the couch spoke up, "Sit down, will you? I haven't got all night."

Nicholas looked over at the man, who was motioning with his beer-wielding hand to the armchair opposite him. His assertion that he didn't have all night at one in the afternoon was strange, but Nicholas didn't push the matter. Nicholas hesitated for another moment and then sat in the chair. The man took a long swig from the bottle.

"So, what would you like to know first?" the man asked.

Nicholas was completely stunned. What to ask first? About the werewolf? Mr.Lloyd's incident? The town? After a moment, the only question that seemed logical was the simplest.

"Who are you?"

Again, the man raised a single brow. He didn't need to say it. Nicholas knew after everything that had happened in the past twenty-four hours, finding out this man's identity was the most mundane thing he could ask. But Nicholas didn't care; he wanted to know if this man was a good guy or just another monster.

"The name's Dusk," the man finally said.

"Dusk what?"

"Dusk nothing. It's just Dusk."

Nicholas thought about prying further, but he decided that was enough for now. Dusk took another swig of his beer and placed the bottle on the coffee table. As he leaned forward, Nicholas backed away a bit in his chair.

Dusk chuckled, "A bit jumpy, aren't we?"

Nicholas waited to relax until Dusk returned to his casual position on the couch.

"I guess after the night you had, it's only natural," Dusk continued.

His hand came up to his face, and he scratched his rough chin. It was strange how calm the man was. It was as if last night was just another night out.

"In fact, I'm surprised to see you out and about in the woods so soon. You don't have a death wish, do you?"

"No," Nicholas answered.

"Good," Dusk said, "I'd hate to think all the effort it took to save your ass was wasted."

Dusk looked away toward the window, obviously bored by the conversation.

"Thanks for that, by the way," Nicholas mentioned, almost as a side note.

Dusk

Dusk looked back from the window.

"It's what I do."

Nicholas was quiet for a second, and then asked, "What is?"

"Huh?"

"What is it, exactly, that you do?"

Dusk looked away at the ground. It was strange; Dusk put up this façade as a guy who would gloat about every little thing he was involved with, and yet, he hesitated as if he was ashamed.

"I am, you could say, a detective of sorts," Dusk finally said.

Dusk looked up from the ground to Nicholas. Nicholas looked back.

"A detective?"

"Yes, a detective. Specializing in only the," Dusk took a moment, "most monstrous of cases."

He smiled wryly.

Nicholas felt a cold chill run up his spine. "By that, you mean cases involving," flashes of teeth, fur, and gore flew through Nicholas's mind, "actual monsters."

Dusk wiped a hand over his face and nodded solemnly. Nicholas took a moment to take in what Dusk was saying.

"You're a monster hunter," he finally said.

Dusk shook his head, not in disagreement, but in annoyance. "If you'd like to romanticize the world we live in, I guess you could say that."

"But how is this possible? Where did you come from? Where did they?" The questions didn't stop now. Nicholas wanted to know everything, and he didn't want to wait any longer.

"Slow down, kid, slow down. Now, I know this is a lot to take in, but I don't have all the answers."

Does anyone? Nicholas thought.

"I'm sorry for what happened," Dusk said, a faint

arrogance creeping into his voice. "Last night, I mean. It's something I try to avoid at all costs. Believe me."

Dusk shifted in his chair. Nicholas couldn't believe the man's demeanor. If Nicholas had to put a word to how Dusk responded, it would probably be 'annoyance.' A boy, almost slaughtered to death the night before, travels back into the woods where he almost got killed, and Dusk is annoyed to see him.

Now, it was Nicholas who was annoyed. "Well, I'm sorry for being an inconvenience."

Dusk looked at Nicholas, surprised. A smile cracked across his face. "Alright, I hear ya," he said, making sure Nicholas got the point. "I guess I do owe you some sort of explanation."

Nicholas was proud, but taken aback by the stranger's response.

"Ask away," Dusk continued, with a wave.

Nicholas started to speak, but Dusk hushed him with a finger. "But please, keep it to one at a time. I was up late last night, and my head is killing me."

Nicholas pushed forward, slower this time. "Last night, that was all real?"

Dusk shrugged, "Depends on your idea of real."

Nicholas shot Dusk a look without realizing he was doing it. The kind teenagers are gifted with. Their 'Don't bullshit a bullshitter' look.

"Yes," Dusk finally relented, "last night was very real."

Nicholas nodded, taking it in. "And that thing?"

"Werewolf," Dusk supplied.

Nicholas, getting used to Dusk's candid attitude, continued unhinged, "That werewolf was real?"

"Yes."

"And you killed it."

"Unfortunately, yes. I killed him."

Nicholas made a mental note of Dusk's specification of

the monster, but didn't comment. "That's good, right? It could have killed you."

Again, Dusk shrugged, "Could be killed by many things. Mauled by legend doesn't seem too terrible a way to go."

"But you killed him anyway," Nicholas pressed.

Dusk eyed the boy, and sighed, "Yes, yes I did. It's what I do."

"Killing monsters."

"Murder," Dusk quickly shot back. "Murder is my business. Yes, it's true most often my jobs involve a certain type of target, but it's murder all the same."

Nicholas thought about this. Although he had seen the man dead on the ground, saw him well and saw the hole in his head even better, he didn't realize until right now that a man died along with that monster last night. The fact that he could overlook this made goose bumps run up his arms. The only thing that calmed his nerves was one thought.

"But it's over right?" he said hopefully.

Dusk raised an eyebrow.

"It's dead; monster defeated. A job well done, right?" Nicholas was almost pleading now.

Dusk's lips lifted in a half-hearted smile, "No. It's never over, kid."

Nicholas could hear the lump in his throat go down.

Dusk sighed again and wiped a speck of dust from his shirt. "By the looks of things, our little, old town has at least two visitors in its midst."

At least? It took everything Nicholas had to believe in one of those things. Now, Dusk was telling him there were, in fact, more of them.

Nicholas began to feel woozy. His eyes wandered and then glazed over at the thought of riding home later, and every night from then on, for that matter.

"No worries, kid," Dusk said, making Nicholas raise

his eyes again. "I've been doing this here for a while now. I have it under control."

These are the words every little boy wishes to hear from their hero, which Nicholas guessed, in this case, Dusk was. But there was something off about it. It could have been Dusk's unshaven, unkempt appearance. Or possibly the almost-gone beer he once again held between his fingers. No matter what it was, the words didn't reassure Nicholas, especially about the gunslinger in front of him.

"So, you're going out again?"

Dusk again did one of his becoming-famous shrugs and said, "Someone's gotta do it." He took the final swig from his beer and placed the bottle on the table as he stood up. "You got anything else? I gotta get some things done before nightfall."

Nicholas just shook his head. He had more questions, plenty of them, but he already had to take in so much. He didn't know if he could take more right then.

Dusk nodded solemnly, "Front door's that way. Out in the hall and take a right."

Nicholas stood up and headed for the hall to leave. Something indescribable happened when Nicholas reached the doorway. He stopped. There was something like a force field blocking Nicholas's exit. There was nothing there, of course. Nicholas could see the dust particles float in and out of the doorway in front of him, but his body remained still all the same.

Nicholas's eyes dropped to the floor, seeing his feet on the threshold of leaving the room. His eyes shifted up the door frame. They traced all the way up until the empty spot on the wall caught his eye again. He looked at the spot for what felt like forever. He knew what he had to do.

"I wanna go with you."

Nicholas said it before realizing the consequence of saying it. His eyes never left the blank spot on the wall.

Dusk

"What?"

Nicholas turned to see Dusk, looking back at him, one eyebrow raised.

"I wanna go with you," Nicholas repeated.

Dusk took a moment to look the boy over. "You're serious?"

"Of course," Nicholas said, hoping to sound confident, but coming off weak.

Dusk chewed on his lower lip. "Naw, sorry. Ain't gonna happen."

Dusk turned around to leave. Nicholas pushed forward.

"Wait. Why not?"

"Why not?" Dusk mocked.

"Yeah. Why not?"

"Oh, I don't know, maybe because you see one dead body and you faint for eight hours. Now, I consider myself sort of an expert, and I can assure you that a good monster hunter that does not make."

"Come on," Nicholas pleaded, still trying to get Dusk to stop. "At least give me a chance."

Dusk stopped his progress toward the kitchen. He turned to look at the kid he had saved from a mess of carnage just the night before.

"Look, kid, you're tough, I'll give you that. But this world," Dusk paused for a moment, thinking it all over, "this life. It isn't for everybody. It's one that's supposed to go by unnoticed. Last night was a close call."

Dusk's eyes drifted away from Nicholas and glanced at the empty spot on the wall. "Too many close calls turn into something more. Some things you can't get back, kid."

Nicholas didn't say anything. He just stood his ground. Nothing he said would have been right.

Dusk saw this, and a small gleam of admiration sparkled in his eyes. He looked the boy up and down again.

"Be here tonight, eight o'clock sharp. One minute later,

and you're riding home alone."

Nicholas smiled and then hid it away. He nodded. Dusk waited for him to leave, but he stood there.

"Well, go on then."

Nicholas jumped, realizing he was still there, and spun on his heels. He was past the hall, outside, back over the gate, and pedaling away before he realized what he had just signed on for.

It was funny to think that not more than thirty minutes ago, Dusk had almost shot the boy. He guessed that's how the world worked sometimes.

"Well, go on then," Dusk said, waving the boy away. He watched as the boy left without a look back. Even though Dusk couldn't see the boy's eyes as he left, he knew what they held. Admiration and excitement mixed with youthful ignorance.

Dusk forgot about his past progress toward the kitchen and went out into the hall after the boy. He followed all the way to the front door, which the kid left open in his haste. Leaving the door open, Dusk leaned against the frame, empty bottle in hand.

If someone asked him why he had told the boy to return later that night, Dusk wouldn't have been able to answer. There seemed to be an aura around the boy, a sense of being more important and vital to everything than either of them realized. This was not the real reason, however. The real reason was something much more personal for Dusk. Something only he and another would have understood.

He's a good kid, Dusk thought. Without realizing it, he spoke aloud, "You would have liked him."

A cool breeze from the water rolled over the yard to the door. It sent a quiver all the way through Dusk's bones. After a quick look about to make sure he was alone again, he receded inside, closing the door on the outside world behind him.

Dusk

Head pounding, stomach churning, and unable to stop the constant shaking in his hands. This was how Andy Wallace awoke that morning, and that was how he had spent his entire day.

Andy's head felt like a piece of metal had been bounced around in his mental blender. He had felt this way before. Too many times to keep track of, if truth were told. Most of the time, he downed some aspirin followed by a large cup of coffee and was all set. This time it was different. He had taken almost three times the usual amount of aspirin, but his head still reverberated with the unforgiving pounding.

The lake rolled over and over against the rocks below. It smacked and licked the steep sides of the cliff. Andy's legs hung over the edge of the wharf where he sat. He had made his way from the place he awoke to the open water hoping the fresh air would clear his head. This usually did the trick for any sickness he ran into. A lucky trait for a fisherman. More than one time, it had saved him from a lost paycheck.

Unfortunately, like the aspirin, the cool air did nothing to calm his head or stomach. The strange uneasiness was only one of his many worries. He could not remember a single thing from the previous night.

Not true, Andy thought sourly.

He could remember going to the bar, ordering a drink, and chatting up a lovely waitress whose legs went all the way up, if you could dig it. There was some time where things got a little foggy. He could see glimpses of trees flashing by, the moon, and red. A thick, dark red.

His hand came up to his face and rubbed his temples. He wanted a cigarette. The other hand went to his chest pocket, but found it empty. Of course it was. He had his cigarettes with him last night and had woken up without them. That wasn't really surprising, however, for he also woke up without his clothes.

The hand fell away from his face, and as his eyes refocused to the light of the setting sun, Andy tried to remember more from the night before. His birthday suit morning had been an unsettling phenomenon. In the past, if he had woken up naked, it was usually next to a woman, and one lucky night, two women. Of course, he couldn't remember any of their names, didn't care to, but he would've given his entire paycheck to have woken up next to one of them today.

On top of his stark naked awakening, he had awoken to paint all over his body. He wished it to be paint, because the other option was too outrageous to consider. Unfortunately, his wishing didn't make it true. Andy Wallace had awakened, naked and drenched in drying, clotting blood.

His stomach took a flop, and he groaned. A dip in the lake, three showers, and many hours later, he could still feel the warm, sticky presence of blood all over his body. It made his skin crawl.

He really wanted a cigarette.

Unable to stop the feeling of dread pulsing through his blood, he spent most of the time alone. To keep him company, he had only a shivery, unshaken feeling of washed-away blood, clammy palms, and a cool sweat. He felt sick, tired, and strained, and he really, really wanted a cigarette.

Checking his watch, he had to be heading down to the dock soon, so he could check on the boat. He turned to look south toward the dock and saw his vessel.

Andy didn't even know who he was working for. Name, what they did, or who they did business with. Nothing. He didn't know what he was shipping. He had been turned on to the job by a guy at his local pub in Grand

Haven. The guy wasn't a regular; Andy had been sure of that. He was too well-kept and well-spoken. He told Andy about some guy who needed some stuff shipped down the coast to the small town. The same town Andy found himself in today.

"What kind of stuff?" Andy had asked, between sips of beer.

"A top secret kind of stuff," the man had replied.

Every fiber of his being told Andy not to take the job. It just felt wrong. His interaction with the man in the bar was even stranger than the usual bar speak he'd run into. One minute he was talking with the guy, and the next, he was waking up in his own bed, fully dressed, with a cut across the inside of his hand. Another night when he had one too many.

The cut was probably from a bottle or glass. Andy was constantly getting nicked in his drunken states. This one had been a bad one, jagged, not like the other cuts. Glass cuts were usually straight. This time, however, something had ripped through his hand rather than sliced it. Right then, he should have known to not show up to accept the job.

But Andy was tight on cash and needed to pay rent, so he did show up at the time the man instructed him to. The crates were all packed up and waiting for him. He loaded up the crates, shaking the bad feeling. They were stamped with the word 'FRAGILE' and 'THIS END UP' in worn red letters. They also had a strange emblem on the sides, a dark green triangle Andy wasn't familiar with.

The sun made its final dip down and disappeared, sending the small town into a darkness broken only by the silvery sliver of moonlight.

Andy sighed and made a move to stand. His muscles cried in protest, but he pushed through. His back cracked as he gained his feet. He stretched, readying himself for the trek ahead, and moved to step away from the wharf.

Pain racked his stomach. It was like an electric shock that riveted all the way down to his bones. His hands went to the lower, right side of his stomach where the surge originated.

Andy cried out, trying to counteract the suffering that ravaged him.

The pain began to subside, and Andy was thanking God for the relief. Just as it was about to be gone, another shot pierced his muscles higher up in his chest. It hit him like a sledge hammer. He stepped back on his left leg to steady himself from the blow.

His hands were on his chest now; the pain was overwhelming.

Dear God! Andy thought, feeling as if he was going to die on the spot.

There was a new lump of discomfort now rolling around in his stomach. It went through him like a wave. His stomach was on fire, and it was rising to his chest. His hands lowered, and he grabbed the end of his shirt. He raised the shirt, expecting to see a fire licking his skin, but what he saw was much worse.

His skin was rippling like the water below. Suddenly, there was a loud series of noises.

Pop, pop, pop.

Andy's ribs were cracking violently under his muscled flesh. They snapped one after another and then expanded. Andy could have sworn that if this pain was really happening, he should have been knocked unconscious, but there was no reprieve as his stomach began to sink in and muscles hardened to rocks. As his ribs expanded, he dropped his shirt and looked around for help. There was no one in sight.

That's when the third bolt came. More powerful than previously, he was thrown from his feet backward over the wharf's edge.

The pain was so strong that Andy didn't notice he was falling until he hit the water below, splashing into the cool waves. His weight thrust him down into the inky blackness of the water. No bottom seemed in sight. Agonizing pain was still ravaging him. He spun and floated about in the water.

The water was cold, icy even, but he felt hot. He was burning up. His hands, or at least he thought they were his hands, felt wrong somehow, and came to his neck to loosen the collar of his shirt. The shirt ripped open. Andy was bare chested in cold water, but still he felt overheated.

Andy screamed out, but the sound was muffled in a swarm of bubbles. His stomach began to mellow with the sensation of what could only be described as stretching. His legs felt like they were being pulled down to the depths as his arms were yanked the other way. His feet began to flatten, elongate, and finally burn. Then, when he thought it couldn't get worse, his face began to follow suit.

The experience was excruciating. Every inch of his body ached, crying out for the world to stop. The muscles in his limbs began to bulge, ripping his clothes from his body. Nails and teeth ripped through the flesh surrounding them. The water around him darkened as red wafted in tendrils.

The world grew dark. The blood, his blood, stained the water around him. There was a quick blip before everything went pitch black. Andy could see, and eventually feel, the fur ripple onto his body, covering him from head to toe.

On the coastline of Pointe's Hollow, a beast emerged from the water. It was tall, covered in fur from muzzle to claws. Still dripping, the beast raised its head and sniffed the breeze. Its upper lip curled back as it caught a scent on the air, a scent every monster desires. The scent of freshly spilled blood.

Chapter 6

The second trip to the old house was much more haunting. The sun was already below the distant horizon casting long shadows and creating a warm darkness. Within the unknown around Nicholas, there could have been countless terrors, and yet he pedaled on.

It was strange. Although Nicholas had called Pointe's Hollow home for most of his life, if he travelled no more than a few miles in either direction and put distance between him and the town, he could have been in another country.

This mixed with the added, premature darkness should have frozen Nicholas in his tracks, forcing him to turn back, tail between his knees, and screaming in terror. But it didn't. It sent shivers across his flesh, of course, but the shivers were waves of anticipation, excitement even, not fear. Tonight was the beginning of something new. Nicholas had peeked at a world that no one was supposed to know existed, and tonight was the night he entered that world, became a part of it.

As he left Winter's Hall earlier in the day, he knew the idea of skipping out on the whole ordeal would cross his mind more than once. That idea had been a tick constantly digging through his mind. But the idea was the only thing that ever came up. Not once did the actual option ever arise. He knew he had to do this. It was an inner force steering Nicholas in the correct direction.

Although he couldn't let his aunt know what he was doing, he felt bad about lying to her. His aunt didn't deserve to be lied to even if it was a white lie. If Nicholas had had another option, he would have taken it, but there wasn't. If someone asked his aunt where Nicholas was this evening, she would answer with the same lie he had fed her.

"Nicholas is down at the library again, reading some more of those darn books he's so fond of."

Of course, Nicholas had no intention of going to the library tonight, but he had no worry his lie would be spoiled. Even if his aunt checked up on him, which she never did, Nicholas was sure Mr. Lloyd would cover for him. He hadn't prearranged this with the librarian, but he knew if he needed Mr. Lloyd to lie for him, he would without question. Especially now. It was his job, his purpose in this story. He knew Mr. Lloyd would know that, or at least hoped he would.

He slowed the pace of his pedaling as he neared the entrance to the great, big house on the hill. Dusk's home. A strange man, Dusk. Even after their discussion, Nicholas couldn't quite put his finger on the man. There was a darkness that was obvious, but that demeanor and his attitude were almost the exact opposite. It was light, joking. Even when they talked about the murdering or the monsters, he still took moments to poke fun.

Nicholas saw the entrance just as he thought he had passed it again. He swerved around the debris.

Now that he was between the trees, the dark was all but complete. His eyes adjusted, but it was still a chore to ride, feeling his way along the path. Small stones crunched about his tires on the path that led Nicholas to the old, iron fence and the house behind it.

After securing his bike where he had before, climbing over the gate, and landing on the other side, Nicholas walked toward the front door, feeling his nerves rise within his throat. Nicholas had placed his first foot on the old step of the front stoop when the front door flew open. For the second time that day, Nicholas was in a staring contest with a gun barrel. He froze instantly and looked at the gleam of moonlight bouncing off the weapon. The man behind the gun was shrouded in shadow.

There was a moment of silence, and then, the gun disappeared back inside as a lantern was thrust in Nicholas's face.

"Ha, I didn't expect to see you again," a rough voice said from the darkness behind the flame. The light lowered, and after a moment, Nicholas saw Dusk standing in the doorway, long coat draped about him, gun in holster, and smirk on his face.

"Well, you said no later than eight," Nicholas said, blinking colored circles from his vision.

"That I did."

Dusk looked the boy up and down. Nicholas looked down at himself and then back to Dusk.

"Are you ready, then?" he asked.

Nicholas swallowed, and then said, "Yeah."

"Good."

Dusk placed the lantern to the side and reached in his jacket. When his hand came out, it was holding a flashlight with a long, silver handle. He clicked the light on then off rapidly to make sure it was working and handed it to Nicholas. Nicholas took it and clicked it once for himself; then, he, too, turned it back off.

Dusk turned around and disappeared back into the house. He returned with a white bucket of considerable weight in one hand and an object with a long handle resting on his shoulder in the other.

"Let's go, kid," Dusk said as he pushed through.

As he passed, Nicholas could hear sloshing from the bucket and smelled a foul odor on the breeze. Even though the bucket seemed to be of cumbersome weight, Dusk's speed wasn't hindered in the least. After a moment of hesitation, Nicholas clicked on the flashlight and jogged after him.

The flashlight bounced along in Nicholas's hand. As it bounced, it caught something gleaming in the night. It was the object Dusk brought out on his shoulder. The shape, although hard to define in the dark, was distinguishable once enough was seen. It was a tomahawk.

Nicholas thought of the revolver holstered within Dusk's belt. A strange combination of weapons, but he assured himself, deadly nonetheless. Flashes from the night before crept to mind.

Wait a minute, Nicholas thought, abruptly stopping his progress. "I haven't got a weapon."

He didn't realize he said it out loud until Dusk also stopped and turned to look at him. Dusk took the tomahawk off his shoulder and looked it over. He looked at Nicholas, who was staring at the vicious curvature of the blade. The backside had a deadly, fine spike on it. Not long like a needle, but stout and very sharp. It was hard to see its complete make, but Nicholas could see that it was definitely old, much older than the man holding it.

Dusk plopped the bucket on the ground and laid the tomahawk on top of it with a laugh. "I think that's a little too much iron for you to handle, kid."

He reached behind him within his coat and pulled out an object. Before Nicholas could see what it was, it was tossed at him. Fumbling, flashlight still in hand, Nicholas caught the object.

A dagger, Nicholas thought, but as daggers go, it was more of a butter knife. The blade, nestled in a smooth sheath, was no more than six inches long ending in a point. Its handle was old leather, worn down from years of use. It looked like it would fall apart at any moment, but it still felt powerful.

Nicholas marveled at it and then looked at Dusk. "Thank you," he said.

Dusk let out a harsh bark of laughter. "Don't be thanking me yet. We've got a long night ahead of us."

He reclaimed his things. Breaking the tree line, he pushed forward, disappearing beyond. Nicholas watched the man go. He felt he was beginning to understand Dusk and, in turn, was beginning to admire him. His grasp tightened on the knife, and then he placed it in his belt and followed Dusk.

They walked through the trees, going deeper and deeper into the darkness. Unlike Nicholas's prior trek, they walked within the trees and not on a discernible path. The oldest residents of The Hollow would have been lost within the first few minutes. Dusk acted like he knew exactly where he was every step of the way.

The flashlight, although comforting, proved quite useless as Nicholas trudged through the woods. The beam cut through only a few feet of darkness before it hit a tree. After a while, Nicholas's eyes adjusted to the thin moonlight between the branches. He placed the flashlight in his back pocket, barely fitting the large handle in. It wobbled about with every step, and a few times, he had to adjust its position to make sure it did not fall out.

At some point during the walk, Dusk began to whistle an old song Nicholas recognized, but couldn't name. Dusk made no attempt to make his approach slowly or quietly. It was strange. Although Nicholas had never gone hunting, he still understood the basic ideas. Be quiet, the element of surprise, and all that. Dusk apparently wasn't aware of such ideas.

After a few more minutes of trampling about the woods at night, Nicholas became aware of the notion of Dusk and him alone in the woods. What did Nicholas know about this man? Not a whole lot, he concluded. Maybe Nicholas had become a threat, and Dusk needed to extinguish that threat.

While Nicholas began to truly consider this sequence of events, Dusk stopped abruptly. "This will work," he said, canvassing the area.

A small clearing between the thick evergreens stood around them. Nicholas thought it was fitting. The moonlight poured into the clearing, illuminating the area just a bit more than the surrounding forest.

Taking it all in, Nicholas stood with his hands on his hips breathing heavily from the walk. Dusk picked up his whistling again and stepped into the middle of the clearing. He placed the bucket onto a soft patch of grass. He took the tomahawk from his shoulder, spun it in his hands, and swung hard at the bucket.

The blade sunk into the lip of the bucket with a hard thud. Then, Dusk removed the blade with a soft plop and whipped it down into the dirt. Using the hole he had just created to remove the lid from the bucket, Dusk opened the bucket and tossed the lid aside. Heaving the load up, he began to pour the contents out onto the ground.

Nicholas stepped closer to get a better look at the scene.

"Is that…," but Nicholas couldn't finish.

"Blood?" Dusk looked up at the boy and smiled. "Don't worry, kid. It's not fresh. Just some extra I collected from a friend."

Nicholas's stomach churned, but he kept his face steady. He just nodded and looked away, trying not to hear the splashing coming from behind him.

Dusk drained the bucket and tossed it across the

clearing. It clattered about the ground and disappeared into the darkness. After checking his watch, Dusk reclaimed his tomahawk and pulled the gun from its holster. With pistol in hand, Dusk surveyed his work and nodded in acceptance.

Nicholas began to feel like the time of silence was growing short, so he asked, "Shouldn't we take cover?"

"What?" Dusk asked back.

Nicholas raised his voice a bit, "Shouldn't we hide?"

Dusk let out a rough chuckle, "Usually, you'd be right, kid. But you don't really hunt werewolves."

A loud, wailing howl flew in on the breeze. It could have been a million miles away or just on the other side of the trees. Its ferocity made it impossible to be sure.

"They hunt you."

Mr. Lloyd was halfway through a pile of papers on his desk when the phone clattered. He lifted it off the receiver on the third ring and in an unintentionally exasperated tone, said, "Pointe's Hollow Public Library."

"Yes, Mr. Lloyd. Hello. It's Sherri, Sherri Wake."

"Ah, Miss Wake, to what do I owe the honor of hearing your lovely voice this evening?"

"Oh, Mr. Lloyd, you flatter me," she said in a childish giggle.

Mr. Lloyd smiled. He loved hearing from Miss Wake. Always in a good mood and pleasant to talk with. Never one to let a conversation drag on nor to cut one short.

"I was just checking on Nicholas," she continued, a smile discernible through her words.

"Nicholas?" He found it odd for Miss Wake to ask him about Nicholas. Mr. Lloyd hadn't seen Nicholas since their talk earlier in the day. He was hoping to see the boy again. Hopefully, to clear up the things he found he couldn't say during their earlier conversation. It was strange how when people needed to know something, it was always harder to tell everything that needed telling.

"Yes," Miss Wake's voice took an uneasy tone, "he said he was helping you late again tonight with something or another at the library. Is he there?"

Mr. Lloyd's face ran cold. Blood drained away, but he was able to keep the fear out of his voice and talk in a calm tone; at least, he believed he did.

"Ah, Nicholas, of course. I am sorry, Miss Wake. The boy is such a hard worker I had almost forgotten he was here."

"Oh, well, I'm glad to hear it." Her tone had regained its lighthearted feel. "I don't know why I felt the need to call. He's such a good boy. I think he's just at that age, you know. I remember when I was sixteen."

"Yes," Mr. Lloyd said, mind racing.

"Well, I don't want to bother him. Please, don't tell him I called."

"Your secret is safe with me."

"Thank you. You have a good night, Mr. Lloyd."

"You too, Miss Wake."

There was a click on the other end, and after a moment of hesitation, Mr. Lloyd hung up the phone. His hand immediately went to his mouth. He could feel the slight tremors running through his fingers. Trying to hide it from himself, he tapped his index finger on his lips.

Images flashed in his mind, none better than the ones before. His hand went from his mouth to his eyes, trying to wipe away the thoughts.

Mr. Lloyd turned until he faced the opposite direction, peering out the window behind him. Again, he saw that terrible line of trees. The night was black as sin, but even in the darkness, the line of trees was darker.

My God, Nicholas. What have you done? Mr. Lloyd thought as a faint howl fell over the night and echoed about Pointe's Hollow.

Nicholas thought about taking the knife from his belt and wielding it for the upcoming battle, but his muscles refused to respond. His eyes slowly scanned the surrounding tree lines. Sounds came from the silence. A scurry about the floor, twigs snapping under foot, and the hoot of an owl.

"Dusk," Nicholas whispered under his breath. His voice wavered; he couldn't help it.

Dusk quickly hushed him as he hunkered himself down in preparation to pounce. The whole of the world seemed to disappear from the two of them, and heartbeats could be felt throughout the clearing: all three of them.

The beast burst from between the trees, not aiming at Dusk or Nicholas, but at the puddle of blood. It fell on all fours, snarling and biting at the ground. The blood splashed onto its paws and muzzle, staining the fur a dark maroon. The eyes, an evil red surrounded by putrefying yellow, scoured its kill zone for the meal it had anticipated, but there was nothing.

At the moment of realization of its empty catch, the beast looked to Dusk and Nicholas for its next target. Neither of them moved. They watched as the werewolf cocked back onto its hind legs. Posing more like a man than an animal. Its lip curled back, revealing a line of sharp, ravenous teeth.

Dusk smirked in response, showing his own teeth. His fingers rolled across the handle of the tomahawk and the grip of his revolver.

Dusk

In a flash, the monster leaned back and launched itself across the clearing, aiming for Dusk's throat. Dusk quickly countered, spinning on his heel and firing his pistol. Once, twice. The bullets ripped through the air. The first flew over the werewolf's left shoulder while the second impacted its arm.

The blast didn't hinder the beast in the least. It thrashed forward unrelentingly. Nicholas thought the thing would rip Dusk apart, but just as it was about to reach him, Dusk smoothly stepped aside.

Nicholas was relieved to see Dusk was unharmed, and his skills were in full force. His enjoyment was short-lived, however, for the beast didn't turn back for Dusk. It plowed forward toward him. He knew he had to move. Had to run, or dive, or just step aside as Dusk had, but he couldn't. His muscles tightened and everything just froze. It was like the night before. If he didn't do something, and quickly, there wouldn't be a next night.

"Move, kid!" Dusk's shout ripped Nicholas awake.

Within seconds of death, Nicholas dove to the left. Blood droplets from the beast's claws and muzzle plopped on his back as he escaped.

The air was ripped from Nicholas's lungs as he hit the ground. He had no time to catch his breath. He rolled over on his back as the beast turned back toward him. The monster had found the weakest link, and it was pushing to break it, hard.

Thinking as fast as he could, Nicholas reached for the dagger he had put in his belt. It was gone.

The jolt of the fall must have knocked it loose. Not wanting or even able to pull his eyes away from the attacking monster, Nicholas pattered around with his hands trying to find the dagger. All he felt was dirt.

The beast advanced. Nicholas could hear the gunshots ripping from Dusk's revolver.

Bullets whistled through the air, missing their target, and still Nicholas collected only dirt between his fingers.

Yards turned into feet, and then feet dwindled into inches. Then, Nicholas felt a handle and wriggled his fingers around it. He thrust it outward toward the advancing beast.

But the handle didn't belong to his dagger; it was the flashlight.

Son of a…. But Nicholas didn't have time for thoughts as the werewolf advanced. Nicholas did all he could think to do and held the flashlight out in front of him like a crucifix warding off evil.

When the beast hit, it knocked Nicholas to the ground. Nicholas opened his eyes to the warm, wet breath landing on him wave after wave. The snout of the wolf was mere inches from Nicholas's own nose. His arm was inside the thing's mouth all the way up to the elbow. The only thing saving his arm from amputation was the flashlight.

When the beast had moved to crush Nicholas's skull, the flashlight had caught within the beast's mouth, wedging the jaw open.

Nicholas looked right into the thing's eyes as it stared back, confused. Its lip curled, and it began to thrust its head side to side trying to finish its bite. Nicholas was whipped back and forth, as if he was a rag doll. Finally, the thrusting became too much, and Nicholas was tossed aside, rolling across the ground.

When he finally came to a stop, he faced the beast and saw its powerful jaw snap the flashlight like a twig. Its teeth met with the ferocity of a bear trap.

That could have been my arm, Nicholas thought. *That could have been my neck.*

The monster spat out the flecks of flashlight as it used its front paws to wipe the fragments from his muzzle fur. Growls bubbled up from the monster's throat as it caught Nicholas in its eye again.

Dusk

Nicholas gulped, *Not again.*

Dusk stepped into the picture, snapping his revolver shut with the flick of a wrist. With the revolver reloaded, he held fast, pointing the barrel at the beast.

"Come on, beastie," Dusk said coyly.

The beast howled again, the sound piercing in such close quarters. Nicholas's hands came up to his ears, but Dusk stood steady. His unrelenting strength appeared to anger the beast. It rushed again, bounding toward the two of them, Nicholas on the ground trying to regain his footing, and Dusk standing strong.

When the monster was a few feet in front of them, Dusk made his move. Instead of firing the revolver, the gun dropped down, creating the counterweight for the blade in his other hand. The tomahawk flew from Dusk's hand, flipping end over end in a perfect line. The blade sliced through the beast's shoulder like butter, nearly severing its arm.

The wound took effect almost immediately, putting the beast to the ground. The inability to use its arm caught the beast off guard. It rounded in a circle, favoring its opposite side. When it became evident it wasn't going to regain the use of its gore-covered appendage, the beast turned to escape.

BANG!

Dusk fired the revolver. The shots flew, one after the other until the chambers were clean, but still the beast tore through the woods, slowed but not stopped. It went between two trees and disappeared into the dark.

"Shit!" Dusk cursed, whipping his arm down in frustration. "Come on, kid. Get up."

Nicholas looked away from the trees and up at Dusk. Even after his sudden frustrated outburst, Dusk was smiling, his revolver smoking in one hand and the other outstretched to help Nicholas up.

"We've got him on the run."

Nicholas took a moment and then accepted Dusk's

hand and raised himself to his feet. Dusk turned quickly, recovered his tomahawk, and called for Nicholas to follow.

Nicholas started to follow, but then thought of something. He went to reclaim his own weapon. He found the dagger a few feet away from where he had groped for it. He removed the blade from its sheath and admired its shine. He followed Dusk into the trees to chase down a monster.

It was not a hard trail to follow. Branches and grass were torn apart in a straight line toward the thing. Even though it was wounded harshly, Dusk and Nicholas had to run over the root-infested ground to keep up with the beast.

They ran for so long and so fast that Nicholas felt like his chest would explode. He didn't relent, however. If Dusk could keep running, he could, too.

As they gained, blood pools began to appear about the ground. First small, then larger and larger. They were getting closer. Nicholas felt his hands begin to sweat as the next battle grew closer.

Dusk burst through a collection of bushes and disappeared from Nicholas's view. Nicholas picked up his pace and a moment later crashed through just as Dusk had. He immediately skidded to a stop, almost running into Dusk who had come to a stop ahead of him.

The wolf stood a few paces ahead of them, its right arm hanging in a red, tattered mess, useless and limp. It peered out toward the open water from the edge of a cliff. Cornered, with nowhere left to go, the beast snorted and growled at the cliff, an unbeatable enemy. No matter how bad his bite or bark was, the wolf would never beat the fall.

Dusk took a step forward, advancing on the beast without fear. The beast sensed him advancing and turned around, head whipping back to see the man. Dusk stood tall and strong, eyeing down the beast.

Suddenly, Nicholas felt sorry for the creature. It took on the appearance of a wounded puppy. Arm bloody, fur matted, and its own mortality strong in its heart, its eyes darted between Dusk and Nicholas, pleading. Nicholas thought about asking Dusk if they had to, but as soon as he opened his mouth, Dusk raised his revolver.

Murder is my business, Nicholas thought as the revolver fired, ringing through the night. The bullet clipped the beast's head, spewing gore violently in all directions. The force of the blow pushed the wolf stumbling toward the edge of the cliff.

As Nicholas began thinking the worst was now behind them, the wolf began to change. Fur poured off its body like water running down a gutter. Its head tilted back, but Nicholas could still make out the muscle crunching its way back into the owner's head. The wounded arm appeared to lose its fur the fastest, but that could just have been a trick of the eye. It was so red, it was almost impossible to tell what lay underneath the blood.

Before long, the beast who had been standing in front of them was gone, and in its place, an average man stood, dying. The wolf was gone, and the man stood. Only then did Dusk lower his pistol.

Nicholas turned to Dusk. He was calm and collected. As if everything had gone according to plan. But in his eyes, Nicholas saw doubt. Dusk took off at a sprint. Nicholas turned to see. The man must have tripped on something, for now he was backpedaling toward the cliff and a deep plunge.

Dusk was already most of the way to the man when Nicholas took off, not knowing what they were doing, but following nonetheless.

The man's feet hit the edge, and he began to tumble. Dusk reached the man in time, grabbing his arm, but the forward motion was too much to overcome. The man fell over, and Dusk dropped to his knee to keep from falling himself. Nicholas made it to the cliff and reached out, trying to help. His hands grasped the first thing that he felt. Warm blood oozed between his fingers as Nicholas caught the man's nearly-severed arm.

There they were, Dusk and Nicholas holding a dead man over a cliff that ended in the churning and slapping water of a cold lake.

Why not let him fall, Nicholas thought wryly as the strain in his shoulders began to burn. He adjusted his grip, and his fingers slipped.

"Pull," Dusk said through gritted teeth. "Pull him up."

Nicholas acquiesced without question, wanting the whole thing to be over. They both heaved, and slowly, the man was raised from his hanging position. The man's body dragged along the edge of the cliff. When he was nearly halfway up, Nicholas yanked hard, wanting to speed the process along.

There was a slight ripping noise, a pop, and then Nicholas was flying backward. The breath was forced out of him as he hit the ground. Something hit his body with a wet, solid plop. A warm wetness saturated his face and chest. He looked down and was greeted with the sight of the man's severed arm, laid out across his chest, fresh blood seeping into his clothes.

Nicholas's throat caught. He rolled over and vomited. The arm rolled from him and fell a few feet away. As Nicholas composed himself, Dusk walked over and collected the arm. He turned it over in his hands and then tossed it on top of the man's body, which was now on solid land.

Dusk looked around with his hands on his hips. Nicholas glanced up at him, ashamed for getting sick over the whole ordeal. Dusk looked at him and let out an over-emphasized breath.

"Well, I think that went rather well." Dusk smiled at Nicholas, "How was it for you?"

Nicholas rolled his eyes and fell onto his back. Dusk let out a hearty laugh. Nicholas knew he wasn't laughing at him, but he was embarrassed by the sound. Dusk stopped laughing as he inspected the boy on the ground, next to a pile of bile.

Nicholas looked back up at Dusk, expecting to see him back at the body or with his battle scowl on. However, he was quite different. Dusk held his gaze with a smile so big it sliced his face in two.

A man, garbed in black, worn clothes, with a holster on his hip, face unshaven and hair unkempt was standing in front of Nicholas with the smile of a boy on Christmas morning.

Nicholas's own face betrayed him as it broke into a smile of its own. They lasted only a few moments before they both broke into a fit of laughter. The sounds drifted away into the night, unheard by all but three. Dusk, Nicholas, and another.

Sheriff Gordon had his fingers deep in his belt, his normal stance for circumstances such as these. He stood, chewing over all that had been going through his mind. Usual things, nothing out of the ordinary, which was the way he liked it. A simple man, living a simple life in a simple town.

The sheriff was a proud man. The Hollow was his world, and he liked it that way. Many dream of faraway places or read stories to escape their life. Sheriff Gordon only wanted his days to go smoothly. A good life for his daughter, a cold Coke every now and again, and him on the couch with a game on the television was all he ever needed.

Some people might look down on his way of life. They might think there is personal potential being wasted or that it's boring, but that was the way Sheriff Gordon liked it.

Simple, Sheriff Gordon thought.

He raised his hand, wiping his mustache in a nervous tick. Letting out a breath as he replaced his fingers in his belt, Sheriff Gordon turned and looked over his cruiser into the night-filled woods. He raised his right arm and leaned on the hood, playing with his fingers.

The red and blue flashes from the car's lights painted the sheriff's face. He looked into the woods where a small collection of flashlights bounced about. When the call had come in, he was collecting his things to go home for the night. He didn't want to take it, but that was the job. After he had taken it, he wished it wasn't his job.

Gravel crunched behind him as another car pulled up. Sheriff Gordon didn't need to turn to see who it was. He had called the doctor himself. It was rare when a call came over the wire like this one. Pointe's Hollow is a small town. It was rare to hear words like body, dead, and murder.

The doctor was out of his car, striding up to the sheriff, a pale look on his face.

"Lawrence," the doctor said, with his hand outstretched.

Sheriff Gordon took the hand, shook it, and replied, "Doctor, thanks for coming."

The doctor, David Ballwin, was a small man with a thin, white beard. His glasses were small circles in front of his eyes. If pressed for a single word to describe the doctor's physical stature, Sheriff Gordon would have said 'round.'

"Of course." The doctor released his grip and fidgeted with the jacket around his girth. "So, how bad is it?"

Sheriff Gordon shrugged, "Not sure yet. I was waiting for you to go have a look."

"Thanks for that," the doctor joked with a wry smile.

Sheriff Gordon raised a hand, and the doctor walked toward the crime scene. He took the walk slowly, taking his time. That, combined with the stoutness of his legs, made the progress into the woods sluggish.

"I don't understand why you always request me on these calls, Lawrence. I'm a doctor. I usually get ahold of people before they're dead, not after."

Sheriff Gordon spoke quietly, not out of fear someone would hear, but out of the personal nature of the comment. "I need someone I can trust in circumstances like this. Those are few and far between."

Sheriff Gordon and the doctor had been good friends and classmates back when they were just Larry and David. They had lived in The Hollow all their lives. They had both experienced loss and, over the years, bonded closer than brothers.

"I am flattered, Lawrence. Truly, I am," the doctor said with a sorrowful tone. He stopped moving and turned to the sheriff. "But next time, just call me over for a game and a cold one. Deal?"

The doctor's morbid tone lightened, and he smiled. Sheriff Gordon smiled, too; it was something he did only in front of David these days. Both of them knew a drink would never happen. They had given up drinking after the months of drowning sorrows over things better left unsaid, but it was nice to imagine.

David turned again and stepped into the crime scene as Lawrence followed, becoming Sheriff Gordon once again. Along with them in the small circle was the deputy, Donald Huckle, a thin man who was more a boy, good in heart, slow in mind; the coroner, Steven Steely, a quirky fellow who made Sheriff Gordon uncomfortable; and another officer by the name of Chris Redding. Pointe's Hollow had only three officers, not including Sheila, the department's secretary. To have all three at one crime scene was unheard of. Most crime in Pointe's Hollow could be handled by one officer, two if it was dire.

"Donald. Chris." Sheriff Gordon greeted them both in turn. They both responded with a curt, "Sheriff."

"Sheriff, good to see you as always," Steven said, without looking up from the scene below.

"Steven," Sheriff Gordon said shortly, "So what's the word?"

Both Chris and Donald said nothing; they looked at each other and pointed their lights at the body laying below Steven. Sheriff Gordon and the doctor looked down. The sight was hard to take in.

"My God," the doctor said, a hand coming up to his mouth.

The sheriff, a strong man who held the respect of many, said nothing and did not react. He stepped forward and bent low next to Steven. The sight was haunting, a sight Lawrence would flee in a flash, but Sheriff Gordon stood strong and investigated thoroughly.

The body was that of Earl Hutchins. Third-class fisherman, first-class drunk. Although Sheriff Gordon had to put Earl in the tank for a night more times than he could count, he never looked down on him. Earl had gone through a lot in his time. War does terrible things to people. Drink is often an easy calm for them.

It was an easy calm for much more than war, Sheriff Gordon thought, remembering times long past.

The identification was not the terrifying part about this scene. He would have expected a local; not many tourists this time of year. The only tourists The Hollow had this time of year were lost travelers passing through. So, in the end, Sheriff Gordon expected a local, but did not expect the condition of the body.

It was stripped naked and laid out flat in a pocket of fallen leaves. The skin was the color of ivory. It was even paler than a dead body should be. Upon further inspection, Sheriff Gordon realized the body was missing both its arms. Its appendages were sliced clean off at the shoulder. In their place were sponge-like circles of pink flesh.

"Funny thing, ain't it," Steven said.

The sheriff turned to him with a raised eyebrow.

"There's no blood," Steven explained, "not inside or outside the body."

Sheriff Gordon turned back to the body to check for himself. It was true. The body was there and the severed arm wounds would easily have spilled blood, but there was none.

No blood. Anywhere.

It seemed like an evil ritual. Appendages removed, drained of blood, and posed to be found.

"There's nothing funny about it," answered Sheriff Gordon as he stood, trying to imagine who could do this. The idea of 'what could do this' never even crossed his mind.

Chapter 7

After they collected the man's body, Dusk and Nicholas returned to Winter's Hall. Dusk told Nicholas to get cleaned up while he took care of things outside. Dusk didn't need to say what he needed to do outside; Nicholas knew he would be taking care of the body, a task Nicholas wanted nothing to do with.

Once inside the house, Nicholas found a bathroom that had seen better days. At that moment, however, Nicholas didn't care; he cared only that the water still ran. After a groan from the old piping, it did. He cleaned himself up. The jacket was too saturated with blood to salvage. Luckily, his pants had been spared most of the spatter. The last thing he wanted to do was ride home in nothing but his boxers.

He looked himself over in the dirty mirror above the sink. His face was red from the scrubbing, and there were small specks of red in his hair around his temples. Overall, though, he was alright.

Leaving his jacket in the wastebasket in the bathroom, Nicholas ventured back into the main part of the house looking for Dusk. He walked through a hallway littered with a myriad of closed doors. They showed no signs of having been opened for a long time, and Nicholas thought it best to keep it that way.

He found Dusk standing in the same room they had gone in before. Nicholas found it strange: an entire mansion, and Dusk never went any deeper than the kitchen.

Dusk, who was standing by the crackling fire in the fireplace, turned to see the boy as he entered the room.

"Well," Dusk said, biting into an apple he held, "you look good." There was an awkward minute, and then Dusk clarified, "Without all that blood, I mean."

Nicholas nodded, not really knowing what else to say. Dusk nodded back at him and surprised Nicholas by asking, "So, how was your first monster hunting experience?"

"I'm not," Nicholas began, hesitated for a moment, then continued, "I'm not sure what happened." Dusk stopped chewing for a moment. "I mean, did we kill that man tonight?"

Dusk paused with the weight of Nicholas's words. As if nothing happened, he began chewing again, "No, we killed a monster."

Nicholas had quick flashes of the werewolves from the past few days and knew what Dusk said was true. But there was also a feeling, a bad taste in the back of his mouth, telling him it was also wrong.

"But it wasn't just a monster," Nicholas said.

After taking another bite, Dusk waved it off, "They never are."

Nicholas sat there in a stupor. The idea that they had committed murder never really occurred to him before this moment. He knew they went out with good intentions and with the means to kill, but murdering a seemingly innocent man was something Nicholas didn't want anything to do with.

I'm an accomplice, Nicholas thought with horror. *But it's not as bad as it seems,* he tried to console himself. *If we hadn't, others would have died. We're heroes.* It sounded like a lie even in his head. *How do I live with this?* Nicholas looked over at Dusk to see him take another bite into his apple. *How does he?*

"Never are?" Nicholas finally said as an epiphany came to him. "How long has all this been going on?"

Dusk's smile faded for a moment as if he was aware of what was coming next. He sighed heavily as he answered, "Who knows? Forever, I guess."

Forever? Nicholas internally choked on the word. "That can't be," he said, rejecting the notion.

Dusk shrugged in response, "Why not? As far as I can tell, evil has always been around."

Nicholas's fear and confusion finally became anger, "Give me a goddamn answer!" He could barely believe he had said it.

Nicholas's breaths came out in heaves. He didn't want to anger Dusk, but he was tired of the riddles and half-truths. They were like the things people had told him when his parents died. 'They are in a better place,' or 'you'll see them again one day.' These were common phrases spat at him as he dealt with the loss. He hadn't realized until that moment how much they bothered him. That, mixed with the nonchalantness of Dusk's attitude, just pushed Nicholas over the edge.

Dusk just stared. With a look of annoyance and sympathy mingling about his face. Nicholas's own temper quickly cooled down, leaving him a kid alone in a discarded house with a murderer.

Once again, Dusk sighed. He tossed his apple into the fire and wiped his hands on each other as if to signify he was done with it.

"Alright, I guess I owe you some answers, but," Dusk

put emphasis on the last word, making Nicholas shrink back a little, "if you were anyone else and we were in any other situation," Dusk walked toward Nicholas, "I would have shot off your tongue without a second thought."

Nicholas's throat constricted as he gulped down the fear. He felt the blood run from his face, but he stayed strong. Dusk smirked a little and winked at him. Nicholas let out the breath he was holding.

Dusk went over and fell on the couch with a slight chuckle, "So, go ahead. Ask away."

Nicholas was still feeling woozy from the exchange, so he took a moment to choose his question. "How long have you been doing this?"

Dusk scratched his face, thinking, "Nine years now."

Nine years? Nicholas thought, completely surprised. *No wonder none of this bothers him. I'm sure blood, guts, and monsters are usual occurrences for him.* The idea made Nicholas uneasy. To deal with this day in and day out. *Is that what I've signed up for?*

"How did this all begin?" Nicholas stopped, then revised, "With you, I mean. How did you get into all this?"

Dusk's face turned solemn. The absence of humanity was terrifying.

"The result of fortuitous events," Dusk finally answered. Nicholas was about to complain, but Dusk raised a hand. "I am not dodging the question. I am still privileged to my own secrets, and I plan on keeping it that way."

Nicholas decided it was Dusk's right to keep some secrets for himself. He nodded in agreement.

"Where did these things come from?"

"The Other." Dusk's voice was low and hollow. Nicholas wasn't sure he heard him right.

"The what?" Nicholas asked.

Dusked nodded. "The Other. At least, that's what I was told it was called."

"What is it?"

"It's a place. A place where all this evil comes from. It's dark and terrible."

"Where is it?"

Dusk chewed on the inside of his lip for a moment. "It's a... It's a different world."

Nicholas had to take a moment with that. He said, "A different world? Like an alternate dimension. As in science fiction?"

"Not so much of the fiction part. It may be scientific, but I see it more as mystical."

Nicholas could only shake his head. He rejected the thought as any person of sound mind would, but at the same time, he believed it. The part of him that not so long ago believed in Santa Claus, the Easter Bunny, and....

Monsters, Nicholas thought. He realized that part of him wasn't so small, wasn't so long ago, but was here, now, and vibrant.

Dusk sighed and said, "This is how it was explained to me. Our world, the one you see around you, it's just one of many. Worlds sit on top of each other and around each other. Imagine a collection of bottle caps."

He grabbed three bottle caps that lay on the table in front of him. He put them together in a triangle.

"They all sit independent." His finger indicated the caps, each in turn. "They are able to stay separate and adjacent because of these empty spaces."

The curves of the bottle caps created gaps where table could be seen. No matter how hard he tried, he could never get two circles to attach completely. There was always empty space.

"Those spaces aren't what concerns us. What concerns us are these," Dusk pointed to the places where the caps touched. "This is where the worlds collide. Thin spots where the two worlds meet."

Nicholas took a moment to let what Dusk was saying set in. Then, he said, "And Pointe's Hollow is one of those thin spots?"

Dusk raised his hands as if to ask, 'What do you think?'

"And our world sits adjacent to another world," Dusk said.

"The Other?" Nicholas guessed, although it wasn't a guess, not really.

"Yes," Dusk answered. "It's not the only world I presume, but it's the one where these things come from."

The Other, Nicholas thought. His bones seemed to quiver at the thought, as if this other world had its own power.

"Are they everywhere?" Nicholas asked, trying to get warm in a room that suddenly felt so cold. Dusk didn't need any clarification. 'They' referred to the grizzly monsters that Nicholas and he had been fighting.

"Not everywhere," Dusk answered. "Just a few places."

"Why here?" And again, quicker than before, Nicholas revised it, "In Pointe's Hollow, I mean."

Dusk shifted in his chair and said, "I'm not sure, but it comes and goes here."

Finally, something Dusk had said caught Nicholas's attention. He leaned forward, putting his forearms on his thighs.

"What do you mean? The…" Nicholas searched for the right word, couldn't find it, and settled on, "things go somewhere else for a time."

"No," Dusk said, lines cutting into his brow, "it's not like that. They don't move from place to place. What I meant was that they come and go. There will be times when there won't be any sightings for weeks, months even. Then, other times, they swarm. It's as if something draws them out."

Nicholas was still confused. "What do you mean?"

Dusk raised his hands in exasperation.

"Look, kid, I know this isn't what you wanted. I don't pretend to have all the answers. What I know is this," Dusk leaned forward, "evil is real, and it's my job to keep that truth out of this world. Keep it hidden, so people like you can live their lives, free of fear. It's not a job I wanted or one I like, but it's what I got."

Dusk paused for a moment, looking seriously at Nicholas. "That is all I know."

He leaned back as if the words had taken a physical toll. Nicholas chewed over his words. It was strange to think just a few days ago he was going to school and his biggest worry was how to get people to notice him. Now, he was hunting down and hiding from monsters.

Nicholas was diving deeper and deeper down in self-thought when Dusk spoke again.

"It's late. You should get home."

As Nicholas came out of his stupor, he was about to ask what Dusk had said when he realized that it was almost morning, and he was still not home. His aunt was a generous woman and great caregiver, but staying out all night was a frowned-upon offense at the least. He quickly stood up to leave. Dusk followed suit without a word, ushering Nicholas toward the door.

They both entered the entrance hall, Nicholas heading toward the door and Dusk climbing the stairs. Nicholas was about to turn the handle when Dusk once again spoke up.

"You did good tonight, kid."

Nicholas thought he had misheard him. He turned to see Dusk partially up the stairs standing in the moonlight of a window. Dusk was looking out the window at something. Pain filled his eyes. It was a strange thing to see after the past night's events.

"Not many people could have seen what you've seen, done what you did, and still kept a cool head," Dusk looked away from the window. A smirked cracked his solemn demeanor. "Pretty brave for a kid."

Nicholas felt warm admiration for the man on the stairs and basked in the compliment. In that moment, Nicholas knew what it was like to have a proud father.

"Thanks," Nicholas said, a little quieter than intended. Dusk nodded his approval and smiled widely. Nicholas was going to leave it at that when he had a second thought, "Doesn't mean a lot to be brave in the presence of someone who's fearless."

Dusk's smile faded a little, "We're all haunted by something, kid."

Nicholas didn't know why, but he suddenly felt like he had overstayed his welcome.

"I'll see you later," Nicholas said over his shoulder as he slipped through the door and left the grounds.

Dusk watched the boy leave. Their talk had left him with a heavy mind. Problems that he didn't want and things he didn't want to think about clogged his head. It threw questions in his face that he couldn't answer.

Although Dusk had asked himself some of the same things over the years, Nicholas had somehow shined a new light on everything. It made Dusk re-evaluate the whole situation, as if he could find the answers if he really wanted to, but they were just out of reach as of yet. Maybe soon all would be revealed, but for now, things were still cloudy.

'Someone who's fearless.' The words rang in Dusk's ears.

Fearless?

It was all wrong. No one, anywhere, was fearless. Everyone feared something. Just as Dusk had said, *Everyone is haunted by something.*

"Everyone has ghosts they bear," Dusk said aloud.

He turned back to the window once again. Something stood on the lawn. It was white and wispy, like a memory. Something that was there one minute, gone the next, and then back again. It was standing, but it almost floated as well. Dusk saw it, saw it well as he always had and just as it always had, it turned and walked away, disappearing behind the trees.

I need a drink, Dusk thought sadly.

Before he climbed another stair, he turned back to the main floor toward the kitchen. His body moved toward a cold bottle dripping of condensation and filled with his personal addiction, but his mind wafted a million miles away.

Chapter 8

Nicholas spent the next day inside the house fussing about from room to room. Too tired to go out, too stir crazy to sleep the day away. It was a terrible state, and Nicholas's mind began to wander.

Luckily, he was able to slip in last night without alerting his aunt of his absence. When he awoke, groggy and shambling about, she merely remarked about his new position at the library. It took him a moment to realize what she was talking about. Once he shifted through the memories of snarling, blood-pouring werewolves, he realized his ruse and played along. She just smiled and went about her business, mostly leaving him alone for the day.

He thought long and hard about everything. Before, his thoughts were ruled by the contemplation of what was real and what was false. Now, he knew what was real, what he had gotten himself into. He didn't know the how or why and only some of the what, but he did know that the world he knew was only a farce for the true world underneath. It made him feel cheated in a way words couldn't explain.

Even with the feeling of being cheated and ripped out of his simple life, he knew he didn't have the worst of it.

Dusk, Nicholas thought.

For years he had been dealing with the burden Nicholas had been messing with for only a couple of days. Dusk said he didn't know much more than Nicholas, and Nicholas was inclined to believe him. There was no reason for Dusk to lie, at least, none that Nicholas could see. In essence, Dusk was a soldier sent to fight a war with no knowledge of who or why he was fighting. Nicholas was sure Dusk had his own reasons for getting involved, reasons he didn't want to share with Nicholas. It was irritating, but Nicholas understood.

In his room, he read book after book, but none seemed to help him deal with his problems. He got up from his bed and began to meander about his room. He landed in his desk chair, staring at the wood in front of him, one finger picking at the grain. After thinking for a long while, he pulled his eyes away from the desk and saw his father's typewriter.

When he was younger, he played with it, pretending to be his father typing away in an imaginary stupor between reality and fiction. His father had been a journalist, but he had come to Pointe's Hollow hoping to write the novel every writer believed was in them. Nicholas had been five. To him, they were just visiting his aunt. To his father, it was his chance to write the book he was meant to, the book he never had the chance to finish.

When Nicholas wasn't pretending, he would watch his father. As he listened to the clicking, he would admire his father as only a son could.

The memories brought tears burning to the brim. Nicholas wiped both eyes and massaged his temples, feeling pain, both mental and physical. He let his hands drop, looking at the typewriter again.

Suddenly, without warning or reason, a chill ran down Nicholas's spine. Before he knew what he was doing, he was reaching for the typewriter, moving it from the corner of the desk to the center.

His hands ran over the keys, kissing the cold metal with his fingertips. Ever since his parents' death, he had not so much as touched the typewriter. It had stayed on his desk because of the feeling of days gone that it lent him. He didn't want to forget them, bury them away in some basement box or toss away any sign of them. So, he had taken the typewriter and proceeded to stare at it, unused.

A notion, strong and vibrant, rushed through him like a poison. It was simple.

"Write."

It crawled about his mind, whispering and taunting him. It became so strong he almost jumped up to find paper. But in the end, he dropped his hand away, turned out of the chair, and plopped back onto his bed.

In the end, one day was not long enough to figure out his total array of problems. He went to bed that night just as he did the one before, confused, tired, and afraid of the world.

In the morning, Nicholas went to school still in turmoil over everything. He decided he would try to forget everything and go back to his normal life. The first few classes went by in a blur. As the day went on, he was able to find things to distract him.

Nicholas's fourth period was history. He did well in history, but that wasn't why he enjoyed the class. His teacher, Mr. Fidel, was someone Nicholas considered a friend. A tall, fit man with long hair tucked behind his ears, Mr. Fidel had taken Nicholas under his wing. He was a new teacher to the school. Younger than the rest of the faculty by a large margin, it was easy to understand how Nicholas could look up to him. Unfortunately, Nicholas wasn't in the mood even for Mr. Fidel today.

When he entered the class, Mr. Fidel smiled and

commented on Nicholas's 'ghostly appearance.' The term sent a shiver down Nicholas's spine and pushed his mind to less comfortable ideas. Nicholas responded with a mild hello and took his seat.

After Mr. Fidel's comment, he couldn't shake the thoughts of the past few days, an absentmindedness that didn't go unnoticed. Periodically, Nicholas caught Mr. Fidel's eyes looking him over, concern written on his face. This wasn't unusual. Often, Mr. Fidel made comments about Nicholas needing to get out and make more friends. Fighting monsters with a gun-toting stranger was probably not what he had in mind.

Nicholas smiled when he noticed Mr. Fidel looking at him, but Mr. Fidel looked unconvinced.

When the bell rang, Nicholas had already collected his things. He slipped out of the classroom before Mr. Fidel could notice. Nicholas liked Mr. Fidel, but he wasn't in the mood to fake emotions today, especially to someone who wouldn't understand. Most likely, Mr. Fidel would console him with words of wisdom on one hand and use the other to call the nurse. Nicholas wouldn't blame him. His story would be a hard one to swallow, impossible even.

Nicholas pushed through the rest of his classes, trying to find anything to take his mind away from the problems of days past. After school, he found no respite from his thoughts. Usually, he would go to the library and dive headlong into a book, but Mr. Lloyd would be there, and Nicholas wasn't ready to face him, either.

When he pushed off the sidewalk, mounted his bike, and pedaled away from the school, he wasn't sure where he was going. After some time of mindless pedaling, he found himself down at the docks. He turned into the gravel parking lot, locked his bike to a post, and wandered.

The weatherworn wood rocked and creaked underfoot as he strolled around. He needed space to think, but it seemed that no matter how much space he found, he still couldn't think straight. His mind had categorized monsters, ghouls, and hauntings in fiction, falsehoods created to frighten and entertain. But now, Nicholas was forced to reconfigure a few things.

What is real? he thought. *How much of those stories are just history mutated and thought of as fakes because of long absences?*

Nicholas sighed heavily, letting his head drop loosely. This was getting him nowhere.

He lifted his head to find he had perched himself against a railing looking out over the dark waters of Lake Michigan. Following the water, Nicholas looked to the lone island and, in turn, the lighthouse. Even though the light wasn't on, Nicholas could imagine it spinning slowly, turning around and around, welcoming fishermen home with its light.

As Nicholas was about to slip back into his thoughts, he heard a conversation behind him.

"Strange thing, isn't it," a voice said.

"Yeah, you hear what they're saying about the body?" another said, with an accent, so the word 'about' was pronounced 'aboot.'

Nicholas's interest was piqued by the talk of a body.

How did Dusk get rid of the body? Did they find it?

Nicholas nonchalantly pushed himself from the railing to follow the conversation as the men drifted away from him. He turned to see two fishermen walking toward land. They were smoking cigarettes and gossiping back and forth like teenagers. The smoke wafted back into Nicholas's face as he followed closely behind them.

"Yeah, I did," the first voice answered the second's question. "Creepy, if you ask me. I mean, who would do that to a body?"

Nicholas's blood slowly began to run cold. *Goddamn it, Dusk. What did you do?*

"Some kind of freak that likes ripping a body apart, I guess."

There it was, the confirmation Nicholas knew was coming. His stomach started to flip and turn over itself. Sickness started to come over him, making it hard for him to walk.

The two men turned, heading toward the parking lot. Continuing to follow, Nicholas turned as well, suddenly wanting to be anywhere else.

"And to such a good guy, too," the first guy said, growing sad.

They knew him, Nicholas thought, feeling a sense of shame.

"Yeah, a drunk bastard he was, but Earl Hutchins was a good man."

Earl? Nicholas was confused now. Earl Hutchins was a local man in town. Known for his drinking as much as anything else, Earl was a familiar face, familiar enough for Nicholas to know the man he and Dusk had killed was not Earl.

A weight seemed to lift off of Nicholas's shoulders. Then, he felt bad for feeling so relieved. He had still killed someone, but because he knew he wasn't getting caught, he felt relieved. It should still weigh on him just as much. A man was still dead.

So is Earl, apparently, Nicholas thought now, picking up speed to hear the rest of what the men were saying.

"Even a drunk don't deserve what happened to ole' Earl," the first man said, sad tone rising in his voice. "I mean, arms cut off? What kind of sick...." His voice trailed off.

The second man spoke up now, "You know what else I heard? I heard that his body was completely white and hard, like rock."

"Really?" the first man sounded surprised, voice slipping from sadness to interest.

"Yup, stone cold, you could say," the guy said, raising a finger and stopping his forward progress. Nicholas slowed and turned to the railing as if to look out over the water. The man's next words were so low, Nicholas almost missed them. "The police are saying his body was completely drained of blood. Like some sort of horror movie."

Nicholas's stomach took another flop, and he felt his face grow white.

"You're full of shit," the first guy said, resuming walking.

Nicholas hoped the first man was right.

"No," the second insisted, "no, I ain't. I heard it right from the deputy's mouth. Ran into him in Richie's late Saturday. Said he had just come from the scene, and he needed a drink."

"Dear God," the first one said, believing the story after all.

Nicholas also began to believe the story. Although completely outrageous to hear in normal circumstances, Nicholas didn't find the story that hard to swallow after the past few days.

The first man continued, saying, "That's just terrible, just awful, just…."

"Monstrous," Nicholas said quietly enough so the fishermen remained ignorant to his presence. The men continued to chat back and forth about the amazing events, but Nicholas no longer followed. He had heard everything he needed.

After unlocking his bike, he debated about going home. About letting the world take care of itself, so he could go through his own life just as he used to. No worries about monsters or ghosts coming to get him in the middle of the night. The only worries he would have were the constant pains and pressures of teenage years. A normal future.

With a deep sigh and a reluctant attitude, Nicholas

turned his bike toward the house on the hill, pedaling toward a not-so-normal future.

Dusk's head was pounding when he finally stirred from his room. It was no surprise to him. After having a night like he had, when one drink turns into a few, a bit of lightheadedness was expected. Pulling his numb appendages together and collecting himself, he pushed forward toward the bathroom.

After cleaning the night off him, Dusk got a fresh drink. He reopened the fridge and pulled out a leftover pizza box. He claimed his cold slice of a prize and went to the other room to fall on the couch to enjoy his breakfast.

Although he had no intention of accepting it, Dusk's life had become complicated all too quickly in his small part of the world. In a single weekend, he had gone from lone ranger to... well, he wasn't sure what he was now.

Doesn't matter. Kid's had enough adventure for a lifetime, Dusk thought, chuckling slightly at the kid's reaction to the bloody tango he had with the arm.

He joked, but Dusk knew it was rare for anyone to survive a brush with their first monster encounter, let alone be willing to go hunting the next day. It was different, strange, special even. The kid was something else, and Dusk couldn't deny that.

Yeah, special or just insane.

After a moment of consideration, Dusk decided it was probably a little of both, a perfect combination. However, Dusk probably shouldn't have told the kid so much. It was always sketchy letting people into this world. Word travels fast in a small town. He had done many jobs during his time in Pointe's Hollow and becoming invisible was becoming more and more difficult. Not that it completely mattered. These things always had a way of working themselves out.

It was not by accident that Dusk continued existing in Pointe's Hollow. It was like the appearance and disappearance of the evil. Things just seemed to happen, but only when something was going on. Dusk didn't know what it was, but he knew that he, Winter's Hall, and the evil would not be found by the world because that was not the way it was designed. What 'it' was, Dusk didn't know. If he had been one to care, the uncertainty in his life would have driven him crazy, but he had given up caring a long time ago.

Dusk took a long pull on his beer, almost finishing the bottle with a single swig. He devoured the pizza in a couple bites. As he wiped his hands together, cleaning off the crumbs, he had to admit that cold pizza from Fellini's was still better than any pizza, any temperature, from anywhere in the world. Strange thing to imagine finding a pizza joint like that in Pitsville, Michigan.

After finishing off the dribble in the bottom of the bottle, Dusk decided yesterday was probably the last he would see of the kid. Of course, he would want to know more, to find all the answers, but it was just too much for a kid, or anyone, to handle. If what happened to him hadn't happened, Dusk wouldn't have been able to handle it. If handling was what he was doing.

Collecting his empty bottle, he left the room with the desire to slip out and walk the grounds for a while. As Dusk went through the front hall, three loud thuds came bouncing through the house.

He paused, staring at the door, confused. Then, the realization came to him that he had been so wrong.

"Shit," he said under his breath as he went to answer the door.

Nicholas was about to knock again, but he thought it might be better to go around back as he did before. That's when the memory of a barrel poised at his head made him consider knocking again as his first option.

Before he could raise his hand again, the old, oak doors opened inward revealing Dusk, hair half wet and empty bottle in hand. Dusk looked as if he expected Nicholas to be the one at the door. Neither spoke.

Just as it began to look as if they were never going to speak, Nicholas spoke up, "Isn't it a bit early?" His hand came up, gesturing at the empty bottle in Dusk's hand.

Dusk looked down at the bottle after a moment of hesitation. "Yeah, well, I was all out of Kool-Aid."

Nicholas looked at him, wondering if he was serious, and then a smile cracked his face. Dusk smiled, too. Over the past few days, Nicholas had thought of Dusk as a stranger or murderer or gunman. But now, Nicholas saw that one day, he could see him as a friend.

"Come on in," Dusk said, waving Nicholas in. "Knowing you, this won't be quick, and I'm empty."

Nicholas pushed by Dusk in the doorway, and after shutting the door, Dusk followed.

"And you're sure that's what they said?" Dusk asked after Nicholas had finished
recapping everything he heard from the two fishermen down at the docks.

"Yeah, I'm sure."

Dusk nodded, then looked away, thinking. After a moment of silence, Nicholas couldn't wait any longer.

"So, what do you think did this?"

Dusk looked up from the floor, "I don't know."

Nicholas looked dumbfounded at him, "What do you mean 'you don't know?' You're supposed to be the expert."

"I am," Dusk said, mockingly insulted. "But it's not like there's a monster hunting handbook. You kind of learn as you go."

Nicholas suddenly realized he was going to have to be the focused one of the two. Dusk seemed content with playing everything on a whim, something Nicholas would have to change, or one of them would end up dead. Probably him.

"Alright, what's next then?" Nicholas asked.

Dusk wiped his face, scratching against stubble. He looked distant again, and just as Nicholas thought he was going to have to ask again, Dusk stood, heading for the door.

"Come on," he said.

Nicholas jumped up and followed, "Where are we going?"

"We need more information. We're going to go talk with Earl."

Nicholas stopped in the main hall. "Wait. Earl? You mean dead Earl?"

"Yup," Dusk said, grabbing his long, dark coat from a coat rack. He shifted the coat until it laid comfortably. "What are you waiting for?"

Nicholas stared at him. After a little bit of thought, Nicholas decided after the week he was having, nothing seemed impossible. He pushed forward, saying, "Oh, what the hell."

Chapter 9

By the time Dusk and Nicholas arrived at the Sheriff's Department, night had fallen. Nicholas followed Dusk, pushing his bike through the nighttime city streets. Once they arrived, Nicholas was afraid they were going to break into the one place in Pointe's Hollow where real trouble could be found, real trouble in the form a large mustache, under a hat and behind a badge.

After hiding his bike behind the shed in the parking lot, Nicholas dashed across the brightly lit lot to find Dusk with his hands on his hips looking up to the sky. Nicholas followed Dusk's sight line and saw he was inspecting the roof. Nicholas didn't like where this was going.

"Are we going to sneak in through the roof?" Nicholas said with a tone of trepidation.

Dusk looked down at him and then back up, saying, "How do you think we'd get up?"

Nicholas sighed, scouring the back wall of the station looking for anything that would help them scale the height. A dumpster was pressed against a rain gutter. "How about the dumpster?" Nicholas suggested.

Dusk looked over, considering the possibility.

"Then, up the gutter, you see." Nicholas pointed out further.

Again, Dusk considered the option, nodding at the idea. Dusk turned and walked in the opposite direction, toward the department's back door. When he reached it, he simply turned the handle, and it opened.

Dusk looked inside in mock amazement. After a thorough inspection, he looked back at Nicholas. Nicholas, feeling foolish, quickly walked over, keeping his eyes diverted from Dusk's. As he slipped into the building, Dusk said, "Gotta love small towns."

Nicholas ground his teeth in retort and ignored the chuckling coming from in front of him. They disappeared into the halls of the department as the door shut behind them without a sound.

Nicholas stopped after a few feet, unsure where to go. Dusk took point, walking through the pale-colored halls with familiarity. They exited the back hallway and entered a large room filled with a few cubicles.The cubicles were sectioned off by waist-high walls, which led to a spacious office on one wall and the front desk on the opposite. It seemed very cozy.

On their right, Nicholas noticed a cork board. Peppered along the cork board were papers, missing persons signs from the previous months. Nicholas was alarmed by the number of people on the wall. A man, around thirty years old, stared out at him with frozen eyes. 'MISSING,' typed in red, was printed along the top of the image.

There is something very wrong with this town, Nicholas thought.

They walked around one cubicle and exited the main room to a second hall. Just as they were about to leave, Nicholas noticed a dim light illuminating from the office. The light silhouetted the letters on the glass of the door. They read 'Sheriff Lawrence Gordon.' Nicholas swallowed hard, thinking of the sheriff and the hell they'd pay if he saw them.

Getting out of the line of fire, Nicholas and Dusk disappeared down the hall. After passing two doors, one without a label and another reading 'Holding,' they came to a door labeled 'Morgue.' Dusk looked back at Nicholas, making sure the kid was still with him. Nicholas looked back, acting tough as his stomach flipped and flopped about. They opened the door to the morgue, revealing steps that led to a basement.

As they descended, Nicholas heard the echoes of whistling bouncing off the walls. The sound reverberated as if it was coming from everywhere at the same time. They hit the bottom when Nicholas realized the whistling was coming from someone else in the basement.

"Dusk, wait," Nicholas said, but Dusk didn't stop. He stepped from the dark stairway into the brightly lit room through the only doorway to the left. Nicholas hesitated, but decided if he had come this far, it would be a waste to stop now.

Turning into the room, Nicholas saw white walls with steel fixings. On the far side was a wall of small doors with silver handles. In front of them stood a table illuminated by an almost blinding white light. Hunched over the table was a small, thin man in a lab coat that was too big. His whistling was high pitched and cheery. He circled around the table. Once he was on the other side, he noticed Dusk and Nicholas.

Nicholas tensed, readying himself for shouting and threats. He was surprised to see a look of happy expectance on the man's face.

"Dusk, it's good to see you," the man said, smiling.

"Ah, Steely," Dusk said, "keeping busy, I see." He strutted forward with Nicholas in tow. "Steely, do you know young Nicholas here?"

Nicholas had seen Steven Steely here and there about the town, but had never actually spoken to him.

"No, I do not believe I've had the pleasure." Steely held out his hand for Nicholas to shake. As Nicholas reached forward to accept, he realized Steely's hand, encased in a rubber glove, was covered in blood and bits.

Steely noticed Nicholas's hesitation and then looked at his own hand. Laughing out loud, he said, "My apologies. You get so used to the feeling of flesh on your hands, you forget it's there."

Nicholas nodded as if he understood, but he was pretty sure he could never get used to that feeling. Visions from the night before came to mind, and he had to look about the room to ignore them. As he did, he realized the body below the blinding light was covered by a sheet from the waist down. However, its top half was completely uncovered. The chest was cut open and hollowed out of all the innards. Nicholas subconsciously felt his hand come up to his mouth.

"Steely, you mind?" Dusk said. Nicholas looked at him, and Steely did as well. Dusk was motioning to the body in front of him. "It's a bit gross."

Steely looked down at what Dusk was referring to and berated himself for not realizing sooner. Nicholas was aware that Dusk had done it for his benefit. He nodded a thanks to Dusk, thinking how strange the whole situation was.

After Steely covered the body, he explained it was an out of town man involved in an automobile accident on the outlying roads.

"Son of bitch was doing ninety around a curve when," Steely brought his fist together with his palm, creating a pop of a sound, "he got real friendly with a tree." Steely chuckled at his joke. Dusk shook his head, which made Steely stop, cough roughly, and say under his breath, "God rest his soul."

Nicholas was able to collect himself as he walked over to the counters at the foot of the autopsy table. He found papers in manilla folders laying out, along with a sink, a box of rubber gloves, and a bowl of Dum-Dum suckers. Nicholas stopped at these. He fingered the white sticks thinking how out of place they were down here.

"Help yourself," Steely said from behind him. Nicholas turned and thanked him, but left the suckers where they were. He didn't want to put anything from this room in his mouth.

Dusk asked, "Where is he Steely?"

Steely looked at Dusk, confused. "Where is who?"

Dusk sighed heavily, "Steely?" This time, there was an edge in his voice.

After a moment of hesitation, Steely gave in. "Alright, alright, Dusk, you win." Steely turned to the wall of doors and began to look for what Nicholas and Dusk had come for.

He opened the door of a chilled drawer and slid another covered body out of the wall on a silver table.

"Order up. One bloodless man, minus arms," Steely said, snickering once again. He threw back the sheet as Dusk and Nicholas came closer.

It was unmistakably Earl Hutchins. Nicholas would have recognized the stout beard and weathered face anywhere. Although Earl had been a drunk in the last years of his life, the muscled body of a fisherman was still evident under the signs of age and fat. Starting at each of his shoulders, two incisions cut through his flesh, connected at his sternum, and continued in a single line all the way to his navel.

Where his arms should have been were large, pink circles of flesh. Other than the paleness of his complexion and missing appendages, the body looked normal, as if Earl was only sleeping.

A few days ago, Nicholas would have been disgusted and repulsed by the body, but now he was glad to be saved the sight of more blood. He inspected the body with immense attention. As far as Nicholas could tell, a dead body was a dead body. Nicholas looked to Dusk for more assistance.

Dusk was inspecting the incisions with a crafter's eye. "How exactly was the body found?"

Nicholas looked back to Steely. "Almost exactly as you see here. No blood anywhere, inside or outside, arms amputated between the humerus and scapula. Stark naked, just outside of Richie's."

Nicholas looked back to Dusk. "You have to clean the body once you got it here?"

"Not too much, a little dirt, but it was mostly clean when it was discovered."

"I see," Dusk said, taking it all in. "These cuts look surgical."

"Almost better than I could do," Steely confirmed.

Dusk's hand came up to his chin, and he scratched, considering all the implications of the facts. Nicholas looked over the body once again.

"Looks a lot different from the work of your usual," Nicholas hesitated on the words, unsure of what he could say around Steely, "cases."

Dusk glanced down on him. The look said his effort was useless and 'how would you know' in the same instant. Nicholas shot his own look back. Dusk smiled, "Yes, it is different."

"There was something else," Steely said. Dusk turned back to him. "Right here," Steely explained. "A small puncture wound right here on the back of his neck." Steely pointed with his pinky at the lower right side of Earl's neck.

Dusk lowered down on his haunches and inspected the spot. Nicholas followed suit. He saw a small speck of red surrounded by a pinkish circle. "It looks like a mosquito bite."

"Yes, but it's much more than that. That right there is a needle puncture. Earl here was injected by something very shortly before he died. Unfortunately, we won't have the toxicology report for a few days."

What kind of monster uses a needle? Nicholas thought.

Nicholas shifted his eyes down to Dusk, who was already looking at him. They both shared a moment of concerned confusion.

Dusk looked back to Steely, "Anything else, Steely?"

"Ah, no." Steely sighed heavily. "Of course, I only work with what I have, and what I have is a clean, dead body in a clean crime scene."

Dusk nodded, "Well, luckily for us, I have a little bit more."

Nicholas caught the quick wink Dusk sent his way. He reached into his coat and pulled out a small vile of dark green liquid. The small, glass vile was stoppered by a little cork. Dusk raised it and wiggled it between his fingers. The liquid began to glow deeply within its recesses.

Dusk stepped forward, uncorked the stopper, and leaned over the body. Both Steely and Nicholas looked at each other, confused, and then both looked at Dusk.

"Now, let's see what old Earl has to say about all this."

Nicholas was about to ask a question when Dusk squeezed out a drop of the green liquid between the slightly agape lips of the corpse in front of him. The green liquid slipped between the lips, past the teeth, disappearing into the dead body. For a moment, nothing happened.

A low sound came from deep within Earl's corpse. It sounded like a balloon deflating as it ran out of air. The sound started quietly and grew even quieter. As the sound dissipated to nothing, Earl's chest lifted, and the corpse inhaled fresh air. Earl jumped, coughing for breath. The body coming to life made both Nicholas and Steely fall back. Steely grabbed Nicholas's arm, yanking Nicholas forward between him and anything that would come at him.

Dry air came out of the body's mouth, and fresh air rushed in to take its place. Earl's eyes shot open, but they held no color. The pupils were grey and vacant, and the pigments were cloudy. Once the fit had subsided, the body lay as if awaiting orders.

Dusk's eyes darted up at the two onlookers as he smiled. He turned back to the body and whispered, "Earl?"

The body inhaled and exhaled, in again, and then on the exhale, the dead man said, "Yes." The voice was airy and vacant.

Dusk readjusted to get closer to Earl's ear. "Do you know where you are?"

Earl kept breathing heavily. His eyes didn't blink; they just stared toward the ceiling without warrant. "No," he said, and his face contorted into fear.

"Do you remember what happened to you?"

"Remember? Yes."

Dusk shot a cautionary glance at Nicholas and Steely.

"What happened, Earl?"

Earl's breathing began to quicken, his eyes grew even wider. "Died."

Hearing the realization of a dead man that he was, in fact, dead made Nicholas feel an overwhelming sense of sadness. This man's death was so terrible, and now, however impossible it was, they were making him relive it.

"Yes, Earl," Dusk said, talking with more compassion than Nicholas had thus far heard in his voice. "You are dead."

The breathing quickened even more. Nicholas stepped forward, not wanting to see this go any farther. Dusk raised his arm, forcing him back.

"We are here to find who did this to you," Dusk continued.

Earl's breathing slowed slightly, and his lids lowered a little. It was as close to a thank you as he could give. It made Nicholas feel better, but he still wanted this to stop.

Dusk tried again, "Who did this to you, Earl?"

Suddenly, Earl's breath caught and rushed faster than before. "Shadows," he breathed. Dusk looked confused. Earl's breath continued to come faster and faster. "Man. In. Shadows."

"Man in shadows," Dusk repeated.

"Man," Earl repeated again, followed by, "Shadows." His breath rapidly rushed faster and faster until Nicholas couldn't take it any more.

"Dusk," he said. Dusk shot him a look.

"Earl," Dusk pleaded. "Who is the man in shadows?"

Earl's eyes widened to a size that was impossible for a live person to achieve. "Do... Do...."

He doesn't know, Nicholas thought.

"Do... Do...." Earl repeated, until his breath came in and out, too quickly to form words. His chest rose and fell, eyes darted back and forth, breath rasped until it finally stopped. There was a moment of silence, and then Earl let out a final, hissing breath, and his lids once again closed together. Earl Hutchins was dead, for a second time.

For a moment, no one moved. Finally, Dusk stood, pinching his nose between his thumb and forefinger, thinking hard.

"That was awesome," Steely said, letting out his breath as if he had been holding it through the whole incident.

Nicholas gave Steely a look of derision, and then his eyes dropped down to Steely's hand, which was still wrapped around his arm. Blood and guts were falling off his hand and onto Nicholas's jacket. He ripped his arm from Steely's grip thinking, *Will there be a day when I don't get blood all over me?*

He looked over to Dusk who had turned away from Earl's body. He was pacing, now deep in thought.

"Man in shadows," Dusk repeated.

"Mean anything to you?" Nicholas asked.

"Nope, beats me," Steely said. Nicholas gave him an

annoyed stare. Steely mouthed, S*orry*.

"Me, neither," Dusk finally replied. "Well, thank you, Steely." Dusk looked over at him, smiling.

"Always a privilege, Dusk."

Dusk waved his good-bye and started to leave, when Steely spoke up, "Dusk?" Dusk turned to Steely. "Got any more of that, ah, green stuff?"

Smiling widely, Dusk turned away, "Good-bye, Steely."

"See ya, Dusk. Oh, and no worries, I didn't see anything." Steely followed the last part with a wink.

Nicholas waved his own good-bye and followed Dusk to the stairs. They weaved through the station in silence. Exiting through the same door they came in, they slipped away without a sound.

Once they were outside, Dusk stopped, placing his hands on his hips. Nicholas stopped as well. The entire experience had left Nicholas with more questions than answers. It was aggravating. However, Nicholas was learning he just had to be patient.

"So," Nicholas said.

"So?" Dusk repeated.

"What exactly happened back there?"

"Standard procedure," Dusk joked.

"It's standard procedure to bring people back from the dead?" Nicholas said.

"No, I didn't bring Earl back from the dead," Dusk said seriously. "When we die, there is a small time where memories can be exhumed. If we had gotten here sooner, Earl would have been stronger, and we could have probably had more time."

Dusk looked off, chewing on his lip, frustrated. Nicholas was still confused. "He was back, though. Breathing, talking."

"No," Dusk said, shaking his head. "His body was still

dead." Dusk took on a very serious look. "Now listen, kid, because this is very important." He paused to let his words sink in. "There is no way to bring anyone back from the dead. It is the only finality in this world."

Dusk's face grew grave, and he took on the appearance of a skull. Nicholas could see there was more than what he was saying behind his words, a story Dusk didn't want to share.

"You understand?" Dusk asked.

Nicholas wanted to pry, but decided there would be other times. He nodded. He also found his eyes burning with the threat of tears as he thought of the deaths in his own life.

Dusk let out a breath and wiped the look off his face. Nicholas watched him walk away.

"Now what?"

Dusk stopped moving and turned to look at Nicholas. "Well, it ain't the best of circumstances, I'll give you that. But there are some things we can look into."

"Man in shadows?" Nicholas asked.

Dusk shook his head, "No, that's gonna have to wait for us to have a little bit more." Dusk again brought his hand up to his chin. "The body is what concerns me."

It's concerning me, too, Nicholas thought roughly.

"There are only a few circumstances I can think of in which a body would be drained of blood. None fit in this case." Dusk let his hand drop as an idea came across his face. "Luckily, I know of an expert in these matters."

"Expert?" Nicholas said, confused. "Who would be an expert in something like this?"

Dusk smiled, "There is only one thing you can talk to about blood draining." Dusk looked over at Nicholas. Nicholas's head tilted, still confused; then, an idea came to him, and as soon as he thought of it, Dusk said it.

"A vampire."

Dusk

Sheriff Gordon felt like the entire world was caving in around him. So many things had come out of nowhere, things he didn't want or need on his plate right now. A sheriff's job is hard enough. Add being a single parent to a teenage girl and a sick killer draining the blood of their victims, and you had the mess that was his life.

"Jesus Christ," Sheriff Gordon said under his breath as he let out a sigh. He leaned far back in his desk chair until he was almost horizontal. After stretching, he leaned forward again, putting his elbows on his desk.

He had been working on Earl Hutchins's murder all night, flipping through the crime scene photos from front to back without any progress. For an officer, there was nothing more irritating than a fresh case with no leads that was going cold fast.

He decided to take one more look, and if he still didn't get anything from everything, he would go home and sleep on it. He hoped coming in the next day with fresh eyes would help him see things he missed. Sheriff Gordon sighed heavily and restarted his usual ritual of flipping through the crime scene photos.

Twenty minutes later, Sheriff Gordon locked the front door of the department behind him. His coat was thrown over his arm and files were in his hand. After his final look through, he decided to take the files home in case something came to him in the night.

The car door creaked slightly when he opened it. He placed the coat and files on his passenger seat. He followed in, landing on the driver seat. He cleared his throat with a rough cough and adjusted his seat.

After closing his door and buckling his safety belt, he

was putting the key in the ignition when he saw a man emerge from the back door of the station. His car was on the edge of the front lot, so he could just make out the back side of the building.

Below the brightly lit back lot light, the door swung open as a man in a black coat emerged. He walked into the center of the lot and stopped, looking up into the sky.

"What the hell?" Sheriff Gordon said. He moved to undo his seat belt and confront the man.

Once the seat belt was off, he checked again, seeing not one, but two people now standing in the back lot. The newcomer was none other than the boy Sheriff Gordon had seen with his daughter the day before.

"What the hell?" the sheriff muttered again, under his breath.

He didn't know the identity of the man in black. Not a local, that he was sure of. Being sheriff of a small town, it was his duty to know everyone. That man, he did not know. The appearance of an outsider in town with the killing happening was beyond unsettling. The fact that he was conversing with a kid who was under the sheriff's protection just threw salt in the wound.

They stood in the back lot and talked a while. Sheriff Gordon knew he should go back there and confront them both; however, something stopped him. He wasn't sure what it was. An idea possibly. An idea that there was more to the story than what he had gathered so far. He decided he would collect all the information and then confront both of them.

Suddenly, the man in black said something and left, with the Wake boy chasing after him on his bike.

Sheriff Gordon buckled his safety belt to leave. Finally, he had a break in the case. The key turned in the ignition, and his car growled to life. He threw the car into gear and headed home. He was going to need his rest for his investigation, an investigation of the man in black.

Chapter 10

As it had always done in the past, the alarm clock's ring racked Nicholas with its annoying clatter far too early for his liking. Nicholas quieted the clock with an exaggerated arm slam. After a lull, the form that was Nicholas slinked out of bed and to the shower.

After cleaning up, Nicholas entered the kitchen feeling like just a cleaner version of the sleepy blob that had slid out of his bed. He rubbed his eyes while wondering how it could be so bright in his little corner of the world.

"Morning, sunshine," Aunt Sherri said, whipping the pancake batter.

"Uh, huh," Nicholas mumbled back, falling into his chair at the table.

His aunt smiled at his discomfort. "A boy your age should be able to handle the late nights and early mornings with ease. You get to my age, and you'll really begin to feel tired."

Nicholas just rolled his eyes, thinking, *How many kids*

over the years have heard the 'Just wait till you get to my age' talk. He concluded the number was probably astronomical, and he was too tired to think too deeply about it.

"Besides, most kid's heads are pounded dead by party music, so a few quiet nights should be easy for you to handle."

Quiet nights? Nicholas just stared at his aunt, confused. *What about the past few nights had been at all quiet?*

She didn't notice his look. She was bouncing about the kitchen, her mind on her cooking. After a moment, however, she commented on the silence. "You know, at the library."

Nicholas still didn't know what she meant. The last time he had been at the library was when Mr. Lloyd had told him about the terrible events leading to Nicholas's discovery of Dusk at Winter's Hall.

Now, Aunt Sherri noticed Nicholas's confusion. She stopped her busying about and leaned on her elbows over the counter.

"You've been at the library," she paused for a moment, but after Nicholas made no move, she continued, "helping Mr. Lloyd with stocking the books or whatever it is librarians do at night. Right?"

Finally, the story came back to him. "Oh, yeah. Of course," he said, less convincing than he had hoped. If he was going to continue with this, he would have to become a better liar. Luckily, he was good enough for his aunt, who shot back, smiling, "Even more tired than I thought," she said.

"Yeah, must be." He was beginning to feel even more tired. There were so many things going on at once.

He, Nicholas Wake, was helping a lone, gun wrangling, monster hunter named Dusk track down a murderer while simultaneously lying to his aunt and dodging the only real friend he had, Mr. Lloyd.

135

Dusk

"Mike said you were talking with Emily Gordon down at the diner the other day." His aunt's words shook him back into the kitchen. She peeked at him out of the corner of her eyes, "Anything I should know about?"

Nicholas slowly shook his head. Then, there was Emily. So far, there wasn't much to him and Emily, but they had talked outside of school, which was far more than he could say about his interaction with any of the other girls in The Hollow.

What a mess, Nicholas thought. He was about to fall back asleep when his aunt clattered a plate down in front of him. He jumped slightly, but the aroma of hot syrup hit his nostrils, and suddenly, sleep wasn't the strongest of his desires.

"Alright, fine. Just keep me in the dark. But if you ever need dating advice, you know who to come to."

Nicholas was already on his second bite, so he was more than able to ignore his aunt's comments and continue eating.

He finished eating, collected his bag, and pedaled off to school, waving good-bye to his aunt. Just like any other day in paradise for most everyone in Pointe's Hollow.

As he rode, Nicholas began to see the small town he had grown up in for the first time. It was the perfect, little town in the daylight, but once you had seen the shadows, as Nicholas had, it seemed a much more mysterious place. With potential terror creeping around every corner, Pointe's Hollow was an enigma of the mind. Looking one way one second and the exact opposite the next.

He arrived at school with plenty of time before class, as he always did. The halls were filled shoulder to shoulder with kids yelling, taunting, running, goofing, and living. Although there weren't many people, let alone teenagers, in The Hollow, there was always a commotion when a collection of them were shoved together in tight spaces. The high school's halls easily constituted a tight space, creating a cacophony of adolescent nonsense.

Making it to his locker, he was surprised to find Emily Gordon leaning against it looking through the crowd of kids clambering about in the last few minutes of freedom. Nicholas was so surprised that he stopped in the middle of the hall, getting bumped by two classmates as he did.

Her hand came up in a drifting tuck, placing the strands of loose crimson hair behind her ear. Was she looking for him? The idea was so foreign to him, he immediately rejected it. Even though he thought the idea was absurd, he saw her begin to turn his way, and he slid to the side, hiding in a door frame.

Feeling childish, he peeked out from his hiding place to see what he thought would never happen: a girl looking for him. After a moment, he decided he had a choice to make: either hide in door frames for the rest of his life or confront the girl. He let out a sigh and turned to Emily.

Emily was already looking at him. Warmth rushed across his cheeks, made worse when Emily smiled and waved. She was completely intoxicating to him, and there was no way he could ignore her pull. It was like gravity. Before he knew it, he was just a pace away from her smiling face, mumbling, "Hey."

"Hey," she said in return.

There was a moment of silence. Nicholas could feel the air grow thick, so he said the first thing that came to his mind.

"That's my locker." He pointed where Emily was leaning. After following his finger, she looked back at him and smiled.

"I know," she said with a nervous laugh.

That was beyond stupid, Nicholas, he berated himself. He also questioned humanity's future survival if this was how teenagers conversed with the opposite sex.

He waited for Emily to speak and save him from more embarrassment. Luckily, he didn't have to wait too long.

"I have something for you." She reached into the space between the books she held in the crook of her arm. She removed a small slip of paper. Nicholas couldn't make out what it was, but as Emily handed it to him, it was clear it was a photograph.

It was a simple print, but the image was spectacular. It showed a bird perched on a dock post, cascaded in silhouette by the sun, which hung right behind the bird's head. The bird had an angelic look as a halo of light encircled its head. The image was framed in white.

"This is cool," he said, lost in the picture and forgetting about Emily for a moment. When he looked up to see her smiling, he adjusted his statement. "It's beautiful. Did you take this?"

She nodded, evidently pleased with Nicholas's enjoyment. "I took it down at the water the other day."

Nicholas again looked at the picture, taking in the entire scene. "You're really good."

He felt like he was the most inarticulate chump on the planet. He wanted to tell her how stunning and absolutely encapsulating the image was, but 'really good' was all that would come out.

Thankfully, Emily didn't seem to mind. She perched on her tiptoes pointing at the picture with her free hand, the other still tightly squeezing the books.

"You see," her finger outlined the bird, "it's a raven."

Nicholas brought the picture closer. With the highlight of a glowing sun around its head, it was hard to identify the bird at first glance or even second. Now, Nicholas could see it, its tall stature and straight beak were dead giveaways.

"As soon as I saw it, I thought of you."

Emily's words puzzled Nicholas. *Why does a raven remind her of me?* Out of all the circumstances Nicholas could think of, none of them were good. He looked up at her and was pained to see a somewhat hurt look on her face.

"You know," she said, proceeding slowly, "like the poem."

Nicholas had to think only a moment to be reminded of the famous Edgar Allen Poe piece, *The Raven*, something Nicholas had read and enjoyed. It was one of his many favorites, along with *The Tell-Tale Heart*.

"You know it?" she asked with a pleading look on her face.

He realized he had been silent for far too long. "Yes, yes. I know it very well, actually."

A weight seemed to fall away from her. "Good. I was afraid I was going to look stupid there for a second," she said, smile and glow returning.

"No," Nicholas said. "No, never."

She nodded, accepting the compliment, but not taking as much stock as Nicholas had put in it. "Besides, I felt like I owed you for giving me your amazing drawing."

Nicholas felt his face falter and his cheeks grow red as he thought of his drawing in comparison to the picture from her that he now held. He wanted to say that his napkin sketch was nothing like the work of art he held now, but the words seemed to get caught in his throat. After a moment, he said something to make sure he didn't spoil the whole encounter.

"I'm glad you liked it."

"Liked it?" she said with a slight giggle. "I loved it."

Nicholas nodded, but didn't really know what else to say. Even though he thought he had said everything he could, he still quickly added, "And I love this."

She looked down, "Not too morbid?"

Her words mirrored his own about his sketch from a few days ago. He smiled, knowing the mocking wasn't by accident and enjoying the idea that their conversation had been heavy on her mind.

"No, not at all. I really love the way the…."

The school bell interrupted Nicholas with a jaw-wrenching clatter. Suddenly, the hustle and bustle of the kids around them went into frantic overdrive. Like a crescendo in a song, the crowd raised quickly in volume and then began to fade away as the kids filtered into their classrooms.

"Well," Emily began, bringing Nicholas back to their conversation, "I guess I'll see you around."

Nicholas once again led with a nod and a quiet, "Okay."

After another of her world class smiles, Emily spun on her heels and disappeared into the thinning crowd of people.

'Is there anything I should know about you two?'

His aunt's words repeated in his head again and, for the first time, Nicholas thought he might have lied to his aunt about that, as well as everything else. Was there something between him and Emily? *No, of course not,* Nicholas thought sourly. However, he couldn't help but feel he was lying to himself now, too.

He was almost to his class when he adjusted the strap on his backpack and froze. "Ah, shit," Nicholas cursed under his breath.

He quickly spun on his heels, rushing back to his locker. In the mess of everything, he had forgotten to open and, in turn, store his bag.

Once everything was stored nice and cozy, he paced down the empty hall, arriving late to first period. His tardiness did not bother him nor his teacher, Mrs. Denver, who merely shook her head as he entered. It was now becoming a day-to-day occurrence for him, but what made today different was that instead of dealing with monsters, he was dealing with girl problems.

For a teenager, those two problems might be considered the same thing from time to time.

It was strange that after everything he had been through

in the past few days, he could think only of Emily.

For years, Nicholas had admired her from afar, as most boys do with pretty girls, he assumed.

Especially girls with sheriffs for fathers, he added with a feeling of dismay forming in his gut. But now they had not had one, but two conversations outside of a classroom. They had given each other presents. To be fair, she had taken hers, but Nicholas was pretty sure that still counted.

It could mean nothing, but it could also mean something. What that something was Nicholas had no idea, for his love life had been nonexistent for as long as he could remember. Libraries are filled with books that tell the story of young love, and only a few had the ending Nicholas desired.

What am I thinking? There are bigger things to think about. Nicholas decided he would spend no more time thinking of this, at least not today.

"Taking a break from the norm, I thought we'd talk about something a little unorthodox."

Nicholas was now sitting in fourth period. The whole day had blurred by like he was in a trance. The conversation with Emily had been so captivating that Nicholas had barely even noticed his classes beginning and ending.

"Reanimation," Mr. Fidel continued.

Nicholas was confused, and he thought he misheard Mr. Fidel. Mr. Fidel looked about the class with interest, as if he was waiting for someone to counter him.

No one did, but not out of intimidation. Mr. Fidel was the most easygoing teacher in the entire school. Kids were encouraged to speak their mind, and even when kids took it a little too far, Mr. Fidel never got angry. He would just tell the class to settle down, chuckling to himself.

"Reanimation," Mr. Fidel repeated. "Does anyone know what that is?"

Nicholas knew what it was, of course. No lover of horror and suspense would be ignorant of reanimation, but he kept silent. Usually, Nicholas would love to answer Mr. Fidel, but his recent interaction with the act in question made his throat swell and brow break out in a sweat.

"No one?" Mr. Fidel looked about the room.

Nicholas was afraid Mr. Fidel would call upon him to answer. His eyes scanned the room and were about to hit Nicholas when he quickly diverted toward another.

"Jennifer," Mr. Fidel said, looking at a young blonde in the second row who was not paying attention. Jennifer looked up from her desk, slightly unnerved by being called to action. "Do you have a guess?"

Jennifer, or Jenny as her classmates called her, shook her head. She was a quiet one. Nicholas had seen her a few times outside of school around town, jogging down the streets, bouncing back and forth day in and day out. Running was something Nicholas never thought of as a hobby, but if he had, he would say Jenny had an unhealthy addiction to it.

"No?" Mr. Fidel said, saddened slightly.

"Doesn't it have to do with cartoons?" Jerry said with a wave of his hand as if he was recalling something from a long-forgotten conversation. Probably was, but in his burnt-out mind, there wasn't much to recall.

"No, Mr. Collins, that's just animation. Reanimation." Mr. Fidel looked about the class in desperation. "Oh, come on, people." He sighed heavily. "Alright, reanimation in normal terms is bringing something…" Mr. Fidel paused here and lifted his arms in a Frankenstein imitation, and his voice took on a cliché horror tone "…or someone back from the dead."

The whole class let out a laugh at the teacher's expense, thinking he was joking. Mr. Fidel smiled at this, "I know, I know. The stuff of the B-rated horror movies down at the drive-in, but the idea of reanimation was not always a plot device in the movies."

Mr. Fidel had captured their attention, and he had them locked. Like a magician finishing the first step of his act, and rounding into the turn, Mr. Fidel spoke with the skill of a master storyteller.

"All the way back to the seventeen nineties, an Italian physician by the name of Luigi Galvani demonstrated the ability of the body's nerves to react to stimuli even after death. He did this by sending volts of electricity through the legs of dead frogs. When he did this, Luigi saw the muscles twitch."

Mr. Fidel paused, looking at the eager faces around the room. They were eating up his words and asking for seconds.

"Of course, this was very far from bringing dead flesh to life with lightning on a metal table, screaming, 'It's alive'!" Mr. Fidel threw up his arms in exaltation, making some students jump in their seats. "But every book begins with a single word," he finished, bringing his arms slowly back down to his desk, leaning forward toward the class.

"It all seems very gruesome," Sarah said, speaking up. She always stated her opinion whether or not it was asked for. Not out of some idea of her knowing more than the teacher, but just so the teacher knew she was paying attention. Anything for a grade was Sarah Cohen's motto, not that she needed the help.

"A bit distasteful, I'll give you that, Miss Cohen." Mr. Fidel's response was proper and respectful. He never talked down to his students, one of the many reasons Nicholas liked him. Being treated like a child was beyond irritating.

"Besides, Mr. Fidel, what could possibly come from bringing a dead frog back to life?"

Mr. Fidel stopped as if the answer was obvious. He took a moment and ran a hand through his hair.

"Is that how all of you feel?" he asked, looking about the room. Luckily for Nicholas, Mr. Fidel had become entranced by the class as a whole, so he didn't see Nicholas's complexion pale, so that if someone looked at him, they would know he himself had seen a form of reanimation just the night before.

Flashes of Earl trying to catch his breath and the glow of the green liquid ran through his head, making him feel as if all the eyes were on him, when that was the furthest thing from the truth. In fact, the entire class was so entranced by Mr. Fidel's topic of conversation, they were absently nodding their heads to his question. This seemed only to further irritate Mr. Fidel. He took a moment and then began to circle his desk.

"Alright," he began, approaching the idea in a different way. "But let me put it to you this way." He continued to circle his desk, rubbing his fingers across the grains as he did.

"If humanity could bring someone back from the dead, what would a disease mean to us?"

The question was strange. It hung in the air. and no one dared to answer. Mr. Fidel continued, his pace and words mesmerizing, "Cancer? It would be a mere annoyance. War? Pointless. Men would go to die, then be revived and go out again. The supply of manpower would be never ending, and nations wouldn't get into never-ending conflicts."

The students sat, taking everything in. Nicholas listened, too, aware of the romantic spin Mr. Fidel put on everything, but unwilling to disagree.

"With the fear of death gone and immortality at our fingertips, what couldn't mankind do?"

Everyone took in the idea Mr. Fidel proposed. Mr. Fidel himself seemed to be taking it all in. Then, he did something Nicholas did not expect. He smiled, a wide, unyielding smile, like a child with a terrible plan to annoy his sister.

"But what if it rained cotton candy and money grew

along the side of the road for everyone to pick?"

The class relaxed and smiled. Some even chuckled at the quick turn on the subject. Mr. Fidel laughed as well. "I am just a teacher, after all. I know less about what would fix this world than I know how to do my own taxes."

Everyone laughed, and suddenly, it was back to a standard day in class. Mr. Fidel went behind his desk and sat in his chair.

"Anyway, I bring this up because the idea of bringing people back from the dead or making deals with or for the afterlife comes up a lot in history, and as we explore the evolution of scientific theory, it will come up a lot." He waved his hand as if he put no weight in all the hubbub history is filled with.

"From the birth of ancient and modern day religions even to rumors of Hitler's scientists doing strange tests on monkeys during World War II, the entire span of history is filled with the endless struggle between humanity and mortality." His attitude had flattened, and his energy was down, but he still held the whole room's attention.

"I also recall reading recently in one of my magazines about a doctor in the military doing some research of his own about the void afterlife. Theories that I had never heard before," Mr. Fidel was building speed and excitement again.

"He proposes ideas about the heart being more important than we realize and all other kinds of theories. There was a single picture of him; he stood holding a beaker of a dark green, glowing liquid. The glow lit his face with an eerie light." Mr. Fidel shivered as if the picture had given him the creeps.

"There were also times during the famous witch trials of the late sixteen hundreds where the line between life and death blurred. Even in our small town here there were questionable times where...."

Nicholas stopped listening. He was too concerned with

what Mr. Fidel had been saying before. 'A beaker of a dark green, glowing liquid.'

Son of a bitch, Nicholas thought so abruptly he almost said it out loud.

After the bell rang, Nicholas approached Mr. Fidel. He needed to find out more about this doctor.

Mr. Fidel's eyes were focused on some papers on his desk, so he didn't notice Nicholas when he came up.

"Oh, hello, Nicholas. I didn't notice you."

"Hey, Mr. Fidel," he said. "How's it going?"

He sighed, slightly lifting the papers on his desk. "The work of a teacher never ends."

They both smiled. Nicholas didn't know how to begin. It was common for Nicholas to talk with Mr. Fidel after class about all kinds of topics. Now, however, Nicholas was asking out of more than just general curiosity. It made Nicholas nervous.

"Did you need something, Nick?"

Mr. Fidel looked at him, confused. Nicholas knew he had to say something, so Mr. Fidel wouldn't get too suspicious.

"Yeah. Well, I was just wondering about the doctor," Nicholas stumbled through his words. Mr. Fidel began to nod, as if he understood what Nicholas was saying.

"Intriguing, isn't it? Would you like to see the article?"

Nicholas smiled, thinking this had been much easier than he anticipated. "Yeah, if I could, that'd be great."

"Alright, hold on a second," Mr. Fidel said, reaching down below his desk. When he came back up, he held a magazine in one hand. Before handing it to Nicholas, he flipped through the pages. He stopped at a page, flipped the cover around, and reached out toward Nicholas.

Nicholas gazed down at the open page and saw exactly what he thought he would see, but didn't want to. In the picture was a man wearing an oversized, white lab coat and thick glasses. His face was slightly obscured by the glowing vile in front of it. The glowing emanated from a strange, green liquid, the same green liquid Dusk used to bring Earl back the night before.

He knew he had to play it cool, so Nicholas proceeded cautiously. "Weird." The word slipped out of his mouth in a long, amazed tone. "Does it say anywhere in the article what the chemical is?"

It was a strong push, but Nicholas knew no other way to say it.

Mr. Fidel didn't seem to notice, shrugging and saying, "No. It just briefly describes his research and his theories, but nothing too in-depth. When the article was written, he was still in the early stages of his research."

Nicholas was discouraged, "Well, is there any way to know if he's found anything since?"

Mr. Fidel shook his head with a frown, "Unfortunately, the research was canned shortly after it began."

"What happened to him?"

"Probably got thrown onto a different project and disappeared into the military," Mr. Fidel said, shrugging it away. "I'm not sure, honestly."

Looking down at the picture, he saw the caption for the first time. It read 'Dr. Alfred Murdock, 1954. Photograph by Giovani Price.'

He took one more look at the picture and handed it back to Mr. Fidel, who took it and looked at the picture himself. Nicholas waved farewell behind him as he left the classroom. Mr. Fidel waved back, not looking away from the magazine, beginning to reread the article.

Dusk

Nicholas saw this and thought it was funny. It was something Nicholas would do with one of his books.

Chapter 11

Nicholas lay with his hands behind his head waiting for night to fall over Pointe's Hollow. The information he gathered from Mr. Fidel's article and speech had been minimal, but he thought it was important. He hoped Dusk would think the same.

After school, Nicholas pondered the idea that it was possible Dusk already knew about the doctor. After all, Dusk had some of the same liquid the doctor was using, and he didn't say where it had come from. Realizing he knew very little about Dusk and everything he was getting himself into, Nicholas thought he might be overreacting. Dusk may have gotten the ooze from the doctor or vice versa, and he may be nothing more than another of Dusk's 'friends.'

Or he could be so much worse, Nicholas thought.

His eyes began to hurt from the roundabout thought process he was entertaining. The pressure from his fingers around the bridge of his nose felt so good he almost fell asleep.

Forcing himself to stay awake, he raised himself up

from his bed and ventured about his room. In the midst of his busy schedule, the room's tidiness declined rapidly. He bent down, collecting articles of forgotten clothes. He deposited them into the basket he kept in his closet and decided the room was clean enough. His mind's constant wandering made him too restless to continue cleaning.

Without realizing it, he found himself sitting at his desk on the west wall of his room. The old typewriter was at the forefront of his desk, but Nicholas wasn't looking at that. His attention was captured by the recently hung picture on the wall directly above the desk.

The picture, like its giver, was completely intoxicating. The absence of color and the harshness of the black and white contrast only accentuated its haunting beauty.

Nicholas was about to look away when there was a sudden flicker that caught his eye. Thinking it was a play of light, he disregarded it. But it happened again. The movement was so quick, Nicholas couldn't be sure it had happened at all. What made him even less sure was the fact that the movement seemed to come from within the picture.

But pictures don't move, Nicholas thought reassuringly.

Yeah, and werewolves don't exist, dead people don't talk, and old Earl died from natural causes, his mind argued.

Its argument was hard to ignore. He leaned toward the picture, squinting hard, trying to decipher every line. The picture remained just as it was: still. Perturbed, Nicholas moved in even closer. Yet, nothing moved.

Raising up on his hands, he moved even closer, his nose almost touching the picture. He stared at the dark raven in the picture. The picture stared back, unrelenting and unmoving.

Sighing, Nicholas sat back down just as the flicker happened a third time. He caught it out of the corner of his eye. Head whipping around, Nicholas's hand slipped, and he fell onto the keys of the typewriter. The harsh click made him jump back, falling into his desk chair. The picture fell from its perch and landed on the desk with a soft, almost inaudible puff.

The entire room was still. Breath returning to his lungs, Nicholas laughed to himself. He concluded the picture's perceived movement was its slow descent as it fell.

After a moment of further reflection, Nicholas reattached the picture to the wall. This time he pressed down harder on the tack, hoping it would stick for good. Leaning back, he watched the picture, bidding it to stay. And it did.

Nicholas's eyes dropped to the typewriter, admiring its own haunting beauty. The contrast of the typewriter's hard angles and smooth surfaces were just as harsh as the black and white of the picture of the raven. The mechanics crisscrossed about the inside of the typewriter.

An idea suddenly occurred to him. He intended to use the typewriter later in life; it was his father's, after all. But it seemed that so far, he had nothing important enough to type on the machine.

His father did great work on this typewriter. Nicholas didn't want to ruin the future potential of this machine with the dribble that he supposed he'd come up with if he used it prematurely.

Nicholas had not used the typewriter to type a single word. Now, however, he wondered if it was a good idea to use a typewriter every once in a while to be sure everything still worked correctly. As far as he knew, the typewriter had laid dormant for the past ten years.

Nicholas licked his lips as he thought. There was a pull to the typewriter. A desire Nicholas couldn't quite put his finger on. The desire, however, was also mottled by fear.

Fear of what?

Nicholas wasn't sure, but a shiver rolled over his skin every time he looked at the typewriter. The feeling made Nicholas pull the typewriter out of storage in the first place.

Dusk

After a moment of internal struggle, Nicholas got up from the chair, retrieved the pile of loose-leaf paper he kept by his bed for drawing, and brought it over to the desk. He put the pile down and picked up a single sheet.

His hands shook slightly as he moved it toward the top of the typewriter. The page slid into the slot as if it were a sandwich and the slot was a starving man's mouth. Once it went in as far as it could before hitting the rollers, Nicholas used his right hand to spin the mechanism inside, sending the paper around the roll to come back up in the front.

With a slight push, the roller was put in the beginning spot, so it was ready to capture thoughts. Nicholas leaned back in his chair and looked over the machine. It looked more powerful with the sheet loaded into it. A hand came up and wiped over his mouth. He leaned forward again with every intention of writing. To write what, he wasn't sure, but he was going to write something to make sure the machine was still functioning.

As he was about to type the first letter, a voice came from below.

"Hon, I'm going out. You good for the night?"

"Yeah," Nicholas shouted back, "I'm good."

"Okay," his aunt said, extra cheery for some reason. "There is some leftover spaghetti in the fridge if you get hungry later. I'll probably be back late, so don't wait up."

"Where are you going?" Nicholas asked.

"It's karaoke night at Richie's."

Nicholas rolled his eyes so much, he was glad she wasn't there to see him. "They brought that back again?"

"It's only one of the busiest nights for Richie's."

"Yeah, it is until *you* get up on stage."

"Oh, boy, you're asking for some trouble you ain't never gonna get out of," Aunt Sherri shot back.

"Have a good night," Nicholas said, still laughing from his joke.

"Night," his aunt said.

Then, he added, "Be careful."

There was a moment when he thought she might not have heard him.

"I will," she said.

There was a strange tone in her voice. But before Nicholas could place it, he heard her start singing a mutilated chorus of *American Pie*. "Bye, bye sir Nicholas-pie. Drove my Chevy to the...."

Nicholas again rolled his eyes and shook his head. He turned back to the typewriter.

He thought about typing something, but the moment had passed. He checked his watch, and as he did, his aunt's car backed out of the drive and disappeared toward Richie's.

It was still probably a little early, but Nicholas decided he had waited long enough. He went to his closet, collected his jacket, went downstairs, slipped on his shoes, and headed out toward another dark night in Pointe's Hollow, the place of karaoke and murder.

The sheriff took another pull on his drink. Given his past, the drink consisted of nothing more than ice-chilled Coca-Cola. Almost as harsh as the hardest liquor, the cold, carbonated liquid slipped down his throat with a tortuous pleasure.

After smacking his lips and sighing from quenched thirst, he spun on his stool, surveying the crowd. It had been growing steadily throughout the night, and it would continue to grow the later it got.

Sheriff Gordon was not the biggest fan of Richie's karaoke night. As many would imagine, he was not a man of musical sorts. But this was his town, and most of the people in his town would end up here by the end of the night. The ones who didn't would probably be in bed soon, if they weren't already.

He would have been there most likely on any other karaoke night, but this night was different. There was a wolf between the pines, and it was picking off the sheriff's flock one by one. A calculated, primal hunter with a taste for blood and an unquenchable appetite.

There had been only one death as of yet, but Sheriff Gordon was not a stupid man. He could tell the difference between a spur of the moment kill and one that served a greater purpose. Was it for the sick bastard's enjoyment, or was there some meaning behind the death of Earl Hutchins? The sheriff didn't know, but he sure knew it wasn't over. The wolf still prowled within the shadows and stalked the night.

The sheriff's mind went back to the night before when he saw the Wake boy with the mysterious man in black. Sheriff Gordon didn't like mysteries. He wasn't a fan of riddles, and he sure as hell didn't like having a stranger in his town while people were turning up dead. That was why he liked The Hollow. Not that it was the safest place on Earth, but secrets didn't last long in a small town, especially if you were the sheriff.

An awkward reverberation sounded from the corner of the bar. The Dresser boy, Michael, or Mikey as his family called him, was on a makeshift stage messing about with cables for the soon-to-be life of the party. The poor boy looked like a spider caught in its own web. Lanky arms and legs tangled about in a myriad of cables and equipment.

Shaking his head at the boy, Sheriff Gordon took another swig of his drink. He lowered the glass and inspected the room with a familiar and professional eye. It was a bar through and through. Wood floors with wood paneled walls decorated with large nautical themed ornaments. A fishing net hung on one wall intermingled with pieces of ships, while on the other wall a harpoon gun and buoy were perched precariously.

Old Richie was down at the other end of the bar, to the sheriff's right, wiping down the countertop with a rag. The old barkeep handled his bar like those in the old western movies.

Passing by him stepped Peggy, or Legs as the fellas referred to her after a few rounds. The bar's one and only server dressed in her usual tight shirt and short skirt. She was pushing fifty, but had a body like a twenty-year-old, and she enjoyed flaunting it.

She delivered drinks to a small circular table where Mr. and Mrs. Hanover sat. This couple was one you had to catch on the right night. One night they'd be everything a good couple should be, and on others they'd be at it with the mouths of sailors and the tempers of grizzly bears. Luckily for everyone involved, tonight seemed to be one of the better ones.

After the drinks were placed, Peggy moved on to another table. She exchanged quick words with Eddie Wood, an elderly chap who loved to tell stories of days long gone. She rounded the tables, placing a soft hand on Mr. Lloyd, who sat sipping a spoon of soup, and finally passed the only pool table, which currently sat vacant, to return behind the bar. Her movements were graceful, yet quick and snappy as if she was dancing with the crowd, bounding up and down, round and round with an air of professional sensuality.

Richie's was usually a quiet place. The locals didn't throw much fuss over anything. The only time the pub became rowdy was when sailors were in port. Most of the time, they were just small scrapes. A couple of guys who had too much getting too loose with their mouths and then turning to fists. The sheriff would roll in, clean up the few stragglers, and have them all spend a night in a cell. By morning, everything was back to normal.

The sheriff took a final swig, draining the drink to nothing, and returned it to the bar. Richie quickly claimed the glass and dropped it in the sink, creating a sudsy wave that bounced off the steel walls. He knew the sheriff all too well. Only one glass. Just enough to say he had been around, and then he was off. Although the sheriff had no intention of leaving, he did intend to step out for a bit, because young Mikey seemed to have finished working on the stage.

The sheriff stood from the stool, readjusted his pants, keeping his appearance clean cut. The crowd began to shuffle as it became obvious that the night's entertainment was about to begin. Sheriff Gordon knew it was the perfect time to slip out, before it became too lively in the bar. As he slowly made his way to the door, Mrs. Hanover moved toward the stage.

The door was closing behind the sheriff as the applause began to quiet and music began to rise for Mrs. Hanover. It closed as the first note rang from her lips, and then there was only muffled sounds from inside.

The sheriff padded to the edge of the bar's porch and leaned against the post by the stairs. Cars sat in neat rows all about the bar, some in the front, a few on the side, and many more in the back.

Mr. Fidel was walking between two of the cars in the front lot. He was fiddling with his keys, getting ready to slip into the driver seat of his forest green Ford Jeep that had a brown, tarp roof.

"Not staying for the festivities?" Sheriff Gordon called to him.

Mr. Fidel turned, and seeing it was the sheriff, smiled and waved, "Howdy, Sheriff. Not tonight, I'm afraid. Papers to grade, and besides, it's a school night."

"That it is," the sheriff agreed. "Well then, you stay safe out there, alright?"

Suddenly, two kids rushed past Sheriff Gordon.

Flinging the bar door open wide, they introduced Mrs. Hanover's less than charming voice to the night. It's squeamish tone cut through the dark like a knife. Then, the door snapped back, and it was quiet once again.

Mr. Fidel's smile grew bigger as he said, "Yeah, you, too. Alright?"

The sheriff sighed, looking around and then back to the teacher. Nodding his acceptance at the sheriff's answer, Mr. Fidel opened his car door and waved a final time. The sheriff gave his own curt nod.

The green Jeep backed out of the spot and sped away. It was quickly replaced by the small, blue car of Miss Sherri Wake. The sheriff smiled as he watched her park the car. He had always liked Miss Wake. A flirt by most standards, but she never caused unnecessary trouble and was always available when she was needed.

Unlike that nephew of hers, thought the sheriff.

His moderate disdain for the boy wasn't because of his appearance with the stranger. It was because of Emily. Like any father, Sheriff Gordon didn't believe any boy was good enough for his little girl. They never would be. He refused to believe he would sooner or later have to give his blessing to one of them to take her hand.

The thought of the boy gave the sheriff an idea. He straightened his posture and pulled on his belt, realigning his uniform. By the time he was ready, Miss Wake was ascending the stairs of the porch on the old bar building.

"Evening, Miss Wake," Sheriff Gordon greeted her.

Miss Wake looked up at him, "Oh, Lawrence, how many times have I told you to call me Sherri?"

The sheriff smiled and nodded slightly, "Too many times to count, Miss Wake."

Miss Wake eyed him up and down in a strong, yet flirtatious manner. She passed him on the porch and continued forward toward the bar door.

Dusk

She turned her head to say over her shoulder, "I hope you're not gonna stay out here all night. It's cold; come on inside, enjoy the music, and have some food."

"I will, Miss Wake. Just had to get some fresh air."

Miss Wake turned and smiled, "Yeah, I'm sure that's why you're out here."

She turned back toward the bar, but the sheriff spoke up again. "Miss Wake?"

Stopping, she looked at the sheriff with a questioning look. The sheriff took a step forward, "Have you been seeing anyone recently?"

The question took Miss Wake off guard as Sheriff Gordon knew it would. It was meant to slightly, but not the way she took it. It was his interrogation method. He needed to be in control of the situation and have power over the detainee. Even if it was Miss Wake, and she was not a criminal by any stretch of the imagination.

She smiled again, "No, Sheriff. Spending these nights as lonely as ever."

The sheriff nodded as if this was brand new information, but he had assumed as much. Miss Wake was a free spirit, anyone could see that. But he didn't have his answer yet, so he pushed forward.

"Have you noticed anyone peculiar around town recently?"

Miss Wake grew serious, "No, not really. Sheriff, what is this about?"

I'll be asking the questions, Sheriff Gordon thought, but he didn't say it.

"Nothing." The sheriff looked around to make sure no one else was around to hear their conversation.

"Has Nicholas been hanging around any new people, or any new friends been hanging around the house?"

For another moment, Miss Wake looked concerned, but soon after, her face cracked and split into a wide smile.

"Sheriff, you had me worried. How dare you scare me like that?" She batted her hand in his direction as if to wave him off.

The sheriff was now the one who looked confused. He put his hands on his waist and shifted his weight to his other leg. After a moment, Miss Wake continued.

"I know it's scary for you. My father was absolutely terrified when I started dating," she said, a motherly tone weighing her words.

The sheriff was still confused.

"Look, Nicholas is a good kid, and Emily is a lovely girl. It was bound to happen sooner or later. I'd just be happy that it wasn't some other kid that grabbed her attention. She could do a lot worse than my Nicholas, you know."

After another slight moment, Sheriff Gordon finally understood. She thought he was talking about Emily and her nephew talking, or dating, or whatever it was kids did nowadays. The sheriff chewed over this for a moment and in the end decided not to correct her. He took big strides to make sure his townsfolk were comfortable. There would be no mayhem on his watch. The proof that someone from his town could be so calm and concerned with normal things when there was a murderer on the loose was a win in his book.

"Yes, ma'am," he answered, smiling and acting as if he had been caught doing something he shouldn't.

Miss Wake nodded and smiled, thinking she had caught the sheriff in a tight spot. "Good. Now if you must know, I haven't seen Nicholas but here and there for the past few days. He's been working with Mr. Lloyd down at the library."

"Doing what?" Sheriff Gordon said before he could catch himself. Luckily for him, Miss Wake didn't notice his accusing tone and answered.

"I don't really know. Restocking books, helping

alphabetize the rows. Honestly, I'm not sure what taking care of a library actually entails."

"Was he there last night?"

Miss Wake's smile dropped slightly, "Yes, in fact, he was."

Sheriff Gordon wanted time to ask more questions, but she was already leaning toward the bar door, and he didn't want to push his luck any further. "Alright, thank you for your time, Miss Wake," he said with an over-exaggerated, professional tone.

Miss Wake took the cue and with a little curtsy said, "Of course, Sheriff Gordon, anything to help the police keep track of the boys their daughters are interested in."

She flashed a big smile and turned away toward the bar.

The door opened and the quiet night was bombarded once again with the sound of terrible karaoke. A warm smell of food and beer wafted past her, and then she was gone. As the door slipped closed, Sheriff Gordon spied Mr. Lloyd in the bar, clapping along.

Thudding shut, the door closed the night off from the lively bar, leaving Sheriff Gordon alone once again. He wanted to rush in and question Mr. Lloyd. Not about Miss Wake's nephew per se, but if he was supposed to be with Mr. Lloyd last night and instead he was with this stranger, then it was a good assumption Mr. Lloyd knew something about it. No matter how much the sheriff wanted the answers, he wouldn't ask the questions. He didn't want to disturb the bar's merriment. Besides, if he talked with Mr. Lloyd after talking with Miss Wake, it might raise her suspicions.

The sheriff sighed and rubbed his forehead. He wanted to keep the majority of his town's people safe even if it meant he had to wait for answers.

Unfortunately for Sheriff Gordon, the night was still young.

Chapter 12

Nicholas had grown accustomed to the ascent to Winter's Hall, so it didn't feel like it was too long before he stashed his bike in the brush and hopped over the wall. Walking up to the house, he was again amazed by its overwhelming size and presence beside the bluff. It was as if the house overlooked the entire world, Mount Olympus overlooking the entirety of Greece and housing the gods set to protect the people.

A sometimes half-lucid, gun-wielding god with a knack for jokes and quick wit, Nicholas thought. He was about to laugh out loud when something caught his eye.

The front door to the house was swaying slightly on its hinge. Nicholas felt a growing chill rush up his arms. He looked about the front yard to see if there was any sign, whatsoever, of foul play. The breeze flooded over the grounds, picking up leaves and playing with them until they once again fell to the ground. The door was the only thing that seemed out of place.

Dusk

Nicholas reached behind him with one hand and pulled out the dagger hidden there. It was the same dagger Dusk had given him just a few nights ago when he had taken Nicholas into the woods to confront the werewolf. The sheath silently slid off.

Nicholas advanced, wielding the knife in front of him in his right hand and the sheath in his left. The world seemed to become all but silent around him. He ascended the first step on the porch, then the second. On the third, the porch reported with a harsh crack. Nicholas paused, but when it seemed he was still unnoticed, he continued forward.

Without a sound, Nicholas slid through the gap between the door and the frame. He padded into the main hall looking all around, ready to be attacked at any moment. The staircase on the opposite side of the room spiraled up to the second floor in the falling darkness with no sign of disturbance. He looked from wall to wall, floor to ceiling, and then he noticed that the room where he had conversed with Dusk before was being licked by the orange light of fire.

His limbs began to shake as he grew closer to the door. The warmth of the flame and the sweet musk of smoke came to him with a punch. Beads of sweat broke out on his forehead, and his breath began to hasten.

Nicholas stopped outside the door. He took one breath in and then let it out. Following another intake of breath, Nicholas stepped into the room with a slight jump. The fireplace was roaring with a large fire. It grabbed Nicholas's attention, and then movement from the right corner of his eye caught him off guard. He turned in response, raising his knife in defense.

Dusk stood on the other side of the couch with a plate in one hand and a slice of pizza in the other. His jaw rolled and chomped on an excessively large bite as he eyed Nicholas up and down.

"What the hell are you supposed to be?" Dusk said

through his mouthful of food.

Nicholas sighed and dropped his arms. "I thought," Nicholas paused. What did he think? "I thought," he repeated, but, again, didn't get anywhere. Dusk was still chewing, waiting for Nicholas to finish.

"I thought you were being tortured or had been killed or were in trouble."

Dusk continued chewing, and then suddenly stopped. "Why?"

"The door was open," Nicholas said, exasperated. His breath was short as if he had run a mile.

"Yeah?" Dusk said, raising his arms. "I knew you'd be by, and I didn't want to have to get up when you got here."

"Don't you think that's dangerous?"

"I live on a remote bluff in a small, rural town; walk around with a loaded gun; and fight monsters. An open front door isn't high on my list of creditable threats."

"I smelled smoke," Nicholas continued erratically.

"I started a fire."

"I... I... I...." Nicholas stammered angrily, relieved and embarrassed all at the same time.

Dusk smiled and took another bite of his pizza. Falling down on the couch, he kicked his feet up and placed them on the table in front of him.

Nicholas looked around the room, turning his back to Dusk. The fire crackled and popped, creating a cozy feel. Nicholas had not been coming to Winter's Hall long, but this was the first time he could actually see the old building as a home. The orange glow created a sense of warmth that contrasted with the cold grey of the walls. It was hard to believe they existed in the same world, let alone in the same room.

Nicholas turned back to Dusk once his breathing had calmed down. His hands still shook slightly, and he found himself wondering if he would ever get used to this feeling.

Dusk

The man looked different in some way. It wasn't an obvious change, but it was different. His hair seemed better kept, and his clothes appeared less wrinkled. However, it was his eyes that really held the change. The slight vacancy that had made him so frightening when they first met had vanished, and his look was welcoming.

Dusk swallowed hard and then pointed with the slice of pizza in his hand, "Mind putting that away; you're making me nervous."

Nicholas looked down at his hands. He was still holding the knife and sheath. Loosening his grip, he put them back together.

"I'm making you nervous?" Nicholas said with a slight waver in his voice.

"Yeah," Dusk said, and his smile widened. "Not for my own safety. I just wouldn't want you cutting yourself and getting blood all over the floor."

Nicholas shot a look his way, which Dusk answered with a quick bite of pizza and a smug chewing session.

On the opposite side of the table from the couch, Nicholas noticed two lounge chairs, cascaded in shadows from the fire. Nicholas took one, almost falling into its embrace. A hand came up to his forehead, wiping the sweat from his brow.

Dusk shoved the last bit of pizza into his mouth and smacked his hands together, wiping the crumbs from between his fingers.

"So," Dusk began, until his mouthful became too much for words. He chewed for another few seconds and then finished with a large gulp. "So, any news from the town below?"

Nicholas just shrugged, "Not really."

Dusk sent him a quick look. Nicholas caught it and responded in kind. "Look, I know I may look it, but I don't have my finger firmly pressed on the pulse of the town."

Dusk kept his look up for another moment longer and then nodded with an over-eccentric frown. "Well put," he finally said.

Nicholas shook his head, chuckling slightly to himself. Then, it hit him like an avalanche. The whole reason he had rushed over here tonight. "Where did you get that stuff?"

"What stuff?"

"The stuff," Nicholas said, waving his hand like Dusk should just understand him. "You know, the green stuff from the other night."

Dusk chuckled slightly, "It's very impressive how you can be so verbally prompt one moment and so blunt and stupid the next."

Nicholas just stared at him, waiting for an answer.

"Look," Dusk began, realizing Nicholas had grown serious. "There are some things I won't be able to tell you. You're just going to have to accept that."

Nicholas was immediately furious. Keeping his calm, Nicholas said, "I saw it."

Dusk's eyes narrowed slightly, but he didn't say anything.

"Today, I mean," Nicholas clarified. "In class. My professor had a magazine with an article about a scientist from World War II."

Still Dusk remained silent.

"He was messing with that stuff in the picture they had of him."

For another moment, Dusk remained silent. He was quiet so long Nicholas wanted to jump up and shake him. Finally, Dusk spoke, "Did it say anything about what he was working on?"

Nicholas shook his head, "No, not really."

Again, Dusk went silent. He brought a hand to his chin and began to contemplate something.

Suddenly, Dusk jumped up and went for the door.

Nicholas was stunned by his quick movement, but he followed Dusk out the door and into the hall.

"Where are you going?"

"To talk to an old friend," Dusk answered as if that was all Nicholas needed. Dusk's cryptic response further frustrated Nicholas.

"You're gonna have to start telling me things."

Dusk didn't stop. He kept moving, collecting his coat, checking his holster, and grabbing his tomahawk. As Dusk opened the door, Nicholas finally broke his silence.

"Dusk!"

Dusk stopped in his tracks and turned back to Nicholas. Not with anger, nor annoyance, but with actual curiosity.

"You will have to start telling me things. I can't be left in the dark forever." Dusk looked at the kid, and his eyes softened. Nicholas's tone dropped, "I know you didn't want this and neither did I. But now that I am in this, I need to know what I am in. You have to start telling me things."

Dusk let out a long sigh and said, "We'll see."

The words caught Nicholas off guard, and before he could say anything else, Dusk was out the door and off. The door swung open and just hung there, waiting for Nicholas to follow.

With everything that had happened, Nicholas's thoughts bounced about without cause or means. Out of that madness, Nicholas could find only one thing to ask. He shouted after Dusk through the open door, "Aren't you gonna put out the fire?"

Dusk, without looking back, yelled over his shoulder, "No. If it burns, it burns."

To Nicholas's surprise, after a long walk, they ended up at Pointe's Hollow's Catholic church. It was positioned on the outskirts of the small town within a small clearing of trees. The building had an aging, white exterior with black roofing tiles. It had a single spire that rose up into a point with a cross perched atop its precipice. Its door, and even the shutters, were a faded white. Even though it had been there forever, its brilliance was unmatched.

Nicholas had been to the church only once: for his parents' funeral. He hadn't been able to bring himself to go near it since. It hit Nicholas hard when they broke through the surrounding brush and were face-to-face with the church. The surprise was enough to stop him in his tracks.

Dusk continued forward for a few steps until he noticed Nicholas wasn't moving. He stopped and turned to see what was holding Nicholas up. Nicholas's face was staring at the cross, eyes wide, jaw slack, and color drained from his face. Dusk followed his gaze and wasn't impressed.

"It's just a building, kid."

Nicholas jumped at the suddenness of the words. He was able to rip his eyes away from the church to look at Dusk. Dusk had a look of stern support, "Nothing more."

Nicholas nodded, but felt the weight of the building's eyes upon him. He had never been religious; his parents had never been, either. No matter how irreligious he was, Nicholas still knew the power behind a single idea that unified millions, and the idea scared him.

They mounted the steps, and Dusk opened the church's doors. A profound silence came from within the church. The air was palpable with stillness. Dusk either didn't notice or ignored the sensation and entered the church. With chin up and eyes staring, Nicholas followed.

Their footsteps pattered against the worn, tiled floor. The room seemed bigger on the inside than it did on the outside. The ceiling rose so high above the rows of pews laid out in front of them that Nicholas could almost imagine clouds materializing below the peak.

At the far end of the church, a raised platform stood at the forefront with a podium placed in the center. It was three steps high and wrapped all the way around the front. Around the backside of the podium, shadows wavered and flickered from the light from small flames.

But what drew Nicholas's eyes from everything else was the oversized cross that hung in front of a giant, stained glass window. The window was made of what seemed like thousands of blue, purple, and yellow shards designed in elaborate patterns to be the most pleasing to its onlookers. Moonlight sliced through the window, masking the cross in silhouette.

"Richard."

The voice echoed about the church, bouncing off the walls and ceiling. It was hard to pinpoint where it came from. Nicholas looked around the room trying to find who had spoken. He saw nothing until a man emerged from the left side of the room walking in front of the first row of pews, looking back at him and Dusk.

"Hello, Christopher, it's been a while," Dusk said, a slight smile on his face.

Nicholas felt like he'd been hit by a stampede.

Dusk's name is Richard, Nicholas said.

"Richard, how many times have I asked you to call me Father?" the man said as he made his way toward them.

"Probably just as many times as I have told you to call me Dusk," Dusk retorted.

The priest, draped in a white robe, waved his hand in response, "Richard Dusk, that is your name. I call you Richard, for that is what your mother and father wished of people."

Richard Dusk, Nicholas thought, looking over the man next to him in an entirely new light. It was strange how many times Nicholas was reminded how little he knew of this stranger. The strangest thing was how much Nicholas trusted the man, believed in him.

The priest finally reached them, putting both his hands

on Dusk's shoulders. This was quite a feat, for Dusk stood almost half a foot taller than the man.

"It is good to see you, my boy, whatever you wish your name to be. And who is this?"

"I'm Ni...." Nicholas tried to answer, but Dusk cut him off.

"He knows who you are; don't let him fool you."

Nicholas looked at Dusk and then at the priest. The priest was looking at Dusk, but turned to Nicholas, smiling. With a wink, he said, "Hello, Nicholas, how have you been? It's been a long time since I have seen you around here."

Nicholas took a moment to find his voice, and then he answered, "I'm good."

"Glad to hear it," the priest answered, smiling even larger. "So, what brings you two to my neck of the woods?"

Dusk sighed, putting his hands on his waist, "We have some questions."

"Questions. Well, then by all means, ask them, for I have answers."

"I will." Dusk shifted his footing. "We also have questions for Clara."

The priest's demeanor changed slightly, but he held his smile. "I see. So, you look for forgiveness as well as answers."

Dusk nodded, "Not for me. I'm long past saving. But," Dusk looked to Nicholas. Nicholas looked between the two of them.

The priest's head lifted as he said, "Ah, I see."

The words came out with the weight of knowing more than was actually being said. The man's wisdom was beyond that of normal minds. Father Christopher was able to read between the lines while thinking outside the box and finding hidden meanings all at the same time.

"Nicholas, if you would be so kind as to follow me."

He raised his arm, ushering Nicholas toward the front

of the church. Nicholas hesitated and then moved forward. When they were about halfway to the front, the priest called over his shoulder, "And Richard, no one is beyond saving. Not even you, my son."

Nicholas didn't see or hear a reply from Dusk, but he could imagine the eye roll and pessimistic look.

They made it to the front of the church and turned, heading toward the area the priest had come from when they first arrived.

It suddenly became clear what was happening. It became clear as soon as Nicholas saw the two wooden doors right beside each other in front of him. The priest quietly said, "The one on the left is yours."

Nicholas's hands went clammy, but he knew there was no backing away. He entered the confessional booth, closing the door behind him.

There were no sounds. Nicholas had the unshakable feeling of being alone but watched. For a moment, there was silence and then a shuffle next to him. Nicholas realized it was Father Christopher entering his own confessional booth.

After he settled down, there was a soft grazing as he opened the small window between them. They were able to speak, but couldn't completely see each other. The window was adorned with an ornate wood carving that created empty spaces.

There was silence for a moment. Nicholas knew he should speak, so he began sputtering. "I'm not really sure how to...." Nicholas slightly trailed off and was about to pick it back up when Father Christopher chuckled.

"Oh, Nicholas, don't worry yourself."

Nicholas was taken off guard. When Father Christopher spoke, his smile was clearly visible through the holes, "In your entire life, you have done nothing more wrong than not finishing your vegetables at the dining room table."

So much was happening, it took Nicholas a moment to

respond.

"What? How could you possibly know that?"

There was a slight twinkle in Father's eye as he said, "Nicholas, my boy, I am sure you have realized there are forces in this world that cannot be explained."

Nicholas wasn't sure what to say. Even before his parents' death, the idea of God or a higher power had confused and frightened him more than comforted him. Now, he seemed to be shoved into an entire world of unexplainable things he must accept. Would he sooner or later have to accept a higher power as well?

Father Christopher let out a warm bark of laughter, "Not unless you wish, my lad."

The blood ran cold in Nicholas's veins. *Did he just....* But Nicholas couldn't even think the thought, for if he did, and Father could, then he would know. His head began to spin, and he wondered if any of this would ever begin to make any sense.

"In time, it may." Father Christopher's words brought Nicholas back to reality, answering another question Nicholas hadn't even asked. "But it may not as well. That is the way of some things. However, anything worth knowing is worth the time it takes to learn it."

Nicholas was nodding, but he wasn't really sure he understood. It was possible he wasn't supposed to quite yet. He decided to push forward in a different direction.

"So, what are we gonna talk about?"

Father Christopher looked at Nicholas through the window for a moment.

"I know it doesn't seem so, but Richard is actually a very emotional and righteous man. Fate has not been kind to him. Yet, he carries himself better than most would given the circumstances."

Nicholas's brow furrowed. He opened his mouth as Father Christopher raised a hand to quiet him.

"I will explain myself; do not worry. This is a time for answers, but I will give them to you in my own time. Do we have an agreement?"

Nicholas thought for a moment and realized he had no other choice. He looked back at Father Christopher, who was politely waiting as if he didn't know what Nicholas was thinking.

"We do," Nicholas said.

Father Christopher nodded, "Good. Now, get comfortable. This is not a short story nor can it be rushed."

Chapter 13

"It was a little over ten years ago when I first met Richard Dusk. He was much different from the man who waits outside. His hair was shorter, combed into place, and he was clean shaven with soft features. And always on his arm, there was Angela, a girl angels envied. They were so happy, so perfect together, and as fate deemed it, destined for tragedy.

"They were not churchgoers nor were they Pointe's Hollow natives. It had been Angela who talked Richard into an extensive vacation in our quaint, little town. They had been married for a few years at that point, but rarely had spent much time together. Richard was a very successful businessman in the big city and wasn't home much. She pressed harder and harder for them to take a trip somewhere outside of the city and away from big business. At first Richard told her he had too much work to do, he couldn't afford the time off. But in the end, as she always did, I imagine, Angela got her way.

"When they rolled in, I was at the market picking up

some food for dinner later that night. I saw their car slowly crawling down the street and sensed a glowing light within a cloud of darkness.

"They stayed in a motel closer to the interstate. But they always came into town during the day. They came through and quickly became a temporary, but very true part of our town, making friends with everyone they met. You know as well as I, small town living is hard for outsiders, but Richard and Angela seemed to be one of us. Within a few days, they were family.

"About a week later, as they were thinking of returning home, Richard learned why Angela had requested this trip and had been so adamant about taking it. She had leukemia. The town had known them only for a short time, but it hit everyone hard when she began to get worse. Richard, as you can imagine, took it as if it was his fault. He gave up work, he gave up sleep, barely ate. All he did was take care of her. When she slept, he watched over her, wishing there was something he could do to save her.

"Angela Dusk died six weeks after their arrival in Pointe's Hollow, creating another notch on the belt of our town's bad luck with death. Richard shut down, dove into himself, and no one could reach him. His mourning was deeper than I have ever seen. I personally tried to go see him at the house, but he wouldn't come to the door. I was afraid he would hurt himself, but there was nothing I could do.

"Soon, the town forgot about Richard and Angela. Not because they didn't care but because they had to. When you live in a town like ours, the ability to forget is a blessing, as well as a curse.

"One night, as I was finishing up around the grounds here at the church, I heard something drifting from the bay. Sounds of anger and pain. I rushed to see if anyone was hurt. That's when I saw him.

"Richard was standing thigh deep in the water off the

shore, a half empty bottle of scotch in one hand, a newly acquired revolver in the other. He looked like a ghoul in the water, a terrible copy of his former self. So thin, vacant, almost transparent, as if I could see through him.

"He was shouting. He cursed the shapeless evil that had taken his love and in turn, his life. He cursed Angela for leaving him. He cursed himself for not being able to save her. He shouted until his voice was hoarse and all that came out were rough gasps of hot air. He was looking for something to fight. That which had taken his wife from him. That which he could not fight.

"Staggering a bit, he looked down to the gun in his hand, and then to the bottle and back to the gun. I knew what he was thinking. It wasn't if he was going to shoot, just if he should take another drink before he did.

"I came out from the brush, running blind and shouting at Richard to put down the gun. I reached toward him, willing him to lay down his gun. At first, he acted as if he didn't notice me at all. Then, he slowly spun around, looking in my direction.

"Facing me, he tilted his head, slightly confused. I shouted for him to stop, because this wouldn't be what Angela would want for him."

"'How would you know?' he shouted back in retort. 'She was my wife, my love, my life. And I couldn't save her. I couldn't keep her safe. I said I would, but I couldn't. I couldn't, couldn't.'

"He shook his head from side to side, and I felt he was too far gone for me to save. I wanted to tell him there was already too much evil in the world, too much death, for him to do this, but it was no use. I silently prayed for something to intervene, to do what I could not.

"As Richard looked back toward the gun in his hand, a faint glow began to appear in the space behind him. It had no true shape, but I knew I had seen it before.

"The gun began to rise closer to Richard's mouth. As it did, the light grew brighter and brighter. As he placed the barrel between his lips, the light became so overwhelming I had to look away. I tried with all my might to see what was out there, but it was too much.

"Before I knew what was happening, I heard the crack of a gunshot and the light was gone. My eyes took a moment to adjust to the darkness, but when they did, I found what I did not expect. Richard was still there, alive. He stood with his back to me again, looking out over the water after something.

"The bottle fell from his hand. It hit the water with a soft thud and disappeared. His newly free hand reached up toward the distant horizon, reaching for something, or someone, who was just out of reach.

"My breath caught, and I was so relieved to see him there, I could barely believe my eyes. There was something that touched me. Deep within myself, I knew this was the man I had been waiting for. The man who had died and yet still lived, a man destined to save us from our evil.

"You may not believe in God, Nicholas, but it doesn't matter if you do. There is no denying there is good and evil in this world. Creation is a terrible power. No matter where it comes from."

Nicholas realized he had been holding his breath, and his eyes burned with the threat of tears. He had heard of such stories in books with fictional characters, but to know someone who had gone through such an ordeal, with or without the metaphysical occurrences, was hard to face.

Even with the overwhelming nature of the story, Nicholas was still aware there were answers missing. He turned toward Father Christopher. His chin was pressed against his chest as he contemplated something.

"Father," Nicholas began. "What did you mean he was the man you needed?"

Father Christopher shook slightly as if he was being awakened from a dream. "For a number of years, I had noticed changes in the world, especially in Pointe's Hollow."

In Pointe's Hollow? Nicholas thought. It was funny how much he had been hearing that recently. As if this small, little speck of a town had some great power over the whole of the world.

"And it may," Father Christopher said, eyeing Nicholas. Nicholas stopped again, flustered by the priest's gift. "I am not sure what it is about this town, or the people in it, for it has something to do with the people. But there is some deep power in this place."

Nicholas thought it over for a moment. "And that power is what is creating the monsters?"

"In a way, yes." Father Christopher exhaled deeply, "And in others, no."

Nicholas's brow furrowed, not liking what he was hearing.

"I know," Father Christopher said, looking at Nicholas through the small window that separated them. "This does not answer everything. Nothing I have to say will. No one has all the answers; that is why many reach for religion, Nicholas. It is not an evil thing; it is something to help people understand things that are hard to understand."

Nicholas looked away from the window, hoping to hide his discomfort about the subject and his rejection of it. Father Christopher smiled slightly, obviously knowing what Nicholas was concerned with, but not saying.

"What I do know is for many years, this place was not settled because of superstition and legends of terrible things. Monsters, ghosts, demons, and above all, evil taking root here. But as I am sure you are aware, it is human nature to have short memories."

Nicholas was nodding, thinking he understood, but how was he to know? He was just sixteen; he didn't know much about the world. He was still trying to understand eleventh grade, let alone this secret power in his hometown. He nodded, because he felt like he was beginning to get some answers. Vague and light, but answers nonetheless.

"In the early 1800s, Pointe's Hollow was settled. It was a great port location for the lake and thrived quickly. Soon after that, however, there were the terrible witch trials, which you have heard legends about, I'm sure. From then on, evil comes and goes through our town like the fall season."

His words trailed off, and Nicholas was still nodding. Nicholas had heard everything Father Christopher had to tell him, but he also felt like the man was hiding something from him.

"You see, Nicholas. The world isn't like most think it is."

You can say that again, Nicholas thought sourly.

"There isn't just one world; there are many."

Nicholas nodded, even though he knew Father wasn't looking his way. He had heard this all before, from Dusk. *The Other,* Nicholas thought again.

"And these worlds," Father Christopher continued, "have certain thin spots."

"Thin spots? What do you mean?"

"Spots where the worlds overlap too closely and things may pass from one to the other. No matter how much we don't want them to. This other world is a very dark world. A world designed with only fear and hatred."

Different worlds? Nicholas hadn't really believed it until now. *God, this world is hard enough. How can I deal with things from other worlds?*

Without realizing it, Nicholas's eyes flicked up to the priest, knowing he would know what he was thinking, but this time Father Christopher wasn't looking at him.

"So, why did Dusk want me to come talk to you? He doesn't know you're telling me all this, does he?"

Father Christopher looked up to meet Nicholas's eyes, "No, of course not. Richard is not one to share things. Especially Angela." Father Christopher's eyes drifted a little, and he looked away. "You are the first person since Angela that Dusk has even been remotely close to. As much as he doesn't want to show it, Dusk is afraid to lose you. For years now, he has been fighting demons that he can shoot, maim, and kill. He is terrified by the idea of losing you to something that he cannot fight."

Nicholas thought for a moment, "Like Angela."

"Like Angela," Father Christopher agreed.

Nicholas thought about everything he was listening to and how heavy it all was. "What about you?" Nicholas spit out abruptly. Father Christopher's brows raised, surprised. "He's known you for ten years now; he's not afraid of losing you."

Father Christopher went quiet for a moment, almost morbid. Then, as if everything shifted and the sun beamed down upon him, Father Christopher perked up and said, "Richard and my relationship is that of a different sort."

Nicholas felt he was not hearing all the truth, but he decided he had enough answers to last him a good long while.

"Well, then," Nicholas said, unsure of what else to say.

"Yes. Let's go make sure Richard hasn't shot anything, shall we?"

Nicholas took a moment as his mind slipped back to Dusk thigh deep in water at his wit's end. Father Christopher looked at him, smiling. Nicholas took that as a sign the priest was more worried about others, rather than Dusk. Nicholas smiled in return, and they left the confessional.

Luckily, they found Dusk with his gun still holstered, leaning against one of the pews, twiddling his fingers.

Nicholas felt awkward seeing Dusk again. Knowing what he did, Nicholas saw and understood more of Dusk than he had before. Although he knew more about the man, he felt as if there were things he didn't know about Dusk and possibly would never know about him.

"We all good here?" Dusk said, looking over to Father Christopher, who raised his hands to either side in a shrug.

"As far as I could tell, you always were," he said, smiling.

Dusk looked away, shaking his head, and as he did, Father Christopher sent Nicholas a quick wink.

"Alright," Dusk said, turning back to the two of them. "We have a problem."

Father Christopher grew slightly more serious. He did not lose his friendly smile and cheer, but his eyes grew weary. "What's the matter?"

Dusk motioned for Nicholas to tell Father Christopher what he had told Dusk. Nicholas relayed the story about Mr. Fidel and his magazine. He told Father Christopher about the doctor and the mysterious green ooze that had brought Earl Hutchins back from the dead for a short time.

As Nicholas told the story, Father Christopher's face fell more and more, as if the information was piling upon his own shoulders and weighing him down. He seemed especially concerned when he heard about the ooze and, as far as Nicholas could tell, that the doctor had gone missing when his research was abruptly halted.

Once Nicholas finished, Father Christopher took a moment. "Well," he finally began, rubbing his chin. "That is troubling."

"That's the same conclusion I came to," Dusk said, scratching his face roughly.

Father Christopher looked distant for a moment and then nodded as if in acceptance. He turned back to Dusk and Nicholas with a smile.

"But it's nothing to worry about."

Nicholas was taken aback and Dusk must have been as

well, for his mouth hung agape for a moment before he said, "Nothing to worry about? How could this possibly be nothing to worry about?"

Raising his hand, Father Christopher hushed Dusk. "I know this may be hard to swallow, Richard, but not everything is yours to control. This has been a long time coming. Science is always encroaching on the mythical. Where things seem to be broken, there are always those who try to fix it."

Nicholas was nodding along with Father Christopher's words, but he was aware of Father Christopher holding back. It appeared knowing what people were thinking and what may come were not the priest's only gifts. He had a power to persuade beyond the normal. Nicholas thought he could sell bottled air, and people would buy it.

"But this power cannot fall into the wrong hands," Dusk complained further.

Father Christopher was quick to agree, "No, no, it cannot. It is an imperfect solution to a permanent problem. But there is only so much we can do. People will always see through, even slightly as they do now."

Nicholas stopped nodding. He was officially confused.

"It is a lot to handle, Nicholas, I know." Father Christopher turned to him, eyes full of concern. "People, normal people, see only what they want to see. There is a lot in this world people wish they could explain or wish they knew. They would have it all if they were just to look at what is right in front of them. But, alas, mankind is a fickle race of slow learners."

The way he said 'mankind' made Nicholas feel like Father Christopher was excluding himself from that category. Nicholas wished he could ask, but he was afraid to find out what he had meant. Luckily, Dusk pushed forward unaffected.

"But they do learn, and right now they are meddling in

things beyond them."

Sighing, Father Christopher clasped his hands together at his waist. "Someone, somewhere is always meddling in God's domain. They question, they push the boundaries. It is what makes this world great. We are here to make sure they do not push too hard." Father Christopher's tone grew heavy, "And make sure nothing pushes back."

Dusk looked at Father Christopher crossly, "You know something more than you're letting on." It wasn't a question.

Father Christopher smiled, "I always do." Dusk didn't like hearing that, and Father Christopher knew it. He continued with, "Everything will come in time. What you need to worry about right now is this string of murders in Pointe's Hollow. I strongly believe if you solve that mystery, more pieces will fall into place."

Nicholas could see Dusk wanted to push further, but they had apparently had this dance before, and Dusk knew the music had stopped. He nodded, biting back more words.

"Good," Father Christopher said. "Well, you two best be off. It is getting late, or early depending on your outlook. The sun will be up in a matter of hours."

"Yeah," Dusk said halfheartedly. He turned away from Father Christopher and headed for the door of the church.

"Good-bye, Richard. Until next time." Father Christopher waved his farewell after Dusk, who threw up his own hand in a weak wave over his shoulder. Nicholas was standing by Father Christopher when he realized Dusk was leaving him behind. Nicholas was about to take off after him when Father Christopher stopped him with an outstretched hand.

Nicholas looked up at the old man and was surprised to see overwhelming sadness in his eyes.

"You will take care of him, won't you?" Father Christopher's words wore heavily on Nicholas, and he realized his answer was going to be binding, more than just words.

Nicholas nodded, unwilling to say the words. Although he had been unable to say it, Father Christopher smiled. "Good. That's good." Father Christopher looked after Dusk. "You two are more closely linked than either of you realize. We all are."

It took Nicholas off guard. Dusk and him linked? What did he mean by that?

"You coming?" Dusk shouted from the doorway of the church.

"Yeah," Nicholas shouted back after a moment's hesitation. He trotted down the center aisle toward Dusk. When he reached the door, he turned back one last time to look at Father Christopher. He gave Nicholas a stout nod and a friendly wave. Nicholas smiled slightly and shut the church door behind him.

Chapter 14

After a few miles of trudging through the dark woods, Nicholas thought about Father Christopher and his cryptic words. He had said the night was almost over, but between the thick, branched trees of the woods, night was on full patrol hugging the forest in darkness.

The two of them walked without talking. There wasn't a whole lot to say. Nicholas felt the silence was awkward, but didn't know what to do about it. So, he continued forward, in stride behind Dusk, further into the forest. Without warning, Dusk slowed. Nicholas looked around and tensed in preparation for an attack. He had no reason to believe anything was around them. He hadn't heard or seen anything, but he had come to learn that when Dusk slowed his pace, danger was most likely near.

Far off in the distance, there was a warming in the darkness. A small spot that seemed slightly less dark. Not bright, just less dark.

"What is it?" Nicholas finally asked, unable to stay quiet.

184

"A trap," Dusk said, without turning around to look at him.

Nicholas didn't like the sound of that. He double-checked that he still had his dagger. He asked, "What do we do?"

Dusk shrugged, "Spring the trap, of course."

With that, he returned to his normal pace. Nicholas followed reluctantly, staying a little closer to Dusk than he had previously.

They had gone a few more yards when the spot first grew and then began to define in shape. It was a lantern, an old lantern from the Civil War. It was attached to a small wooden rod, which led to a small structure that stood a few feet off the ground supported by wheels. It was covered in strange odds and ends and worn colors. It reminded Nicholas of the old man's cart Dorothy ran into before the twister had picked her up in the film *The Wizard of Oz.*

The flame in the lantern flickered lively, illuminating the small section of surrounding woods and a hooded figure who sat next to the cart. The hair on the back of Nicholas's neck stood on end.

Wind brushed by his ear, and Nicholas heard a word carried on the breeze. The flame in the lantern flickered feverishly, and Dusk quickly turned around. Nicholas did the same.

He saw nothing, only trees and darkness, but he had not missed that feeling. The feeling that Dusk had just a moment before him.

They were being watched.

"Nicholas," the wind whispered again, freezing Nicholas's breath.

There was a sudden rush of noise behind him, and Nicholas turned to see Dusk standing there frozen as well.

Behind Dusk, with her arms wrapped around his waist, stood a woman. She was so stunningly beautiful that

Dusk

Nicholas was instantly intoxicated by her. Her soft, dark features made him feel warm all over. Her nose lightly grazed Dusk's exposed neck, and her lips parted slightly to reveal sharp fangs.

"What is this? I've caught a monster hunter in my web?" the vampire cooed toward Dusk. Dusk only smirked at the thing, struggling slightly to get free.

Vampire, Nicholas thought. He scuffled a bit with himself, trying to grab his knife from his waist. Getting the knife free, Nicholas pointed it accusingly at the the woman, prepared for a fight.

The vampire, however, barely glanced at him. "You best put that away, dear, before you cut yourself."

Nicholas tightened up. Her voice was condescending, but something else lingered: a combination of seduction, confidence, and complete omnipotence. As if she knew Nicholas wouldn't and couldn't do anything to her.

"Be nice to the kid, Clara," Dusk said. "He's still young."

Clara's eyes sparkled for a moment as she looked from Dusk to Nicholas. "Oh, fresh meat," she cooed, licking her lips.

Nicholas felt sweat slide down his temples, and his throat caught on his fear. The dagger felt uncomfortable in his fingers, and as he adjusted, Clara smiled, startling him. He started to drop the knife, leaning forward to catch it.

When he looked back up, Clara was standing in front of him. She didn't move at inhuman speeds. She was fast, no doubt, but what made her so dangerous was that she glided so quietly, as if she hadn't moved at all.

It took all Nicholas had to not fall to the ground. His knees were weak, and his lower stomach felt heavy. Clara was looking at him, not as one person looks at another but as a lioness looks at a gazelle.

"Clara, we have some questions." Dusk's voice was

conversational as if they were in no danger, as if they weren't in the presence of a bloodthirsty vampire. It both calmed and unnerved Nicholas at the same time.

"Questions?" Clara asked Dusk, while staring at Nicholas. "Why do you always come to me with an agenda?"

She turned to Dusk now, putting all her weight on one leg. It made her look modern, even though her attire was anything but. She wore a white blouse with a neckline that fell on her upper arms, exposing her ebony shoulders. The blouse ended below her bosom, replaced by a dark maroon corset. Her legs were covered by long, flowing, overlapping red and brown material, creating a fiendishly beautiful skirt.

"You never just come to say hello," she continued, feigning distress. Nicholas felt sorry for her, as if her emotions controlled his own. Nicholas couldn't understand how Dusk could stand as he did, solid and unaffected.

"What can I say, Clara, I've been busy. Killing monsters, saving innocents. You know, the usual day-to-day."

Clara passed Dusk, smiling at him as she did. She bent down and picked up a dark brown cloak, which lay strewn about behind the chair. Nicholas put two and two together realizing Clara had been the hunched figure in the chair all along.

Tossing the cloak into an open door on her cart, she plopped down in her chair and kicked her feet over the arm, crossing them at the ankles. It was unbelievable how graceful she was. No matter where she was or what she was doing, she was stunningly beautiful.

"So," Clara began, settling into her chair. "What is it you wish to know?"

Dusk looked at Nicholas and ushered him forth. After a moment of hesitation, Nicholas moved in and replaced his knife in its sheath.

Dusk began his interrogation. "Have had a few more

murders and disappearances in Pointe's Hollow this year. Know anything about it?"

Clara's mouth dropped open in shock, "You think I have something...."

"We had a victim completely drained of blood," Dusk said, cutting Clara off.

This caught her off guard. She stared at Dusk as if he was joking. Dusk stared back, like an old-time lawman staring down the accused. When she realized he wasn't joking, Clara smiled again.

"I understand why you would come to me, Dusk, but, unfortunately, I know nothing about what you say. I just got back into town tonight."

Dusk nodded, but the look on his face said he wasn't buying it at all. "Blood drained from bodies, Clara. Sounds like some vampire activity to me. Maybe not you," he said as she was about to protest once again, "but I'm sure you've heard something. Maybe just a whisper?"

Clara hesitated for a moment and then smiled fiendishly. "There are always whispers. A girl can't help but hear 'em."

Dusk shot her a stare that seemed to be as pointed and hurtful as a bullet from his gun. Clara saw it, too, but it must have missed its mark, for she flicked her hair and smiled.

"No matter what the world may believe, Dusky, we vampires are not few in numbers." She hesitated as her smile dropped slightly, "However, no matter how many of us there are, and no matter how unquenchable our thirst is, it would take days for one of us to drain an entire body."

Dusk shifted, crossing his arms and nodding slightly as if he expected this answer, but needed confirmation. Nicholas felt sick. Clara kept shooting hungry glances his way, making blood pump into his face and redden his cheeks.

Her entire presence was captivating. When Nicholas read *Dracula*, he did not fully understand the control the count had on his female victims. Now, he could feel Clara's pull for him to come in closer, let his guard down, give her everything, and she was barely paying attention to him. Nicholas could only imagine how powerful she would be if she wanted him.

"We get full, just as you do," Clara continued, snapping Nicholas back to the conversation.

"So, we're not looking for a vampire?" Dusk stated in a half question.

Clara was shaking her head, "Or vampires. We are lone hunters."

Dusk again nodded at her words, confirming that what Clara said Dusk took as fact. Nicholas was wondering what could be behind this killing if it wasn't supernatural. Vampires had been their best lead; now, it looked like they were back to square one.

"I see," was all Dusk said. He rubbed his chin. It was evident Dusk was thinking the same thing Nicholas was. "And that's all you have for us?" Dusk asked.

Clara's brows raised, as if to ask, 'Who me?' Dusk squinted, trying to see through Clara. Nicholas determined this process was more of a dance than a conversation, a dance where they each fought to lead, without stepping on each other's toes.

"I'm sorry, Dusky," Clara said, raising her arms. "That's all I can say." She smiled so sweetly.

Unluckily for Clara, Dusk was the kind of man to look right through a smile no matter how sweet. "Alright," Dusk shrugged. "I guess we've wasted enough of your time."

Clara's smile dropped, "You're leaving already?"

For the first time, Clara's strength wavered. It was evident mostly in her voice, which quivered as she spoke. Nicholas slowly began to understand what was happening.

"Yeah, we have too much to do, too little time," Dusk said, toying with Clara. Clara looked down to the ground trying to think of something else to say. "If we have more questions, we'll find you. You'll be sticking around town for a bit, right?"

Clara looked up, "Well, I don't...."

"Of course you will, nowhere else really to go, right?" Dusk interrupted coldly. "You'll be hearing from us." Dusk turned from Clara.

She suddenly stood up from her chair, "Wait!"

Dusk stopped, looking toward Nicholas, away from Clara. He waited for her to continue.

"There may be something else," Clara continued.

Dusk looked to Nicholas, smirking slightly. Nicholas fought the urge to smile. Clara had gone from tough loner chick to wimpy little girl in no time flat. Her reasons weren't completely unfounded. Nicholas had never thought of it, but he could imagine the life of a vampire was very lonely. Eternity spent moving from place to place, getting close to people only to be driven by thirst to kill them.

"Oh, really?" Dusk said, swiftly laying on a snide tone with practiced ease. He winked at Nicholas, which only made it harder for Nicholas to keep a straight face. Turning, Dusk continued, "So, what is it?"

Clara quickly looked around the woods, expecting someone to be listening to them. Her frantic search made Nicholas look around. There were only trees and darkness.

"All I know is, something is different about this place." Clara's voice slowly grew quieter as she spoke, which interested Dusk more than what she had said. Nicholas could see that her worry troubled Dusk.

"What do you mean?" Dusk said, speaking softly as well. Not because he was afraid. Dusk was never afraid.

"There's," Clara began, looking for the words. Nicholas wondered if English was Clara's native language. She spoke with no accent, but something in the way she hesitated made Nicholas believe she was trying to remember how to form words, while thinking of the right ones.

"There's a thickness in the air," Clara said. "The air is heavier. The night darker." Dusk looked seriously at Clara. There was something seriously worrying Clara, and Dusk did not like the idea of something in his town that would scare a vampire. Nicholas knew he was terrified by the same thing. It went back to what Mr. Lloyd had said when he had talked with Nicholas about how there was something very wrong with Pointe's Hollow.

"There is also a whisper. No, not even that." Clara once again had to think of a word. "A notion, of something brewing here. Some great evil."

"Like a person," Nicholas said, without thinking. "Like a bad person?"

Clara looked to him, shaking her head, "A monster."

Come on, only one more mile to go, Jenny Harper thought as she huffed and puffed her way through the trees just outside The Hollow.

Jenny was a long distance runner on the high school's cross country team, and she wanted to beat her personal record. It was her senior year, and she didn't know when or if she'd ever be in such great shape again in her life. Her legs were tight with muscle, her stomach was flat, and her hair was long with a sheen of sweat.

Her Nikes pounded the soft ground. Two miles ago, the shoes padded across the ground as if not even touching it, pushing her forward. Now, they pounded, weighed down with the weight of exhaustion.

But I only have one more mile to go, she told herself again, trying to push herself mentally as much as physically.

She wove in and out of the trees, ducking branches and being careful not to trip on debris. The weather was cool, but Jenny didn't mind. It was a Michigan November, which meant it hadn't snowed yet, and the air still felt like fall. The air felt good as she ran, and it was just cool enough to keep away all the mosquitoes that she constantly battled during the warmer months. It was a good night for a run, or so Jenny thought.

She was running up a rather large hill in the woods when she first noticed something was off. Thinking it was her mind's way of trying to get her to stop her pace, she ignored it and kept going. She was on top of the hill now, and she turned to run along the ridge, saving the downhill trek for later.

A sudden whoosh of air caught Jenny's attention enough to pull her eyes from her path. She was used to running in the woods, so when her foot caught on some underbrush, she stumbled, but she knew how to catch herself. Unfortunately, to do so, she had to stop her pace.

"Shit," Jenny breathed between gasps of breath.

With knees bent, she hunched over, trying to catch her breath. She remembered a lecture from her coach. She stood up straight and laced her fingers behind her head. It hurt more to breath this way, but she knew it was proper form.

SNAP!

Jenny whipped around. No matter how tired she was, she knew she had heard something, whatever it was. She looked around, expecting to see another runner or possibly a deer trotting through the trees. There was nothing, only shadows hugging the dark trunks of the pines. Jenny was turning back around when it happened again.

SNAP!

"Who's there?" Jenny called into the darkness.

Her hair whipped around and smacked at her shoulders, making her skin crawl. It felt like the fingers of death clawing at her neck.

The woods didn't answer her demand. They stood silent and resolute as Jenny looked around angrily. "I know someone's there. Answer me!" she yelled into the night, hoping to scare out a response. Unfortunately, the only person who was getting scared was her.

"Whoever is there, this isn't funny."

Her words were getting weaker and weaker. Her eyes began to dart wildly as the woods seemed to close in around her.

Jenny began running at her usual pace to prove to herself she wasn't afraid. She ran along the top of the hill toward home.

She tried to forget the snapping sounds she heard and tried to ignore the feeling of uneasiness enveloping her, but it was no use. Out of the corner of her eye, she saw shifts of movement. She never stopped to see if it was real or her imagination. She just ran faster.

The motions grew more frequent, pushing Jenny harder. Soon, Jenny was no longer running with form. Her arms flailed wildly as she sprinted as fast as her tired legs would carry her. Her breathing became more labored, and she began to cry from the pure terror she was enduring. She tried screaming for help, but only weak sounds came out of her dry throat.

As Jenny rounded a large tree, there was something waiting for her on the other side. It appeared so quickly, Jenny couldn't make out the shape. She only knew it wasn't human. Jumping back from the encounter, she tripped on the underbrush at her feet. This time, she couldn't catch herself, and she spiraled down the left side of the hill.

She rolled end over end until she shifted her weight enough to cause her to roll more like a log, saving her neck from unwanted tension. Momentum failing, Jenny stopped rolling at the bottom of the hill with her face in the dirt.

Dusk

Her eyes darted upward to look at the hill and the thing that had startled her. There was nothing there. She breathed heavily, whimpers of pain and fear escaped her. She looked left, then right. There was nothing. Her breathing calmed.

Suddenly, there was a cold wisp of air as an icy grip grabbed Jenny's ankle. She tried to turn, but before she could, the thing ripped her body, dragging her across the forest floor.

Five yards, ten, twenty. Jenny was helpless. She reached out frantically, grabbing anything to slow her progress. It was useless. Roots ripped out of the ground. Her nails dug gouges in trunks causing them to rip off and her fingers to bleed. Twigs and rocks scraped her legs, stomach, and chest as her body bounced across the ground.

Jenny cried, she screamed, and she prayed for this to stop. Able to peer behind her for fragments of seconds, she couldn't be sure what had her. Jenny raised herself up on one arm and tried to twist onto her back. She was unsuccessful, falling back down onto her stomach.

But she had seen something. Something that shouldn't, no, couldn't be real. The only thing that appeared to have her in its grasp was darkness. Shear darkness, blacker than even the darkest night. Darkness so deep that you could get lost in it just by looking for too long.

Then, just as suddenly as she had been ripped away, Jenny's body stopped. Shaking, she flipped around, hair whipping, looking to defend herself. Her eyes burned with tears as the dark figure came forth out of the shadows. She froze with confusion, hatred, and sadness. She whispered one word, "You?"

Then, Jenny Harper was silenced, forever.

Chapter 15

Perspective is a strange thing. It can change so easily. A few days ago, Nicholas walked through his little town of Pointe's Hollow without a second thought to the outside world and anything that was happening there. Now, he was wondering if there were other places like this and other people dealing with the same evil he was.

After visiting Clara last night, Nicholas and Dusk had talked about other options. Nicholas had thought it was a somewhat beneficial encounter, while Dusk saw it as a dead end.

"Why haven't you...."

"Killed her?" Dusk asked, already knowing what Nicholas had meant. "If she ever gives me reason to I will, but unlike most, she's one of the good ones. Well, mostly."

Dusk assured Nicholas these happenings were not completely local to Pointe's Hollow, but it was a hot spot. It had something to do with this piece of Earth and its history. Father Christopher had called it a thin spot between two worlds.

"He told you about The Other?" Dusk asked, shocked.

Nicholas felt bad about divulging what he and Father Christopher had discussed in secrecy, but he figured Dusk would know eventually. Once he explained, Dusk nodded as if he expected nothing less from Father Christopher. He also warned Nicholas.

"Father Christopher always knows more than he says. It has to do with his sight." He wiggled his fingers in front of his eyes to emphasize. "He sees a lot. Perhaps the whole picture, but I doubt it. He only tells you what you need to know."

Nicholas found the thought disconcerting.

"Don't worry, kid. I've known Father Christopher for a long time, and if he's keeping secrets, it's for a good reason."

Clara had mentioned other vampires and other monsters roaming the world. It was strange. In this day and age when there was little left to be discovered, the realization that these things were out there made the world seem so much bigger. It made Nicholas feel a lot smaller.

"They just seem to slip through," Dusk explained. "Somehow, they found a rift and have been walking through into our world for some time now."

All the things that go bump in the night were real and were out there now, just waiting. It made someone like Nicholas feel very small. What did he, a kid, have to give to a world filled with terror and monsters? He hadn't even been able to save his parents from a car crash. How was he supposed to help save the world from monsters. Thinking of his parents made his eyes burn deep in his head.

He was so consumed by his thoughts he was unable to keep from tossing and turning the night before. Now, he was stumbling from class to class rubbing his eyes, trying to stay awake. Next class was Mr. Fidel's, which didn't help. He needed to concentrate on what he was supposed to be learning and less on the terrible mystery plaguing his own town.

"Yeah, I heard she was bled out. Just like Earl."

Nicholas was instantly shaken out of his own reverie when he overheard the conversation between two kids a few seats behind him. Randy Hodeman was turned around in his chair chatting with Michael Richmond.

They were two of the troublemakers in Pointe's Hollow High, jokers with potty mouths and a craving for the town gossip. They were talking about someone who had died. Who had been bled out, just like Earl.

Just like Earl, Nicholas thought again. He leaned back in his chair, trying to get a better position for listening.

"Well," Michael was saying, trying to one-up Randy. "I heard she was found naked out in the woods."

Randy chuckled slightly, "I wish I had found her then. She was so hot." He winked and ticked with his mouth. Michael laughed in response, but he was shaking his head.

"No, you don't. I overheard my mom talking on the phone with Tommy's mom, said she had no legs."

A chill ran over Nicholas.

"What?" Randy said, "You've got to be shitting me?"

The line made Nicholas think of the sailors on the docks and how similar the situation was. It was as if clues were just falling into his lap. He wasn't complaining.

"I swear." With more animation, Michael continued, obviously pleased he had Randy's attention. "She was out there, naked, bloodless, and no legs."

"Fuck me," Randy said, shaking his head. "Well, it only figures."

Michael looked at him, questioning. Randy smiled, "I mean, if I could, I would have stole her legs, too, if you know what I mean." Randy made a rude gesture with his hand.

Michael smacked Randy's hand. "You're sick," he said.

First arms, Nicholas thought. *Now legs? What the hell*

is going on?

Nicholas was weighing the pros and cons of turning around and asking Randy and Michael who they were talking about when he first felt it. A low rumbling coming up from the floor through his feet and into the pit of his stomach. No one else reacted. Nicholas thought it was just him, but then slowly, the others began to react as the rumbling became more intense.

The rumbling got so bad, pencils on desks began to rattle. Crystal, a small girl with large glasses, sitting on the far side of the room by the windows, stood up and said, "Look!"

Nicholas looked over while kids began to stand up and go to the window. He tried looking around the crowding bodies, but he wasn't able to see anything. Nicholas stood up and went to the window. What he saw surprised him. In a million years, Nicholas probably couldn't have guessed what was coming into his town.

Four large army trucks, flanked by two green Jeeps, were bumping their way down the street.

"What the hell are they doing here?" Randy said a little too loudly.

"Randy, watch the mouth, or you'll be in detention for the rest of the week," Mr. Fidel said, loud enough to be heard over the mumbling kids.

Nicholas looked toward Mr. Fidel, hoping he'd maybe have an idea of what was going on. Mr. Fidel shrugged slightly and looked out the window toward the war machines. Nicholas looked to the trucks as well.

This is not going to be good, Nicholas thought.

He watched until the trucks disappeared further into town, and a little after that, Mr. Fidel called everyone back to their seats. Nicholas wanted to listen to what Mr. Fidel was saying, but he couldn't. His mind was consumed by thoughts of dismembered bodies, military police, and what Dusk would make of all of it.

So many people, Sheriff Gordon thought as he looked over his plastered cork board. Pages upon pages of missing persons posters hung with individual thumbtacks of ranging colors. This year, there had been more disappearances than usual in Pointe's Hollow and the surrounding area. There was an exact copy of this board in the main lobby of the sheriff's department.

In a small town, an unusual number of disappearances was very hard to keep under wraps. Luckily, most of the people were outsiders, so the talk had been limited to vague whispers and rumors. Not the best thing for an investigation, but the only thing Sheriff Gordon could ask for in The Hollow.

The cases had been the focus of the sheriff's days before he had found Earl Hutchins's body drained and missing limbs in his woods. Then, they got pushed to the side. So many missing sons, daughters, fathers, mothers.

"Goddamn it," Sheriff Gordon said under his breath as he wiped his lips.

He had hoped taking his mind off the current file on his desk would help, but it only made him more agitated. Sheriff Gordon moved back behind his desk and fell into his chair. The manilla folder lay open, displayed for him to look over. Covered with paperwork and pictures, it stared back at him tauntingly.

Eighteen-year-old Jennifer Liane Harper, found dead, naked in the the woods, completely drained of blood and missing both her legs. Severed at the hips, her body laid mutilated. Murder cases in his town put a salty taste in the back of Sheriff Gordon's mouth, but murder cases involving teenage girls made him sick. He wanted people who could do a thing like this to be hunted down, immediately and relentlessly.

The whole thing was worse because he had his own daughter. Every time he saw Jennifer's face there on his desk, cold and pale, he couldn't help imagining Emily's face. The thought hurt deeply, the way only a father could hurt for his daughter.

Sheriff Gordon wiped his eyes and rubbed his temples. *Getting too old for this shit,* he thought. The case was not making any progress. If anything, it was moving backward, something he could not afford.

He looked around the room. On one wall hung lots of posters of missing persons, another wall had windows looking out at the officers working on the murder of Earl Hutchins, and on his desk lay the file for Jennifer Harper. Death surrounded and suffocated him.

He rubbed his lip with one finger, a habit he had since he gave up the drink. In his first year sober, his lips bled and cracked from being rubbed so much. His hand dropped away, and he began to flip through the file again, hoping to see something that he had missed before.

There was a commotion growing out in the lobby. He tried to ignore it, but it became too great. He looked out and saw everyone crowding around the department's front windows. He got up to see what was happening.

"What in the Sam hell is going on out here?" Sheriff Gordon said as he exited his office.

"Aw, man," Donald said. "You're not gonna believe this, Sheriff."

Sheriff Gordon sighed, "Why don't you try me, Donald."

Donald turned around to face the sheriff. "Well, by the looks of things, the entire National Guard is rolling up to our front door."

Sheriff Gordon didn't grace this with words; instead, he shot a look at Donald.

Donald just shrugged and said, "I just call them as I see them, Sheriff."

Sheriff Gordon was going to respond to Donald's outrageous statement, but the front door to the station burst open. Five men in full army fatigues filed in with guns slung on their backs. Once they had all entered, they stood at attention.

A man entered the station behind them. He held his head high with a smirk of arrogance and slicked-back hair. Two silver bars rested on his shoulders signifying his rank of Captain. They shined with a gleam that could only mean they had just been graced with fresh polish. Overall, the kid, which he was in the sheriff's eyes, because he was in his early thirties at the oldest, looked like he knew how to bark orders, but knew nothing about leadership.

"I am looking for the sheriff," the captain announced. No one answered him at first. Donald looked to Sheriff Gordon, who was looking the captain up and down. The captain became irritated. "Is the sheriff of this town here or not?"

"Yup," Sheriff Gordon finally spoke up. "Right here, Captain."

The captain gave the sheriff a once-over glance. "So you are," he finally concluded. "Sheriff, if I could have a moment of your time. There are some pressing matters we must discuss."

Sheriff Gordon gave the captain a look that seemed to say, 'Well, alrighty then, spit it out bucko.' When the captain didn't continue, Sheriff Gordon spoke up, "Alright, well, you better come into my office."

"Yes, I believe that would be best."

The captain pushed past his soldiers and right by

Sheriff Gordon into the office. Sheriff Gordon looked at him as he passed. Sheila gave him a confused look over her glasses, which lay low on her nose. The only thing the sheriff could think to do was shrug and follow the captain.

As the door shut, Sheriff Gordon walked around the captain, who had already taken the seat across from the sheriff's desk. "So, to what do we owe the pleasure?" the sheriff asked as he fell into his own chair.

The captain looked around the office. His eyes fell upon the cork board full of missing persons posters. "I see you've had some trouble keeping track of your people recently, Sheriff."

The words came as both a dodge of the sheriff's question and an insult. But Sheriff Gordon was a hard man to rattle. "Not my people, strangers mostly passing through. City folk get lost out here all the time. We do our best to keep them safe as they pass on through, but some just can't handle country living."

A flicker of agitation on the captain's face confirmed Sheriff Gordon had gotten his point across. The irritation fell away quickly, however, as the captain looked back to Sheriff Gordon.

"Well, anyway, that's not what brings me here," the captain went on.

"What does bring you here, Captain…. I'm sorry, I must have missed your name," Sheriff Gordon said slyly.

"Captain Hayward," the captain said, adjusting his coat so he looked his best. "And yours?"

Following suit by not giving a first name, the sheriff said, "Sheriff Gordon."

The captain was definitely part of the military, but not from any infantry branch. There was a symbol on his chest next to his badges that Sheriff Gordon couldn't place.

Probably some newfangled scientific division. Sheriff Gordon had heard about different kinds of testing that had been going on behind the scenes, but never thought he'd be face-to-face with someone behind it.

The captain nodded, "Yes, of course. Well," the captain began as he slouched back slightly in his chair. "I have some troubling news, Sheriff. It appears that we have a common enemy."

Sheriff Gordon nodded at this, "Oh, and who would that be?"

"The man who seems to be cutting up your townspeople, Sheriff."

That hit Sheriff Gordon like a boulder. He didn't like that this man had come into his town and had his nose in the sheriff's business.

"You see, this M.O. of killing people, draining them of their blood, and harvesting their parts is someone we have been tracking for quite some time."

"He's done this before?" Sheriff Gordon asked.

"Ah, yes, but not as easily as he has here. People in Pointe's Hollow seem to be dropping like flies."

Sheriff Gordon clenched his jaw. Captain Hayward just smiled. "Don't be offended, Sheriff. This man, if you can call such a creature a man, is one of the very best. My men and I have been following for a few weeks now. We are the best of the best, so do not feel bad that you have failed so far."

The blood in Sheriff Gordon's veins began to boil. He was a good man, but when pushed the wrong way, he could be quite a force to reckon with.

"Besides, we are here now and will have this matter cleaned up in no time." Captain Hayward stood up.

Sheriff Gordon remained seated, "I see, and what do you want from us?"

"I will need everything you have on the two confirmed victims so far. Files, pictures, leads, and the bodies, of course," Captain Hayward said as if it was only to be expected.

Snot nose, brat, Sheriff Gordon thought, but he said, "Unfortunately, I can't just give you files without written consent from someone a little higher up."

Captain Hayward twinged slightly at Sheriff Gordon's words. From his jacket, Captain Hayward pulled out a stack of neatly folder papers. "I believe you will find everything to be in order."

Sheriff Gordon took the papers and began scanning the documentation. As the captain said, it all appeared to be in order. Without a leg to stand on, Sheriff Gordon said, "I'll have Sheila make up copies for you and have Dr. Steely, our coroner, set aside some time for you to look at the bodies."

The captain paused for a moment. "Apparently, I was unclear. This is a military matter now, Sheriff. I will need every scrap of info you have on this case. You are to turn over all the info to me within the hour, and there is to be nothing left here."

"Well, maybe if you could give me a little more about what you have to do with all this, I might understand a little bit better."

"Sheriff, you do not need to understand. You just need to give me and my men what we need and stay out of the way."

Sheriff Gordon had had enough. He stood up, shouting, "Now hold on, Captain. This is my town, you can't just come in here...."

"Yes, I can," Captain Hayward cut him off. "And I am." He straightened and glared at the sheriff. "You have stumbled on something far above the pay grade of a sheriff in a pit stain town such as this. I am here now, and this is my investigation from here on out."

Sheriff Gordon glanced down at the file on his desk and a thought occurred to him.

"Do I make myself one-hundred percent clear, Sheriff?" Captain Hayward straightened again.

Sheriff Gordon began to think that if the captain straightened anymore, he'd turn into a plank of petrified wood and fall over.

Sheriff Gordon looked up and put on the biggest fake smile he could muster. "Of course, Captain. Anything to help our service boys," the sheriff's voice sliced with malicious intent. "In fact," Sheriff Gordon began, shuffling the file on his desk. "Take this, the latest victim."

He handed the file to the captain with a single, crime scene photo clipped to the outside of the manilla folder. Captain Hayward saw the picture and turned green.

"Jennifer Harper, eighteen years old. Last seen going out for a run before she was found drained and mutilated in the woods."

Captain Hayward didn't move to take the folder. He tried to look away from the picture, but Sheriff Gordon wouldn't let him.

"A little different seeing it than just hearing about it," Sheriff Gordon cooed. "Aye, Cap'n?"

Captain Hayward stiffened as he realized he was being tested. He reached up and grasped the folder, but Sheriff Gordon didn't let it go.

"This isn't just your guys' case, is it?" Sheriff Gordon asked as he pulled Captain Hayward closer. "You see, when I was younger, I took a summer job as a janitor."

The captain tried to pull the file away, but Sheriff Gordon held on tightly. "Now, it was the worst job in the world; I just couldn't stand cleaning up other people's messes. Especially ones that were so easy to avoid."

Captain Hayward's eyes met the sheriff's. "Looks like you don't have a problem with that. Now do you, Captain?"

Finally, with a quick yank, Captain Hayward ripped the file away. After a quick adjustment of putting the picture back on the inside, the captain readjusted his person once again, sliding his hair back into place, and said, "If you know what's good for you, Sheriff, you'll keep your nose out of this." Captain Hayward smiled, "Cause I may clean up, but I have no problem creating a few messes of my own."

The captain stepped forward one more time. "Is there anything else I should know about, Sheriff?"

Sheriff Gordon thought about the mysterious man in black he had seen with the Wake boy only two nights before. The man was definitely something strange in the sheriff's book and something he was going to pursue without a doubt. It could be vital to finding Earl's and Jennifer's killer. The sheriff knew the captain should know about him.

"Nope, not a thing."

The two men stared each other down before the captain smirked as he turned to leave, "Good day, Sheriff." He opened the door and walked out through the front lobby.

By the time Sheriff Gordon got up from his chair and over to the door to his office, the last soldier was filing out of the station. The big, green trucks thundered to life. Donald was still by the window watching the men pile in and roll out, but Sheila had made it back to the sheriff's office with a warm cup of coffee in hand.

"What was that all about?" Sheila asked as she handed the sheriff the cup.

Sheriff Gordon took a sip of the hot liquid before he said, "I'm not sure." The last truck was rolling away now, a stream of black exhaust parading out behind it. "But I'm going to find out."

Chapter 16

By the time Nicholas had finished relaying the day's events to Dusk, night had fallen and Pointe's Hollow was cascaded in darkness. Dusk asked Nicholas if he knew who the second victim was. Nicholas reported that the second victim was a girl from his school named Jennifer Harper, which he had found out through the whispers at lunch.

"So, what's next?" Nicholas asked.

Dusk scratched his beard and took a sip from his beer, finishing it off. He placed the bottle next to the other empty.

"Not sure," Dusk said.

Nicholas had a funny feeling Dusk had been thinking of something other than the case.

"The military showing up like this makes everything much harder. They'll be on the lookout for anything weird."

"Like giant werewolves, vampire gypsies...."

"And a man toting around a gun," Dusk finished for Nicholas. "We're going to have to play our cards a little closer to the vest now."

Nicholas nodded. Being caught with Dusk had never

occurred to him as a bad thing. He had been so concerned with staying alive against monsters that the thought of being seen with Dusk as a bad thing by some of the townsfolk never crossed his mind.

Only then did he remember that he still needed to talk with Mr. Lloyd about everything. Every night Nicholas had been out, he had told his aunt he was at the library. Mr. Lloyd had covered for him, but Nicholas was not sure the librarian would keep doing so.

I'll talk to him next chance I get. After school tomorrow, Nicholas concluded.

"First thing we should do," Dusk said, jumping up from the couch, "is go see our old friend Steely."

An icy chill ran over Nicholas's skin. Their last visit with Steely the coroner was one Nicholas was trying hard to forget. Steven Steely wasn't a bad guy, just creepy. Nicholas knew if they were seeing Steely, they were going to have to see a dead body, something Nicholas had not and would not get used to.

"Come on," Dusk said, already by the doorway leading to the main hall. "Never polite to leave the dead waiting."

Nicholas rolled his eyes, groaning with discomfort. He got up, fixed the glasses on his face, threw his jacket over his shoulders, and followed Dusk out the door.

They arrived at the station without seeing the new military force in The Hollow. Slipping through the back door, Nicholas and Dusk once again maneuvered through the dark station and into the basement.

If it was possible, the morgue felt even colder. Nicholas surveyed the room and found that everything looked the same. It appeared no matter how careless Steely seemed to be, he was very tidy. Everything was exactly where it was the last time; the place was more like a museum display than a working morgue.

"Dusk, Nicholas. What a surprise!" Steely said as he

turned to see them.

He was working on a corpse whose chest was pried open. A section of ribs sat in a bowl off to the side of the table. A bone saw was resting near it, still plugged in. Steely was covered head to toe for the autopsy: a white apron on top of white scrubs ending in ugly hospital green gloves and boots. On his head sat a strange device that magnified what he was looking at, but to an onlooker shrunk his eyes to pea size.

"Actually, that's not quite true, is it?" Steely looked between the two of them, his magnifying device bouncing slightly as he did. "I knew you two would be showing up again as soon as I saw the body."

"Jennifer Harper's body?" Dusk asked.

Steely nodded emphatically, "Which other body could I mean?" Steely pivoted as if remembering something. Turning back to Dusk and Nicholas, he pointed over his shoulder and said, "Not this guy. This guy just hit my table earlier today. Heart attack, I think, but still digging."

"The one you're looking for was much worse," Steely said, shaking his head. "Poor girl, only eighteen. But death does not judge on age. When it's time, it's time." Steely chuckled. An odd sound that made Nicholas feel uncomfortable.

Nicholas felt a twinge of pain as he realized he knew Jennifer. Not all that well, mind you, but he had known of her, everyone in The Hollow did.

"Strange," Dusk said. "To have two victims so different killed by the same killer."

Steely nodded, "An old drunk and a young, hot teenager. Add in an abused mother and fire-starting son, and there you are, a cliché family set for disaster." Again, he chuckled that awkward laugh. Dusk smiled, amusing Steely, but his smile quickly faded.

"Well, let's pull her out and see what she's got to say,"

Dusk said, reaching for the small vile of green liquid he kept.

"Ooh," Steely said, raising a finger. "Sorry, man. No can do. She's not here."

"Not here? Where is she?"

Steely took off his magnifier and dropped his arms in a shrug. "Gone. Taken from me. Along with Earl. Some army guys came in right after I got back from lunch. Collected everything we had about the two deaths. Files, pictures, and the bodies."

Dusk gritted his teeth. "They took everything?"

"Yep. Down to the last paper clip."

Dusk turned away, frustrated. "Is there anything you can remember? Anything different about this body?"

Shaking his head, Steely said, "Not much. I didn't get to go into detail on her like I did Earl. All I could tell was she had been knocked out just like Earl, needle to the neck. Her body had been completely drained of blood, and she was missing both her legs."

Nicholas knew all this, but he was nodding as if this was the first time he was hearing the news. On the other hand, Dusk was moving his hand in a circular pattern begging for Steely to continue. He had heard all this before. He wanted new information.

"That's all I got," Steely said, exasperated. "Like I said, I didn't get much time with the body."

Dusk stopped his hand and walked around, trying to think of anything that might be helpful. "She was from Pointe's Hollow?" he finally asked.

This time Nicholas was the one to answer, "Yeah, she went to my school."

"And she was found in the woods, just like the first body," Dusk said, more to himself than to the others.

"Yup," Steely said. "Not in the same spot, but close around there. Just about a hundred yards from the coast south of town."

Dusk began to pace, "How long ago did she go missing?"

"Mother said she left for a run around seven o'clock last night."

This made Dusk stop in his tracks. "Last night?"

"Yeah," Steely repeated. "After identifying the body this morning, the mother said she had last seen Jennifer the night before as she left for the run. Poor woman. I've never seen a person so heartbroken."

"Steely, focus!" Dusk said sharply. "Jennifer left her house at seven last night. Her body was found at what time this morning?"

"Eight twenty. By a dock worker who walked into the woods to take a piss."

"Eight twenty," Dusk repeated. "And how long had she been out there before she was found?"

Steely shrugged as he tried to find words, "Hard to say without blood. Body temp was ice cold. But taking into account the overall appearance of the scene, I'd say two, maybe three hours?"

"Okay, that gave the killer about," Dusk did some quick mental math, "eleven hours to abduct, drain, and clean the body; sever the legs; and get it back into the woods without being seen."

Steely shrugged, "Okay, that's pretty quick, but not impossible. With the right suction, the human body can be drained in just about nine seconds."

A shiver wormed its way down Nicholas's spine. It also concerned him that Steely was so quick to come up with that number. Hoping for the best, Nicholas concluded Steely had the answer for an exam in coroner school.

Dusk gritted his teeth. He felt like he was on a roll, getting somewhere with these questions, but, alas, he had hit another dead end. As Dusk began to pace again, Nicholas thought about the whole case, listing off what he knew

Dusk

Both bodies were drained. Both missing limbs. Earl's arms, Jennifer's legs. They had been dumped deep enough in the woods to be hidden, but close enough to be found. Both dumps were close to the docks. Both had lived in Pointe's Hollow and were known by almost everyone.

As much as Nicholas wanted to come up with something, he was drawing a blank. He went over and over the list trying to think of anything. In the end, he had to give up.

There were a few more tense minutes as Dusk paced around the coroner's morgue, but he finally relented, too. They were all out of ideas and running out of time.

Steely again said he was sorry for not knowing more. Both Nicholas and Dusk reassured him he had done all he could. As they left, Steely told them they could come by any time to talk to him, even without needing a dead body, but bringing a cold one wouldn't hurt. Nicholas hoped Steely was referring to a beer, but he had a sneaky suspicion he meant something else entirely.

They ascended the stairs, walked through the station, and exited without a word. Nicholas once again felt like he had failed Dusk for his lead had become a dead end. First, Clara raising more questions and now the military taking Jennifer's body, leaving them without the means to get answers. It was very clear this whole detective thing was not as easy as it had first seemed.

They marched back to Winter's Hall, making sure to keep a sharp eye out for any wandering soldiers or evil monsters.

Dusk turned to Nicholas when they reached the front door, and his face looked even more haggard than usual. "We can't meet up tomorrow; there's something I've gotta take care of," he said, sounding very sad and old.

"What?" Nicholas said, thinking he had misheard Dusk. "Is this about tonight? I'm sure we'll do better tomorrow." As he said it, Nicholas knew he didn't even fully believe it.

Dusk smiled at the boy, but it fell away quickly. "It's just something I gotta do."

Nicholas wanted to push further, but Dusk spun around and went into Winter's Hall without another word, leaving Nicholas on the stoop, alone and confused.

His ride home was not much better than the walk back to Winter's Hall. The same questions kept rolling around in his head.

Who is doing this?

Why are they doing it?

Why here?

Why me?

More and more questions piled up, creating an endless current of inquiries.

Nicholas arrived home without knowing how he had gotten there. It was late, or early depending on how you looked at it, and his aunt was asleep. He was careful to make as little noise as possible as he gathered a midnight snack from the kitchen and headed to his room.

The cereal he had grabbed from the kitchen crackled as he poured milk into the bowl. Cap'n Crunch's Crunch Berries was one of Nicholas's favorite meals, but even its scrumptious bite-size puffs were not enough to extinguish his discomfort. So, Nicholas dug out his remote and clicked on the television.

Darkness Falls was still on. The episode was about an alien attack on a little town. Nicholas usually liked monster shows better than aliens, but recently, he had had enough of monsters. Aliens were just fine with him.

He set his empty bowl on the bedside table and laid his head down and fell asleep. The television continued to play, showing scenes of mayhem and the destruction of a small town by an unbelievable force.

Dusk

Mr. Lloyd was replacing the last few books he had left before he could go home for the night. His nights seemed to be getting longer and longer, and he seemed to be moving slower and slower.

He put *Moby Dick* on the shelf and moved to the next row. Putting books away was usually one of Mr. Lloyd's favorite tasks as a librarian. It was a time for him to be alone with the stories. He'd talk to the books as if they were old friends and let his mind wander to anything it seemed to find important.

But that was dangerous, the reason why the task had lost its luster for him. Ever since Nicholas had talked with him and he had been face to face with that man again, Mr. Lloyd couldn't shake the feeling of impending doom. There seemed to always be this presence looming over him, his own personal rain cloud he couldn't shake.

No matter how much Mr. Lloyd tried, he couldn't get away. The feeling was palpable, so much so that at times, he could taste it. Like a leftover taste from a bad meal. He thought putting the books away tonight might help soothe his wandering mind. It didn't even come close.

As Mr. Lloyd was rounding the corner down his final row, a flicker of movement caught his eye. Far down on the other side of the library, Mr. Lloyd could almost make out a silhouette of a man.

"Hello?" Mr. Lloyd called. "Anybody there?"

Moving forward to get a better look, Mr. Lloyd noticed the shadow faltered slightly. It no longer looked like a man, just the ordinary shadows of a dark building late at night. "Old eyes playing tricks on me," Mr. Lloyd concluded under his breath.

But just as he was about to go back to his books, there was another flicker of movement. This time, Mr. Lloyd froze, looking back toward the other end of the library. He was not a gullible man and neither was he stupid. He knew what he saw.

He walked to the small reading area where he had seen the shadow. Four small, round tables sat in a diamond pattern. Each table was surrounded by four chairs. Mr. Lloyd stood in the middle of the tables turning about, looking for someone or something.

A whisper of noise came from behind him. He spun to find only darkness. This was followed by another, and then another. Both times, Mr. Lloyd turned to find nothing.

A chill grew over Mr. Lloyd. He fought it, but the more he did, the colder he felt. Death himself was breathing down the back of Mr. Lloyd's neck.

He whipped around to once again see a shadow of a man, so faint that if Mr. Lloyd changed angles just a little bit, he was sure the image would disappear. His breathing slowed.

"Is this what you want?" Mr. Lloyd said aloud. His voice wavered slightly. The room grew dark, darker than night.

"To take an old man? Take him away from his books, his life?" Mr. Lloyd continued.

The air became thinner and tasted stale as Mr. Lloyd drew in breaths. Mr. Lloyd sniffled slightly, finding himself having to fight back tears. He was scared and sad, but he was also angry.

"My life was taken from me long ago, so come on. Do your worst."

The shadow stared back as if it was confused. An icy finger of a breeze cut along the back of Mr. Lloyd's neck. He braced himself for whatever was to come.

Dusk

A sudden rush of wind and thunderous noise rocked the library. Chairs toppled over, and a window burst open. As it did, air rushed out of the room. Darkness seemed to follow it, and the room grew light once again.

Mr. Lloyd let out his breath and inhaled clean, beautiful, fresh air.

He decided he had put enough books away for one night. He collected his things from his office, locked up the library, and left for home.

Chapter 17

After a short sleep, Nicholas woke up less tired than the day before, but still felt worn down. He dragged himself to the bathroom for his morning ritual of peeing, staring into the mirror to check for acne, and then splashing his face to wake himself up as he prepared for a shower.

Nicholas dressed and grabbed his school things. He was about to leave his bedroom when he took a moment to look around. His room looked the same as it always had, but it seemed to have a more potent feel. People seemed to be disappearing and dying too regularly in Pointe's Hollow to not think about the little things. Nicholas was sixteen, not really the age to have thoughts about his own mortality, but with everything happening, Nicholas didn't think it was a bad idea to start early.

His eyes scanned the room and fell upon the typewriter once again. It seemed to be the hundredth time in the last week. His eyes began to burn. He looked away, trying not to think that his parents hadn't had time to enjoy the little things, and then left his bedroom.

Dusk

As Nicholas pedaled to school, he felt pretty optimistic. It was sunny, quite warm for this time of year. But this was Michigan after all. Time of year and weather rarely matched. His good mood was no match for the sight that greeted him when he arrived at school.

In the parking lot of the school sat the huge army trucks positioned in a half circle pattern. It shouldn't have surprised Nicholas. The school's parking lot was really the only lot large enough in The Hollow to house the vehicles.

For some reason, it made Nicholas angry. He had never particularly liked school, but this was his turf. The whole town was his turf, but the school especially. The army's disregard for his territory was beyond irritating.

It was the first time he had a good look at the trucks, and he realized that no matter how close he got to the trucks, they looked the same. They were completely green with army singularity. The only distinguishing mark was a triangle symbol on the side of each vehicle. Nicholas didn't recognize the symbol. He was left with no clues about which branch of the military employed these trucks. And, in turn, why they were in his town.

Throughout the day, Nicholas felt the trucks out in the lot watching him. Even in rooms without windows, Nicholas felt as if the trucks bore through the brick walls and tried to pull information from him. Nicholas decided to fight the trucks. Attempting to glean clues from them instead. He stared back. The flat, colored bumpers and wheel wells gleamed. The tarps over the back of the trucks wobbled slightly in the breeze from the lake. Nicholas saw through all this. He knew there was more behind the olive exterior. They were reverse Halloween masks, a calm and normal exterior hiding a monster within.

What are you here for? What did you do with Jennifer? What do you have to do with the killer? he asked the trucks, coaxing the information from them, but nothing came.

His day was made worse when he saw a soldier walking the halls of his school. Nicholas stopped dead, and his blood ran cold. An instant traffic jam ensued as people piled up behind Nicholas, bumping into him and knocking him to the floor. His math book, a notebook, and a collection of pencils scattered across the tiles. Nicholas didn't care; he was too focused on the soldier walking down the hall. As Nicholas looked up, he realized the soldier wasn't a soldier at all, just a kid wearing an oversized army jacket.

"Have a nice trip?" someone shouted from behind Nicholas.

"See you next fall," another chimed in.

Nicholas collected his things as the snickering died down. By the time he reclaimed all of his belongings, the halls were clear, and he was late for class.

When the bell rang to end the school day, Nicholas let out an audible sigh. The front doors burst open, letting the flood of kids rush into the town. Nicholas moved slowly between them, eyeing the trucks as if waiting for them to make a move.

"Eerie, aren't they?" a voice said to Nicholas's right. He turned to find Mr. Fidel. He was standing with his hands in his pockets and a magazine tucked under his arm. Nicholas pushed up his glasses on his nose and recognized the magazine as the one with Dr. Murdock's story in it.

Mr. Fidel looked at Nicholas and smiled. "Yeah," Nicholas said, turning back to the trucks. "They creep me out."

Mr. Fidel only nodded.

"You know why they're here?"

"Not sure, Nick," Mr. Fidel smiled. "But I have my theories."

Nicholas looked away from the trucks. Mr. Fidel winked at him, "Ah, I see that grabbed your interest."

Nicholas nodded.

"Well," Mr. Fidel continued, "it goes back to this magazine." He took the magazine from under his arm. He flipped to the page with the story about Dr. Murdock. Mr. Fidel wrapped the front cover around to the back. When he handed it over, Nicholas was looking only at one page.

"You see anything familiar?"

Nicholas scanned the page. It was the same story Mr. Fidel had shown him before. The image in the magazine depicted the doctor holding the vial with the dark green glow of revival liquid. He read over the caption to make sure he hadn't missed something, but that, too, was the same as it had been days before.

Frustrated, Nicholas looked up to Mr. Fidel for help. "Look closer," he said, and pointed.

Nicholas's eyes went back down to the picture. He looked over the image behind the doctor, all the rows of utensils hanging, the desk with the glowing green liquid. Around and around Nicholas looked. As he was about to give up, something caught his eye. Above a pocket on the left breast side of the doctor's lab coat was a very familiar symbol. Nicholas looked up to the truck and then back down to the magazine.

Son of a bitch, Nicholas thought. The symbols were identical.

"What," Nicholas began but stopped, suddenly finding it difficult to breathe. "What does this mean?"

Mr. Fidel shrugged, "I don't know, Nick. Just interesting, wouldn't you say?"

Nicholas looked at the magazine intently, "Yeah, very interesting."

Pieces of the puzzle began to drop into place. As if he was hearing the whole story for the first time, Nicholas was connecting things that seemed so distant from each other, they hardly belonged in the same world. The doctor, the murders, missing blood, chopped up bodies. It was all coming together. Ideas were rushing together so fast, Nicholas barely had time to make sense of them, but he knew he was right.

Nicholas realized he was staring at the magazine for far too long. He handed it back to Mr. Fidel and said, "Well, see ya later."

The words sounded forced and awkward.

"Ah, okay," Mr. Fidel said, his brows dropping into a quizzical look. "See ya, Nick."

Nicholas rushed toward the bike rack. He knew he should have said more to Mr. Fidel, but he also knew he had to go tell Dusk. Nicholas had figured it out. Dr. Murdock was in Pointe's Hollow, and he had most likely brought his research with him. That was why the military was here. They were looking for the doctor.

And the military believes that Dr. Murdock is the one killing people. Nicholas wasn't sure why they thought this, or how a doctor obsessed with the idea of bringing people back from the dead would kill people, but it felt right. Nicholas couldn't explain it. It was like instinct. A gut feeling that, if he was right, was truer than any other logical thought.

His bike jumped out of the rack. He spun it around on its back tire, but let out an, "Oft," as he suddenly bumped into someone.

Nicholas looked up and saw a blurry image of a girl. His glasses had shifted down his nose in the shuffle. Readjusting them, Nicholas realized the girl was Emily.

"I'm sorry," Nicholas stammered out.

"Don't worry about it," Emily said, smiling. "I should have been watching where I was walking."

She smiled even bigger, and Nicholas smiled in return. They stood there, both smiling dumbly for a second.

"Have you done any more drawings recently?" Emily finally asked.

"Ah," Nicholas thought for a moment. "No, actually. Not at all."

Emily's smile faded, "Oh, I see."

"Not that I don't want to," Nicholas quickly added. "I just haven't had time recently. You know, school and stuff."

Yeah, stuff being werewolves, dead bodies, and mad doctors.

Emily smiled again, "Yeah, midterms. They're a bitch, aren't they?"

Nicholas was taken aback for a second. Had he ever heard a girl swear? His aunt swore like a sailor, but a girl? Nicholas didn't think so, which only made him like Emily even more.

"Yeah, they are such bitches."

Even as he said it, Nicholas knew it sounded dumb. Emily apparently found it funny, because she let out a soft giggle. Nicholas smiled, feeling his face turn red.

A rumble from across the lot interrupted their conversation. One of the army trucks was starting up. The sight reminded Nicholas of what he had been about to do and how dire it was.

"So, I was wondering," Emily began, but Nicholas cut her off.

"Well, I have to get going. My aunt will be waiting for me."

"Oh," Emily said, worry replacing her glorious, glowing smile. "Alright. I guess I'll just see you tomorrow?"

"Yup," Nicholas said as he placed his foot on the pedal of his bike. The truck was now pulling out of the parking lot and onto the road. "Bye."

He pedaled off at a frightening pace, trying to get in front of the puttering truck. With the deaths of Earl and Jennifer and the realization that monsters do exist, Nicholas didn't have time to think of Emily looking after him as he left her standing alone.

Sheriff Gordon usually prided himself on being the guy everyone in town came to when something was wrong, but usually they didn't all talk to him at once. Most circumstances had Sheriff Gordon dealing with two or three people at a time. He had become good at being a mediator for the small town squabbles. If a problem was big enough to sweep a town into a mayhem-infused whirlwind, Sheriff Gordon had it figured out, under control, and cleaned up before it could begin.

That's what made this town meeting so nerve-racking. In all of Sheriff Gordon's time as the sheriff of Pointe's Hollow, he had to call an impromptu town meeting only twice before. Once because of a proposal to put new docks into the residential side of the marina and the other because of a coyote infestation they had a few months ago. In the latter, the public had been pretty upset over the rise in pet disappearances.

Now, not only had their town been overtaken by outsiders, but their own lives seemed to be in danger. Sheriff Gordon wished that the people could understand that he disliked the military's presence as much as all of them, but they couldn't understand. Mostly because Sheriff Gordon had to make it appear that the military's presence was a normal response to what their town was going through to keep the panic down. Of course, that wasn't true at all. Sheriff Gordon had no idea how the military had heard of and responded to their issue so fast.

Sheriff Gordon shifted his stance in the front of the school gymnasium. He stood in front of the stage that was usually constructed for graduation ceremonies, but today it

223

had been raised for him. Turning around, Sheriff Gordon eyed the microphone positioned in the middle of the stage. The silver stand made the sheriff shake his head.

Two years ago, Henry Carpenter, Pointe's Hollow's mayor dropped dead from a heart attack. After his passing, some names were kicked around to take his place, and Lawrence Gordon was the top contender. But he was no public speaker. Stages and speeches were for politicians and comedians. Two things Sheriff Gordon would never and could never be. But that didn't stop the town from hoping. Hoping so much that they had neglected to name anyone else as mayor as if to say, "Once you come to your senses, Sheriff Gordon, the job will be here waiting for ya."

Behind him the gym was filling up, and people were taking their seats in three hundred folding chairs. When Sheriff Gordon had seen the giant collection of chairs, he had been sure there would still be chairs free when this all started. Now, however, the sheriff could see people were going to be lined up along the back wall and against the collapsed bleachers to either side of the chairs.

The sheriff straightened his back and adjusted his belt as he prepared to mount the stage. He looked at his watch and saw the second hand count up to fifty-six, fifty-seven, fifty-eight, fifty-nine, and then it was five o-clock. The meeting time had been set so they'd finish before the sun went down, so no one had to be out in the dark. There wasn't an official curfew over the town, but there was an understanding that folks shouldn't go out alone after dark unless absolutely necessary.

Once again, Sheriff Gordon adjusted his belt. This time it was more as a nervous tick than an actual need. Once he felt that he couldn't procrastinate any longer, he began making his way up the stairs. As he stepped toward the microphone, the entire room quieted. He took a moment for the room to completely settle, and then he spoke.

"I'd like to thank all of you for making it on such short notice." He never liked the way his voice sounded coming through the sound system in the gym, but today it almost made him cringe. His low baritone and commanding voice that shrunk weaker men came out tinny and with a crackle of static.

"Now, I know the last few days have been rough on all of us, but I want to assure everyone that everything is under control."

There was a low rumble at this. Not in disagreement, nor in argument, but concern for truthfulness. Sheriff Gordon knew that concern could quickly turn into fear. He hoped that he could do his job well enough to avoid that.

"I also know that the military's presence has caused some of you to worry, but again I assure you everything is under control. We are doing everything that we can to keep everyone in town safe."

"So, are you going to be starting a curfew?" a voice came from somewhere in the back. It was so abrupt, Sheriff Gordon had missed who it was.

"As of right now, we believe we are able to go forth without the need of a mandatory curfew. This doesn't mean you should be reckless."

This time the rumble was louder, and some people even shook their heads. He was about to speak when the voice spoke again.

"Then, you have a suspect?"

The voice was that of Mrs. Dresser. Sheriff Gordon knew why she was asking. He remembered watching Mikey, her son, fussing with wires on karaoke night. What stopped him from being next, she must be thinking. Sheriff Gordon looked around at all of the people's faces. Many of them had kids and even more had known Earl. He had to handle this cautiously, or he was going to lose control. Small town fears quickly turned into big time trouble.

"Mrs. Dresser, we have leads we are currently following. I can't tell you anymore, but I can say we're getting close." Sheriff Gordon tried to sound calm and sure, even though he wasn't at all. It must have done the trick, because Mrs. Dresser nodded and quieted.

"Are these your leads or the army guys' leads?" John Horton said. A good man, but he was cursed with a quick mouth. Saying whatever was on his mind no matter the consequences.

"We are closely working with the military, so from now on, you can think of us and them as one in the same." Sheriff Gordon wanted to vomit just hearing himself say the words, but his town needed him to say them. Needed to believe them.

"I don't think we can, Sheriff," John said, standing. "I was talking to some of the boys in green, and they are a little unsure of what they're even doing here."

"Come on, John," Sheriff Gordon said in his best I'm-on-your-side voice. "You know how the army works. It's a need-to-know kind of world. I'm sure they just don't have the specifics."

John Horton had no affiliation with the military, so Sheriff Gordon was hoping he would bite at the bait. Unfortunately, John took it a different way.

"All I know is there is something you're not telling us."

The crowd began to mumble back and forth. Sheriff Gordon felt himself losing the crowd. He could see the tension in their faces. During the day, on the street, they looked like they always did. But here, gathered and discussing the terror stalking their town, they were getting scared and angry.

"I am telling you everything I can, John. You know I can't openly talk about an ongoing investigation."

John raised a hand and then dropped it against his thigh. It clearly said, "Do you believe he's feeding me this line?" The townsfolk seemed to agree, because their voices grew louder. Sheriff Gordon heard snippets of what was being said, and it wasn't good.

This was why Sheriff Gordon could never be mayor. He knew the words to say, but didn't know how to say them. He was a blunt man. A man who told it like it is. Not a man who could spin stories and play word games. He was going to try again when the door to the gymnasium opened.

The sudden clatter hushed the room as people turned in their chairs to see what had made the noise. People who were standing against the wall near the door backed away. Soldiers noisily stomped into the gym, making sure their presence was known. The soldiers entered through the open door and positioned themselves around the room.

Jesus Christ, not this again, Sheriff Gordon thought.

After a moment of suspended silence, Captain Hayward entered the gym. His black boots thundered on the waxed gym floor. One second the town had been on the verge of a revolt, and now you could hear a pin drop. At least, the pin dropping between the pacing of the ever-advancing captain.

Captain Hayward reached the stage, turned left, and proceeded up the stairs onto the stage. He walked right up to Sheriff Gordon and without a word or motion waited for the sheriff to step away from the microphone. Against his better judgment, but still wanting to keep the illusion of coordination with the military for the hundreds of townsfolk in the gym, Sheriff Gordon stepped back.

He moved back far enough to give Captain Hayward room to speak, but he didn't leave the stage. He still needed to be seen as the man in charge of this thing. No matter how much it was out of his control.

Captain Hayward stepped up to the microphone and cleared his throat. The sound hit the microphone and was amplified throughout the gym.

"Hello, Pointe's Hollowers. I am sorry for barging in

on your town meeting, but I am sure, given the nature of what I have to say, your sheriff," he turned to look at Sheriff Gordon, "won't mind sharing the spotlight."

A quick moment of desire to beat the captain into a small puddle flooded the sheriff's thoughts. Keeping his composure, Sheriff Gordon nodded his approval, and Captain Hayward turned back around.

"In the past few days, your small community has been plagued by a monster and for this you have my deepest sympathy. Luckily for you, though, we are here," the captain smiled his charming Boy Scout smile.

He could be a politician, Sheriff Gordon thought sourly. *He's got this speaking thing down. Even the bullshit smile is top notch.*

"As I am sure you could tell, we are a special branch of the United States Military concentrated in scientific and experimental exploration. In simple terms, we are the people that test new research from the country's brightest minds. Due to our extensive knowledge in the advanced techniques of war and given the obscure nature of these kills, we believe we are the perfect team to help you through the situation you currently find yourselves in."

"So, you've done things like this before?" John Horton said, breaking the crowd's silence.

Captain Hayward didn't miss a beat. He just smiled and said, "Many, many times."

Horse shit, Sheriff Gordon thought, remembering how the captain had reacted to the picture of Jennifer's body. If he had done things like this before, that picture wouldn't have made him blink.

"Now, as I'm sure your good sheriff has told you, your noble police force has handed everything they have on the situation over to us. From this point forward, any information that pertains to this case should be disclosed directly to me. You can get word to me through any of my men stationed throughout your community here."

Sheriff Gordon could feel his hands tighten into balls. The captain was unknowingly contradicting what the sheriff had just said. Sheriff Gordon quickly remembered the captain looking back at him and what he had said when he first arrived. Suddenly, Sheriff Gordon had the feeling Captain Hayward knew exactly what he was doing.

You sneaky son of a bitch.

As the captain continued, Sheriff Gordon could almost hear him say, 'This is for that picture trick you pulled back at your office, Sheriff.'

"Other than that, we just want everyone to remain calm and safe. Make sure if you go out after dark, you don't do it alone, and if anyone sees anything suspicious, I want it reported right away."

Captain Hayward smiled again and raised his arms to the side. "I know if you work with me and let us do what we do best, we will be able to take care of this situation, and I'll be out of your hair in no time. Thank you for your time."

The captain leaned back from the microphone. When he moved to leave, he sent a smirk over his shoulder at Sheriff Gordon, who could only look on, unwilling to lose his composure in front of his town. The captain's feet once again pounded the wood floor as he exited the gym followed by his entourage. Just as the door closed behind the final soldier, hell broke loose within the gym. People began standing up and yelling at the sheriff. Some yells were in fear, some were in anger.

"Looks like you're working closely with jack-shit, Sheriff!" John Horton yelled over the bubbling crowd.

Sheriff Gordon raced to the microphone in an attempt to calm the crowd. "People, people, please. Clearly, there are some things that need to be cleared up, and if you give me a moment, I can do just that, but you have to settle down."

The sheriff could have been talking to a brick wall for

all the good it did. People began yelling at each other now. Conflicted ideas about what to do, stirred up old rivalries, and hatchets that had been long buried were brought back to light. It was pure chaos.

Sheriff Gordon's fingers tensed, and his knuckles whitened as he clenched his fists harder and harder. As his nails bit into his palms, he imagined them on Captain Hayward's throat. Sheriff Gordon wasn't a violent man, but he knew how to hurt if he wanted. And right then, he would have liked nothing more.

Nicholas remembered what Dusk said the night before: They were not to meet today and there was something Dusk 'had to see to.' Nicholas knew Dusk was not a man he should bother, but he also knew that Dusk needed to know that the doctor who had been messing around with the green ooze was somehow connected with the military presence in The Hollow as soon as possible.

He didn't even feel the least bit guilty as he hopped over the wall onto Winter's Hall's grounds. Nicholas was at the door to the great mansion when he heard a cracking sound coming from the backyard.

His body went on high alert, but Nicholas knew by now that the sound was most likely just Dusk. He went around the corner of the house without another thought.

As Nicholas rounded the corner and saw Dusk, he noticed two things. One was the large liquor bottle in his left hand, which dangled nearly empty. The second was the tomahawk stuck into a tree surrounded by littered pieces of wood.

Nicholas stopped as he surveyed the scene. Apparently,

it was longer than Nicholas realized, because he shook when he heard Dusk ask, "What are you doing here?"

Nicholas couldn't speak for a second. He was too stunned by everything. Dusk was standing there in front of him, no mistaking it. But at the same time, it wasn't Dusk. Just a shell of what was normally Dusk. A terrible, feeble, scotch-smelling shell.

"I said we weren't to meet today," Dusk continued, his words slightly slurring into each other. He walked forward, and as he did, Nicholas could see his eyes were red, as if he had been crying. The sight made Nicholas both scared and sad at the same time.

"I figured it out," Nicholas finally said.

Dusk stopped uneasily. "Figured what out?"

Nicholas rolled his eyes. "The murders. The dead, bloodless people that have been popping up all over town. I figured it out."

Dusk squinted for a moment as if trying to remember. He snapped his fingers as if he knew what Nicholas was talking about, but then his face grew sullen again. "Come back tomorrow; we'll talk about it then."

Nicholas was dumbfounded. "Did you hear what I said? I figured it out!"

"And I said come back tomorrow," Dusk said, forcefully, but with a hint of sadness.

Nicholas couldn't believe what he was hearing. *Tomorrow? You want me to come back tomorrow?*

"Bullshit!" Nicholas said. "People are dying! Don't you understand?"

Dusk had already turned around by the time Nicholas responded. Dusk looked over his shoulder. "People die everyday. There ain't no stopping it."

Nicholas felt his hands clench. Anger was mounting up inside of him like a bomb getting down to its last inch of wick. "Dr. Murdock thinks there's a way."

Dusk

Dusk looked confused for a moment and then turned fully around. Nicholas walked forward, fists clenched at his side. "That's who's doing this. I don't know why he came here, but he's the one that's been killing people. He's trying to perfect bringing people back."

Dusk and Nicholas were within arm's reach. Dusk sighed, the smell of booze wafting out, "Then, he's a fool. There is no way to bring someone back. People die, and when they do, they are gone for good."

"That's not true. I've seen you with my own eyes bring people back. Dead corpses talking. I've seen it."

"That is not life," Dusk said, exasperated. "It is a farce of life. Prerecorded memories, that's all."

Nicholas could not stand Dusk this way, so uncaring and completely ignorant. Mr. Fidel believed in this doctor's work, and he was a teacher, a sound-minded man. What was Dusk on the other hand? Just a drunk.

My parents can be saved, Nicholas thought. He hadn't realized how hard he had been holding onto that thought until now. *I will save them.*

"What if the doctor can do it? What if he doesn't have to fake life? What if he can actually bring people back?"

"He can't!" Dusk yelled. Nicholas jumped back. Dusk sighed and said, softer this time, "No one can."

"How do you know, though?" Nicholas was shouting now. He was so angry. How could Dusk be so stupid?

"Because I do," Dusk said sternly.

Nicholas wanted to pull his hair out in clumps. He was shaking his head in denial.

Dusk turned away from Nicholas, but continued to speak over his shoulder, saying, "I know you want to believe your parents could come back, but they can't."

Nicholas exploded on the inside. Anger and sadness melded together into a steel so hard it shot at Dusk in words.

"And neither can Angela."

Nicholas didn't even know where the thought, let alone the words, came from. He had never even said her name out loud to himself, let alone to Dusk. Dusk didn't give him much time to reflect on bringing up Angela. Before Nicholas knew it, Dusk had turned around, ripped the tomahawk from the tree, gripped Nicholas by the shirt collar, and pinned him in the air between himself and the tree.

Kicking wildly, Nicholas fought to get free. His back rubbed on the bark of the tree while Dusk swayed slightly from side to side with drunken rage. The tomahawk was upraised, gleaming in the fading sunlight, asking for its thirst of blood to be quenched. For the first time, Nicholas thought Dusk would actually kill him, strike him down like the monsters he had been killing for so long.

Dusk's grip readjusted on the raised weapon. Nicholas closed his eyes and waited for death. But it never came.

Slowly, Dusk lowered Nicholas. He felt the familiar feeling of solid ground beneath his feet. He opened his eyes. His glasses had been disheveled, but he could still see Dusk's face. Fresh tears rolled down Dusk's cheeks, and his lips trembled.

Dusk's hand unfurled from Nicholas's shirt, and the tomahawk fell to the ground with a soft thud. Nicholas was still terrified, but more than that, he was angry, completely infuriated that Dusk had ignored him, blown him off, and then tried to kill him. The anger swelled even more as he thought about this incident and Dusk's behavior. He didn't need to help Dusk; he had been risking his own life every night and for what? To be threatened by a gun-happy drunk.

Bullshit, Nicholas thought again.

He stomped around Dusk, leaving him by the tree, surrounded by the shattered remnants of its trunk. He had gone about two or three paces when he heard a shuffle behind him.

Dusk had fallen to his knees. The once-great monster

hunter was broken and nothing more than a lump on the ground, but Nicholas was too angry to feel sorry for him.

With his mind clouded by anger and hatred, Nicholas said, "Some hero you turned out to be."

If it was possible, Dusk shrank even lower. Nicholas felt a pang of regret, but he swallowed it hard. He left Dusk there and hopped the wall once again without a look back. He was on his bike and pedaling away as his own tears threatened to fall. He rubbed his eyes, trying to stop the encroaching sadness, but it was inevitable. He just pedaled home, ignoring the tears that fell.

"What have I done?" Dusk asked, his voice barely audible above the soft rustle of trees. The trees that surrounded him blanketed the entire backyard with sounds and shadows.

Behind Dusk, between him and the retreating Nicholas, a soft, white figure materialized. She stood, billowing in the wind like a cloth hung on a clothesline to dry. Her angelic features were enhanced by a soft, inner glow. The woman, as beautiful in death as she was in life, looked at the man on the ground. Then, she looked off toward the boy, who pedaled away in angered haste. She could do nothing but look on helplessly as the two became farther and farther apart.

Dusk stirred, becoming aware of the ghost's presence. She came back to him, longing to hold him and love him as she did so long ago. But as she thought about what could have been, she knew it would never be so.

As the sun began its final descent below the trees, the woman faded, until she was nothing more than a cherished memory. Dusk felt her presence leave the yard, and once again, he began to sob.

As Dusk cried in his backyard surrounded by growing shadows and splintered wood, Nicholas cried, riding his bike back into a town that had its own fair share of shadows and broken pieces.

Chapter 18

Nicholas's tires wore at the pavement as he rode back to town. He passed Marsh Street, which led into the small subdivision where his aunt's house sat. As much as he wanted to cover his head and ignore the world, he didn't want to go home. There was a good chance his aunt wouldn't be there, but even with the odds on his side, Nicholas didn't want to take the chance of running into her.

Before he knew it, Nicholas found himself deep in downtown Pointe's Hollow, night completely overtaking the town. Shadows and darkness were plastered around every corner and within every crease.

The town was normally warm and welcoming, like the friendly and homegrown backyard of America shown in Coca-Cola commercials. Now, it felt cold and slimy. The darkness wasn't the only thing that made the town feel that way. The feeling was because of everything he now understood. As Mr. Lloyd had said, evil was among them.

Nicholas rushed through downtown as if he was being watched. An absurd idea considering that as soon as the sun went down, Pointe's Hollow residents disappeared into their homes. No one was out and about.

Besides me and Dusk, Nicholas thought, fighting back a deep burning in his eyes.

Nicholas wondered where he would end up if he just kept pedaling. He then saw a light in the distance, across a field that should be completely dark. For a moment, it scared him, and then he looked around and realized where he was.

And him, Nicholas thought as he pointed his bike in the direction of the light.

"Now, where are you going?" Sheriff Gordon said, scratching his mustache.

He hadn't intended to tail the Wake boy, but sometimes things just fell into his lap, and he didn't usually let them fall back out. The boy had sped by his patrol car positioned out on Coast Line Road. Sheriff Gordon usually parked out there for a few hours late at night trying to catch high school kids speeding around with open beer cans.

Teenagers, Sheriff Gordon thought as he sat out there shaking his head. *If they only knew what they were risking and what could happen in the blink of an eye.*

Sheriff Gordon knew, knew what happened to people in car crashes. Knew how they looked flattened to a pulp. Knew how bad needing a drink could become, but also knew what would come with one more taste.

This time, however, he wasn't looking for teenagers; he was just trying to figure out what he should do next. The town meeting had gone terribly wrong. After a lot of consoling and a lot of pleading, he was able to calm the crowd. Tensions were still high, probably higher than they were before the meeting, but the crowd had left without burning the sheriff at the stake, which, given the circumstances, Sheriff Gordon took as a win. It wasn't the win he had hoped for when he had set up the meeting, but a win nonetheless.

Sheriff Gordon shifted his car into gear. He kept the headlights turned off and followed the Wake boy into The Hollow. Sheriff Gordon hoped that wherever the boy was going, he would lead the sheriff to his win. The boy looked off into the distance, and Sheriff Gordon followed his gaze. The boy was looking toward the library. Oddly enough, there was a light on. It was well after closing time, but it appeared Mr. Lloyd had decided to stay late.

The Wake boy pointed his bike toward the library and sped off. The sheriff turned down Second Street. He would circle back around the high school and head to the library from a different angle. His pace was slow, calculated. He wanted the boy to arrive well before him, so he could pull up and watch.

The library came into view as Sheriff Gordon drove past the high school and crossed to the other side of Main Street. In front of the library, the boy's bike sat within the bike rack. Sheriff Gordon couldn't see into the library, but he knew the kid was in there.

Continuing his progress past the library, Sheriff Gordon pulled to the side of the road about fifty yards past the library's lot and turned off the engine. He peeked in the rearview mirror and made sure he could see the entire library building.

"Don't worry, boy," Sheriff Gordon said between a yawn. "I can wait all night."

There was a hollow clang as Nicholas shoved his bike into the rack. The sound, although slight, sounded much louder in the night. Nicholas looked around him to make sure he was alone. The night was dark and ominous, but appeared empty except for shadows.

Nicholas looked at the two-story building. He let out a sigh and then walked up to the library.

The door was locked. So, Nicholas went around the building and looked into the only window with light. He saw Mr. Lloyd sitting at his desk looking over some paperwork.

CLICK, CLICK.

Nicholas knocked on the window. Mr. Lloyd glanced up as if it was a normal distraction, sure that when he looked up, he'd see an empty window. This time, however, he saw Nicholas. Nicholas waved, and Mr. Lloyd smiled, holding up a finger pointing toward the front door.

Nicholas nodded, leaving the window.

It took only a moment for Mr. Lloyd to reach the front door. There was a soft click, and the door swung open. Mr. Lloyd looked down at Nicholas, and suddenly, Nicholas felt very small. He wanted to say something and explain everything that had happened since their last talk, but he didn't know where to begin.

Mr. Lloyd sighed while nodding his head as if he understood everything without Nicholas saying a word. In that moment, Nicholas realized just how much of a friend Mr. Lloyd was.

Mr. Lloyd stepped back and beckoned Nicholas in. Without saying a single word to each other, Nicholas stepped into the library, and Mr. Lloyd locked the door behind them. They continued in silence. Nicholas walked around the library replacing books on shelves as Mr. Lloyd did paperwork in his office.

It was nice to have something to keep him busy. It was dull and repetitive, but that's what made it perfect for

Nicholas. There was so much going on in his life, a life that had seemed so simple just a few weeks ago. Nicholas needed some time to think through it all. Unfortunately, thinking it through made Nicholas think of Dusk, the man Nicholas had grown to admire and who, just like that, had shut him out and given him an extremely close shave with a tomahawk.

Nicholas shoved a book into place as his thinking turned to anger.

He's being so stupid! Nicholas thought.

After the last three days they had spent trying to find this killer, and Nicholas had found the answer. All the answers fell right into his lap as if he had already known them, as if they had been presented to him on a silver platter. But now Dusk was too lost in the bottom of his bottle to listen.

So stupid, Nicholas thought.

In the end, it seemed to be more helpful for Nicholas to talk with Mr. Fidel instead of Dusk. Mr. Fidel had unwittingly uncovered the answers to their questions. Nicholas thought about how Mr. Fidel would react to the idea of monsters and mad scientists plaguing the small town. He was sure Mr. Fidel would initially crack a quick joke, but then he would completely freak out.

Nicholas chuckled and looked down at the book in his hand, Matthew Night's *'Til The Sun Comes Up*. A great vampire book in the spirit of the original *Dracula* style. No matter how good the book was, it didn't belong here. Nicholas was currently putting books back with author's last names that started with 'F.' 'Night,' at least the last time Nicholas checked, started with 'N' not 'F.'

Turning away from the book, Nicholas peered down the row of books toward the back of the building. The 'N' row was against the far wall. There the rows jumped the walkway and came toward the front of the building. So, the front rows, the 'A' and 'Z' rows, were opposite each other in the front of the room.

THUD! THUD!

Nicholas turned toward the front doors as the resounding knock echoed through the books. Mr. Lloyd looked up from his desk and then to Nicholas. After a moment, Mr. Lloyd smiled, trying to console Nicholas. Nicholas smiled back, still on edge.

The librarian stood up, left his office, heading toward the knocking, and opened the door. Nicholas could not see who was there.

A voice came from the outside, "Where is he?"

It was quiet, which made it difficult for Nicholas to hear the words. The voice sounded familiar, but he couldn't be sure who it was. Mr. Lloyd turned back to Nicholas for a momentary glance; then, he walked outside to talk, shutting the door behind him.

Nicholas stayed there for a moment thinking he should probably be getting home. He didn't know who was out there, but it was obvious they had been looking for him. People would expect to find him here at this hour. This had been his cover to go monster hunting with Dusk. Suddenly, Nicholas felt a ping of guilt when he thought of Mr. Lloyd staying late only to keep his cover.

Nicholas looked back down to the book in his hands. He made a mental note to thank Mr. Lloyd for all his help. Readjusting his grip on the book, Nicholas headed for the back of the library. The light in the library was dim, supported only by the moonlight from the tall windows. Once he got to the back row, Nicholas had to squint to find the proper spot for *'Til The Sun Comes Up*.

Nicholas slid the book into place and backed up.

THUD.

Nicholas's blood instantly ran cold. He stepped out from behind the back row.

"Mr. Lloyd?" Nicholas's voice wavered.

There was no answer.

The library seemed to grow darker for a moment, then brightened. Nicholas slowly moved forward. He reached behind him, hoping to find the knife Dusk had given him, but found empty belt loops. The knife sat on his dresser in his bedroom. He had gone to Dusk's and to the library right from school, so he didn't have the blade with him.

THUD.

Nicholas jumped. The library grew dark again and then once again, it brightened, as if the whole place was a lung inhaling, then exhaling. A few rows from the front of the room, Nicholas looked down a row to find a book laying flat on the ground. He turned right and found yet another book on the ground.

THUD.

The noise came from behind Nicholas, making him spin around. *'Til The Sun Comes Up* lay flat on the ground in the middle of the walkway. Past the book, right next to the back row, stood a person. Or at least it seemed to be a person.

The figure was inky black and slightly transparent. It stood tall and lanky, its face slightly brighter than the rest of the body. It was a terrifying figure that Nicholas felt, more than saw, deep within his bones.

"The man in shadows," Nicholas breathed, and he was slightly aware the room had grown cold as his breath came out in puffs.

The figure seemed to hear him, tilting its head like a confused dog. Then, it shook its head slowly and raised its hand. The fingers were long and as thin as wires. It reached out toward Nicholas, but instead of reaching out in three-dimensional space, the arm spread out along the carpet as a growing, grasping shadow heading toward Nicholas.

Nicholas's brain knew he needed to run, but it took his body a moment longer. As he moved away, the shadow hand left the carpet and grasped his ankle. Before Nicholas knew

242

what was happening, his own momentum put him to the ground. Nicholas was yanked back toward the far end of the library.

With all his effort, Nicholas flipped onto his back and saw the shadow's head tilt just enough to signify a smile. Nicholas knew it was no use, but he screamed anyway.

"You know he's just a boy," Mr. Lloyd said. His voice had taken on a fierceness it rarely held. "He can't handle all of this. It's too big. Too dark."

"He can handle more than you think," Dusk said. "And even more than he knows."

Mr. Lloyd scoffed rudely. Nicholas had come to him to get away. At the time, he didn't know why, but now Mr. Lloyd could tell. Dusk smelled of booze and had circles under his eyes two sizes too big for a single missed night of sleep. The man was a pathetic husk. Mr. Lloyd had seen enough darkness in his life to know it latched onto this man like a disease.

"He shouldn't have to handle this," Mr. Lloyd continued. "He shouldn't have to handle you."

For a moment, Mr. Lloyd thought Dusk would strike him, for the anger that riled up behind Dusk's eyes was terrifying. But Dusk looked off distantly and sighed.

"No, no, he shouldn't," Dusk agreed.

Mr. Lloyd expected him to say more, but he didn't. His eyes drifted off to where the field across the street from the library stopped and the woods began.

"Look," Dusk finally said. "I didn't want this either, but I think...." Dusk wasn't able to finish, for at that moment, a scream ripped through the quiet night like a fire burning through dried twigs.

"Nicholas!" Mr Lloyd said.

They turned around and burst through the front doors of the library.

Nicholas felt the icy breath of cold death all along his spine as the shadow creature nearly had him. Any moment now, Nicholas would be covered in shadow for all of time. He flung himself back onto his stomach and began clawing at the ground, trying to escape the death grip this shadow had on his ankle. It was no use. His fingers grazed harmlessly over the soft carpet.

Before Nicholas was swallowed up by blackness, there was a loud commotion in the front of the library followed quickly by a soft whoosh-whoosh noise. It all ended with a defiant thud. Nicholas stopped, moving, and his leg was released.

Without waiting for an explanation, Nicholas scrambled away like a spider whose hiding place has just been discovered. Once he felt like he was far enough away from the thing, he flipped over to look at the monster. Right in the middle of the thing's head, stuck into the wall, was a tomahawk.

Whipping his head around, Nicholas saw Dusk standing between the 'A' and 'Z' shelves of library books. A few paces behind him was Mr. Lloyd, his face pale and hand over his mouth. Nicholas smiled as he turned back to the shadow creature.

The creature turned its head like it had before as if puzzled by the new arrivals. Its arm detached from the wall and pulled the tomahawk from its head.

Held up only by shadow, the blade twisted and turned in the air. The shadow looked over the weapon as if it was the most astonishing thing. Suddenly, it became disgusted and tossed the weapon aside. The tomahawk twirled once and then stuck into the floor. Nicholas felt the vibrations it made from where he lay.

That's not good, Nicholas thought as the shadow's arms reached out, pushing Dusk right off his feet and sending him into one of the reading tables. As the hands came back, they grabbed Nicholas again.

Nicholas fought against the shadow's grip, but his blows passed through without resistance. The shadow creature began to pull Nicholas to him.

No, not to him, Nicholas realized. After him. The thing's wild, licorice-type arms were still extended, but its body began to move about the walls. Nicholas's body was a towline being dragged behind the shadowy monstrosity. It turned and disappeared behind a few bookshelves, bringing Nicholas along for the ride, almost thrusting him right into the side of one of the shelves. For the next moment or two, Nicholas didn't know which way was up. He rolled, hopped, spun, and dodged things as the shadow danced along the walls.

Nicholas could register Mr. Lloyd and Dusk yelling back and forth at each other and to him. Nicholas wanted to shout back, but was afraid he'd bite his own tongue off if he opened his mouth.

Nicholas was wrenched across the ground, and he felt his body begin to lift. Nicholas was no longer grinding against the carpeted floor. He was being dragged across the wall, bouncing upon books properly sequenced on wooden shelves. His arms, legs, back, and head rebounded like a tennis ball in a Wimbledon match.

Just as Nicholas was sure he was going to be knocked unconscious or vomit, there was a blood curdling screech from the shadow, and Nicholas fell free.

In a daze, Nicholas was faintly aware which way was up as Mr. Lloyd ran over to him. If Nicholas's understanding of up and down was right, Mr Lloyd had learned how to walk on the ceiling.

"Nicholas? Nicholas, are you alright?"

Nicholas wanted to say, "Yeah, fine. Just a little dizzy," but the sound that came out was like a mouth full of mashed potatoes.

He flipped himself right side up. After the room stopped spinning, he looked over at Mr. Lloyd, "What happened?" he said.

Mr. Lloyd turned from Nicholas to the shadow that bounced about the walls. Dusk stood up against the beast like the lone gunman he was, armed with nothing but the spitfire in his own gut. His tomahawk was still stuck into the floor in the back of the library, and his holster sat empty.

"I'm not sure," Mr. Lloyd sputtered. "It looked like that thing was gonna run you right out the front door." Mr. Lloyd shrugged his shoulders and dropped his hands.

Nicholas was pretty close to the whole ordeal, but he didn't know any more than Mr. Lloyd. It seemed like the beast had been hurt by something.

But by what? Nicholas scanned the room. Books upon books laid scattered about the library, but Nicholas was sure those books hadn't caused the pain. Then, Nicholas saw where he was laying. Right in front of Mr. Lloyd's office.

The light, Nicholas realized. "Mr. Lloyd, get me a flashlight, and then go turn all the lights on."

For a moment, Mr. Lloyd looked confused; then, he understood. He didn't nod or say anything; he just jumped up and disappeared into his office. A moment later, a silver-handled, large bulbed flashlight sailed toward Nicholas, who snatched it out of the air with one hand. He was up in a wink, wavered a bit, and then steadied.

The shadow was tossing books across the library at Dusk, who was easily dodging them, but it was only a matter of time. Nicholas looked down at the flashlight and clicked it on. The light blared into his eyes, stunning him for a second before he pointed it at the shadow. As soon as the light touched the dark, murky body of the shadow creature, an ice-crunching screech wretched forth from the thing's mouth.

Dusk looked around to see what was happening. He saw Nicholas holding the light and smirked. Nicholas smiled, proud of himself for contributing to the fight, instead of just being the monster's victim.

The fight wasn't over, however. The creature ducked behind bookshelves, shielding its figure from the light. Nicholas tried to weave the beam within the rows, touching the creature as much as possible. It screamed and yelped as it creeped up the far wall enough to get around the shelves. It dove at the tables as if to slip into a pool.

The thing flung the closest table toward the three of them. Dusk dove out of the way, sprawling, as did Nicholas, losing his grip on the flashlight. It tumbled from his hands, and the light went out as the flying table collided with another table that hit Mr. Lloyd. He yelled and fell to the ground, trapped.

Nicholas wanted to go to his aid, but the beast was advancing on Dusk, who was crawling on his back. Nicholas swiped up the flashlight, clicking the switch on and off. Nothing happened.

"Come on," Nicholas shouted at the flashlight.

He pounded on the flashlight, and the bulb flickered in and out, but didn't come on. Nicholas looked up and saw the beast was almost to Dusk. Without thinking, Nicholas rushed over and stood his ground between the two of them.

The figure backed away momentarily, but then reached forward toward Nicholas. He hit the flashlight harder. But still only flickers were ignited.

Dusk

The cold hand reached closer and closer to Nicholas.

THWAP.

A flicker of light.

THWAP.

The creature's forefinger was inches from Nicholas's cheek.

THWAP!

The lights in the library burst into full bloom. White light exploded about the room, blinding Nicholas.

The shadow let out a blood-curdling scream that was a mixture of a deflating balloon and a ratchet toy that kids spin at New Year's.

Shielding his eyes, Nicholas looked over at the front of the library. Mr. Lloyd, breathing heavily, with a small cut that was bleeding on his forehead, was standing with his hand on the light switch.

The shadow shrunk smaller and smaller, and then with one final effort, it jumped out a window and slipped into the dark. Without warning, the room grew suddenly still and quiet. With an ironic twist of fate, Nicholas noticed that the flashlight in his hand was alright, its beam barely visible in the bright room.

He clicked off the light and turned to look at Dusk. Dusk had stood up and was dusting himself off. Nicholas nodded to him, and Dusk nodded back. He looked toward Mr. Lloyd. The old man was doubled over, breathing heavily.

Nicholas rushed over, asking, "Are you alright?"

Mr. Lloyd looked up. "Yes, yes. I'm fine. A bit winded, but fine. Are you alright, Nicholas? That thing dragged you around like something I've never seen."

"I'm fine," Nicholas said, and he meant it. A few bumps and scrapes, but nothing a good night's sleep wouldn't fix.

"The kid's strong," Dusk said as he walked up behind the two of them.

Mr. Lloyd glanced at him. There was a quick, silent conversation between the two of them that Nicholas couldn't help but notice. Then, Mr. Lloyd brought his attention back to Nicholas, "It appears so."

Mr. Lloyd sighed and then continued, "You two better get going."

Nicholas was about to ask how hard Mr. Lloyd had hit his head, when Dusk spoke up, "Yes. I think that would be best."

Nicholas was looking between the two of them as if they were crazy. How could they have just gone through what he had gone through and now just leave without a word.

"But, but...." Nicholas began, but Dusk cut him off.

"I know you have questions. So do I, but now isn't the time to talk about it. With the military roaming around town, we can't risk being seen here in this mess."

Nicholas had to admit he had forgotten about the military. Somewhere between flying around the library and that thing's scream, it must have slipped his mind.

"Couldn't have said it better myself," Mr. Lloyd said.

Nicholas took a moment as if he was going to say something else when Mr. Lloyd cut him off. "Now, get going."

Nicholas looked down, "Yes, sir." He reached out to give back the flashlight, but Mr. Lloyd shook his head.

"You keep it; it might come in handy."

Nicholas nodded, thinking, *It'd probably be more handy if it worked all the time.* He tucked it in his back pocket all the same. He and Dusk made their way to the door.

After they exited the library, there was a moment where they just stood there in silence. The night was still and dark, although not as suffocating as it was when Nicholas had left Winter's Hall.

"So," Dusk said, shuffling. "What are we going to do about that doctor?"

And with that, the fight was over. It wasn't like it didn't happen, but it was all in the past. Dusk was a man of few words, especially when it came to apologies. Aunt Sherri had told Nicholas once that his father had been the same way.

After Nicholas collected his bike, they walked toward Nicholas's home, where Dusk would drop Nicholas off on his way to Winter's Hall. The whole while they talked about what Nicholas had found out, what needed to be done about it, and where they were going to begin tomorrow night.

Mr. Lloyd had his back to the night as he locked up the library when a voice made him jump.

"Evening, Mr. Lloyd."

Mr. Lloyd found himself face-to-face with Sheriff Gordon. He let out a huge sigh of relief.

"Oh, Sheriff. It's just you."

"You were expecting someone else?" Sheriff Gordon said, half joking, half waiting for an answer.

"No, no one at this hour anyway. You just surprised me, that's all." Mr. Lloyd took a moment to catch his breath. "What brings Pointe's Hollow's sheriff all the way over here in the middle of the night?"

Sheriff Gordon looked around at the library as if trying to see inside, "Nothing big, Mr. Lloyd. Just making my rounds. Saw you were burning the midnight oil and thought I'd come by, ask you a few questions."

Mr. Lloyd felt the blood run out of his face. He hoped the darkness would conceal his panic from the sheriff. "Fire away," he said, smiling.

Sheriff Gordon looked the librarian over, as if sizing him up. Mr Lloyd knew that this was no friendly visit. It was all business.

"I was just wondering if you had noticed anything strange in town recently?"

Mr. Lloyd appeared to be thinking back over the last few days, but all he was thinking was how not to mention what had happened in the last few minutes. Mr. Lloyd held no illusions that what he was about to do was wrong. Lying to the authorities was one of the last things Mr. Lloyd wanted to do, but he also knew he couldn't tell Sheriff Gordon about Nicholas and what he was doing. Not because he didn't trust the sheriff, but because he knew how it would sound.

"Nope, can't say that I have," Mr. Lloyd said easily.

"Really?" Sheriff Gordon said, raising an eyebrow. "Not anything out of the ordinary? No new people about town?"

"You mean other than the army," Mr. Lloyd said. This seemed to take Sheriff Gordon off guard.

"Yes, other than them."

Mr. Lloyd thought, and then once again said, "I'm sorry, Sheriff. If it isn't happening right here in this library, I don't pay it much attention."

Sheriff Gordon raised his eyebrow. "You sure now?"

The sheriff was prying. Had he seen something? Mr. Lloyd couldn't tell. Luckily, Mr. Lloyd had a few tricks up his sleeve that always put people in their place.

"I'm sure. I may be old Sheriff, but I ain't daft yet," Mr. Lloyd said with a listen-here-sonny tone. The approach worked. Sheriff Gordon backed off slightly and dropped his eyes to his boots.

"I'm sorry, Mr. Lloyd. I don't mean to be a bother. It's just with all these murders, we can't afford to leave any stone unturned."

Mr. Lloyd let out a breath, "I understand, Sheriff. These are troubling times for all of us."

"Troubling times indeed," Sheriff Gordon said slyly.

"How'd you get that bump right there?" Sheriff Gordon pointed to Mr. Lloyd's forehead.

Mr. Lloyd raised his hand to his forehead. His fingers came away sticky, warm, and red. Mr. Lloyd felt his body go rigid.

"You know it was the darndest thing," Mr. Lloyd chuckled, half nerves, half acting. "I went to put a book away, a real heavy one, and…. Well, it must have not been on the shelf all the way, 'cause it toppled off and knocked me right in the head. I thought it had stopped bleeding."

Mr. Lloyd smiled weakly.

"Best put some ice on it when you get home. Looks like it may swell."

Mr. Lloyd sighed, "Will do."

Sheriff Gordon looked him over again.

"Well," Sheriff Gordon said, shoving his thumbs into his waistband, pushing his belt forward, and shifting his weight to his right foot. "You have a good night, Mr. Lloyd."

Mr. Lloyd smiled and nodded. "You as well, Sheriff." He gave the Sheriff one last smile before walking past him on the way to the car.

"Oh, and Mr. Lloyd," Sheriff Gordon said. Mr. Lloyd looked back. "Best start locking up earlier. It's dangerous to be out late at night anymore."

Mr. Lloyd smiled and said, "Can't remember a time when it was safe in this town."

There was a moment of silence before Sheriff Gordon gave Mr. Lloyd a friendly wave over his shoulder as he walked away to his car.

The door to his cruiser closed behind Sheriff Gordon

with a soft thud. He was not a stupid man. Mr. Lloyd knew more than he was letting on. He didn't get to be the sheriff in a small town without knowing how to tell when someone was lying to him. However, he didn't have any evidence, so he would have to be patient.

Unfortunately, he had been too patient, and the past few days had finally caught up with him. Once the boy had disappeared into the library, it wasn't long before Sheriff Gordon found himself stirring awake in his car. After rubbing the sleep from his eyes, he looked toward the library. The kid's bike was gone, and no one was in sight. He was about to drive away when he saw Mr. Lloyd come out of the library. He had questioned the librarian in an attempt to salvage his missed opportunity with the boy.

Why hadn't the sheriff pressed Mr. Lloyd for more details?

Wasn't the right time.

If Sheriff Gordon pushed too hard, Mr. Lloyd would inform the man before the sheriff could find him.

Also, the sheriff appreciated and liked the librarian. He didn't want to make Mr. Lloyd the bad guy, because he wasn't. Sheriff Gordon didn't know his part in all this, but he knew it wasn't bad, couldn't be.

Sheriff Gordon sighed. He needed to be getting home. The whole night had taken way too long. Emily would no doubt be in bed by now. She knew not to stay up for him. Sheriff Gordon would crack her door to check in on her. It would be just as he always did. When she was younger, he would sit and watch her sleep for hours. He would trade the entire town for a chance to peek in at her. His town was important, but his daughter was precious.

The dark clothed stranger would have to wait until tomorrow. His family was the most important thing. Sometimes, that importance consisted of the entire town, but not tonight. Tonight it was all about Emily.

Dusk

Sheriff Gordon turned his key in the ignition, yanked the car into gear, and drove all the way home without a single look back at the library.

Sitting in the front pew of his church, Father Christopher awaited a visitor. As a child trying to cope with this sight, Father Christopher, just Chris then, had tried to explain the phenomenon in a lot of different ways. He thought he might be a wizard of some sort. Like Merlin from King Arthur's Court. This was high on his list until he was disappointed by his attempts at doing true magic.

Luckily, once he learned how to control his gift, he didn't need to figure out what it was. A great voice told him what he was. An angel.

At the time, Father Christopher believed it was God, but over time he realized that God was just a title for something people didn't understand, something even Father Christopher couldn't explain, even in the vaguest terms.

What could be proved was that there was honest good in the world, which he saw in Richard and Nicholas. There was also evil in the world; what came out of The Other proved that beyond a shadow of a doubt. Sometimes, these two forces of white and black mingled into a grayness, but there was always those two. He didn't know what came before these two or if anything would stand once they were gone. He knew only that he was part of it. He was a protector, put on this Earth to look after this town, Richard, and most importantly, Nicholas.

There was a slight creek from behind him. He tilted his head ever so slightly. A small, soft smile came across his face.

"I have been waiting for you," Father Christopher said.

He stood, turning to face his end. The man who stood in front of him, for it was just a man, was not one of the monsters Father Christopher helped Dusk fight off over the last years. Of course, Father Christopher knew who the man was. He knew everyone in Pointe's Hollow, and it was no real surprise. He had been seeing this man approach him and kill him for years.

"Waiting a long time," Father Christopher continued.

There was a flash behind him, followed by a cold rush of gooseflesh over his neck. Father Christopher closed his eyes. He heard the man approach, but he seemed slow and sluggish. When the man finally reached him, it was over quickly and without pain. There was coldness, but Father Christopher felt warm all over. It was easy to accept something he had known was coming for so long. It felt good to be confirmed, to be fulfilled.

As everything went dark, this is what Father Christopher thought about. He was a protector, a guardian, an angel, and he was going home. Wherever home was.

Chapter 19

School went by in a blur. Nicholas was too busy thinking about where they would search tonight for the doctor. He and Dusk had planned the night before. Back and forth, they tried to determine logical places that the doctor from the magazine would work. In the end, the only conclusion they had drawn was that Pointe's Hollow was not a place to be for any scientific work whatsoever.

No progress on finding the murderer was seen from the military. Of course, that hadn't slowed them down, only pushed them harder. Their presence had doubled, if not tripled, in the past forty-eight hours, which made what Nicholas and Dusk were trying to do so much harder.

But they had to do it. They were so close, Nicholas could almost taste it. Like an aftertaste stuck on your tongue after eating a spicy salsa. They needed to finish this, and if luck was on their side, it would be tonight.

Unfortunately, luck would be on their side, but in the worst possible way.

The school bell rang. Nicholas hopped on his bike,

stopped by his house to pick up the knife Dusk had given him, and was halfway to Dusk's before he even thought about everything he was riding into and who he was riding away from. His aunt, Mr. Lloyd, Mr. Fidel, Emily.

Emily, Nicholas thought, remembering their last encounter.

He should have apologized today, but he was too busy being an emotional zombie. Lost in thought in a different part of the world.

Damn it. Life was so much easier before... all of this. Nicholas thought that this was just life. Juggling things like relationships, work, and play.

And monsters, can't forget monsters.

This time Nicholas didn't knock. He walked up, turned the handle, and entered, like one does at a best friend's house. It suddenly occurred to Nicholas that it was exactly like that. He didn't really have any friends, but if he had to choose a best friend, it would be Dusk. It was made stranger only because they had known each other only for the past week. But their connection went deeper than that, somehow. Nicholas couldn't explain it.

Dusk was right where Nicholas had expected to find him, sitting on the couch in the room off of the left side of the great hall. It was a surprise, however, to see him drinking a can of Coca-Cola instead of his usual beer.

"I know, I know," Dusk said as he saw Nicholas looking at the Coke. "Don't get used to it. I've put back about five of these in the last few hours, and I'm still thirsty."

Nicholas smiled and raised his hands in a defensive gesture as if to say, 'Hey, I'm not saying anything.' He took his own place in a large armchair across from the couch Dusk sat on.

"So, what's the plan?"

Dusk raised a finger as he drained the last of the Coke. "I've been thinking about that." He put the can down hard on the small coffee table. It made a hollow clang, and then Dusk sat back once again. "I think the best thing to do is to pay a little visit to your teacher, Mr. Fido."

"Fidel," Nicholas corrected.

"Whatever," Dusk said, waving his hand. "If he really is as into this doctor as you say he is, it'd be a good idea to find out what he knows."

It seemed too easy, like cheating, like seeing the card before the actor began the charade. Nicholas knew this was absurd; there was no cheating when trying to stop a murdering psychopath, but it still felt wrong. But when Nicholas thought of the bodies of Earl Hutchins and Jennifer Harper, he shook the feeling out of his head. Nicholas was about to respond when a shrill noise cut him off.

Nicholas realized it was the telephone. In the far corner of the room on a small table sat the warbling telephone. It was as if it had been placed there for this exact moment, staged almost.

Dusk looked over at it. Nicholas could read the concern on his face. Nicholas didn't know what the phone meant or who would be calling Dusk. Only a handful of people knew he existed, let alone lived in Pointe's Hollow. Without a word, Dusk stood and went to it. It had time to ring once more before Dusk lifted it off the cradle. Dusk raised the handset to the side of his head, but didn't say anything. Nicholas could faintly hear the sound of a voice on the other end. Nicholas immediately felt cold. The voice didn't affect Nicholas, but the color running out of Dusk's face put the ice in Nicholas's veins.

There was a soft click, loud enough for Nicholas to hear through the phone. Dusk moved the phone in front of his face to look at it as if to make sure he was actually holding it and that what he heard hadn't been a dream.

"What is it?" Nicholas asked, afraid of the answer.

Dusk hung up the phone and looked out the window

toward town. "Nothing good," he said, voice wavering. "We need to get to the church."

"Right now? What about Mr. Fidel?" Nicholas asked.

"It'll have to wait," Dusk said quietly with a hint of sadness. "Let's go."

Dusk hurried out of the room. Nicholas fell over himself trying to follow. They both rushed out of Winter's Hall on no discernible path, but in the general direction of the town.

Steam billowed from the boiling pot as Emily poured in the noodles. For as long as she could remember, Emily had been in charge of making dinner. If she didn't, her father would eat some grease-filled burger or pizza from one of the shops. He'd eat that crap every night if it wasn't for her. Now, she wasn't a chef nor a miracle worker. Mostly, she made dishes that were quick and easy. Once she tried to make a healthier dinner by starting with a salad. Her dad had just scoffed, called the spread rabbit food, and ordered a pizza.

America, Emily thought. *Clogged arteries only a phone call away.*

She stirred the noodles in the bubbling water. The noodles began to soften and tangle into a stringy mess within the water. The steam hit her face, and she wiped her brow thinking, not for the first time, that it was warmer than normal. She had spent her entire life in The Hollow, and in a normal year, she would have her sweaters and coats on stand-by in her closet. As it stood, she was still sporting her short sleeve shirts and, sometimes, even shorts.

Leaving the noodles to do what noodles do, she went to

the cupboard and pulled down two dishes. After placing the plates on the table, she also grabbed two forks and two napkins. Once they were properly placed on the table, she returned to the noodles. They were almost to the point of tasting.

She once again went to a cupboard and pulled down two glasses. One glass she set on the table, the other she took to the sink. After filling it up, she took two long drinks of the liquid, feeling instantly cooler. She refilled the glass and placed that one on the table as well.

This time, when she returned to the noodles, she fished one out. Being careful not to burn herself, she bit off half the noodle and chewed. *Not bad,* she thought. *But can it pass the real test?* She wound back and tossed the rest of the noodle at the cupboard from which she had pulled the glasses. The cooked noodle stuck to the wood in a squiggly knot. After a moment, the noodle began to walk down the cupboard like an intoxicated slinky.

Perfect, Emily thought as she turned off the burner and placed the strainer in the sink. Now that everything was set, Emily's mind wandered onto more interesting things. Like Nicholas Wake. She found herself thinking about Nicholas more and more. At first she thought the boy was into her as much as she was into him. But now she wasn't so sure. Their conversation, if you could call it that, after school had been less than spectacular.

Spectacular? I would have settled for okay.

The noodles bounced about as she shook the final drops of water from them. As she poured the noodles back into the pot, she heard the cruiser pull into the drive, followed by the slamming of a car door and the opening of the front door.

"Hey, Dad," Emily called over her shoulder.

"Hey, honey, what's for dinner?"

"Spaghetti."

"Mm, my favorite."

He said that no matter what Emily made. Except 'rabbit food,' of course; then, pizza was his favorite.

"I'll be in in a sec. Just gotta lock up and wash up."

This was another one of his sayings. Every time he walked into the house when he was coming from police business he'd 'lock up and wash up,' which meant he went to lock up his gun in the small gun safe he kept in the top drawer of his nightstand and then wash his hands. He'd always wash his hands. Even if they weren't eating, he'd go into the bathroom and scrub away. Emily saw it as cleaning the sheriff off of him. Once he was locked up and washed up, he was her dad and nothing else.

"Alright, I'll get your plate ready," she said, getting louder as he disappeared farther and farther into the house. She placed the pot of noodles on a cool burner and popped open a jar of Ragú. The sauce spilled into the pot, and with a few stirs of her spoon, dinner was done.

Emily scooped out a more than generous helping onto her father's plate and followed that up with a more reasonably sized pile on her own plate. When the plates were returned to the table, Emily heard her dad entering the kitchen, wiping his hands on his pants.

"Everything looks great," he said.

"Thanks," Emily returned. "Hurry up and sit before it gets cold."

Her dad walked around the table and took his seat. He had his fork in his hand before Emily replaced the pot on the stove.

"What's the green flecks in the sauce?"

Emily just shook her head, "It's Ragú sauce, Dad. You like Ragú."

He just huffed and took a small bite. After a few seconds of chewing, he said, "So I do."

Paranoid old man, Emily thought lovingly. Before she sat down, she went and opened the fridge.

Dusk

"Emily, did you grab me a...." He stopped mid-sentence as she held out a can of Coca-Cola. "Thanks," he said, cracking open the pop and pouring it into the glass.

"You're welcome," Emily said as she took her own seat and sat down. They ate in silence for a moment, enjoying the food. Then, as she always did, she asked how his day was.

"It was alright, not done yet, though. I'll be out late again hoping to make some progress on this certain case I got right now."

Emily didn't know why he said it like that. She, of course, knew which case he would be working on. She had known Jennifer Harper fairly well, and her death was all anyone could talk about at school. *Except Nicholas,* Emily thought sadly. *It doesn't seem like he can talk about anything, at least not to me.*

"Any leads?"

Her dad chewed through a mouthful of spaghetti as he just shrugged. He wouldn't talk about cases, not in front of her. She believed it was his way of keeping her safe, and she appreciated it, but she also wished she could know more about what was going on.

"What about you? Got anything going on with school?"

Emily took a cue from her dad and just shrugged. "Same old, same old. Teachers, homework, hormones."

Her father scoffed at this. She liked poking fun at her dad about teenager stuff. It always made him uncomfortable. If she didn't know any better, she would have believed he had never been a teenager. People around town always talked about him as an old, tough, and fair man.

"Speaking of that, I was wondering if you had talked to the Wake boy recently."

The mention of Nicholas's name caught Emily off guard. "What?"

Her father looked right at her. "The Wake boy?"

262

"You mean Nicholas."

"Yes, him. You two talk recently?"

Emily looked down at her plate. "No, not really." Their last conversation played back in her mind, and she felt her cheeks grow warm.

"Good. That's good."

"Why is that good?" Emily's voice came out a little harsher than she had intended. It was not directed at her father; it was just her anger at Nicholas.

"I just think it's better that you two keep your distance from each other."

"Dad," she said, brushing his concern aside. There hadn't been many boys in Emily's life. A few crushes here or there, but not much. No matter how little the thing was, however, her dad was always there to disapprove.

"I'm serious, Emily."

"But why?"

"I just think it's for the best. You don't know what that boy is like and with everything happening, I think it's safest to just keep everyone at arm's reach right now."

Emily was stunned by this. Her dad had always been protective, but if he was suggesting what she thought he was suggesting, well then, she didn't know what to think anymore.

"You think Nicholas has something to do with Jennifer's death?" The words just came out. Once she heard herself say them, they sounded even more absurd.

"I'm not gonna talk about that at the dinner table."

That wasn't a no, Emily thought. She couldn't believe what she was hearing. This had to be against some rule somewhere. Sure, dads are supposed to dislike the guy their daughters are interested in. That's standard, but to suspect them of murder?

"There's no way," Emily spit out. "There's no way Nicholas has anything to do with what's going on."

"Emily, you don't know that. You don't know him. I've seen him with some very shady characters, and he's too quiet. You can't trust a boy that's too quiet."

"You suspect him because he's quiet?" Emily's voice was rising. She didn't know why she felt the need to defend Nicholas to her father. He had blown her off the day before and had not talked to her at all at school today. But in a way, her father was attacking her judgment, her choice, and in the end, her.

"That's not what I said. I only meant...."

"No, Dad, that's what you said. You said you couldn't trust a boy that's quiet. You just said it."

"Yes, but that's not what I meant. I've seen him lurking around town."

"Lurking?" Emily said frantically. "You've seen him lurking?"

"Emily, look, I'm not going to get into it with you. I just want you to be safe."

"And you're saying Nicholas is dangerous. You're saying Nicholas is killing people?"

Her father looked down at his plate. "I said I'm not going to talk about this."

Emily shook her head, unwilling to accept his resignation. "But that's what you think. It has to be, or why else would you bring it up."

"I said, I'm not going to talk about this, Emily!" Sheriff Gordon pounded his fist against the table, making everything shake.

Emily jumped back, away from the table. There was a second of complete stillness, and then Emily spoke up, "I've got a lot of homework to do, so I'm going to finish dinner in my room."

She collected her dinner things and left the kitchen. Her dad sat at the table, tired and sad, but Emily refused to look back.

As they walked, Nicholas began to realize it was a lot warmer than it had been when he arrived at Dusk's. The air felt heavy and wet. A muggy feeling had thickened the air and made it feel like the Amazon rather than Northern Michigan in November. They should be expecting snow soon, not hot weather.

Through the trees, Nicholas caught glimpses of the lake, the lighthouse perched on its isle and the waves slowly rolling in.

And the clouds, Nicholas thought. Giant, dark rain clouds moved in from the horizon. He was sure it would storm soon, and with those clouds, everything outdoors would be getting a bit wet.

They made it to the edge of town. Nicholas was breathing hard, because Dusk had been keeping a constant pace that would have winded a dog. They surveyed the town. The church was on the other side, the fastest way to it was through town. Unfortunately, the military had decided to make tonight a particularly busy night for the small town.

Soldiers walked up and down the streets looking out for anything peculiar. It was bad luck that Nicholas was walking with one of the most peculiar guys in Pointe's Hollow, possibly the entire state. They were going to have to be careful and not draw attention to themselves.

They moved in. Dusk did not want to slow his pace, but did while they were in eyesight of anyone. Every time the person or people dropped out of sight, he would change gears and hustle forward.

Turning a corner onto Harbor Street, Dusk slowed down to a crawl. Once Nicholas caught up, he saw why. A group of soldiers stood only a few yards ahead. Standing in a small circle, they exchanged jokes and cigarettes. Guys were trading brands back and forth as they puffed lit ones.

Nicholas checked to see if they should cross the street. They probably could, but it might look awkward changing direction so quickly to avoid the soldiers. In the end, that could do more harm than good. The only option was to continue forward as they were, straight into the circle of soldiers.

Dusk made a little motion with his hand, and Nicholas moved to his right side so Dusk was between him and the soldiers. Nicholas wasn't sure if this was wise. He was the local. Him, not Dusk. If people saw him walking around, they wouldn't think twice. Dusk would be talked about in hushed tones like all big secrets in small towns.

But knowing it was better to follow Dusk's lead than go his own path, Nicholas moved to Dusk's right, bowing his head a little to stay out of sight.

They reached the soldiers. Nicholas could feel the toxic cigarette smoke scratching at the back of his throat. Voices came through, too.

One guy said, "And then, then she said that she was tired and had a long ride home. I told her to save the cab fare, she could have a long ride right here."

The other men laughed, like it was the funniest thing in the world. A puff of cigarette smoke billowed around Dusk and right into Nicholas's face, burning his eyes. Squinting, he tried not to rub his eyes. He didn't, but as he was preoccupied with that urge, there was a tickle in the back of his throat, and he let out a cough. Low and ragged, it came out in hacks.

The blood ran from his face as he heard the shuffle directly behind them. He turned and met the faces of all the soldiers. Nicholas didn't know if he should run or beg for mercy.

One of the guys took another drag on his cigarette and

then blew a long trail of smoke out of the side of his mouth.

Here it comes, Nicholas thought, cringing.

He said, "Sorry, kid," and turned back to the rest of the group without a second thought.

Nicholas felt the blood return to his extremities, and they moved through town, crossing Harbor Street and disappearing into the woods behind Richie's Bar.

They were through the main section of Pointe's Hollow, but Dusk still hadn't told Nicholas who had been on the phone and what was so urgent that they had to put their plans on hold. In the end, Nicholas was glad Dusk hadn't told him anything. If he had, Nicholas might not have wanted to come.

The church finally came into view. Its peak rose above the top of the trees, just as it had the last time Nicholas had visited. As they rounded the church, Nicholas's bones turned icy.

Dusk stood like a statue in front of the church. Nicholas, jogging to catch up, rounded the corner just a moment after Dusk. He, too, stopped dead in his tracks.

The door to the church was wide open. The interior sat dark, like a dungeon waiting for a brave traveler to enter and fall victim to the horrors within.

Dusk sucked in a breath, then pulled out his revolver and clicked back the hammer. He took one step toward the church, followed by another. Dusk had taken three steps before Nicholas even took one.

They climbed the steps, careful to not move too fast. The door stood at the top like a black hole with an interior so dark it seemed solid. The shutters must have been closed on the windows inside, because no light seemed to penetrate the darkness. Nicholas was lucky Dusk was in front. If he were the first one to face the portal, he knew he wouldn't be able to go on.

The revolver in Dusk's hand was the first thing to

pierce the inky blackness. Its silver barrel disappeared into the shadows followed by Dusk's hand. When his hand hit the darkness, he hesitated for just a second. Then, he rushed in.

A great distance seemed to rise between the two of them, Dusk inside the church, Nicholas on the outside. It took everything he had, but Nicholas swallowed hard and entered.

Once he was in, his eyes took time to adjust. A moment later, things came into view. Dark shapes upon other dark shapes piled on top of one another, creating the interior of the church.

There was a smell Nicholas couldn't place. He was familiar with the smell, but he couldn't remember where from. He stepped forward, trying to catch up with Dusk. Without Dusk next to him, the feeling of loneliness was palpable. Nicholas kept walking forward. Looking around the blackness of dark blobs, Nicholas tried to remember the layout of the church.

Suddenly, he realized that one dark blob he expected to be in the church wasn't there anymore. Dusk was not in front of him. Just as Nicholas was about to whisper his name, his foot slipped on something, and he struggled to catch himself. A hand went out wildly and landed on a church pew. Nicholas steadied himself and released the pew. His hand came away wet and sticky.

What the hell? Nicholas thought as he spread his fingers. Unfortunately, the darkness was so thick he couldn't even see the hand in front of his face.

CLICK.

Nicholas turned around at the sound of the lights above him coming to life. He saw Dusk, gun still at the ready, standing with his other hand still on the light switch he had just flicked.

"God almighty," Dusk said as he looked around Nicholas.

Nicholas was confused. His fingers came together and spread once again. Looking at them, Nicholas saw dark red covering his palm.

No, Nicholas thought.

Through his fingers, he saw his foot was also covered in the dark crimson.

Please, not that. Anything but that. Not....

Blood.

The church was covered in it. The floor, pews, walls, light fixtures, everything that could be reached was drenched in the dark bodily fluid. Some had begun to coagulate, other portions still flowed and dripped.

It was the most terrible thing Nicholas had ever seen. A few days ago, that wouldn't have really meant anything, but now, it was a whole different level. He probably would have fainted or vomited, but he had been preparing himself for something terrible. This, however, he had not expected.

There was a soft shuffle, and Nicholas was aware that Dusk was next to him, but he couldn't look away from the obscene horror laid out in front of him.

"What happened?" Nicholas asked.

An answer was unnecessary, nor wanted, because Nicholas knew in his heart what had happened. Blood poured out over the church pews, displayed for them to see. Blood from Earl Hutchins, Jennifer Harper, and....

No, we don't know that yet, Nicholas thought, cutting off the notion of the probable third victim.

As Nicholas was trying to fight the idea, he saw them: four white bars laid on the steps at the far end of the church. Everything else was stained red except those four bars. No, not bars, they were too round. After a few moments of distant inspection, Nicholas made a startling discovery.

"Are those...." But Nicholas couldn't, nor did he need to, finish.

"Limbs," Dusk said. His voice was cold, distant. He

walked forward, stepping from tile to blood-coated tile as if he didn't even notice the difference. Nicholas, on the other hand, took a step back out of the blood and wiped his hand on his jeans. Dusk's footsteps made plopping noises. Small blood ripples extended from the souls of his boots. They arched out and rebounded off the legs of the pews.

As he reached the limbs, he slowed, lowered himself over them, and picked up each in turn. After he inspected each one, he replaced it on the altar. He stood and turned to the left, looking about the room.

"It's him," Dusk said, still harsh.

Nicholas knew who Dusk meant. Father Christopher.

A burning began in the back of Nicholas's eyes. He didn't want to cry. He really didn't know Father Christopher well, but it still hurt. It hurt that he and Dusk had not been able to stop whoever was doing this before another person had died. But no matter how Nicholas felt, he knew it was only a fraction of Dusk's pain.

A single tear swelled in his left eye. He turned so Dusk couldn't see him and raised a hand to wipe it away.

When he looked away, he saw a single pew in the back row with a clean spot. The spot was pristine. This wouldn't have been so strange, except the outline was that of a body. On the back rest of the pew, faint outlines of arms and shoulders were visible. The seat showed phantom legs as if someone had been sitting on the pew as blood was spilled around the room. It was the only spot that didn't have blood on it and sitting in the middle of that blood-free patch was a Bible.

They were in a church, so a Bible wasn't too far-fetched, but it was too perfect to be sitting there by accident. He went over to the pew to inspect the find. Nicholas picked up the Bible.

It felt heavy. He turned the book over in his hand, feeling the cover and binding, trying to discern anything out of the ordinary. It said nothing but, 'I'm a dirty, old, dingy Bible.'

Nicholas took a quick look up at Dusk. He had moved away from the limbs and was looking for clues, trying not to be affected by the death of his friend.

Going back to the Bible, Nicholas let the book fall open in his hands to whatever page it wanted. The book, that some think holds all the answers, gave Nicholas an answer to a question he didn't even ask.

"Dusk!" Nicholas said, staring at the pages.

Nicholas didn't look up, but he heard the plop-plop of Dusk approaching.

"What is it?" Dusk said.

Nicholas didn't answer; he just held up the book. Dusk took it. Nicholas watched Dusk read the words written in blood on the page.

Sheriff Gordon sat at a small, wrought iron table outside of Berk's Bakery sipping an old fashioned cup of coffee. The cup was so fresh that warm waves of coffee smells wafted through the lid and wrapped themselves around his nose.

It had been a long day, and even though it was much later than his normal time to enjoy a cup of Berk's coffee,

Sheriff Gordon thought it was the exact thing he needed. Not only had the progress on his murder investigation slowed, the military's presence had more than complicated his life. Beginning with his meeting with Captain Hayward and ending with their stunt at the town meeting. All that piled on the fight with Emily was more than Sheriff Gordon could take without a bit of caffeine.

Every day that passed, more and more people seemed to show up in his town wearing uniforms and carrying guns. It upset Sheriff Gordon, because he knew it made his townspeople, his family, feel uncomfortable. Too many guns, in a small area, led only to bad things.

From where he sat in front of Berk's Bakery, Sheriff Gordon could see down Harbor Street. At the end of the street, past the vacant lot, the sheriff could see out across the docks. The cool, blue water rolled in, unperturbed by the military's presence here in The Hollow.

Sheriff Gordon took another sip from his cup. The warm brew slipped down his throat. Once he finished, his lips popped, and he rubbed his mustache clean of remnants. A low rumble came from out over the water. It looked like they were about to get some rain in The Hollow.

Two soldiers walked by him. They were out of place, making the small town community feel like a prison.

A prison, with a psycho murderer on the inside.

Sheriff Gordon raised his cup of coffee again, watching the soldiers walk away. The cup stopped before it reached his lips. Past the soldiers, something caught his eye. Down at the end of the street, Sheriff Gordon saw the man in black walking at a quick pace. In tow behind him was the Wake boy.

Well, I'll be a monkey's uncle.

The sheriff lowered the cup, forgotten. He stood up and walked toward them. He wasn't sure what he was going to do. Arrest them? Question them? Shoot them? Most likely not the latter, but he couldn't be sure.

While in stride, he deposited his coffee cup into a wastebasket on the curb. The two were about to reach his side of the sidewalk. Sheriff Gordon had a lot of ground to make up. If he was going to catch them, he was going to have to....

"Ah, Sheriff!"

Sheriff Gordon had heard that voice only a few times in his life, but it had been a few times too many. It had already been burned into his memory.

"Captain," Sheriff Gordon said, stopping. "To what do I owe the pleasure?"

Captain Hayward walked up, flanked by two soldiers. How had he not seen them?

Damn tunnel vision, Sheriff Gordon said.

He saw the man in black and the Wake boy jump up onto his side of the street and continue off.

Captain Hayward squinted at Sheriff Gordon and then turned to see what he had been looking at. The two had disappeared behind the buildings.

"What were you looking at?" Captain Hayward asked.

Sheriff Gordon wanted to say, 'None of your Goddamn business, you adolescent prick.' Instead, he nodded toward the lake and said, "Storm's rolling in."

Captain Hayward inspected the clouds, frowned, and nodded as if that made sense. "I see." He turned back to the sheriff. "Well, anyway, I'm looking to take a boat and a few of my men out to that island out there in the bay."

Sheriff Gordon's eyes turned to the small island with the lighthouse that sat perfectly in the center of Pointe's Hollow's cove.

"Nothing out there but the old lighthouse building. Ol' Steve McPherson goes out there 'bout once a month to clean up and make sure everything's still working. It's got some pretty views when the sun's going down, but that's all."

Dusk

Captain Hayward frowned again. "With all due respect, Sheriff," the captain began. This only made Sheriff Gordon hate him more. People didn't say, 'With all due respect' unless they were going to follow up with something disrespectful.

"If we took your word on everything, we would still be at square one with these killings."

This irritated the sheriff, but he heard deep within the lines that they had made some progress on the case.

"You have something?" Sheriff Gordon asked.

Captain Hayward smiled, "If we did, Sheriff, it would be classified far above your pay grade." Captain Hayward's eyes narrowed quickly, "Why, do you have something?"

Sheriff Gordon looked off distantly after his top suspects, who were most likely halfway to their hideout by now.

"Sheriff?" Captain Hayward pushed.

"Nope, nothing at all, Captain. Head on down to the docks, ask for Steve. Tell him I sent you. He'll ferry you across."

Captain Hayward nodded, "Thank you, Sheriff. Your cooperation is appreciated." The words were nice, but his tone said otherwise.

"Happy to help," Sheriff Gordon laid it on thick.

Captain Hayward smirked, turned, and headed for the docks, soldiers following in step behind him.

Sheriff Gordon watched them go and then glanced to the island with the lighthouse on it. He continued turning his head to the right, looking along the coast until his eyes saw beyond the buildings directly in front of him the two people who had had his fancy for the past few days.

The sheriff pulled keys from his pocket.

Time for a little drive.

Chapter 20

Wind howled through the forest, and the pines moaned in response. It had grown late, but the clouds rolling in from the lake made it feel even later. A storm was coming, and mixed with the unseasonal warmth, it was going to be a bad one. Thunder rumbled as if to warn everyone to seek shelter.

Dusk and Nicholas fought through the wind toward Winter's Hall. It was an unconscious fear, but Nicholas had the strangest feeling they were running to their own deaths. By the way Dusk was keeping quiet, Nicholas had a suspicion that he felt the same way. It was unsettling to think of Dusk being afraid of the same thing he was, and they both were heading blindly into it.

The gravel shifted, and stones bounced around their feet. Dusk was ahead of Nicholas by only a few feet. When he skidded to a stop, Nicholas had to do everything he could to not run into him. He looked at Dusk, confused.

"Son of a bitch," Dusk said, grinding his teeth.

Nicholas turned to see what he was looking at and was greeted by a horrific sight. The gate to Winter's Hall had been smashed inward. Both sides hung loosely on snapped hinges. The long-time battlefront of the old house had been defeated in one quick blow.

Thinking back to the entrance on the road, Nicholas remembered someone had done the same thing to the brush pile on the road's entrance. Two rows of tire treads had ripped through the faux growth and sent twigs everywhere.

Dusk pulled out his revolver as Nicholas inspected the sight.

"Stay behind me, kid. This will most likely get worse before it's over."

Nicholas nodded, understanding that if it didn't on its own, Dusk would make it worse. His emotions were on high. He was hurt, and he wanted retribution.

They took off again, rushing toward the hall. It had been a sanctuary for them both, but now it seemed to tower over them. They were so distracted by the house and who could be in it that they didn't see the vehicle parked further up in the yard.

Nicholas looked up as if to face off against the house itself.

That's when he saw the shadow. On the second story stood a large multi-paneled window. The window wasn't unsettling in itself, but what was in the window was. There was a light and within the light, the silhouette of a man standing, looking upon them.

"Dusk, look!" Nicholas pointed up at the window, still running toward the door. Dusk slowed enough to get a good look up. He didn't say anything, just snarled and kept moving.

When they reached the house, Dusk kicked in the front door. It flung open, pounding against the side wall. Dusk stopped on a dime, revolver pointed forward, a fire in his eyes.

The house stood silent. Dried leaves rustled across the

tiled floor. Nothing had been disturbed on this first level. It looked exactly the way they had left it.

"He's upstairs, in the library." Dusk motioned toward the stairs.

They pushed forward, slower than the dash outside, but still moving briskly. Mounting the stairs, Dusk ascended with the gun pointed up to the second floor. Nicholas was taking the stairs two at a time to keep up with Dusk. His heart was pounding, and his hands began to shake.

On the second floor, they continued forward faster. Nicholas's heart was racing right out of his chest, his breath coming in short gasps.

They came to a room with a faint, orange glow emitting below the door. Dusk looked back to Nicholas and pointed at the door with his gun. Nicholas nodded. Pushing by Dusk, Nicholas grabbed the door handle, took a breath, and opened the door.

They entered the room.

The room rose to an enormous height. On both walls, bookcases extended the scale of the room and were stuffed to the brim with books. Within the room was a large desk where the lamp sat. In front of the desk were two lounge chairs and a thick leather couch. Everything in the room was covered in a layer of dust. Like a tomb, the air felt stagnate from vacancy.

"It's bad manners to keep your guests waiting, Mr. Dusk," the man said without turning away from the window.

The voice sounded familiar to Nicholas, but in that moment, he couldn't place it.

"Yeah, well, it's also rude to come over unannounced," Dusk retorted, gun arm raised and pointed at the man. "And killing the host's friend is also thought of as bad taste, you bastard."

The man let out a little chuckle. A maniacal tone rushed over the room. "Well, luckily, I'm not one to thrive on ceremony."

Something he said caught in Nicholas's mind. *No,* he thought, *it can't be.*

The man turned around.

Mr. Fidel.

He stepped forward with his arms behind him and a diabolical smirk across his face.

"Mr. Fidel?" Nicholas said, blown away by this turn of events.

"Yes, Nicholas, but you should call me Daniel. I think it's safe to say we are beyond a normal student-teacher relationship."

Nicholas could not believe what he was seeing. Mr. Fidel? The history teacher who barely yelled at students in class was the man dismembering people all over town? It didn't make any sense.

"It can't be," Nicholas said under his breath.

"Ah, but it is. I am very sorry it had to be this way, Nicholas. With you on that side of the room and me on this side." He pointed to the two sides as if to emphasize the differences between them. "I really hoped that we could have come to this crossroad together."

Nicholas felt the pit of his stomach give a flop, and his head began to spin. The man he had considered a confidant was the man behind all of this, the cause of all the deaths and evil in Pointe's Hollow.

"You're the man in shadows?" Nicholas said, still unbelieving.

Mr. Fidel shook his head and looked disappointed. "If that's what you think, Nicholas, I have overestimated you."

Lightning flashed behind him, illuminating the room in stark, white light for a moment. Mr. Fidel turned as if half noticing the lightning. His eyes looked through the large window. Nicholas was across the room, but even from his spot, he saw what Mr. Fidel was looking at.

The lighthouse.

"It's almost time now. That one was close."

Nicholas had a moment of epiphany. It was as if the answers to a test were being fed directly into his head as he sat penciling in the bubbles. His mind's eye flew through the air and was suddenly seeing the lighthouse. A scene from a book he had just recently started rereading came to mind. Flashes only, but flashes were enough. Lightning, a doctor, and a monster.

"He's at the lighthouse," Nicholas said, without realizing he was saying it out loud.

"Very good, Nicholas." Mr. Fidel turned around, his arms still behind his back, facing away from the window toward the two of them once again. "But just a little too late."

Mr. Fidel began to walk around the large, oak desk that stood between them. He made it to the front corner and sat down, leaning on the desk, just as he had done in class a million times.

"I wish he could have been the one to tell you this, Nicholas, I really do. He is the only one that can really spin the mystical web that is his research."

"Is that how he ensnared you?" Dusk asked.

"He didn't have to. I was privileged to have the opportunity to help such a brilliant man. His research is groundbreaking, to say the least."

Mr. Fidel laced his fingers and rested his forearms on his knees. Nicholas wanted to blink and wake up in class. That's where Mr. Fidel belonged. Not here, not as a killer.

"You remember what I told you, Nicholas?" Mr. Fidel continued. "About Dr. Murdock's research?"

Nicholas remembered; of course, he did. It was all Nicholas could think about the past few days.

Mr. Fidel smiled and said, "Well, he did it. He found a way."

If Nicholas hadn't been so used to being slammed with

unbelievable news over the past few days, this would have floored him. Instead, it just knocked the wind from him. *Found a way?* Nicholas thought. *No. It was impossible.*

Nicholas looked at the gunslinger. His arm was raised, and he had not flinched at what Mr. Fidel said. If Nicholas hadn't known Dusk, he may not have noticed, but now it was unmistakable. His pupils shifted left and right just slightly, as if to say, 'He's wrong.'

"Nicholas, did you hear me? Dr. Murdock has found a way to bring people back from the dead." Mr. Fidel became very animated. "Dr. Murdock has found the secret to life."

"Bullshit." Dusk's words shook Nicholas.

Mr. Fidel's features contorted in pure hatred. "Bullshit? What do you know? You're a gun toting psychopath, not a scientist. Not a forward thinker like Dr. Murdock."

The way Mr. Fidel said the doctor's name was the way one said 'God' when a disbeliever challenged his teachings.

"I may like my metal here between my fingers," Dusk countered. "But believe me, I've been down this road and know more about death than most. The one thing I know for sure is that it's a one-way door."

Mr. Fidel clenched his fists for a second, but then waved Dusk's argument away as he spun, stood, and walked back toward the window.

"You think you know. But who are you? No one. You couldn't possibly question a great man like Dr. Murdock."

"Who are you?" Dusk asked. "A follower. A tool. Nothing more. Once he's done with you, you'll be pushed aside."

"NO!" Mr. Fidel screamed. Madness crept into his face, and his nostrils flared. "He didn't leave me when the first test went wrong, he won't leave me now!"

"First test?" This time it was Nicholas who spoke. "First test?"

Mr. Fidel made it back to the window, ignoring the

question. His eyes stared off dreamily toward the lighthouse. When he spoke again, his voice was softer. "He said he has found it. He promised me. He wouldn't lie to me again."

"You don't know for sure, do you?" Dusk said.

Mr. Fidel cringed at Dusk's voice. Then, he straightened. "No, Dusk. I am very sure." He turned. "I give you points for trying; even at this point in the game, your denial is admirable. Foolish, but admirable."

Mr. Fidel raised his hand as he spoke and fixed a few strands of hair that had fallen out of place.

"I'm not the only fool in the room," Dusk's voice cut like a knife.

"Nicholas," Mr. Fidel said, forcing Nicholas to look at him. "You believe, don't you?" Nicholas didn't say anything, but he heard himself swallow hard. "I know what this means to you. Your parents."

Nicholas's eyes immediately began to burn. Tears threatened to fall as a result of the mere mention of them. Or maybe it was more than that. Nicholas didn't want to admit it, especially in front of Dusk, but he really wanted Mr. Fidel to be right.

"How good will it be to have them back. A boy shouldn't grow up without a father, without a mother. You are so alone, I can see this." Mr. Fidel smiled. "I understand your longing. For years, I have feared my own mortality, but I don't have to anymore."

Nicholas felt his head tilt, questioningly.

Mr. Fidel dropped his head, still smiling. "I am immortal now, Nicholas. That is what I got in return for my support."

"You mean killing innocent people," Dusk said.

"Every scientific advancement has sacrifices."

"Is that what the mad doctor told you?"

"Don't call him that!" Mr. Fidel shouted. "He is brilliant; he made me what I am today."

281

Dusk smirked, "Yeah, and what is that?"

"Important," Mr. Fidel said, smiling.

Lightning flashed through the window again. It seemed to arch down straight from the clouds, and it struck behind the peak of the lighthouse, cascading the tower in a silhouette.

"I knew he would do it."

Nicholas looked from the window to Mr. Fidel. Mr. Fidel was also looking out the window, admiration and pure joy on his face. "Nicholas," he said as he turned toward them. "Don't you see now?"

Most people would have been utterly confused, but Nicholas did understand. It could have been because of his obsession with monster stories or the weird sense of detective intuition. Regardless, it didn't matter. Nicholas understood what the lightning meant, what it all meant.

Mr. Fidel raised one hand in an accepting gesture toward Nicholas. "Come on, Nicholas. Don't be foolish like this man." He flicked his hand at Dusk and gestured again at Nicholas. "If you come with me, you can have everything you ever wanted. You can have your parents again, and you can all live forever without fear of death and loss."

Nicholas wanted to rush to that hand, to take it and leave everything else behind. It was the easy way out. If he just walked across the room, he could have everything he wanted. He wouldn't be hollow; he'd be happy. No matter how much Nicholas thought he wanted everything Mr. Fidel was offering, he couldn't shake a feeling deep down. A feeling he couldn't place, or even explain, but Nicholas knew what he had to do.

"I...," Nicholas said. Mr. Fidel smiled, expecting to hear the answer he wanted to hear. "I'm good right where I am."

Mr. Fidel's confidence shook and then crumbled. He scowled, and his outstretched hand clenched. Nicholas glanced up at Dusk, who was smiling ever so slightly. Nicholas thought he may have seen a tear in the man's eye, but he couldn't be sure.

"Very well. Fools, the both of you, until the bitter end."

He replaced his hand behind his back and looked down. He took a moment, calmed himself, and then looked back up at the two of them. "Well," Mr. Fidel said. "I guess there's only one thing left to...."

BANG!

Dusk's revolver recoiled and smoke jetted after a bullet ripping through the air. The slug flew and hit its mark. Mr. Fidel's left shoulder rolled back as if it had been hit by a car, knocking him from his feet and to the ground.

It all happened so fast, Nicholas didn't react. He swallowed down what he could only assume was his heart jumping up his throat as he turned to look at Dusk.

Dusk holstered his gun and said, "Exactly what I was thinking."

Nicholas looked back to the desk where some smoke was still slowly billowing up. He was about to suggest they get over to the lighthouse before the storm really picked up when the laughing started.

It started quietly, but then grew. It was empty and mad. A hand came up and smacked down on the desk. A body began to rise next. It was Mr. Fidel, but at the same time, it wasn't. His left arm hung slack, drenched in blood. He stood, disjointed and awkward, as if he suddenly didn't fit in his own skin. Then, there was his eyes. They were different from before. One was a normal shade of green, but the other had changed to red.

"You know, at first it seemed to be a terrible curse," Mr. Fidel said. "The doctor said side effects would change and cross contamination was only to be expected."

Mr. Fidel's body convulsed in a spasm that rocked him from the inside. He continued unperturbed, making his way from behind the desk.

"What did you think would happen, he said."

Again, another tremor shook the former history teacher of Pointe's Hollow High. Nicholas involuntarily took a step back. Dusk stood, eyeing the thing coming toward them.

"Now, I see," Mr. Fidel continued, but it didn't sound like Mr. Fidel anymore. The voice was scratchy, as if Mr. Fidel had been smoking for years. "The month of turning every night had been a test. A test to see if I was worthy."

This time his arms bent backward and then thrust forward. "A test to see if my DNA would dominate over the others." His legs popped and quaked. Nicholas could hardly watch. "And I did."

Nicholas felt another moment of realization, but he didn't have time to think about it, because a moment later, Mr. Fidel's body ripped apart. Skin and clothes exploded outward, replaced by fur, teeth, and claws.

Not again, Nicholas thought as he was once again facing a towering, fang-bearing werewolf. This time, however, the monster was different. Its arms and legs were thicker, stronger. Its lower back all the way up to its neck bulged with muscles. The head held no human features. It was all animal. The others Nicholas and Dusk had faced were watered down versions of this catastrophic abomination of horror.

There was a clatter next to Nicholas. He looked to the floor and saw shell casings bouncing about. One shell was empty, but the rest still held their slugs. They were lead slugs, not silver, so they were just as useless in the gun as they were on the floor. Dusk was already reaching into a pocket in his jacket, pulling out fresh ammo.

A roar came from the beast that used to be Daniel Fidel. The beast took one step back, lowered itself, and flew across the room. Dusk tried to dodge, but the beast was too fast. It hit him with a thud, and the impact sent them both into the wall and Nicholas to the floor.

Dusk's gun fell free. It hit the floor on the top of the grip, causing it to bounce and then skitter across the floor. The beast roared into Dusk's face.

"Kid, the gun!" Dusk yelled, barely audible over the monster.

Nicholas saw the revolver only a few feet away. There was another roar from behind Nicholas, and he didn't need to look to know that the beast had forgotten about Dusk and was heading straight for him.

He scrambled on his hands and knees trying to get to the gun, but he was too slow. The beast was about to pounce on him, so Nicholas gave up his progress and just went flat. He hoped the beast would overshoot him. It did, but only because as it was about to land, a tomahawk flying end-over-end caught it in the thigh.

Nicholas watched as a large mass of fur, dripping blood, flew over him, hitting the wood and sliding into the wall of books. Large volumes shook and fell from the higher shelves as it hit. Nicholas was stunned until the beast righted itself and looked back to him. He abandoned all thought, turned back to the gun, and started moving again.

The beast's arm reached to the wall and raked the shelves, thrusting books toward Nicholas. One caught him behind his knee, making him yell out in pain before being quieted by another knocking, this time on the back of his head. Reflexively, Nicholas raised his hands to stop more punishment. After two more rounds of books, the bombardment ended.

He looked up to find the gun was gone. Books were all over the floor and somewhere under the novels sat their only chance of survival. Nicholas scanned the piles, hoping to see a quick glimmer of metal, but nothing stuck out. Then, he heard the footsteps of the beast zeroing in on his target once again.

Nicholas got onto his knees and haphazardly tossed books to the left, then to the right. He dug through the books, hoping to find the gun in time, but even if he did, he didn't have the bullets; Dusk had those.

That's when Dusk passed him, running at full speed right at the monster. He stepped, bouncing between the fallen books like a frog jumping from one lily pad to another.

"Dusk, no!" Nicholas yelled, but Dusk didn't slow.

He lowered his shoulder and dove into the beast. The wolf seemed as surprised as Nicholas, because as Dusk jumped, it pulled back. The awkward stance allowed Dusk to take it off its feet.

The two tumbled backward, arms of the beast flailing. Nicholas watched the two fall, but knew he had to pull his eyes away and look for the gun. He urged himself on, saying in a low voice, "Come on! Come on!" Again and again he said it, growing frustrated. The gun had been here a second ago. Where did it go?

Dusk began making noises like an old car with a bad starter. As much as he knew he shouldn't, Nicholas looked to the left seeing the two struggle. Dusk was trying to keep the beast busy for Nicholas, but it wasn't easy.

The werewolf got one leg between himself and Dusk. It kicked forward, and the force was too much for Dusk to fight. He flew across the room like a rag doll, hitting the floor and crumpling.

Nicholas watched his friend fly by him. As he saw him hit the ground, something else caught his eye. A wooden grip with a single strip of metal sticking out from between two books. Nicholas made his way to the book and fished it out with ease.

"Dusk! Heads up!"

Dusk looked toward Nicholas. Nicholas didn't wait for a response. He put the gun on the wood floor and slid it over. Dusk caught the gun, fumbling as he shook his head to clear it.

The beast roared louder than before as he ran forward, ignoring Nicholas. It headed straight for Dusk, who stood unsteadily and began to load the gun.

In a split second, Nicholas made a decision. The beast rushed past him, and as it did, Nicholas reached out and grabbed a hold of the tomahawk lodged in the beast's calf. Nicholas was ripped from his knees and carried forward with the beast and the tomahawk.

The beast growled at the pain. Nicholas pulled on the tool that was embedded in its muscle.

Dusk waited and then easily dodged the beast. It jumped from the ground and began to climb along the wall with Nicholas still in tow.

"Kid, let go!" Nicholas heard Dusk yell.

Nicholas didn't think he could let go.

"Shoot!" Nicholas screamed at the top of his lungs.

His yell was followed by a sharp crack of the revolver. A book exploded next to Nicholas's head as the bullet hit.

"Shoot better!"

The wolf turned, and instead of going up, it began running along the wall. In two short bounds, the beast was at the other end of the room. Then, it jumped to the center of the room, spinning. Suddenly, everything seemed to slow down. Nicholas saw Dusk, arm raised, gun aimed. He didn't hear the shot, but saw Dusk's arm kick back. Blood exploded from the beast's side, rocking the monster off balance.

Nicholas suddenly fell free and hit the ground. After a moment of dizziness, Nicholas saw that he had landed behind the desk, facing the window. In his right hand, he felt Dusk's tomahawk; in his left, he felt the warm, wet feeling of blood. It wasn't his. At least he didn't think so.

The beast stood up. Blood ran down its left side from a dark, oozing wound. Another wound on its calf spilled blood. But still, the beast fought on.

It roared at Nicholas and stepped forward. Nicholas raised the tomahawk to defend himself from the wolf.

BANG!

The beast's right arm whipped back as the bullet hit.

BANG!

Its lower stomach.

BANG!

Between its ribs on the left side.

BANG!

This final bullet ripped through the beast's neck, causing it to spin all the way around. The spinning knocked the thing off balance, and it stumbled backward. As it moved back, the stumbling became worse and worse until it was in a free fall. It hit the large window. The glass shattered, sending shards flying and creating a gaping hole. The wind that blew in was warm, damp storm air. The breeze wasn't strong enough to stop the animal from falling back and out the window into the open air.

In an instant, the thing was gone, and there was only a soft whistling of the breeze.

"Kid?" Dusk said, with a tone of concern.

Nicholas stood slowly, being careful to not cut himself on glass. He turned around and saw Dusk standing there.

"You okay?" he asked.

Nicholas nodded, "All good."

Dusk sighed and popped the revolver open, sending the spent shells across the floor. "Come on, we have to make sure it's dead."

With that, he turned and left the library. Nicholas took one more look behind him at the broken window before chasing after Dusk.

Sheriff Gordon thought his search would end the same as the one the other night. Instead, he was surprised by what he found. Around the bend at a spot that he passed twice when searching before sat a hole ripped through the underbrush. After further inspection, Sheriff Gordon saw scattered pieces of processed lumber.

The sheriff cursed himself under his breath as he pulled into the trees. The road had definitely been forgotten, but it was still easily visible. He rolled along slowly, unsure what he was going to find.

Sheriff Gordon arrived at a broken gate, which he carefully navigated, and then rolled the car to a stop.

"Holy shit," Sheriff Gordon said, in disbelief.

The house loomed over him. Even when he was a kid, this house had stories. He had forgotten all about it. That was strange. Sheriff Gordon knew his town pretty well. Things never changed, and that was just fine. If things were always the same, he knew how to handle them. Change didn't bother him, but the fact that he hadn't thought about the old house or even considered it bothered him. It seemed so obvious now.

It was as if the house was erased from his mind. Sheriff Gordon rubbed his mustache.

He turned off the ignition and got out of his patrol car. He saw the Jeep in the drive, a forest green Jeep with a brown cover. He got to the front of the Jeep and saw the front bumper and grill completely bent in all different angles.

He knew the Jeep. His mind flashed back to karaoke night.

"Mr. Fidel?" Sheriff Gordon said, confused and surprised.

CRASH!

Sheriff Gordon spun toward the noise. What he saw, Sheriff Gordon couldn't rightly explain at first. It was something falling out of a window. Glass shards rained about like hailstones. Within the glass, a thing resembling a body tumbled toward the hard ground.

The sheriff dashed out to the yard and, out of reflex, pulled his gun from his holster. He stopped dead when he saw something he was not prepared for.

The body was that of a wolf with large extended appendages. Blood flowed from wounds all over its body. It flipped end-over-end without any sign of stopping.

The body began to change. Fur spilled away, and it began to shrink down to human size. The muzzle flattened, lower legs turned into feet, claws into nails, and before long, it wasn't an animal falling, it was just a person. Mr. Daniel Fidel.

Sheriff Gordon realized who it was just before the body hit the dirt with a crunch that sent a shiver down his spine. Blood splashed and began to pool quickly around the school teacher.

Mr. Fidel was dead, and blood still oozed. Sheriff Gordon was a strong man; he didn't get squeamish at the sight of blood. But being confronted with an unexplainable event that didn't fit in terms normal people used was enough to make his stomach flop and a cold sweat break out.

Before Sheriff Gordon could rationalize what he saw, the front door flew open and the stranger in black came out with a large revolver in hand. The man made it down the front stoop and three steps into the drive before seeing the sheriff.

Sheriff Gordon raised his weapon and shouted, "Put the weapon on the ground."

He must have been able to pull out those words only because of the years of saying it to crazy locals with twenty-twos. This was, however, the first time he seriously felt threatened.

The Wake boy jogged out of the house and nearly ran into the stranger before seeing Sheriff Gordon.

"Nicholas!" Sheriff Gordon shouted. "Come over here. Get away from that man."

"Sheriff," the stranger said, tone calm, but serious. "I know this is strange, but I must see, I must make sure that man is dead."

Sheriff Gordon thought the stranger was tricking him somehow, but he didn't buy it.

"That man just fell from a second story window and is currently laying in a pool of his own blood. Believe me, son, he's dead. I said, put the gun down on the ground now."

The dark clothed man was about to speak again when Sheriff Gordon cut him off. "I really want to shoot you, dirt bag. Don't give me a reason to."

The man in black eyed the sheriff, and for a moment, just for a moment, Sheriff Gordon thought he would have to shoot him. In the end, however, the man tossed his gun aside and put his hands out to show they were empty.

"Sheriff!" This time it was the Wake boy's turn to speak. He stepped out from behind the man. He was about to speak again when he realized, as did Sheriff Gordon, that he was holding a tomahawk dripping with blood. The Wake boy quickly tossed the blade aside and raised his own hands.

"You don't understand what's going on, Sheriff," the boy continued.

Sheriff Gordon squinted down the barrel of his gun. "You've got blood on you, son."

The gun in his hand slowly shifted to the left. The stranger took one step to stand in front of the boy, blocking the sheriff's shot.

"Don't move!" Sheriff Gordon yelled.

The man raised his hands a little higher as if to emphasize he was defenseless. The boy pushed around him and tried to talk with the sheriff.

"Sheriff, this is very hard to swallow, but that isn't Mr. Fidel."

Sheriff Gordon scoffed, "I may be old son, but I ain't blind. I can see the body right there."

"Okay, yes. What I meant was it's not the Mr. Fidel you know. He wasn't even human."

A flash of the terrible wolf-like creature that crashed through the glass went through the sheriff's mind. He tried to tell himself his mind was playing tricks on him, but now the boy was trying to tell him something else.

"You saw it, didn't you?"

Sheriff Gordon fixed his grip on the gun and looked at the boy.

"You saw the werewolf," the boy repeated.

Werewolf? What does this kid think this is, a God damn science fiction picture? Sheriff Gordon thought, but even as he did, he knew what he had seen.

"I, I...." Sheriff Gordon didn't know what to say.

"Look," the stranger was speaking again. "I know this is rough, but we don't have time to explain it all to you right now. All you need to know is that there is a man who has been organizing these kills in your town in the lighthouse. Doing what? I'm not sure, but you can be damn sure it can't be good."

The man stopped and breathed heavily. Sheriff Gordon didn't say anything in return, he just listened. A rare event in his life.

"We are going down there, and if you feel like you have to shoot us, then shoot us."

The Wake boy quickly looked at the stranger as if he didn't really want that to be the outcome, but in the end, looked sternly back at the sheriff.

Well, you know what to do, Lawrence. Arrest the both of them. If for anything, for carrying weapons and on the suspicion of murder. Sheriff Gordon knew that's what he should do, but he had the nagging feeling that if he did, it would make everything worse.

How could it be worse?

He didn't know, but he didn't want to find out.

Against every bone in his body and every fiber of his professional being, Sheriff Gordon lowered his gun.

"Go."

"Sheriff, I need to make sure...."

"I said, go!" Sheriff Gordon didn't yell, but he made sure he was heard. "I'll take care of... it."

There was a shuffle in front of him and after a few minutes, he could see out of the corner of his eye the Wake boy walking past him, followed by the stranger.

"You're doing the right thing, Sheriff." The man had stopped and was now whispering quietly enough for only them to hear. "I know it doesn't feel like it, but it is."

When the man moved to leave, Sheriff Gordon grasped the stranger's arm tightly. The man didn't fight; he just waited.

"This isn't over," Sheriff Gordon finally said. His voice was rough due to his emotions.

The man nodded. Sheriff Gordon let go of the man's arm and turned back toward the house. In normal circumstances, he would have gone with them. It would have been his job as the sheriff. But these weren't normal circumstances.

The two jogged off without a look back. Sheriff Gordon holstered his gun. The night had grown darker in the last few minutes. Thick storm clouds rolled in over the small town of Pointe's Hollow and blocked out almost all light. Soft sprinkles began to fall about the yard and on the sheriff.

He turned and looked out over the trees; over the town, his town; and over the water toward the lighthouse. The rain picked up slightly to full drops. Sheriff Gordon dropped his head, and he shook it side to side. A moment later, he raised his head back up and wiped the rain from his face.

The storm is here, Sheriff Gordon thought as he

Dusk

returned to his car.

Chapter 21

By the time the two of them made it to the docks and loaded themselves into a small rowboat, they were soaked from the rain. They were so wet, they hardly noticed the worsening weather. Nicholas tried to keep the rain off his glasses, but it was a losing battle. He decided he'd just have to deal with streaked lenses.

The rowboat was a little thing. It could barely stay topside on the waves brewing on the lake. It wasn't Dusk's, Nicholas knew that, but he didn't feel bad about borrowing it. He knew if they didn't, more people would die. Some still might.

Dusk paddled at a rhythmic beat, making Nicholas drowsy. It had been a long night already, and by the way things seemed to go for Dusk and him, it would probably get longer.

They rode in silence, unsure of what they were going to find on the island. It wasn't a large island. The lighthouse building was the biggest thing there. That building and a few thickets of trees was all that populated the small patch of land. On the back side, the island cut into huge cliffs as if the island was meant to continue growing, but someone had gotten lazy and forgotten to finish it.

The sand scraped against the bottom of the boat as they came up onto shore. Once they were far enough up, Dusk got out and held the boat steady for Nicholas.

"Someone else is here," Dusk said.

Nicholas looked over and saw two other boats pulled on shore. One was tucked underneath some ripped branches so as not to be seen from far away. The other was freshly dug into the muddy shore. Who had brought them, Nicholas didn't know.

They pulled their boat up high enough to ensure it wouldn't float away and walked toward the lighthouse. They navigated through a small group of trees before the land opened onto a footpath to the lighthouse. Trees circled behind and to the right of them. To the left, the island dropped off to bluffs.

In front stood only the lighthouse. The structure had two main parts. One was the tower itself, leading to the rotating light. The second was a square building that looked like a small home. Beside it sat a small shed. The rest of the island was clear.

The lighthouse's tall, looming figure told them to turn back. The sides, beaten by wind and water, seemed to plead for help. They could see the door now. It was time for them to meet this doctor who had caused all the trouble.

Nicholas motioned forward, but was stopped by Dusk's hand. He was looking around cautiously.

"What?" Nicholas asked.

Dusk held up a finger, signaling Nicholas to be quiet.

"Hold it right there, boys," a voice broke through the silence, making Nicholas jump.

Nicholas and Dusk both spun around and saw a soldier standing with a pistol in his hand. This would have been strange enough, but what was even stranger was that this man, who usually looked sharp and clean cut, was completely dastardly looking.

His hair stuck out in clumps all about. Clothes hung as mostly rags about his body. Streaks of dirt and what looked like blood painted his skin. If Nicholas was forced to guess, he'd say this man had been dragged by a semi-truck driving down a dirt road in the middle of a thunderstorm.

The constant onslaught of the rain didn't help. Nicholas and Dusk were wet and probably looked pretty ragged in their own right, but this man barely had any clothes on him and was shaking from the cold.

"I knew someone was behind this. I knew it," he said, waving the gun at them. "The others didn't believe me that there was a rational explanation to all of this. Spouting nonsense about demons and... and...." The gun twirled in his hand as if that would help him come up with the word.

Dusk looked at Nicholas. Nicholas gave a slight shrug, but he felt the color run from his face. Whatever it was, it wasn't good.

"It doesn't matter! Because I was right! It's your fault."

Dusk raised his hands in the most diplomatic gesture he could manage. "You said the others. Who are you talking about?"

"What? The others, the two men who came with me to this damned island." The soldier was getting hysterical.

"Where are they?" Dusk asked. "Are they alright?"

The man laughed, but there was no joy in it. "Alright? No, no. Not alright at all. They're dead. Both of them. Ripped limb from limb by those things."

Things? Nicholas thought. He had fought monsters one on one. Well, actually one on two, but to have "things," plural. That couldn't be good.

"But that's okay, 'cause now I have you two. It's your fault. Your fault." The man took a step forward and raised the gun, which had drooped slightly during his rambling. He used his other hand to attempt to calm his wild hair.

"My name is Captain J. Hayward, and by the power invested in me by the United States Military and the President of the United States himself, you are both under arrest for the murders of Earl Hutchins and Jennifer Harper."

Nicholas thought about letting him know that Father Christopher was also dead, but he assumed knowing the information before the captain did wouldn't work well for their defense. Instead, he looked at Dusk, hoping for a sign of what to do next.

"I'm sorry, Captain, but you have the wrong guys," Dusk said. "The man you're looking for is in that lighthouse. Now, if you just follow us...."

"NO!" Captain Hayward screamed. "No, no, no. That's where those things came from. No way, José. I ain't going near that place."

"What things?" Nicholas asked, but as soon as he did, he wished he hadn't.

A low, groaning sound resonated from the trees. Nicholas thought it was just the wind, but after a moment, he realized the noise was anything but natural. All around them the groaning grew louder and louder. Rustling followed, accompanied by twigs snapping and soft yells.

"Not again!" Captain Hayward screamed as he spun around and clasped his gun with both hands.

The smell of putrid meat and garbage came on the cool wind. It came in waves like the water below the cliffs. It made Nicholas's nose wrinkle. At times, it was so strong, he could almost taste it.

Nicholas crouched a little, preparing himself for an attack from the trees. He heard Dusk pull out his revolver, and he pulled the knife out from his belt loop. It gleamed in the dim moonlight, but Nicholas hardly noticed. His eyes were on the trees. Captain Hayward kept up his wild chants about how this couldn't be happening, not again, not to him. Nicholas wanted to tell him to shut up, but didn't dare speak. His eyes scanned back and forth on the tree line looking for any sign of movement.

The first one came from the left. It hobbled on a broken, right leg. In its left hand, it held something up to its mouth as it chewed. The thing was human. No, that wasn't quite right. More like used to be human. Its skin looked transparent. Wrinkles sagged and open wounds covered the dirty body. The wounds didn't ooze blood. They secreted a dark green liquid.

"No, no, no! Please! Not me! Not me! Tell him to stop, please tell him to stop!" Captain Hayward yelled at Dusk and Nicholas.

More beasts began to appear. First, they could see the glowing green around the eyes in the darkness of the trees. Then, appendages would appear, breaking through the tree line and moving forward. They all moved on wounded limbs, but they kept coming. They grew in number until there were at least thirty of the dead walking toward three of the living.

Nicholas again looked at the one who had first appeared. Below the wrinkly skin and molding features, Nicholas thought he recognized the man. He did; he was one of the men from the missing persons wall at the police station.

The thought hit him, *All these people are from that wall.*

These were the missing people, and Nicholas wished they had stayed missing.

Captain Hayward spun around, facing the oncoming monsters. "You stay back, you devils. Stay back!"

BANG!

The gun in his hand went off. The bullet missed everything. Nicholas wasn't even sure if it hit a tree behind the shambling corpses. It could have kept going forever.

BANG!

Another shot rang out. This one caught the leading beast in the chest. It made the beast drop the thing it was eating, which Nicholas realized was a piece of one of Captain Hayward's companions. The thing hesitated for a moment, gave a confused sort of groan, and then continued forward.

"Why don't you die?" Captain Hayward shouted.

Click. Click.

"Oh, no!"

The gun in Captain Hayward's hand clicked with no response. He looked at the gun in disbelief, as if it was the gun's fault that Captain Hayward couldn't shoot and not the fact that he forgot to reload.

The leading beast was now so close to the captain that his arms reached toward the soldier, grasping for his next meal. Captain Hayward pulled his arm back and launched the gun from his hand. It caught the beast in the face, tearing a bit of its cheek free. The flesh and the gun fell to the soft ground with a squish.

Captain Hayward tried to run away, but he took a single step and got caught up in his own feet and fell.

The beast with half his face laying on the ground lowered his gaze to look at the captain. The absence of most of his face was nothing more than a mild annoyance to him. The biggest issue on his mind was the fresh meal laying on the ground in front of him.

"No! No! Please God, not that. Anything but that!" Captain Hayward screamed as he raised his arms in defense.

His arms were no help. The beast fell upon Captain Hayward with the grace of a walrus, squashing the captain and snapping its jaws hungrily.

A few of the beast's companions jumped in on the action. It was like a food trough had just been filled on the farm. Between the sounds of the captain's screams was the terrible sound of skin ripping and organs squashing.

Zombies, it has to be zombies, Nicholas thought.

Dusk raised his own gun. "Enough of this."

BANG!

Dusk's revolver sounded next to Nicholas, and a moment later, the head of one of the zombies exploded into a billion pieces.

BANG!

BANG!

Two more craniums collapsed, sending brain matter mixed with green blood about the scene. Some of the other zombies were bypassing the army captain stew and coming straight for Dusk and Nicholas.

BANG!

Dusk took out the lead zombie. It crumpled to the ground in a heap. Nicholas was starting to feel more optimistic about their chance of survival, but the whole horde was getting closer and closer while Dusk had only two bullets left....

BANG!

One bullet left. Dusk backed up, and Nicholas followed suit. Nicholas stole a glance behind them.

BANG!

The last bullet was spent. Behind them was an uphill slope to the base of the lighthouse. Unfortunately, there were also more of those things in the way.

"Ah, Dusk?" Nicholas's voice wavered as he stopped and began backing up the other way. Dusk opened the gun and began to quickly reload the revolver. He grabbed Nicholas to stop him from backing up into the horde. Nicholas only pointed back. They stood, side by side, facing in opposite directions.

Nicholas saw the shambling cretins begin to group up and keep moving. Behind them, the wrecked corpse of Captain Hayward laid out, forgotten in exchange for fresh meat.

Dusk

There was a soft click as Dusk finished reloading. Nicholas looked around, hoping for a way to help, but there was nothing close by. He stood, knife in hand, as Dusk did all the heavy lifting, shooting down the dead.

Dusk once again emptied the clip of his revolver, hitting his mark every time. His aim wasn't the problem. The problem was that after two rounds of bullets, there were still zombies pursuing them and more coming from the trees. Jaws hung agape, limbs bent awkwardly, and bodies shambled toward them. But the group between them and the lighthouse was smaller and was beginning to thin with every shot Dusk sent forth.

Nicholas kept stealing glances that way, but was still dismayed by how many there were. In addition, he had his own problems ahead of him. The creatures' progress was unrelenting.

Dusk fired. He had reloaded and didn't waste a second blowing away the next zombie in the line, gore flying in a mess behind it. Nicholas's hair, heavy and wet from the rain, whipped around as he tried to decide what to do next. They were surrounded. There was no way out.

Nicholas heard a zombie behind him and turned to see an exploding head as Dusk's bullet ripped it apart. The rain kept Nicholas mostly clean from the spatter, but the sight still caught in his stomach.

"Kid, watch it!"

Nicholas had enough time to register this when a hand fell upon his shoulder. With reflex action, he turned, seeing a gaping mouth and feeling the warmth of breath on his face. Stepping back, Nicholas slipped and fell. The wind rushed out of his chest as he hit the ground. He had only a moment to regain his senses before the thing fell upon him.

Nicholas did the only thing he could think of. He pointed the knife upward and caught the creature below the chin. It let out a final gurgle and then became dead weight on

Nicholas. Because of all the rain, Nicholas was saved the sight of the thing's head skewered by his knife. Before he could push the thing off, a shadow cast over him. Another creature had arrived for his turn in the Nicholas buffet line.

It went to its knees and reached for Nicholas. Its fingers found the dead creature. No matter how rainy it was, Nicholas caught glimpses of what happened next. The thing ripped at the creature on top of Nicholas. Before it could get to Nicholas, the creature had to go through his brother-in-arms.

Emerald blood and innards were ripped out and thrown free from the body. It was a mess of bits and pieces that Nicholas tried to ignore. Splashes and flecks hit Nicholas, and he squeezed his lips tight to make sure none got into his mouth.

Shaking his arms, he tried to free the knife from the monster's skull, but with his hands under the weight of the thing, it was useless. Luckily, the other creature had to get through the creature on Nicholas. Nicholas could feel the creature being torn in two above him. Then, the first fingertips grazed Nicholas's stomach, and Nicholas shook harder.

BANG!

The second beast's head flew back, and then it fell forward. The added weight made Nicholas lose his breath again. There was another hand on his shoulder. This one yanked him back and then up.

"You alright?" Dusk shouted in his ear. He proceeded to fire his gun at another zombie while waiting for Nicholas's answer, which came in the form of a nod. Nicholas was still trying to catch his breath, and he couldn't speak.

"This way, come on!"

Dusk backed up through a break in their line. He shot enough to make a hole. Nicholas started to follow when he noticed his knife. It was still in his hand, but when he was ripped up from the ground, the force also ripped the creature's head from its shoulders. The thing's head was stuck on the blade of the knife. Its neck hung limp, bleeding and in strands. After forcing down a bout of bile, Nicholas shook the head free and followed Dusk, backing up slowly.

They kept backing up. The only problem was that they were backing up toward the cliff. Soon, they would have no more space to back up. Nicholas once again looked around, desperately hoping to find something to help them.

To their left was the southern wall of the lighthouse. Against that wall stood the small shed. Outside the shed sat some odds and ends. Tires sat piled three high. Next to the tires was an old window, a large section missing in the bottom corner. By both of those was what Nicholas was looking for.

A cart.

It had a large bed with a wall around all four sides to make sure things didn't fall out in transport. In the front of the cart, two large, wooden poles extended forth. This is where the horse would stand, and loosely tied straps hung there, waiting for the next horse.

Perfect, he thought. He took a look back at the dead walking toward them. As he watched, a zombie's face drooped and then fell free from his head, revealing a terrible, dark green tinted muscle structure. Noticing Nicholas staring at it, it seemed to smile.

"I'll be right back," Nicholas said. He put the knife back into his waistband and then said, "Hold them off."

"What do you think I'm doing?" Dusk shouted after him, but Nicholas ignored him. He ran to the side of the shed, giving the creatures shambling toward them a wide berth, and assessed the situation. The tires on the cart were flat, and none of the piled tires looked any better. Besides, Nicholas knew he didn't have time to change any of them.

He heard Dusk fire six more rounds. Nicholas wasn't

sure how many bullets Dusk had left to reload.

Nicholas grabbed the front poles of the cart and pulled hard. It shifted, then stopped. Nicholas looked back at Dusk, who had holstered his gun and pulled out his tomahawk. There were still about ten zombies, and they were much too close together for Dusk to successfully take them all.

Nicholas turned back to the cart and draped the ties around his arms and began to pull again. Once the cart got going, it moved surprisingly well. The hard part was turning it so the back was facing Dusk and the zombies.

Dusk now fended off the fiends without bullets. His tomahawk was in one hand and his gun, butt out with the barrel in hand, was in the other. He twirled like a macabre ballerina. The gun would fall, crushing skulls and breaking bones. This would be followed by the slicing and hacking of the tomahawk. Blood and innards spilled out and painted the ground around him.

One of them dodged the massacre as it broke away from the pack and started for Nicholas. Nicholas lowered himself, made sure his grip was solid, and began pushing as hard as he could. The cart gave a little resistance at first, the flat tires not wanting to roll in reverse. But after a few seconds, Nicholas had it moving.

Luckily, the path was downhill, so once the cart got going, the momentum carried it. He hit the first zombie with the cart. Right before the impact, the green-blooded monstrosity had raised a hand as if to defend itself, but the force was too much for it. It crumpled under the cart, and Nicholas heard sounds of tearing and squishing.

He kept pushing through. Faster and faster the cart rolled. After a few more steps, Nicholas looked up and saw Dusk pushing a zombie away, back into the rest of them. They tottered and bumped into each other. They were so close, it was as if they were all posing for a family photo.

Say cheese, you bastards, Nicholas thought as he

picked up more speed and rocked the group of zombies.

The collisions were hard, but the weight of the cart proved too much for the corpse-populated family. They didn't fall under the cart, but seemed to be carried off their feet and pushed forward to the edge of the cliff.

"Let go, kid!" Dusk shouted over the commotion.

Nicholas wanted to yell back, "Duh?" but was terrified by the sight of the cliff so close. His plan had worked too well, and he was going too fast now. If he didn't let go, he'd be over the cliff in seconds.

Both of his hands released their grip, and he tried to slow down. The cart, however, had different plans. The cables he had draped over his arms went taunt around his left arm and yanked. He was suddenly pulled off his feet. His stomach and face hit the ground first, followed by the rest of his body.

It hurt, but Nicholas couldn't think about that now. He had to get his arm free. He reached up to the strap to see if he could untangle himself, but the more he tried, the tighter the strap became.

He caught a quick glimpse of the cliff from under the cart. What he saw made his blood run cold. The first zombies started tumbling over the cliff. Nicholas had just enough time to think how ironic the whole situation was. He had survived werewolves, vampires, shadow beasts, and zombies, but he would end up done in by a runaway cart.

No, the more cynical side of Nicholas's brain thought, *the cart is just a guide, the sudden stop at the bottom of the cliff will be what does you in.*

Then, he was falling, one arm completely ensnared, and his eyes squeezed shut.

"NICHOLAS!" Dusk screamed, his arm reaching toward the kid and the cart. He couldn't reach him, though. The kid was already falling. The kid was gone.

Dusk rushed forward. When he got to the cliff's edge, he dropped on all fours and peered over. He could see nothing. The night and rain obscured the shore below. All he could hear was the sound of waves crashing against the rocks at the base of the island.

He couldn't believe it. The kid was dead. When this whole thing had started, Dusk had expected the kid to not make it. Dusk had learned that if anyone got too close to him, they always paid a price. But now that the time had come and the kid was gone, Dusk refused to believe it.

He can't be dead; he just can't be.

No matter how many times he thought it, he never believed himself. Death was too ordinary an occurrence in his life. It was the normal thing to have happen to him. Monsters, friends, loved ones. They all died around Dusk. He was a grim reaper, collecting souls as trophies.

Dusk dropped his head, unsure if he could ever bring it back up.

There was a groaning from behind him. Dusk turned and saw the one zombie that had gone for Nicholas instead of him laying in the dirt. The kid had hit the thing good. Most of its face was scraped off. Dark green muscle stretched and oozed, distorting the features. Its lower half lay limp about four feet behind the torso. Between the two pieces were organs floating on a river of dark green.

Kid's wheel must have split you in two, Dusk thought.

He wiped his face, trying to clear the rain, but new drops just replaced old. Dusk walked over to the torso of the living corpse and with a swift swipe of his tomahawk, split its head in two.

He gazed up at the lighthouse. He didn't know what was going to happen tomorrow. Without Father Christopher and the kid by his side, Dusk assumed he would be eating a bullet before long.

But that would be tomorrow. Tonight, he was going to finish what they had come here to do. Dusk fit the tomahawk into the small loop at his waist, pulled out his revolver, and reloaded the entire clip.

Once he put his gun back in its holster, he glanced back at the cliff one last time, hoping beyond hope. Then, he headed for the door at the base of the lighthouse.

Chapter 22

The interior of the first level of the lighthouse was exactly what you'd expect to find in a building on an uninhabited small island. The walls were white-painted brick, the floor was stone, and there were a few pieces of furniture about the room. It definitely wasn't one of the most comfortable places, but it served its purpose.

Off this main room, two doorways went in separate directions. One led up to the rotating light, while the other led down to what Dusk assumed was a cellar. His eyes looked over each door in turn. He noticed a faint, orange glow in the one leading down. Once he was looking that way, he could also hear sounds coming from that direction.

Dusk attempted to wipe the dampness from his face. He did the best he could and then readjusted the gun in his hand. Raising his pistol like a seasoned police officer, Dusk stepped forward, descending to whatever was waiting.

The orange light grew brighter as he went lower. Some of the light flickered like a flame, but other portions were constant. The mixture of lighting paraded forth from the room. Dusk kept moving, but was cautious every step of the way. The only time he hesitated was when a sound like a heavy object being scraped across cement bounded up the stairwell.

Once the sound vanished, he proceeded, knowing that he had to face whatever was waiting for him. One way or another.

He reached the final step and then entered the cellar, a room that slightly resembled a cave. The room was mostly square. Four walls, a floor, and a ceiling much like a mirror image of the one above it. But that design had recently been changed.

The far wall had been knocked down and the surrounding earth excavated. Piles of dirt and rock lined the bottom of all the walls. The small room, which had served as the entire cellar, was now an entrance to a cavern. The constant light was lightbulbs in the room, while the flames were torches within the cavern. There was a large boulder in one corner of the room that was oddly rounded as if sculpted rather than excavated.

Within the room were half a dozen tables cluttered with odds and ends. Vials, beakers, and jars of this and that connected by spiraling tubes that bubbled and hissed with foreboding liquids. Strange smells wafted from the liquids and mixed with freshly excavated dirt to create a medieval aroma. Between the glassware, paperwork lay about as if it had fallen from the ceiling and still lay where it had landed.

Dusk continued forward, careful to move soundlessly and to touch nothing. He rounded the makeshift corner and saw machines he didn't recognize lining the walls. They stood as tall as he did, whirling and beeping. A myriad of lights blinked on and off, seemingly at random.

He scanned the room and noticed that a strange, new odor hung in the air. It was the smell of mold and rotten flesh, but most of all it was the smell of death. This could be attributed to the army he had just faced, but it also smelled fresher. As if the source was still there in the room.

His eyes fell upon a table clear of clutter, a table with a single object outlined by a single white sheet covering it. The shape could be only one thing, and Dusk knew no matter how much he didn't want it to be, it was.

A body.

"Why, hello there. We have been expecting you."

The voice caught Dusk off guard, and he didn't usually get caught off guard. His gun cut through the air and took aim at a small, silhouetted figure standing behind one of the machines. The person was obscured by the shadow of the machine. The light licked his chin, but Dusk could not see his face.

"Who's there?" Dusk said, his voice harsh with anger. "Come out, into the light."

The figure moved forward, and there he was: the man the kid had described in the picture. A small, elderly man with a slight hunch and wire-framed glasses. He wore a long lab coat in need of a good washing. Yellow, dark brown, and maroon stains dotted his clothes. The left breast pocket hung loosely from a slight rip on one of the seams.

"My name is Dr. Murdock, and you can put that gun away. There will be no need for that here," the doctor said.

Dusk didn't drop the gun. The doctor walked to the center of the room, strategically placing the table with the white sheet between the two of them.

"Like I said," Dr. Murdock continued, "we have been expecting you."

Dusk's eyes narrowed, "We? Who's we?"

Dr. Murdock smiled. Raising his left hand, he said, "Myself, her," he motioned to the body on the table, "and him." His hand pointed to the boulder.

Dusk saw that the shape was not a boulder at all, but a man crouching. The flickering candle light and the sheer size had tricked him. When the doctor spoke of it, the shape moved. It was massive. It was approximately twelve feet tall. The shoulders hunched, and it kept its neck low so it wouldn't touch the ceiling of the cellar. A brute it was, no doubt, all muscle, no brains. The eyes of the creature had the same dark green glow as the dead outside.

A monster of this size would have been enough to shake Dusk's composure, but as the creature stepped into the light, it got worse. On its shoulders and hips, large seams were visible. The arms, legs, and torso were all different, but as a seamstress might do with scrap fabric, they had been sewn together into a giant monstrosity. The arms were Earl Hutchins's. The legs, surely they belonged to Jennifer Harper. Finally, the torso and head....

"It cannot be," Dusk muttered to himself.

But it was. He was staring into the face of Father Christopher. His features were that of a brain dead chimp, but the face was undoubtedly the preacher's. Dusk could barely take the sight of it. He was so shocked that his gun arm drooped, and he almost let go of his pistol.

"He's beautiful, is he not?" the doctor asked, a mad glee in his tone.

Dr. Murdock had not only created a monster out of the pieces of Daniel Fidel's murder victims, but he had somehow mutated the bodies. Muscle of unbelievable proportions took the place of normal tissue. The strain was so great that all the skin was covered in stretch marks threatening to burst at any moment. The seams that held the beast together groaned with every move it made. Dark green oozed from tears where the tension had become too great.

It had been made of things that were dead, yet against all odds and beliefs, it was alive. In essence, the thing that stood in front of Dusk and Dr. Murdock was the epitome of a monster.

"Do you see now, Dusk?"

Dusk's head was slow to respond, but after a moment, he turned to the doctor.

"I have figured out the greatest mystery in the world. I have figured out the mystery of life itself," Dr. Murdock said, gazing at the monstrosity's form.

The monster simply looked back and forth between the two small creatures while his breath heaved.

"How can this be?" Dusk asked.

"Years of sacrifice and ridicule," Dr. Murdock answered. "But in the end, it was all worth it."

Dr. Murdock looked at Dusk. Dusk was pulled out of his momentary fascination with the beast, but then realizing what had happened, he retrained his gun on Dr. Murdock. The beast grunted, and the sound shook the room.

"Shhhhh," Dr. Murdock hushed the beast.

It quieted and readjusted. Then, the doctor turned to Dusk. "I told you, Dusk, there will be no need for that. We have been waiting for you to come. You're a welcome guest here."

Once again, Dusk was confused. He was here to break up the party, not to be the guest of honor. What was Dr. Murdock playing at?

"You see, as much of a success that this wonderful creation is," Dr. Murdock once again referred to the creature standing in front of him, "he is still imperfect."

"Yeah, I guessed as much, with the whole marshmallow-left-over-the-fire-too-long look he's got going on."

Dr. Murdock's face gave way to a moment of irritation. "Yes, it is a bit much. But at least it is leaps and bounds better than the dead that you ran into outside. Tell me, are there any still alive?"

Dusk just shook his head.

"Thought as much. I guess the boy did a good job clearing a path for you."

Dusk

Dusk's face contorted as if he had been punched in the gut. He readjusted his gun to make sure his shot would kill when it came time to take it.

"That was insensitive, I know. But can you blame me? I have been surrounded by dead things for so long it's hard to remember social norms." Dr. Murdock's tone was sincere and sarcastic at the same time, the way only insane people can sound.

"But," Dr. Murdock raised a finger. "I know how to make it up to you. I have someone here who has been waiting a long time to see you again."

"What are you talking about?" Dusk was getting agitated. He felt at a disadvantage. He was supposed to have the power of surprise on his side, yet, somehow, the doctor was one step ahead of him the whole time.

"Come now, Dusk. You didn't forget about her now, did you?"

Dr. Murdock pointed at the body covered by the white sheet.

A burning feeling began in the bottom of Dusk's heart, and it spread throughout his entire body, to the marrow of his bones.

It can't be, he thought.

"I hate to be the one to hold up a reunion," Dr. Murdock said as he leaned down and grasped the white sheet. In one quick yank, he pulled the sheet free and let it slowly billow to the floor.

Laying on the cold, steel table in the cellar of the Pointe's Hollow lighthouse was Angela Dusk.

Nicholas's head felt like it had just been run over by a

horse wearing soccer cleats. Considering the alternative, he couldn't complain. His eyes winked open, but the falling rain made them close tight again.

He rolled out of his current position as the ground shifted and squished. Once he was sitting up, he reopened his eyes and looked down. Oddly enough, the things that had saved his life were the exact things that were trying to kill him and Dusk just moments before.

The undeads' bodies were piled and spread across the rock faces at the bottom of the cliff. They had cushioned his blow enough to make the fall only bruise instead of kill.

The hand that supported him wiggled a little. Dark green blood mixed with other bodily fluids seeped and squished between his fingers. Then, the smell hit him. Mixed with the smell of muggy lake water, the stench was almost too much for Nicholas to take. On his intakes, he heaved violently as if he was going to vomit, but he kept it all down.

Nicholas found his glasses, which, thank God, weren't broken, and looked up. It was tough trying to block his eyes from the rain with blood-drenched hands. Once he flung the excess fluid away, he was able to see the feat in front of him.

The cliff wall stood before him, imposing. Nicholas thought it would be tough to conquer on a clear day. But now? During all this rain?

It's impossible, he thought. *And I'm gonna have to do it, because Dusk needs me.*

After cleaning his hands with a quick dip in the lake, Nicholas took his initial footholds. He gave himself one second to consider swimming for The Hollow's shore and to return home. After that, he thrust forward and grabbed rocks that jutted free of the rock face.

After a few minutes, Nicholas thought he was making good progress. He snuck a look upward and was faced by a daunting amount of cliff still to climb. That was when Nicholas made his biggest mistake and took a look down to see how far he had come.

Fortunately, it appeared he had made it a long way. Unfortunately, he had made it a long way. The sight made Nicholas's limbs feel like jelly. The feeling of complete fatigue fell over him. It felt like he was carrying twice his body weight along with him.

Dusk needs me.

Nicholas didn't know how he knew this, but he did. He swallowed his fear and reached for his next hold, followed by another and then another.

After what felt like another hundred grabs, Nicholas knew he had to be close to the top. When he looked up again, his left foot slipped. He thought he was falling. The entire experience left him nauseous with his head swimming. For a long moment, he just stood there on the wall. His eyes were squeezed tightly shut. His fingers were bright red with strain.

Please, oh, please, don't let me fall.

Time was ticking. The rain kept falling, and Dusk was in trouble. Nicholas knew he could save him. Didn't know how or what it would entail or if it would end up with him dead, but he knew he had to climb this wall and make it to that lighthouse.

Come on, come on. Nicholas took one breath in, then slowly let it out and continued forward.

I'm coming, Dusk, Nicholas thought as he bared his teeth, pulling himself toward the top of the cliff. *Just hold on.*

Chapter 23

Dusk could not, no, would not, believe his eyes. He had lost her once; he couldn't see her there, because it meant he could lose her again.

Angela's hair spread out in a small fan pattern. Her skin fair, with color of life pulsating through it. She looked beautiful.

Of course she does. She always did.

Dusk felt his eyes brim with tears. He let them. He didn't sob, nor did he try to hide the tears.

He took a step forward, then a second, followed by a third. Before he knew it, he was at the table. If he reached out, he could touch her. But he didn't dare, not yet. He feared if he even attempted, her figure would fade or crumble into ash. It was too much for one man to bear. Why had Dr. Murdock done this? *Why?*

The table, cold steel, looked out of place below Angela's body. She wore her white dress. The same one Dusk had buried her in.

No, I didn't bury her. The world did that. I would never

have let her go. I would never let you go, my love. You are everything to me. That doesn't matter; you're here now. It can be just the two of us, I swear.

Dusk's mind rambled now. Words rolled through his head. Of all the things he imagined he would find here on this island, she was the absolute last. But he was so glad.

Not able to take it any longer, he slowly raised the hand that held the gun. He placed the revolver softly on the table beside Angela. Once the gun was in place, he reached out and brushed the side of her cheek.

For a moment, her skin felt wrong. After he thought about it, he assured himself it was her skin. How could it not be?

That's when he finally broke down and engulfed Angela in a hug. Her body lifted into his arms, lighter than he remembered, but that was to be expected; he was stronger than he had been. Fighting monsters would do that to a person, wouldn't it?

"Angela," Dusk whispered to her. "Angela, my God. I am so sorry."

His tears became sobs. Steady breaths became heaves, and snot dripped. The lone gunman known as Dusk, who hunted monsters in the night, became weak for the one he loved.

The doctor and the monster watched in silence. Dr. Murdock had wanted this. It was exactly what he had expected. It was exactly what he needed.

However, to their eyes, Dusk was not hugging his love's body. He was hugging the shell that had once been her. In Dusk's mind, he still saw Angela, beautiful and whole. In reality, her skin hugged tight against her bones. Her hair broke at the slightest touch. Her frame thin and clothes dirty from being locked below the earth. Which is exactly where Dr. Murdock had found her, dug her up, and brought her here to entice Dusk.

"Angela," Dusk was saying again, alone with her in their own world. He looked up, sniffling. "Angela?"

Miracle after miracle. Angela's eyes were open and staring at him. He didn't believe it, so he said it again.

"Angela?"

She smiled sweetly, "Hello, Richie."

They weren't in the cave-like basement of the lone lighthouse on a small island on Lake Michigan. They were still on an island, one in the middle of a place that was not Earth-bound. Waves crashed along a white, sandy shore. Soft coos of gulls could be heard, but none were visible. Palm trees and soft underbrush lay behind them.

It looked like it belonged on Earth, but the horizon was anything but Earthly. The outlying water melted into white clouds. Not big, puffy, white clouds of the cartoon versions of heaven, but fine white mist that gave way to nothing.

It was beautiful. She was beautiful.

"Stand up, silly. You'll get dirty."

Her voice sounded like his dreams, soft and musical. She extended her arms to help him up.

He looked down and found himself sitting with his toes deep in the sand. His clothes were different. He wore light khaki pants ending at mid-calf. His torso was covered by a breezy white shirt with buttons only part way down. They were open, leaving his chest partially exposed to the cool, ocean breeze.

"Well?" Angela said, gesturing. "Come on."

Dusk took her hands. With a little help from her, Dusk stood on the shore of this unknown place. For a moment, he looked out over the water and was entranced by everything he saw. He looked at Angela, who was smiling at him.

"Oh, Ang." His voice was hoarse and pleading. "I have missed you so much."

"And I you."

He pulled her in tight for a hug; she hugged him back. They parted just long enough to be pulled into a kiss. At first, it was hard and fierce, like they knew it would be one of the only kisses they would get again. Then, it softened, turning into an exchange between kindred spirits.

After they parted, Dusk looked down upon her and began to speak again.

"Angela, I'm so sorry. I can't begin to explain... I'm sorry that this... I should have saved you. Found a way, any way, and saved you, but I couldn't. I couldn't, and I am so sorry."

He would have kept on like that forever, but Angela stopped him with a single finger placed on his lips.

"Do not blame yourself for what happened. These things happen all the time. They are sad, but it is the way of the world."

Dusk moved to argue that if that was the way of the world, he would no longer be a part of that world. They would be each other's world. That was all they needed. But Angela held strong.

"Richie."

My God, how he had missed that name. She was the only one who had called him that, the only one who could.

"I know you feel like you must give up. Things seem hopeless sometimes, but it's because of times like this that we need to keep going."

Dusk couldn't take it anymore. Moving her finger aside, he said, "I have. But I don't need to anymore. I'm here now, and so are you. We can just stay here together."

Angela's smile faded, and she shook her head. "No, Richie. Not yet."

"Not yet? You don't want me to stay?"

"No," Angela put her hand on his chest, and he immediately felt calm. "You don't understand. I want that more than anything in the world. But your part in the story isn't over yet. You need to go back. There is much left for you to do; that is why I brought you here."

Angela looked around.

"This is ours. Our own little piece of paradise. I tried to tell you at Winter's Hall, but I could do little more than watch. Besides, you would have been too stubborn to listen to me there."

Dusk felt his cheeks blush, something that happened only around Angela. So many things are lost when someone loses someone so close to them. It is so much more than just a friend or a lover. It is an extension of oneself. An extension that Dusk wanted back so much. He pulled her in closer to him.

Angela felt the tug and maneuvered in even closer. "Richie, you have to let me go."

"No." The word came out without him realizing. Instinctively, he readjusted his grip on her.

She smiled, "I know it's hard, but it is the only way. Your time will come, and when it does, I will be here waiting."

Dusk slowly realized that she was getting harder to hold onto. Not because of her, but because things were beginning to get cloudy.

"No, no! Not again!" Dusk cried. He frantically looked around, trying to find anything he could use to ground himself there.

Dusk

"Richie, Richie!" She put her hands on either side of his face. "Listen to me. I love you."

No words ever sounded so sweet.

"I love you, too," Dusk said, new tears forming.

"I know, but you have to let me go for now. There will come a time when we can once again be together, but right now, someone needs you more than me."

Dusk was confused. Who could possibly need him? People just died around him. He didn't have time to dwell on that now; everything was fading fast.

"Angela, I love you. I will come back for you."

Angela smiled, "I know you will, and I will be waiting here with open arms. Now go, my love. Till next time."

"Till next time," Dusk echoed.

He came back to the cellar with a thud, one so hard his body thrust forward. Reality came screaming back to him. Pulling himself away, he was greeted by the sight of Angela's corpse tucked sweetly in his arms.

Most would have jerked back, some maybe even screamed. But not Richard Dusk. He looked upon his love as one tear dripped down his face and whispered, "Just as beautiful as ever, Ang." He finished with a soft peck upon her brow and then softly laid the body back down.

"I know it is difficult, Dusk." Dr. Murdock's voice cut through Dusk's mental barriers like a knife. If Dusk wasn't fully back to reality before then, he was now.

"But you see, that is why I have kept you alive so long." Dr. Murdock stepped forward. "Because of your love for her."

Dusk took a moment to give Angela one more look, and then he began to straighten. The movement made him feel every bit his age. Dr. Murdock continued, not noticing the embers alighting in Dusk's eyes.

"You see, he is quite a masterpiece."

The doctor said this while pointing at the monstrous

giant behind Dusk. Dusk had almost been able to forget about tall, dark, and ugly, but then there was that smell of overcooked meat.

"But like I said, he is still not perfect. I don't settle for imperfection, Dusk. I am a scientist, after all. There is no room for imperfection in my world. After all my struggles and after years of painstaking research, I have been able to bring people back from the dead."

This last bit came out as a matter of pride for Dr. Murdock. "But when they come back, they are what you see here and saw outside. Mindless droves of insufferable meat patties."

A harshness tinged his voice. Dusk caught it, and behind him the monster shifted.

"The creature you see before you is an upgrade from the simpletons you fought outside. Far above those things, but despite all his strengths, he is still imperfect. My failure is staring me in the face."

The doctor began to pace. Dusk stood and watched the mad doctor.

"Just as I thought all hope was lost, I had an epiphany. What is at the center of life? What is it that makes our world turn every second of every day?"

Dusk wanted to say that it was a pizza with everything on it from Felini's, but he didn't think the doctor was much of a pizza guy.

"Love!" Dr. Murdock said the word as if it was the answer to everything. In his eyes, it just might be. "Don't you see, Dusk? Love is the answer to life. To create life, two must make love. What makes us different from these things?" He once again pointed a finger at the large beast in the room, his index finger shaking accusingly.

"Emotions, and at the root of emotions is love. Don't you see?"

Dusk nodded, but in all honesty, he thought it was a

load of bullshit a mad man had concocted to make excuses for what he saw as his failures.

Dr. Murdock either didn't care or didn't notice Dusk's true feelings. He just smiled and said, "I believe that I can get this next one to work, with your help."

"With my help?"

"Of course." Dr. Murdock's smile returned. "Taking into account you have already gone through this once before, you are the perfect candidate."

Dusk didn't ask, but Dr. Murdock continued, "When you stood knee deep in the cold water of Lake Michigan with the barrel of that very gun resting against your temple."

Flashes of that dark night came to Dusk in blurry succession. What he remembered the most were the emotions. Sadness, hatred, love, despair, release, and finally warmth.

"You died that night, Dusk. At least, Richard did. That bullet did the trick, alright. Ripped through your brain and exploded out the other side of your skull barely noticing the interference."

"So why am I still here, Doc?" Dusk said, his words oozing with skepticism.

Dr. Murdock pointed, "Because of her." He was pointing at Angela's body. "Because of her love for you, she was able to bring you back from death."

Dusk wasn't sure what had happened that night. He had been so drunk that God himself could have come down to shake Dusk's hand and Dusk wouldn't have known. He knew Angela had saved him, somehow. Beyond that, he didn't care.

"Uh-huh," Dusk said, taking Dr. Murdock by surprise. "Well, that's all good and dandy, doc, but I think you forgot something."

Quickly, Dusk rushed forward, snatched up his revolver from the table, and trained it on the doctor.

A fraction of a second. It would have taken only a fraction of a second longer for Dusk to pull the trigger. But as luck would have it, a fraction of a second was just too long.

The monster behind him reached out and scooped up Dusk with one hand. Dusk flew through the air and came to a sudden halt as the beast clapped his other hand around Dusk. His gun hand, his right hand, was still free, but his left was pinched between himself and the monster's palm. It began to squeeze, making Dusk squirm.

"No, Dusk. I haven't forgotten anything. You see, I needed you to make it here alive, but you need to be dead for me to bring you back to life."

The monster squeezed harder.

"When a person dies," Dr. Murdock continued as Dusk struggled to breathe. "Their soul, or life essence, leaves their body. Once it's gone, it's gone. Nothing can bring it back."

Dr. Murdock stopped pacing and smiled savagely. "Except one thing. Love. Love is the only thing strong enough to root a being to the body."

Dusk struggled against the tightening hold. He was able to free himself enough to talk. He said, "Sorry... to disappoint... but when... I'm gone... I'm gone, doc. I got someone... waiting for me."

Dr. Murdock's smile widened. "I know you do, but you don't understand. I don't think your soul will stay connected to your own body. I believe you'll still be connected to hers."

Dusk would have been dumbfounded if he wasn't so busy making sure his ribs weren't popping his lungs.

"It adds a whole new meaning to giving someone your heart, doesn't it, Dusk?"

Dusk managed a weak, "Yeah." Which was shortly followed by, "And you give... a whole new meaning... to mad doctor."

This hit a nerve. The doctor's face went white, and his

blood began to boil. "I wouldn't be so cocky if I were you," he said through gritted teeth.

"Well... it's a good thing... you're not me, then."

Dusk twisted slightly to give him a moment to take in a quick breath. The breath gave him the strength to raise his gun again, this time at the monster's face.

Again, he was just a fraction of a second too slow. The monster adjusted his grip and squeezed tighter than before. There was a moment of resistance, followed by a horrifying crunch as Dusk's left arm broke.

The pain came so quickly and so overwhelmingly, it was a miracle that Dusk didn't pass out. It took all he had to stay conscious, which included letting go of his revolver, which clattered to the floor. Warmth spilled down Dusk's arm, and he could feel the blood pulsate from around his protruding bone.

It was bad, Dusk knew it. Dr. Murdock knew it. Hell, even the dumb ass who had done the break probably knew how bad it was.

Black spots began to speckle Dusk's vision. He shook them away. He wouldn't give them the satisfaction.

"You're right. Good thing I'm not you." Dr. Murdock's voice was smug and triumphant. "Cause if I was, I'd have a hell of a time surviving what comes next." He nodded, and the monster gritted its teeth, covering Dusk in warm monster breath as it squeezed.

Dusk fought with what little strength he had, but, of course, it did no good. His head tilted back, and blackness overtook his vision. He saw a small spark of light. In his mind, it was Angela telling him to come to her. So he went.

Chapter 24

When he finally grabbed grass instead of another rock, Nicholas felt like the entire world had lifted off his shoulders. After yanking himself up the final few inches, he rolled across the grass and laid on his back. The rain pummeled him, and he welcomed it as he tried to regroup.

Just need one second to catch my breath, Nicholas thought. But he knew he didn't have a second. He rolled over and got to his feet. Dodging the scattered remains of the dead, he ran to the lighthouse.

When he arrived, he found the small room with the two doorways. He heard a familiar voice from the doorway with the stairs leading down.

"Uh-huh. Well, that's all good and dandy, doc, but I think you forgot something."

Nicholas rushed toward the door. He took the stairs two at a time. As he descended, he heard scuffling and the sound of something huge moving about. His mind was telling him to move slowly and assess the situation, but his heart told him he needed to get to Dusk.

Dusk

Nicholas burst into the basement of the lighthouse. The room was strange, this he knew, but it didn't phase Nicholas. What made Nicholas stop dead in his tracks was the abnormally large man holding onto Dusk. Dusk looked like nothing more than a toy within its grasp.

"No, Dusk. I haven't forgotten anything."

A small man walked out from behind the oversized monstrosity. Nicholas ducked behind one of the tables covered in equipment.

"You see, I needed you to make it here alive, but you need to be dead for me to bring you back to life."

Nicholas peeked around the side of the table. He could see all three of them. Dusk fighting for his life, the monster squeezing, and Dr. Murdock pacing with a devilish grin.

Come on, Nicholas! Get yourself together. Dusk needs you.

He looked all over the room for something he could use. As he shifted, he felt something rub against his stomach. It was the knife that Dusk had given him on their first night out.

"...I got someone... waiting for me."

Dusk sounded strained. Nicholas knew he wouldn't last much longer. He pulled the knife from his waistband and slowly unsheathed the blade. It shined with a fiendish glow in the dimly lit room.

He looked around the table once again. The thing holding Dusk was huge, and all he had was this little knife. What could he do with this little thing that Dusk was unable to do with his gun and tomahawk?

"... giving someone your heart, doesn't it, Dusk?"

Dusk managed a weak, "Yeah." Which was shortly followed by, "And you give... a whole new meaning... to mad doctor."

Nicholas heard the strength escape Dusk's voice. It didn't matter if Nicholas had only a knife; he had to do something, or Dusk would die. Trying to formulate a plan, Nicholas shifted to the other side of the table and looked around that way. Between him and the beast were two tables. On the end of the second table sat a large box that looked like an oversized microwave oven. Gears started grinding, and Nicholas had an idea.

"I wouldn't be so cocky if I were you."

"Well... it's a good thing... you're not me, then."

Nicholas barely heard the shuffling and caught only half a glance from the corner of his eye. What he saw clearly, though, was the sight and sound of cracking bones and Dusk's short, loud gasp of pain. This was followed by the terrible clatter of Dusk's gun hitting the ground.

Nicholas instantly went white. He had been getting used to gore, but not when it involved Dusk. The whole situation made Nicholas feel sick. Maybe he was already too late. Maybe Dusk's spine had been what broke, and he was dead right now in the monster's hands.

"You're right. Good thing I'm not you. Cause if I was, I'd have a hell of a time surviving what comes next."

Survive? What comes next?

Dusk was still alive. Maybe for only a few more moments, but long enough. Nicholas didn't wait a second longer. He broke from his hiding place in a dead sprint. Arms pumping, legs propelling, Nicholas flung himself on top of the first table.

Glassware and other odds and ends spilled off the table around his kicking feet. He cleared the gap to the next table in stride. First step, he sent more bottles filled with liquids flying. Second step, he knocked over a beaker in a stand as he raised his foot onto the large microwave oven. Third step, which ended up being more of a jump, sent Nicholas flying through the air.

His adrenaline mixed with the extra height of the oven, sent him flying above the beast. He was afraid he would hit the ceiling, but he didn't. As he reached the height of the jump, his knife glinted in his hands. He brought the weapon down with all his weight. The blade bit into the monster's rotting flesh at the base of the thing's neck.

It was a little knife, not much more than a letter opener, but the beast reacted like it was a bomb that had struck him. It turned, instantly dropping Dusk, and reached for Nicholas. The turning sent Nicholas flying, which was lucky, because if Nicholas had held on, he would have been in the monster's hands.

Nicholas smacked a table, crashing through the materials on top of it, and then fell to the floor with a thud. This was better than Dusk, who hit with a squish and a softer crunch. Nicholas rolled, feeling little pieces of glass cut him, but ignoring that. He saw the beast spin around and around looking for the knife.

Nicholas didn't know how or why, and he didn't care, but this thing was not like the other things they had faced outside. He wasn't sure it felt pain, but it sure felt something from the knife in its back.

Reaching back and spinning about, the beast tried to get the blade free. He was unsuccessful. The knife kept dodging its grasp. The monster became so infuriated and disoriented that it ran into the machines that lined the wall. Sparks burst forth from the front control panels. These sparks danced in the air, and a few hit some of the liquids that now drenched the room's floor.

One liquid, a harsh, yellow color, immediately burst into flame from the spark. The flame then reacted with another liquid, this one purple, and the two created small, popping explosions.

"No! Stop! You're ruining everything!" Dr. Murdock yelled. The beast, either ignorant to the doctor's pleas or too concerned with the knife, ignored the calls.

"You must stop!" the doctor continued yelling.

The popping had hit another liquid, which created green flames. Those flames mixed with the other ones, and very quickly, the basement resembled the inside of a furnace. Fire licked the bottoms of tables, and machines groaned and whined.

Nicholas looked from the stumbling monster to Dusk, who lay there, not moving. The thing's foot took a step and almost landed on Dusk.

Wake up, damn-it! Nicholas silently pleaded.

The monster stumbled about as Dusk remained prone. The doctor stepped forward, fist held high.

"Goddamn you. Don't you see what you're doing, you incompetent...."

Although it looked like it was an accident, the monster got a good shot in. Dr. Murdock was cut off by the beast whipping around and hitting him with a solid back hand. The small, frail man flew back and hit one of the machines against the wall, crumpling to the ground.

Nicholas knew this would be his best chance.

"Dusk!" he shouted as he tried to get to his feet.

Dusk didn't move. He continued to lay there and bleed. Nicholas got to his feet, but his toss about the room took more from him than he realized. His head spun, and he had to retreat to his knees.

"Dusk! Get up!" Nicholas shouted once again.

Finally, the room stopped spinning, and Nicholas stood up. His nostrils flared at the scent of smoke. As he looked toward Dusk, he saw a small glint of something falling and then heard the clatter of a dagger hitting the cement. Turning his head, Nicholas looked up at the beast. It stared back at him, breathing heavily. Its shoulders rose and then fell. Then rose and again fell.

"Shit," Nicholas said under his breath. The monster roared.

His mind went into survival mode. Nicholas dashed for

the stairs. The thuds of the monster's footsteps shook the entire room. The billowing flames swayed back and forth, and dust shook loose from the ceiling above.

A few steps away from the door, Nicholas felt the monster's fingers just inches away from him. Without thinking of the consequences, Nicholas dove toward the door.

The cement stairs were unforgiving. He hit them so hard that they seemed to hit back.

Gritting his teeth and holding his side, Nicholas looked back. The monster was reaching into the doorway, but his girth was too large for him to fit. Nicholas began to calm down and breathe easier.

It seemed like the monster noticed this and found it insulting. He roared again and then pounded on the wall. Dust and small rocks fell from the ceiling. Nicholas could see the beast pound again and again on the wall. Its hands cracked and bled dark green liquid.

Once it realized pounding wasn't working, it began to feverishly pull at the walls. As its muscles tensed, sections of the wall began to give way, and the hole began to widen.

Nicholas had decided he had seen enough and scurried up the rest of the stairs, leaving the monster to pry his way out on his own.

Heat, smoke, burning, agony, blood, pain, moist, pounding. These sensations came at Dusk like an attack. They wrenched and prodded at his mind. A cough tickled the back of his throat. He hacked, but it only caused him to cough harder.

Dusk picked himself up to help his breathing. Pain racked his body from his horribly broken arm.

Doesn't matter, you silly son of a bitch, just get the fuck up.

This he did. It took him a few moments, but in the end, he got up to a sitting position. The room was different from when he saw it last. Back then, there had been a large monster taking up most of the space. Now, flames danced about as if Dusk was sitting in the seventh circle of hell.

The smoke was beginning to get too thick to breathe. Dusk knew he had only minutes before he would be trapped.

BOOM!

Dusk turned to see what had made the noise. The way to the stairs also looked different. A huge hole had been torn through the cement. Apparently, the monster really wanted to get out, and he wasn't waiting for anything.

Can't go that way, Dusk thought.

He turned back to the way he had been facing when he woke up. The doctor was nowhere to be found. Dusk continued his search and saw something strange. One of the machines that had been home to many flashing lights had fallen forward. The absent machine revealed another doorway. The stairs there were cruder than the stairway that Dusk had descended, but he was sure they would lead to the same place. Out. He could smell the damp air through the smoke.

You slimy son of a bitch. I'm coming for you.

Forcing his body to obey, he managed to get to his feet. He stumbled slightly, but he was able to walk over, reclaim his gun, and remain standing without passing out.

All the while, the beast pounded and ripped at the stairway, causing debris to fall all around Dusk.

As Dusk was giving the room a last glance, he saw something that both scared and delighted him. Sitting in the middle of the cement floor was a dagger resembling a stout sword. It was the same dagger he had given to Nicholas on their first night out. The same one Nicholas had carried with him on all their adventures. The same one Nicholas had when he fell over the cliff.

Life had taught Dusk to be a pessimistic man. But when he saw that dagger, he could not help but hope the boy was alive. He shambled over to the discarded weapon, snatched it up, slipped it into a pocket on the inside of his coat, and turned toward the doctor's escape route.

I'm coming for you, you bastard, he thought and stepped forward.

Nicholas had forgotten it was raining when he entered the lighthouse. When he stepped outside, the heavy drops slowed him, causing a moment of adjustment. He moved forward, needing to put distance between him and the monster. Holding up his hand as a brim to cover his eyes from the downpour, he ran.

Once clear of the building, he moved toward the cylinder of the tower. The wind cried, and the rain pummeled. He couldn't be sure, but it sounded like the monster's tearing of the stone had stopped.

Maybe he got stuck? Nicholas thought hopefully. *Or tired?*

This consoled him for a second, and then there was a sound like an earthquake. It seemed to shake the very ground. He looked toward the lighthouse, pushing his glasses up on his nose as he squinted through the spots of rain on the lenses.

The monster had not gotten stuck nor was it tired. In a single bound, much like an explosion, the creature crashed through the side of the building, sending debris everywhere.

Nicholas raised his hands in defense and backed up.

Once the initial explosion ended, Nicholas lowered his arms and found himself face-to-face with the monster. Its face, which Nicholas only now realized was Father Christopher, stared at Nicholas and grinned savagely.

In his head, he heard the thing say in a voice that sounded like gravel, *I've got you now, kid.*

Nicholas continued to back up, trying to escape. It didn't attack. It matched Nicholas stride for stride. It was toying with him.

Nicholas started to step back, but felt nothing below his feet. He caught himself before he fell, but only by the smallest of increments. He looked to make sure he was right, and, of course, he was. Nicholas had backed up to another cliff edge.

It was a miracle he had survived the last drop. He knew he wouldn't be so lucky a second time.

The monster made a low, rumbling sound spawned from the depths of its Humpty Dumpty body. Nicholas imagined it was laughter. There they stood. Nicholas, defenseless and facing a hundred foot drop; the monster towering above him, waiting to tear him limb from limb.

Nicholas should have been afraid. He should have felt helpless and defeated. But he didn't. He was here between a rock and a hard place, and for the first time, Nicholas knew it was exactly where he needed to be. Nicholas straightened up, as if to say, 'Do your worst.'

The monster reared back and charged, roaring all the way. Just as it was about to pounce, a loud cracking sound echoed through the air. It was ten times louder than when the monster had broken through the wall. It was so loud it stopped the thing in its tracks.

Both of them looked around for the source, but found nothing. Then, a slight movement caught Nicholas's attention. It was at the top of the lighthouse. No, scratch that. It was the entire lighthouse. The cylinder beacon of light began to tip forward toward the two of them, its light still spiraling around and around.

The monster couldn't see it, because its back was to the tower, but Nicholas saw it. Oh, did he see it. He turned to his right and began to sprint. There was a sound of disgust from behind him as the monster saw him take off. He was sure it would chase him, but then another cracking sound broke through, and the monster turned to see the falling tower.

It tried to run, but it was too slow, too big, and too late. The brick tower crumbled from the base's structural damage. The bottom sections crumbled inward upon themselves, and the top bent over and fell. The light at the top continued to spin during the fall. Not until it hit the ground, pinning the monstrosity below it, did the light finally blink into darkness.

Nicholas was safe, but only by inches. When the tower hit, a gust of air buffeted his back and sent him flying forward. He landed face downward, eating dirt and mud. Nicholas turned around to see what had happened.

He saw the tower laying flat against the ground. Pieces of it were collapsing inward from the side, which was now the top. The very top, including the actual light and about twenty feet of bricks, hit the cliff edge and broke free from the rest of the tower. It tumbled further, scraping and disintegrating against the cliff face as it went. The water splashed at the bottom, creating the final note to the song.

It took only seconds.

Nicholas sat on his bottom propped up by his hands. The monster was dead, and he was safe. He had accidentally destroyed the town's lighthouse in the process, but he was sure he could forgive himself. As for the rest of the town, who needed to know? Most wouldn't have even believed him. Most didn't even know....

Dusk! The thought hit him like a smack in the face.

He turned back to the lighthouse, which was completely demolished. Some flames still licked the night air from the basement fire, but they wouldn't last long, not in this rain. He scanned the island looking for any sign of the man. Nicholas was sure he was still on the floor, now at the bottom of a pile of bricks.

Then, he saw him. A man in a dark coat walking off into the distance. One arm hanging limp, the other holding a revolver. It was hard to see, but Nicholas could tell he was walking with a purpose toward something.

Without a second thought, Nicholas hopped up and ran after him.

Dusk felt such a relief come over him when he saw the kid sitting in the mud. He had made it out of the lighthouse with time to spare before the whole thing collapsed. But what had worried him was seeing the boy face off against the monster. Just as you thought the kid was a goner again, fate stepped in and helped out.

Now the kid sat there looking at the fallen tower. Dusk wanted to rush over to him. To come up behind him, put a hand on his shoulder, and tell him he did well. Then, he, too, would take a seat, and they would enjoy the view together.

But Dusk had unfinished business. He turned around and could faintly see an outline of a man limping off.

You don't get off that easy. Dusk raised his gun and followed the mad doctor.

How could this have happened? Dr. Murdock had

thought it all out. He had planned. Ran test after test after test. This was not the way things were supposed to be.

It's that damn brat's fault, Dr. Murdock thought. He nodded, agreeing with himself. "All that fucking kid's fault."

He had Dusk. Dusk was dying right there. Right in front of him. His creation had been literally squeezing the life out of him.

"My creation? No, surely something must be wrong. My creation would never have acted so daftly. I only make perfection."

He was nodding again. His leg was hurt, so he slowed his pace, but nodded animatedly. Water dripped and bounced off his body in the rain, making his physique seem even smaller than usual. Clothes clinging to his body just as he clung to the crazed madness within.

"I create life where there is none. I am the only one who can do that. The only one. Who is God? You hear me!" Dr. Murdock shouted into the rain. "Who is God? I am!"

The sky continued to rain. Thunder rumbled in response, mocking the doctor.

"Next time will be different," Dr. Murdock told himself as much as he told the sky. "Next time, I'll be ready. Ready for anything. Next time, I will be able to bring someone back for real. Not like those brain dead bafoons or like the terrible beast. No, no. Next time, it will be for real." Dr. Murdock laughed maniacally.

"What's so funny?" a voice called from behind him.

The voice caught him so off guard that when he turned around to see who it was, he slipped and fell. Dr. Murdock looked up and saw the last man he wanted to see.

Dusk had his gun trained on Dr. Murdock as soon as the old man hit the ground. He wanted to shoot him right then, but he waited.

"No!" Dr. Murdock shouted. "No! Please! Don't kill me!"

His pleas were pathetic and hypocritical. It made Dusk sick.

"I bet that's what your victims said right before they died."

Dr. Murdock shook his head from side to side. "That wasn't me. That was them."

"Them?" Dusk asked, confused. "You mean the teacher?"

"Daniel? Yes, Daniel's one. The other is from the other side." The doctor's voice faded.

"Other side? From The Other?"

"The Other?" Dr. Murdock looked confused. "Is that what you call it?" Dr. Murdock thought very quickly about what he was saying and changed directions. "Yes, yes. From The Other. He's the crazy one. He's the one who told me about you and Angela. It was all his idea. He's the one you want. I am a scientist. A doctor, for God's sake. I am trying to make the world a better place."

"By creating monsters," Dusk retorted.

"I know I've made some mistakes, but I can fix those. I promise."

Dr. Murdock looked up into Dusk's eyes. Through all the wind and rain, the doctor could see Dusk wasn't buying any of it. The doctor began to shake. It was a mixture of anger, fear, and sadness. As he wiped the rain from his face, he spat at Dusk.

"Yes, I created monsters. But what about you? Eh?" Dr. Murdock smirked and then pointed a finger upward, accusingly. "You look down upon me for creating monsters. But what about you? You kill. That is all you're good for.

Dusk

You sulk about your house, leaving a growing body count in your wake."

"I kill monsters," Dusk said, loud and firm.

"Monsters in your eyes, yes. But they have life. Beating hearts, just like you and me. When a werewolf dies, so does a man."

Dusk's jaw clenched. Dr. Murdock pressed on.

"Yes. You kill monsters, men, women, and now even children."

Dr. Murdock's finger panned sideways. Dusk heard Nicholas approach before he saw him. The soft plop-plop of his sneakers in the mud was faint, but audible.

"You killed this boy," Dr. Murdock said, sneering at the both of them. "His innocence at least. He will never be the same."

Nicholas looked at Dusk. Dusk could see his look from the corner of his eye, but he made no move to return the look. Why hadn't the kid just stayed away?

"You see it. I know you do."

Dr. Murdock licked his lips. He felt he was gaining ground, and Dusk was afraid he was right.

"So I ask you, Dusk." He said Dusk's name as if it was a rotten fruit he had to spit out. "What is worse, the monster maker?" Dr. Murdock pointed at himself. "Or the monster killer?" He once again pointed at Dusk.

Dusk's face dropped a little. Just a little, but it was enough for Dr. Murdock to notice. "I guess we're both monsters in our own right, aren't we?"

There was a moment of silence. Dusk could feel Nicholas and the doctor staring at him. Dusk wasn't sure what to do. He knew what he wanted to do, but didn't know what he should do.

"Go ahead, shoot me. Eradicate me with your shining gun of justice. Add another notch to your death toll." Dr. Murdock was egging Dusk on, and Dusk would have loved giving the man exactly what he wanted.

"But," Dr. Murdock said, making Dusk hesitate. "If you do, you might as well use the second bullet on yourself."

Once again, Dusk was hit with flashbacks to a dark night like this where he had this same gun in one hand and a bottle in the other. The memory burned of gun powder and alcohol.

"Well?" Dr. Murdock asked. "What'll it be, Dusk? Be the monster we know you are or let another monster go free?"

The wind dropped to nothing, the rain pattered about the ground, the waves crashed on the rocks below, and Dusk pulled the trigger.

The sound from the gun sliced through the night like a hot knife through butter. It sounded like the earth itself had cracked open. The bullet flew true, striking Dr. Murdock in the head. He fell dead in a muddy, wet, and bloody mess.

Dusk's arm lowered until it was by his side. He couldn't look at the newly dead man at his feet, and he definitely couldn't look at Nicholas. Dusk knew he had to kill the doctor, but he knew the doctor had spoken the truth. His head dropped even lower.

He was a monster.

As Dusk stood there wallowing away, he felt something at his arm. He raised his head just enough to see Nicholas.

Neither said anything. There wasn't anything to say.

After a moment, Nicholas leaned in and hugged Dusk. Dusk pulled back at first. Then, realizing it was exactly what they both needed, Dusk wrapped his one arm around the kid and hugged back. They stood like that in the pouring rain beneath a cloud of smoke as the dust settled, and everything was exactly how it was supposed to be.

Chapter 25

A lot can happen in a week. The unusually warm weather passed with the storm. Temperatures dropped quickly. Most said Michigan just couldn't decide what the weather was supposed to be. Others weren't so sure.

The army had vacated the area rather quickly once their leader had gone missing. Most of the town's residents weren't sure why they left in a hurry. Of course, Nicholas and Dusk knew why. It was because their leader had been eaten alive and their killer had been blown away in the storm. There was no reason for them to stay. Wild accusations about what could have pulled them away began to spring up all over town. Old Eddie even talked about how there had been stories coming out of the midwest about alien abductions, which was probably what they went to investigate. This, of course, led to the tale of his daring escape from his own abduction. These folks live in a world with vampires, werewolves, and mad doctors, so why not throw in aliens, too?

Snow had fallen a few days later, blanketing Pointe's Hollow in a soft, white sheet. Not only did it cover the ground, it seemed to have covered everything that had happened. Of course, this wasn't true. Nicholas and Dusk had been the ones to take care of that. First, by cleaning up the island, tossing the bodies in the wreckage of the lighthouse, letting them burn away. And then the church.

It had been a long night. It was made longer by Dusk's injury. Nicholas did most of the heavy lifting, which he did without complaint; it just made it slow going. Father Christopher's body parts were found, and he was pronounced the killer's third victim. His death was hard for the town to take. He had been a pillar who helped hold up the town. Mr. Fidel was found to be guilty of the murders thanks to a suicide letter and some creative forensics work by Steely. Nicholas was worried about what Sheriff Gordon would say about the whole thing, but Dusk was confident that this was the best way. It would seem Sheriff Gordon thought so, too. He accepted the letter into evidence and marked the case closed. People were shocked, but in time they came to accept it.

Nicholas and Dusk also saved the town from seeing their church as the blood bath it had been. They went back that night and, after retrieving Father Christopher's limbs for the authorities to find, burned the church to the ground. They also retrieved four large, wooden chests from a room in the back of the church. When Nicholas asked about the contents, Dusk promptly opened one and threw back a dark maroon cloth that was draped over the contents. Nicholas saw stakes, knives, and other weapons, but what caught his eye the most was a smaller box filled with small jars of a dark green liquid.

Once Father Christopher and the chests were clear of the church, Dusk poured gas on the blood-stained floor and set fire to it. Nothing was left once they were done.

Luckily, the storm had offered cover for the church's and the lighthouse's destruction. Most people saw the storm as the cause. Some even swore they saw the lightning strike that lit the church ablaze. A few told of fire being seen on the island, but these comments were chalked up to nothing more than small town exaggeration. The whole story solidified when Steve McPherson himself told fellow jabberjaws that he had seen an increase in what he called "structural integrity issues" around the base of the lighthouse for months. In his words, "It was only a matter of time before she fell. I'm just glad I wasn't under her when she did."

Things went pretty much back to normal in Pointe's Hollow after that.

The more things change, Dusk thought.

He was standing on the cusp of the cliff behind Winter's Hall. The water below crashed upon the shore as cold wind blew through the trees. He had a few bumps and bruises, but other than the obvious, he was fine. His left arm was inside his coat, held up in a sling.

Dusk had Steely take a look at his arm. He wouldn't go to a hospital. He wouldn't say why, but he was sure Nicholas knew why. It was because Angela had died in a hospital. Besides, after the jokes about how good Dusk's bone had looked and how groovy the wound was, the surgery had gone well.

In his other hand, he held a small, glass jar. Before they left the island, Dusk went back into the lighthouse wreckage and collected Angela's body. It had been burned in the fire, and all that was left was ash.

It was better that way. Dusk didn't want to see her like that again. He liked the way he remembered her better. The jar held what was left of Angela Dusk, at least in the physical world.

He raised the jar and looked into it. "Well, I'm doing what you asked." The jar stared back at him, which was the best kind of answer. Dusk took another look over the water and then turned the jar over.

The fine ash spilled out, wafting on the air like mist. It flowed up and down on a breeze as it fell to the water below. The last ash drained out, and Dusk lowered the jar. He had done what he had said he would. He had let her go, for now. After another moment of enjoying the view, Dusk turned and walked back to Winter's Hall.

Nicholas pedaled through the front gate of Winter's Hall, the snow crunching below his tires. The metal doors were gone, so this was the first time he pedaled in without having to climb. It left him with a surprisingly good feeling, as if he had finally been accepted.

What also surprised him was what he found at the house. People. Construction workers were everywhere. All wearing dark green hard hats. The color made Nicholas think of a few weeks ago, but he shook his head. It was over.

All over.

Nicholas looked up to the house. Clear tarps and fresh wood covered the large window that led to the library. Other parts of the house were being fixed up as well.

It was strange to see people here. For so long, it had just been Dusk. Now, it was Dusk, Nicholas, and the good men of Dreyfus Construction.

Apparently, shortly after the snow fell, Pointe's Hollow had an old resident come back into town. Richard Dusk. A big city businessman who had vacationed here with his wife finally decided to retire to a rustic setting for hunting. It was almost true. Nicholas had tried to convince Dusk to use a cover, at least a fake name. Dusk had dismissed the idea, stating, "Playing pretend is for kids."

Nicholas had retorted, "So was believing in monsters."

They had both laughed. Nicholas laughed now thinking of it.

"May I help you?"

Nicholas looked up and saw a tall, thin man in a suit. His face was old and wrinkled, but firm. He approached Nicholas with his hands behind him in a manner that looked like he was doing something unpleasant.

"I'm looking for Dusk," Nicholas said and thought how weird that sounded.

"Mr. Dusk is unavailable."

Nicholas had to fight hard not to laugh at this man calling Dusk 'mister.' He was about to lose that fight when he heard Dusk call out.

"Argyle, the kid is fine."

Nicholas saw Dusk walk through the trees and approach them. He looked good. Thicker, with more color in his face.

"Very well, Mr. Dusk. Is there anything I can get for you?"

Dusk thought and said, "A drink would be nice."

"Yes, sir. I will get you a nice glass of ice water."

"I meant a real drink, Argyle."

"Yes, sir. A Coca-Cola it is then."

With that, Argyle walked back toward the house. Dusk shook his head at the man, and Nicholas bit his lip, so he wouldn't laugh.

"You alright?" Dusk said.

Ever since the storm, Dusk had the habit of asking if Nicholas was alright. He wasn't sure if it was because of his fall or because Nicholas looked like he wasn't alright.

"I'm fine," Nicholas said, just like he always did, and he was. "How's everything here?"

They both turned and faced Winter's Hall.

"It's alright. It's weird being part of the world again."

Nicholas nodded.

"He's a real treat," Nicholas said, pointing at the suited man.

"Argyle? He's harmless. Besides, someone will have to keep this place tidy once it's fixed up."

Nicholas nodded. It was a big place. Even though he and Dusk had been in only a handful of rooms, Nicholas understood it was bigger on the inside than it looked. Dusk couldn't take care of it all on his own even if he cared to.

When asked where the money had come from, Dusk explained that he had been a successful businessman. His bank account was quite plentiful, and after nine years of interest, Dusk was considered a rich man.

Dusk continued, "The guys promise me it'll be finished in a couple of weeks. I give 'em two months."

Nicholas smiled. *The more things change,* he thought.

"Well, I better be heading back to town."

"Your aunt still on your case?"

Nicholas's aunt had been on his case. During the storm, his Aunt Sherri had looked everywhere for him and had no luck. When he finally returned home, beaten and battered, she had scolded him.

"Nicholas Wake, where the hell have you been? I have been worried sick! I have called everyone in the tri-state area twice looking for you!"

It went on like that for a while. Nicholas responded quietly with 'I'm sorry' and 'It won't happen again.' Ever since then, Aunt Sherri had been more concerned with where Nicholas was going and where he'd be.

"You know she's upset because she cares about you."

Nicholas looked up at Dusk. Dusk was looking down at him. "Sound parenting advice from a monster hunter," Nicholas said, laughing.

"Big game hunter," Dusk corrected.

They laughed and said their good-byes. Nicholas remounted his bike and then hesitated, turning to wave one last time. Dusk waved back and then walked toward Winter's Hall. Nicholas looked over the scene one last time before he pedaled back to town.

In town, he saw the usual people going about their day. In their small part of the world, nothing strange had happened besides a freak storm that had destroyed their lighthouse and church. Nicholas had wondered if they would ever know what really went on, but he knew deep down most wouldn't have a clue.

He saw Sheriff Gordon in his cruiser stopped at a crossroad. The sheriff saw Nicholas, too. He raised two fingers to his forehead and gave Nicholas a mock salute. Nicholas smiled, but wasn't sure if that was the right response. Sheriff Gordon turned his car and drove away, leaving the situation alone for now.

Nicholas had enough time to let out a breath of relief when he saw Emily step out from behind a car. Nicholas slammed on his breaks and swerved to miss her. His tires skidded in the snow, and he had to work hard to stay up. Once he stopped, he looked over to make sure she was alright. She was, holding the camera that hung around her neck with one hand, while the other rested on her chest.

He still asked, "Are you alright?"

"Yeah," she said, trying to calm her breathing. "Yeah, I'm fine."

"I'm sorry, I must have been distracted."

It was the first time they had spoken since he had left her behind in the school's parking lot. He had expected it to be awkward when they finally talked, and it was.

"Yeah, you seem to be a lot recently."

Nicholas had no answer. So, he lowered his head and didn't meet her eyes. She, too, lowered her head.

"I just saw your dad," Nicholas blurted out.

Emily seemed to shrink even more. Nicholas didn't know why, but he felt like that was the completely wrong way to steer the conversation. So, they stood there in silence.

"Well, I guess I'll be going," she finally said.

"Oh, okay," was all Nicholas managed.

This seemed to hurt Emily worse than the almost bike accident. Her shoulders slouched, and she began to walk off.

Suddenly, Dusk's voice was in Nicholas's head. "Come on, kid, you can face a twelve foot meat doll, but you can't talk to a girl? Grow some balls."

"Emily!" Nicholas said after her.

She turned, still looking somber. Nicholas swallowed hard and quickly looked down to collect his nerves.

"How would you feel about grabbing a bite some time? With me, I mean."

The next second was one of the longest of Nicholas's life. His legs felt weak, and he had an urge to be facing off against a werewolf if it meant he didn't have to be here.

Emily, on the other hand, looked up, smiled, and in an energetic voice said, "Yeah. I'd love that."

"You would?" Nicholas couldn't believe his ears. He felt his face get warm. "Okay, that's great."

Nicholas was so happy. He was sure he had a dumb-looking smile on his face. He was about to pedal away when Emily stopped him.

"Nicholas?"

He turned to look at her again.

"Where we going?"

Nicholas felt so stupid. He had gotten the date, but had forgotten to set it up. "Oh, yeah. Um, I must have…."

"Been distracted?" Emily said, smiling.

Nicholas smiled, too. "Yeah."

She walked closer to him. Raising a hand, she pushed some hair out of Nicholas's face and pushed his glasses up. "You're a strange kid, Nicholas. One day you'll have to tell me what you're so distracted by all the time."

Nicholas smiled and imagined telling Emily

everything. About Dusk, Dr. Murdock, and the monsters that haunted the woods.

"Maybe I will," he said finally.

She smiled. "Good. How about Shores at seven?"

Nicholas didn't even have to think about it. "Sounds great."

"Perfect." She rose up on her tiptoes and kissed him on the cheek. "I'll see you tonight then."

"Yeah, I guess you will."

Emily smiled one last time before turning, hair whipping through the air. Nicholas watched her leave. Just as he was about to leave himself, Emily turned around again, but continued walking, backward now.

"Try leaving the distractions at home, huh?"

Nicholas smiled and said, "I will."

"Good." She turned back around, and then from over her shoulder, she shouted, "Try writing them down or something. You're much too young to have all that stuck up in your head."

And that was it. Nicholas took another moment to take it all in before he, too, left, heading for home.

His aunt asked him a million questions when he got home. Nicholas dodged most of them when he explained he'd be going out that night on a date. Immediately, Aunt Sherri dropped what she was doing, which happened to be dishes, and turned to talk with him. She asked question after question, prying every bit of information out of him.

Finally, the interrogation was over, and Nicholas was free. He made it to his bed and collapsed. The pillow felt good on his face; he wanted to sleep, but thought better of it. Flipping over, he placed a hand behind his head. He stared up at the ceiling thinking about everything and nothing at the same time.

He turned his head toward the television. He must have forgotten to turn it off when he left because Graveyard Jerry was on the screen putting on his usual charade. "Oh my, that was a scary movie, wasn't it?" Graveyard Jerry cued. "I bet those kids thought they were safe when the monster fell from that cliff. If they only knew. True evil cannot be stopped. True evil lives on. No one should ever get too comfortable for if one evil fails, another will take its place." He laughed harshly and over-dramatically.

The normal chill and excitement ran through Nicholas as he shrank into his bed, getting more comfortable.

Suddenly, he felt a cool breeze flow over him and heard a soft, crinkly noise. He turned and saw his window was open, which was strange because he was sure it had been closed when he had left. He assumed his aunt must have come up and opened it. Nicholas could almost see her walking up the stairs with her super sniffer nose, thinking his room needed some air.

Nicholas's eyes drifted over to the desk where the typewriter still sat. Another breeze came in. The paper caught in the roller, shifted, and crinkled. Nicholas thought about his parents and how much he missed them. After a moment, he got up and went over to the typewriter. His finger grazed over the keys.

"Try writing them down or something," Emily's voice reverberated in his head.

"I just await the day I'll be putting a book away with your name on the spine." This time it was Mr. Lloyd's voice.

"You wanna help me write?" Now, his father's. A memory of warm, summer light coming in from a window. His father, Stephen Wake, sitting at his desk, and Nicholas, so small then, looking up at him. His father spoke again, "You wanna help?"

Nicholas opened his eyes from the memory and looked at the typewriter. His hands fell in place over the typewriter. He took a single breath in and then typed a single letter. An 'M.' He took a moment and then continued.

Most people don't believe in monsters, ghosts, or other things that go bump in the night. But for Richard Dusk, it was the only thing, besides his revolver, that he did believe in.

Nicholas hadn't known what he was going to write before he did, but he was happy with the end result. After flexing his fingers once, causing some of them to crack, he continued typing. He typed for hours, retelling every second of his adventures with Dusk. He wrote for so long, he was almost late for his date with Emily. He made it with minutes to spare.

Unfortunately, he was still slightly distracted. Part of his mind was back home with his writing. From then on, there would always be a part of him back there, in front of the typewriter, clicking away.

The small town of Pointe's Hollow thought it was safe. They thought the worst was over. They believed everything was back to normal.

"How wrong they are," a man said.

His voice rolled like oil. He stood on the very edge of the trees to the east of the small town. Hands were clasped together at the small of his back as he surveyed everything in front of him.

Darkness shifted behind him within the trees. Faint shadows from the trees collected and created a dark shape. It was humanoid, but transparent. It clung to everything like a shadow. Once it was next to the man, it pulled itself free from the ground and trees until it stood beside him. Whispers spilled out of the abyss as if thousands of voices spoke through it.

The man turned to look at the creature. "Calm yourself," he said. "Everything is going perfectly. He is writing." He turned back to look out over the town.

"It has begun."

The shadow creature shrank slightly and seemed to nod in urgent agreement. The voices began to cackle as the thing's shoulders bounced.

The man smiled.

As the creature still laughed, it slipped downward and covered the ground. It stretched and fell into place behind the man, becoming the man's own shadow.

The man adjusted slightly, as if to make sure the shadow fit right. Once it felt like it did, the man Nicholas and Dusk knew as the man in shadows walked into Pointe's Hollow.

End of
Book One

Find out what happens next in...

The Hollow Trilogy: Book Two
Pitch

Kickstarter Supporters

John and Sherri Kruscke (Mom & Dad)
Evon Lintern (Aunt Evon)
John Lintern (Uncle Jack)
Corwin "Ryoku" Walker
John Wurzler
Jennifer Halm Bradshaw
Betty and Howard "Nana and Papa" Kruscke
Michelle Rutkowski
Nancy Thompson
Travis and Cassie Lintern
Kalli, Kenadi & Kolten Lintern
Tom & Paula Mulnix
Ethan & Trenton Mulnix
Dave Isbell
Cougar Kara
Max Schaefer
Linda and Mike Kruscke
Robert L. Schaefer
Deb and Brad Fahr
Shannon & Nick Hunter
Spike

Todd and Kim Gavin
Taylor and Aaron Gavin
Betsy Romankewiz
Grant Scott
Alec J. Kruscke
Stormyi Skyi Judd
Roxy Kruscke
Kate Sanford
Bonnie Jacobs
Britain O'Connor
Kyle & Shelly Lintern
Randy Woodbury
Christina Clark
Brian & Stephanie Draus
Courtney & Krystal Draus
Sir Ernest Tyler Swain III of Birmingham
Jon Jacobs
Jessica and Matt Fahr
Cheryl Schaefer
Grandma Herman
Brad Bonnville
Amanda Bonnville
Kerry Bonnville
Aimee Williford
Jayson & Ashley Jacobs
Justin Highroller Brown

Molly Wurzler & Jeff Wurzler
Leighland, Grace & Baby Wurzler
Garry & Barb English
Owen & Madelynn English
Uncle Bill
Michael & Melissa Demps
Kyreese Demps
Kenyeon Demps
Britton Demps
Chad Bowden
The Stevenson Family
Austin Spalding
Amanda Beaton
Karlena Vozar
Ryan A Adkins
Noah Curl
Rick & Joy Schaefer
Tim "L.T." Kingsley
Brianna Kingsley
Klint Kaercher
Josiah Wood has a magnificent pair of pants
Heather Parra
Lupe Dominguez
Amit Chauhan

About the Author

Brent Kruscke is a homegrown cinephile from Leslie, Michigan. He graduated from Lansing Community College with a degree in Digital Media and Film and has had a passion for the mysterious his entire life. He currently resides in Lansing, Michigan with his girlfriend, Kara and lifelong turtle friend, Franklin. *Dusk* is his first novel.

Made in the USA
Middletown, DE
04 August 2016